FRUIT OF TEMPTATION

Mariana eyed the water, the dress, and the moccasins that were now being offered her. And Lone Hawk's words to her had become implanted in her mind. She was to spend the full night alone with him . . . would he do more than kiss her?

She knew that the chances were great that he would try and draw her into a full seduction. And Mariana was afraid that she was not in any frame of mind to deny him. These feelings between them were becoming too strong to deny.

Lone Hawk nodded toward the basin of water. "You will remove the mud from your lovely body," he said, his heart pounding at the thought of touching her all over. . . .

Mariana scarcely breathed, her eyes wide, as his mouth covered her own in a fiery kiss. The drugged passion that was overwhelming her made her toss aside all thoughts of shame for what she was sharing with this Indian. It was their destiny to be together. Nothing could be wrong that was shared between them. . . .

ROMANCE IN THE OLD WEST
by Cassie Edwards

SAVAGE PARADISE   (1985, $3.95)
When a virile Chippewa brave saved Mariana's life, she
never wanted to leave the wilderness of the unsettled Minnesota Territory which she had once detested. Lone Hawk
cursed his weakness for the hated paleface, but for now he
would take her time and again to glory in their *Savage Paradise*.

EUGENIA'S EMBRACE   (1880, $3.95)
At sixteen, Eugenia Marie Scott was ill prepared for the
harsh life she was thrust into: the rough, coarse gold min-
ing town of Cripple Creek. There she was drawn to Drew,
an exciting man of adventure. Drew made Eugenia a
woman, and she fell under a spell she would never break
for the rest of her life.

PASSION'S FIRE   (1872, $3.95)
At first sight, Samantha thought Troy was a cad, but after
one brief kiss, one tender caress, he awakened an unfamiliar stirring from deep within her soul. Troy knew he would
be the one to unleash her passions, and he swore to find
her again . . . to make her burn with *Passion's Fire*.

SAVAGE TORMENT   (1739, $3.95)
Judith should have been afraid of the red-skinned warrior,
but those fears turned to desire as her blue eyes travelled
upward to meet his. She had found her destiny—bound by
his forbidden kiss.

*Available wherever paperbacks are sold, or order direct from the
Publisher. Send cover price plus 50¢ per copy for mailing and
handling to Zebra Books, Dept. 1985, 475 Park Avenue South,
New York, N.Y. 10016. Residents of New York, New Jersey and
Pennsylvania must include sales tax. DO NOT SEND CASH.*

SAVAGE PARADISE
CASSIE EDWARDS

ZEBRA BOOKS
KENSINGTON PUBLISHING CORP.

ZEBRA BOOKS

are published by

Kensington Publishing Corp.
475 Park Avenue South
New York, NY 10016

First printing: February 1987

Printed in the United States of America

With love I dedicate SAVAGE EDEN to a dear, sweet friend, Ella Spradlin, of Nippa, Kentucky, and her special family . . . her husband, Leslie; her son, Leslie Matthew; and her daughter, Addie Francis.

—CASSIE EDWARDS

ACKNOWLEDGMENTS

I wish to sincerely thank historian Don Carney, of the National Park Service in Grand Marais, Minnesota, and Paul James, General Manager of the Grand Portage Lodge in Grand Portage, Minnesota, for sharing their knowledge of both the Chippewa Indians and the Grand Portage area with me.

I now feel a part of the land and the people as do these two fine gentlemen who are fortunate enough to reside in the Grand Portage area, to be a part of it, every day.

—CASSIE EDWARDS

1783--EARLY MINNESOTA TERRITORY

GRAND PORTAGE

Prologue

During the American Revolution the British moved their main trading post supply base to Grand Portage on the shores of Lake Superior, closer to Montreal, the British's Eastern trade center.

Grand Portage was the mid-point between Montreal and the Northwest Territory. It became the fur capital of the West. The Portage was a nine-mile trail that led from Grand Portage, bypassing waterfalls and other natural obstructions on the lower Pigeon River, to Fort Charlotte and inland waters used by Voyageurs. The hardy Voyageurs could carry ninety-pound packs over the trail in two and a half hours.

To the Chippewa Indians Grand Portage meant "Great Carrying Place," or, in Chippewa, Kitchi-onigum. Lake Superior was called Kitchi-gami.

At the Grand Portage Trading Post there were two trapping seasons. The first season began in the autumn after the summer fur had become prime, and lasted until ice and snow made travel and trapping impossible.

11

The second trapping season began in the spring, when the ice began to break up, and continued until the quality of furs deteriorated because of warm weather.

It was now May . . . the second trapping season was in full swing in this land of natural beauty, refreshing lakes and rugged, scenic shores . . . a land that could have been described as another Eden. . . .

Chapter One

Ne'er made less beautiful the blue, unclouded heaven of her eyes.

—LOWEL

1789—Early Minnesota Territory

Behind Mariana Fowler the forest was dotted a deep rose pink with the flowers of the wild crab trees, their wonderful fragrance evoking images as pastoral as any artist ever dreamed. Before her lay what she thought infinity might look like.

Carrying a basket brimming with freshly picked raspberries, Mariana moved cautiously to the rugged bluff overlooking Lake Superior and looked downward to where the water lapped gently at the pebbled beach below her. The rhythmic wash of the waves was like a gentle pulsebeat. To most people this would have been relaxing. It only added to Mariana's frustration and loneliness, however, this huge body of water spread out before her separating her from what her life

13

had once been, forcing her to accept what it had become.

Sighing desolately, Mariana placed her basket of raspberries on a patch of thick moss at her feet and settled down on the ground beside them. Straightening the skirt of her dress about her, she placed her hands on her lap and stared absently into the distance, again caught up in her unhappiness.

She knew that she wasn't alone in this sadness. Her mother, as well as she, missed the social activities they had been forced to leave behind along with their large Tidewater plantation in Virginia. If only her father hadn't gambled to excess . . . hadn't cheated his friends and fled with their money, it wouldn't have become necessary for them to escape to this desolate wilderness uninhabited by anyone except trappers, Voyageurs, and . . . Indians. . . .

Mariana's hands moved from her lap as her eyes were drawn elsewhere, her gaze now shifting, now looking down the long, fluid avenue of water, for possible signs of Indian canoes approaching.

"Indians . . ." she whispered. "Lone Hawk . . ."

Even whispering Lone Hawk's name weakened Mariana's knees and caused a keen thrill and a flush of warmth to spread all through her body. Though he wasn't aware of it, Lone Hawk had become Mariana's lifeline of sorts, a reason for being.

Yet she knew that she was living in a fantasy world to think that anything could ever develop between her and the handsome Indian. She had to keep reminding herself that he *was* Indian . . . she was white.

Though attracted to him, she had been compelled to believe that it must be kept to only herself. Any sort of

14

relationship with an Indian would be forbidden by her father. Though her father took the Indians' furs in trade, he despised them all, looking at them as nothing more than barbaric, savage beasts.

A melancholic pain pierced Mariana's heart. She lowered her face into her hands and emitted a low half sob, having only recently discovered that her father was a ruthless man of few principles other than those of self-interest. She was glad to have inherited her mother's genuinely gentle personality, as well as her physical attributes.

From childhood on, Mariana had been described as beautiful and delicate. At age seventeen, she still fit the same description. She was petite in stature, yet exuded much energy in her restless daily wanderings and explorations.

Her waist-length hair was fiery red, worn loose and free, except for a few soft ringlets that framed her delicately chiseled features. Her large, expressive eyes, fringed with thick lashes, were blue. Her cheeks were pink and glowing, her lips sensually full.

In Virginia, her petite, high-bosomed figure had been shown off in fashionable dresses. But now there was no need. There were no fancy balls. There were no social activities at *all*. She was isolated from life as she had always known it. She had been used to luxuries and servants. Now she had not even one maid, and most certainly no luxuries. She had been forced to accompany her parents to what she could only describe as the end of the earth. So why dress herself in lacy silks and satins?

Even Lone Hawk never seemed to notice her attire. When she watched her father and Lone Hawk

15

transacting business at the trading post lodge, Lone Hawk always focused on her eyes if he happened to look her way, as though looking into her soul.

This day a homespun dress sufficed . . . pink, brocaded with tiny green flowers and silver leaves. The dress had little puffed sleeves and a high waist, displaying high curves of her round breasts above the low, round neckline. The fully gathered skirt of her dress rustled about her ankles as she rose smoothly to her feet, her heart now thundering excitedly as she caught her first glimpse of the convoy of canoes approaching from the west.

Her hand trembling, she cupped it above her eyes, shielding them from the brilliant rays of the sun, watching the movements of the Indian in the lead canoe. Ah, she knew his every feature so well. It couldn't be anyone but Lone Hawk coming to the Grand Portage Lodge to do his monthly trading. She had been right to watch for him! Her heart had told her that today was the day that she would again see him.

Today . . . ? Oh, sweet Lord, she so wanted to do more than just look upon his handsomeness. She so wanted to talk with him . . . be near him . . . be so close she could touch him. Ever since her arrival at Grand Portage she had been strongly attracted to . . . enthralled by . . . Lone Hawk.

Yet, in truth, she had become intrigued by *all* Indians and couldn't understand why. A part of her cried out to understand. A part of her had already been captured by Lone Hawk. She knew that her heart now belonged to the handsome Indian, and they had yet even to exchange one word between them! She knew that the time had come that they must become acquainted.

Picking up her basket of raspberries, Mariana began running along the bluff. The moccasins she wore were like a soft kiss to her tiny feet as she now began making her way down a steep incline, the ground tangle almost causing her to trip.

Quick and graceful in all her movements, her gorgeous red hair flying in the wind, Mariana moved steadily onward. She took an only occasional sideways glance to see how close the canoes were that carried the many Indians to the wharf that reached out away from the land not far from where a cottonwood log stockade formed a great rectangle. Within its walls were the Grand Portage Trading Post and accompanying buildings.

Raspberries bounced from Mariana's basket as her feet carried her faster toward the main gate of the fort. Breathless, she dared not another look toward the canoes, knowing that they were quite close, for she could now hear the steady swishing of the paddles as they dipped in and out of the water.

Mariana's face flushed warmly. She knew that Lone Hawk must have seen her hasty eagerness to return to the fort. She had to wonder if he might guess why. Had he guessed her infatuation with him? Surely he had. She had not hidden it well enough even from her father.

Her father had warned her more than once about the dangers of letting her eyes meet and hold with the Indian's. Her father had called her shameful, had even had the nerve to quote from the Bible, though he had not lived by the word of God himself in his adult years! Everett Fowler knew the Bible well, because his mother had forced him to listen to her read from it each evening when he had been a mere lad. It surprised

17

Mariana that her father had not learned from the teachings any better than he had, for he was a most dishonest man! She had concluded that he had rebelled *because* of having been forced to do something that he hadn't wanted to do.

Mariana knew well enough that she had inherited at least this one trait from her father, for she, too, disliked being forced to do what she didn't want to do. She had a mind of her own; she was a most determined person! And she was determined to make the acquaintance of Lone Hawk this day, no matter if her father scolded her frightfully afterwards for doing it!

Oblivious of various canoes already moored at the wharf, and of schooners having dropped anchor further out into the water, even of the men sleeping under their canoes along the beach getting much needed rest before venturing up the great Portage trail with their ninety-pound packs of trade goods on their backs, Mariana fled on through the wide gate and across the courtyard. Only out of the corner of her eyes did she get glimpses of the activity about her . . . skilled tradesmen performing their daily chores: barrelmaking, canoe building, gun-smithing, and carpentry. She ran on past a warehouse where men were cleaning and packing furs to be sent to Montreal.

Breathless, she ran into the door at the rear end of the great lodge that housed not only the store where all trading was done, but also the Fowlers' private quarters. In her haste, Mariana almost collided with her mother who was busily kneading dough on the flour-dusted tabletop, specks of flour like white powder on her lovely, pink-tinged cheeks, and at the tip of her nose.

"Mariana!" Jewel Fowler said, stopping her kneading to brush a fallen strand of auburn hair back away from her face, adding a touch more of flour to her cheek. "Why on earth are you in such a hurry?"

Her wide blue eyes swept over Mariana, seeing her heaving breasts, the pearl beads of sweat on her brow. A cold fear suddenly pressed into her heart.

Forgetting her flour-dusted hands, she placed them suddenly to Mariana's shoulders. "Did someone try to . . . to . . . accost you? Did you happen along an Indian, by chance?" Her face showed the pain she was feeling inside her heart. "I've warned you about venturing off alone, Mariana. Why must you be so stubborn? One day . . ."

Sorely tired of these sorts of warnings, feeling as though she could fend for herself, even now aware of the cold steel pressed flat against the flesh of her left thigh beneath the skirt of her dress, the knife she always carried for protection, Mariana wriggled free of her mother's possessive hands.

"Don't you see the raspberries I have brought you, Mama?" she said, ignoring her mother's pleading eyes, which followed her around the room. Mariana finally placed the raspberries on the table beneath an airy open window. "My mouth waters even now for the jam we can make."

Mariana swirled around and clasped her hands together before her. She looked nervously toward the door that led into the store where Lone Hawk might now even be, knowing that she must delay going there long enough to calm her mother's stricken nerves. Her mother's fears of Indians were understandable, and Mariana knew that she herself should be just as afraid. But on the other hand, it was this same intriguing

19

frightening quality of the Indians that made her more interested in them than fearful of them.

"Think of the muffins we can even make to please Papa," Mariana blurted, finally having caught her breath from her hasty retreat from the tall bluff. She wanted to tease and laugh, to cheer her mother into forgetting Indians and all other sadnesses.

But Mariana's own smile was drawn away when she saw her mother's usual paleness, the uneasiness in her eyes, and felt guilt plaguing her for having, again, worried her.

Mariana's mother was not at all well. She suffered from some sort of malady that seemed to affect her heart. She was a petite lady, quite withdrawn because of her loneliness. In her early forties, her hair was still auburn, worn drawn back from her face and plaited in a loop at the back.

Beneath her apron Mariana's mother wore a high-necked, long-sleeved dress, yet the plain attire did not take away from her gentle loveliness. She had a perfectly shaped mouth and a tiny nose; her eyes were beautiful, yet in their blue depths appeared always to be hidden some sort of unspoken anguish.

Mariana had never questioned the quiet moodiness of her mother. She had learned to accept it as far back as her early childhood, when her mother had had everything that should have made her happy, surrounded by riches and friends, in Virginia. She accepted it but wondered if she would ever find out the reason behind her mother's silent sadness. She doubted it, since up to this time she had not even one inkling of what it could all be about.

Jewel went to the raspberries and picked one up

20

between her dainty fingers. She plucked its stem and placed the raspberry into her mouth, avoiding Mariana's studious gaze. Jewel realized that as her daughter grew older she was becoming more alert to her mother's moods. Even now Mariana had picked up on her fears of the Indians. Jewel cast Mariana a half glance, knowing that one day Mariana would understand. Fully understand. But not now. Later . . .

"Which would you prefer, Mariana?" Jewel quickly asked, turning to face her daughter, swallowing the last tangy sweetness of the raspberry. "Would you prefer muffins for supper? Or would you prefer helping me make jam?"

Again throwing glances toward the door that led into the store, Mariana nervously ran her fingers through her hair, guiding it back from her shoulders to tumble more loosely down her back. She did not wish to get occupied with anything in this drab kitchen. She already had plans! She *must* find a way to make a true acquaintance with Lone Hawk this morning. If not now, maybe never, if her mother and father had anything to do with it.

Drawing the tail of the skirt of her dress up into her arms, Mariana began walking toward the door, her soft moccasins making no sound on the bare wooden floor beneath them. She held her chin high, her eyes straight ahead.

"Mama, Papa is expecting me to help him this morning," she said, hoping her mother wouldn't hear the strained quality of her voice. "This is the beginning of his busy season with the trappers, you know. Even some Voyageurs have already arrived. Did you not see them sleeping beneath their canoes on the beach?"

21

Jewel went to the window and stared from it, though she was not able to see the water or the beach. The dreaded log stockade blocked her view of what could have been the most pleasant one of all if she had to live here at Grand Portage. At least being afforded the view of the loveliness of the blue waters of Lake Superior could have made her daytime hours less intolerable.

"No," Jewel said, swinging around to go back to her dough kneading. "I never noticed." She flailed a hand in the air. "If you must help your father, then go, Mariana. I'll make muffins alone." She smiled weakly toward Mariana as Mariana turned to give her a wistful stare. "Tell Everett he'll have muffins on the supper table tonight."

"I will, Mama," Mariana said softly. "I will."

With an anxious heartbeat, forcing herself to not think about her mother's strangeness, Mariana rushed from the room, only a few moments away from actually seeing Lone Hawk again! Oh, she *must* speak with him. She must . . . !

Chapter Two

*Her eyes as stars of twilight
fair, like twilights, too, her dusky
hair.*

—WORDSWORTH

The room Mariana had entered was rectangular, with a fireplace opposite the door. The wide boards of the floor were mottled with mud, looking like worn spots on the bare wood. Pegs flanking the door were hung with coats and hats; mud daubers buzzed overhead as they carried mud to their mud nest in the shape of a ball that was being built in a corner of the room.

A wide counter with a large scale stretched across one end of the room. Shelves lined the walls behind the counter, filled with all assortments of trade goods. A desk littered with maps, papers, and order books sat against the opposite wall. Cigar smoke eddied about the room, resembling swirling fog. Men loitered about the fireplace and open door that led out to the courtyard.

With one sweep of the eyes, Mariana saw that Lone Hawk and his Indian companions were not yet at the store. And she cringed when she realized just whose company she was going to be forced to be in. Standing beside her father, weighing pelts brought in by the trappers, Eugene South was her prime target of antagonism each day. Though he was, deep down, a kind and honest man, Mariana couldn't stand his whining voice, nor the fact that he let Everett Fowler rule his each and every move.

Eugene South had arrived from Montreal soon after the Fowlers had arrived at Grand Portage, and he had become Mariana's father's assistant at the trading post. And to Mariana's chagrin, he had immediately become attracted to her. He was just a simple man, too old to even be considering asking for her hand in marriage. He was thirty-five, pale-featured, and, today, as usual, his tan hair was tied at the nape of his neck. He wore a suit of black fustian, brass-buttoned, and his leather brown shoes were immaculately buffed, his linen shirt, with ruffles of lace about the cuffs, sparkling white.

And then Mariana's gaze shifted to another man whom she had learned to despise. Jed Fenris. A trapper who frequented the trading post more than any other. Mariana's insides grew cold when he looked her way and smiled his wicked, yellow-toothed smile toward her through his shaggy beard. She looked away from Jed in a quick jerk. She was never able to blot his ugly appearance from her mind. His skin, from constant exposure, had assumed a hue almost the color of an Indian's, his features and physical structure had a rough and hardy cast. His dark hair, through inattention, had become long, coarse and bushy and dangled loosely over his shoulders. His clothes were of buckskin, and he wore a beaver hat cocked to one side of his head. His narrow gray eyes were squinting, his nose long and narrow, its tip always red.

Even without looking she knew that he wore a leather belt at his waist holding his knife and pistols, while from his neck was suspended a bullet-pouch securely fastened to the belt in front. Beneath the right arm a powder-horn would be hanging traversely from his shoulder, behind which, upon the strap attached to it, would be affixed his bullet-mold and ball screw. He always carried a good rifle. . . .

Jed's high-pitched voice broke through Mariana's consciousness, making her flinch with its nasal twang.

"Ain't the prices too steep this time round, Everett?" Jed complained. "I ain't no Injun you're dealin' with. You cain't pull the wool over my eyes like you do those dark-skinned savages."

Mariana's eyes widened as she looked quickly toward her father, knowing how he hated to be questioned about anything. He was the voice of authority here at the trading post, the agent operating a floating version of the company store, complete with high prices. No one should dare question his honesty, though it was, indeed, questionable. Always. She knew how he cheated not only the Indians, but most assuredly the traders and Voyageurs!

An arrogant man, Everett Fowler was large, standing over six feet tall, packing two hundred fifty pounds of brawn and brutality on a massive frame, his torso and thighs solid and compact. He had a long, straight nose, and deep-set eyes. He wore buckskin attire and carried a holstered pistol at his waist and a

25

knife thrust into a sheath at the side of his leg.

Mariana watched her father control his temper as he smiled toward Jed Fenris, a smile that had little humor in it.

Everett was checking Jed's packs of raccoon, bear, fox, mink, and the prized beaver furs. Most furs traded here were for the English fashions. A lady's bonnet was not thought *comme il faut* unless adorned with a dash of fur . . . a silk pelisse robe with marten trimming, fox shawls, and marten-trimmed bonnets. No proper English gentleman appeared in public without a beaver hat.

"Are you questioning my honesty, Jed?" Everett said in a deep, even tone. "If so, perhaps you'd best do business elsewhere."

Jed shifted his feet nervously. He laughed out of the corner of his mouth, a cynical laugh. "Yeah. Somewheres else," he said, hawking and spitting into the fireplace. The fire sizzled low. He whittled slices off a plug of black tobacco and stuffed one cheek until it bulged like a pocket gopher's. "Now, Everett, you know that ain't at all possible. You're the only tradin' post near these parts. I ain't venturin' in travelin' any farther."

Everett scooted the pelts aside and readjusted his scales to weigh the incoming packs of furs. "Then you ain't voicing a true complaint?" he asked, nodding toward Eugene South, a silent command for Eugene to bring the ledgers to the counter to make records of this sale.

Everett knew that his business structure all but guaranteed that while it was he who supplied the trappers, it would be *he* who would grow rich while the

26

trappers would remain poor. They had no choice but to offer their pelts to him. The trappers even had to buy all their goods for the next season from him. He had them both coming and going.

Jed again shifted his feet nervously. His eyes wavered, squinting into two points of hate. "You goin' to pay me two dollars a pound again for my beaver pelts?" he grumbled.

"Yes. I believe it is my inclination to do so," Everett said, avoiding Jed's eyes. He instead lifted a small chased-silver snuffbox and pinched out a quantity of the brown powder onto the back of his left wrist, drawing up the snuffs with two quick sniffs.

Jed took a bold step forward, closer to Everett. He spoke into Everett's face. "You know damn well that you'll be gettin' six to eight dollars a pound for them elsewhere. It ain't fair, Everett. Like I said . . . it ain't like I'm a fool Injun. I ain't blind. I seen how your markup is two thousand percent when dealin' with them redskins." He laughed throatily. "I'm aware of your credit system with the Injuns. You give Injuns trade goods before the huntin' season, then say the Injuns owe more than they do, later."

Mariana placed her hand to her mouth and gasped, seeing her father's face take on a red cast. Yet she silently admired him for holding his temper when she knew he surely would have liked to wring the filthy trapper's neck.

She went to the counter, to her father's side. She gave Eugene a half glance, taking it upon herself to take the ledger from him. She wanted to make sure this didn't get out of hand between her father and the trapper. So far there had been no actual physical fighting at

27

the lodge.

"I'll help Father with the paperwork," she said softly. "Eugene, you can be free to do other chores that need being done."

"Jed, what sort of supplies do you need this time round?" Everett said, ignoring Jed's accusations. "I'd best get your dealings out of the way, to make room for others." He tilted a heavy eyebrow as he gave Jed a steady stare. "Surely you understand. Time is money, Jed."

Jed grumbled something inaudible beneath his breath, as his eyes began moving along the shelves of supplies. "Give me the usual," he said, again spitting into the fireplace. "Tobacco, coffee, sugar. I need plenty of gunpowder." He nodded toward traps hanging on the wall. "I also need some more beaver traps, Everett. Should be some prime stuff in the forest come June."

Mariana lifted the quill and dipped it into ink, then began writing as her father quickly spilled out the figures to her. She nervously watched the door, knowing that at any moment Lone Hawk had to appear. Her pulse raced, her heart fluttered menacingly, anticipating that first moment when their eyes would meet and lock.

"Tobacco, coffee, and sugar ten cents a pound, Mariana," Everett growled. "Record that Jed is buying six pounds of each." He nodded toward Eugene who silently did as bade by emptying the shelves of the supplies mentioned. "Gunpowder? Record two dollars' worth, Mariana."

He strolled, heavy-footed, to where the traps hung on the wall. He lifted several and placed them on the floor beside the other supplies being put there in gunny sacks. "The traps are sixteen dollars apiece. Make a record that Jed has purchased six," he added casually, then a twinkle appeared in his eyes as he saw the flour dust on Mariana's dress.

He went to her and flecked the dust off with his powerful hands. "You were helping your mother in the kitchen, I see," he chuckled. "What've my two women been up to? What can I expect to find on the table this evening, daughter?"

Mariana laughed lightly, always in awe of her father's capability of changing his moods as a chameleon changes its colors.

She brushed more flour from her dress, now recalling her mother's placing her flour-dusted hands on her shoulders, and the cause of her mother's concern. She blocked the thought from her mind, not wanting to be reminded of why her mother had been so concerned.

"I've been out picking raspberries this morning, Papa," Mariana said, resuming her work, placing the figures that her father had given her on the ledger page. She cast him a soft smile. "Mama is going to make muffins for supper."

"A woman after my heart," Everett said. Then his eyes became like leaden specks as he picked up pelts, examining them, again becoming all business.

Seeing his mood changing, Mariana became quiet. She sprinkled the page of the ledger with sand to dry the ink, then funneled the sand back into its jar and wiped her quill clean on a rag.

All of this was done just in time, for there was a commotion suddenly in the room and when Mariana

29

looked up, she was looking squarely into the dark, fathomless eyes of none other than Lone Hawk.

With a quivering of her heart and a thrill rushing through her veins, Mariana returned his gaze openly, fearlessly, lovingly, for she knew that she did love this Indian. No other man had ever stirred her insides so. These feelings she was experiencing had to be those of a woman having met the man of her midnight dreams . . . the man she was *destined* to love!

Without moving her gaze from his face, she knew his whole figure so well, having memorized it the other times she had seen him. She knew the shape of his long, muscular limbs and powerful chest, most of which were openly displayed, since he only wore a breechcloth. She knew that his feet were shod in moccasins and that his long muscles knotted and rippled as he walked, sharply defined by his leanness.

Lone Hawk was a Chippewa brave near the age of twenty-five. His skin was of a beautiful copper sheen, he was tall and handsome, very proud and dignified. His hair was as black as the blackest nights, worn straight to his shoulder, held in place by a beautifully designed headband. At the back, in a loop of his hair, he wore a hawk's feather.

His eyes held a command in them, dark and fathomless, fringed by even darker lashes; his jaw was firm and square; his nose was prominent, defining him as a man of courage and determination.

But it was his chin that seemed to set him apart from the other Indian braves who accompanied him to the trading post. There was a cleft in his chin, beautifully cut, as though placed there by a skilled sculptor.

He carried a caplock rifle, and across his shoulder

30

was slung a great bow with a quiver of arrows positioned at his back.

Again in the presence of the beautiful white woman who was called by the name of Mariana, Lone Hawk felt his hands, his feet, his head, his insides all very alive, *ay-uh,* yes, all very much alive! Never had any Chippewa maiden turned his heart into some sort of plaything, hammering like a rattle at a Chippewa celebration!

Her hair had most surely been dyed by the rays of the sun, with its brilliant fiery reds, tumbling even now down her back without the hindrance of braids. As daylight poured through a window beside her, the light bathed her face in a soft, reflective glow, limning her throat and delicate neck. With innocent, wide, expressive eyes the same blue color as Kitchi-gami, Lake Superior, and her delicate cheekbones blooming with color, she was a haunting image of loveliness.

His eyes now lowering, Lone Hawk let his gaze settle on the gentle swell of her breasts. His loins ached to touch her there, place his lips to her hardened nipples, express to her in this sensuous way how deeply he felt for her in his newfound love.

Her breasts were now heaving with her sudden breathlessness, and Lone Hawk had to believe that she was touched by the same feelings for him as he was for her.

Up to now he had not openly expressed these feelings to anyone. Not even his best friend, his blood brother, Sitting Tall, with whom Lone Hawk had always shared his most intimate secrets.

But one day soon he would. For it was not only his purpose to keep the white man from trapping in these forests of the Chippewa, to fool and trick the white man in the ways he had learned, it was also his purpose to win Mariana! In his moments of dreaming of her he had already given her a Chippewa name.

Bis-kah-ko-nay-gee-day. Ay-uh, yes, he had already chosen to call her Blazing Heart. Did it not match the color of her hair? Did it not match her fiery spirit? He had watched her from afar as she moved through the forest unescorted. He had sensed her need for freedom. Without her knowing it, he had been there to watch out for her. She was going to be his. Nobody could be allowed to cause her any harm!

Everett's eyes narrowed into a squint, his insides growing cold, again seeing how Mariana was so taken by Lone Hawk and that Lone Hawk seemed to be as infatuated, in turn, by *her.* Everett had seen it before, but had not wanted to believe his own daughter could be attracted to an Indian. He even hated treating the treacherous devils like human *beings.*

But it was necessary. The Indians were the most clever of the trappers in this wilderness of a land. A canoe load of trade goods worth two thousand dollars could be exchanged for furs valued at more than thirty-thousand dollars!

But Everett did not have to stand by and watch his daughter make a fool of herself over the likes of the Indians!

"So where's the furs, Lone Hawk?" Everett spat, his eyes cold and calculating. "Let's get this transaction over with so you can get back to your village. No sense in wasting time, is there, Lone Hawk?"

Her father's snappish tone . . . his voice alone . . . shook Mariana from her hypnotic trance. She

32

blinked her eyes nervously as Lone Hawk moved farther into the store, now looking over all the supplies. Mariana stepped back into the shadows, knowing what her next move must be. She must hurry on from the store, enabling her to be outside when Lone Hawk left to return to his canoe.

But her feet were frozen in place as she saw Lone Hawk choosing only female items from the shelves.

"My braves will arrive soon with their arms burdened with many furs," Lone Hawk said, his chin held high, now closely studying the many trinkets spread out on the counter. "The hunt has been rewarding. My Braves are *nush-ska-wee-zee,* strong and capable. They are even swifter than your white man traps. The arrow is cleaner than the ragged teeth of the traps. One day the white man will learn that it is the Chippewa who know what is best way to hunt."

"You talk the white man language well," Everett grumbled. "If not for the trappers, you would not be able to communicate. Didn't they teach you the way to speak in the white man's tongue?"

Lone Hawk's eyes darkened in intensity as he glared at Everett. "It was the white man trapper who shared his language with the Chippewa, *ay-uh,* yes," he grumbled. "They teach well, but they do not *learn* as well. But this is not something Lone Hawk wishes to talk about again to you. You know Lone Hawk's feelings about the treacherous traps hidden in the forest. It was necessary to learn the language from the trappers so that, in turn, we might teach them the true way to hunt. But they didn't listen. My voice grows tired even now, trying to explain the feelings of my heart to you, so it is finished." He gestured with a hand.

"Mee-ee-oo. Done. I now wish to trade with you, white man Everett Fowler, then be on my way."

Everett's lips lifted into a half smile when he saw the assortment of women's apparel spread out on the counter. He cast Mariana a quick glance, seeing that she also had seen. She must realize, as well, that Lone Hawk was choosing gifts to take back to his woman. Perhaps that would cause Mariana to forget the Indian!

"So you wish mainly to choose trinkets today, Lone Hawk?" Everett said, stepping up to the counter, spreading the articles out so that Lone Hawk and Mariana, as well, could get a better look. "Let's see now. We have us here several strings of colorful beads, brass rings, lace-trimmed handkerchiefs, earrings, and Chinese vermilion."

"All of these for her," Everett added, smiling wickedly up at Lone Hawk as Everett bent his back to lean his full weight against the counter.

"Lone Hawk, take what you please," he added, seeing the many furs now being carried into the room in the arms of the Chippewa braves. "It appears that we have much dealing to do. I like the looks of the furs you've brought today."

Jed Fenris stood aside, quietly watching, seeing the Indian sorting through the female trinkets. His loins were on fire, hungering to have a squaw's sweet flesh against his own.

But then his gaze swept to the door and his gut twisted angrily when he saw the pelts being brought in by the Indians. Whatever pelts the Indians were able to capture represented that many less pelts for him. He was now recalling Lone Hawk's venomous words

34

about the traps in the forest, and remembering all of his traps that had been stolen these past several weeks. Could this Indian and his tribe of braves be responsible? If he ever found out, he would kill them all!

Mariana's heart ached. Her eyes were riveted to the beautiful beads now being held up by Lone Hawk, carefully studying them. And as he chose others, and even colorful, satin ribbons, Mariana's eyes began to burn. Surely Lone Hawk loved someone! Surely he had an Indian squaw eagerly awaiting his return in his village.

But this would not cause Mariana's determination to meet Lone Hawk to falter. She had planned this for too long now to back down. She would wait outside for him and introduce herself to him. She would not let herself be jealous of a woman she did not know. And hadn't he looked at her as though she were the only woman in the world?

But could an Indian have two women in his life . . . ?

Shaking that possibility from her mind, Mariana fled from the room and stood in the outdoor shadows of the lodge, waiting for Lone Hawk, her heart erratic from her excitement.

Everett smiled to himself, having seen Mariana's hasty escape from the store. She had seen Lone Hawk's trading for women's trinkets and she surely now knew that she was wrong ever to think she could have a place in the Indian's life.

Feeling victorious, Everett puffed out his chest and went and helped the Indians into the store with their many prized pelts.

Chapter Three

*I saw her upon nearer view, a
spirit, yet a woman too!*
　　　　—WORDSWORTH

Lone Hawk appeared suddenly on the path that led away from the lodge, so suddenly that Mariana was left shaken with wonder, now only seeing his sinewy back, so straight and proud, as he carried his fine-boned frame away from her. In his soft moccasins, his footsteps were like the panther's, quiet, yet determined, as he moved quickly onward, oblivious of Mariana's being there, staring openly after him.

Knowing that her plan was about to go quickly awry, and desperately not wanting it to, Mariana stepped out of the shadows of the trading lodge and hurried after Lone Hawk, not even caring if her father saw her in what he would call her shameful pursuit of the Chippewa Indian.

She even ignored the other Indian braves who were following alongside Lone Hawk, their eyes now on her, dark and questioning. Lone Hawk was, at this moment, the only other person besides herself in her existence. She must speak with him. She must. Or she might just die waiting for the opportunity to arise again!

Lone Hawk's long stride carried him farther and farther away. Mariana picked the encumbrance of the skirt of her dress up from her ankles and began softly running toward him. When he disappeared around the corner of the canoe works cabin, her heart faltered. Only a few more footsteps would carry him through the wide gate that opened onto the beach and his canoe. If she didn't want to draw undue attention to herself, she must stop him now.

Hurrying her steps, the moccasins cushioning her blows against the hard ground, she finally reached the canoe works cabin, and as she turned the corner, she spoke his name.

"Lone Hawk?" she said, her voice quivering from nervousness.

When he stopped to turn and their eyes met and held, her limbs seemed suddenly to suffer from a bizarre weakness as she drew to an abrupt halt. One more step would have thrown her against his hard frame as he abruptly stopped to turn his attention her way. And the way he looked at her with his burning gaze was leaving her shaken with a passion never known to her before.

The intenseness with which he continued to look at Mariana caused a searing flame to shoot through her. She was aware of her heart, dangerously fluttering. She now even questioned her sanity in having chosen to do this daring deed.

Could she even speak to him now that she had

his undivided attention? Were words even needed? Weren't their eyes saying it all . . . ?

Again Lone Hawk was keenly aware of the white woman's delicate loveliness. Her blue eyes were capturing his soul. Flushed pink, her cheeks shone like petals of a rose, and her lips, only barely parted, reminded him of the berries of the forest, waiting to be tasted . . . to be savored.

Surely they would taste as sweet.

Ah-neen-ay-kee-do-yen?" Lone Hawk said, squaring his shoulders. *"Andi-dush-ay-ah-szhi-on-nee-gee?"*

A frown lightly creased Mariana's brow. "I do not know the language of the Chippewa," she murmured, yet thrilled by the fact that he was actually addressing his words to *her.* This was the first time, ever. Always, in the presence of her father, Lone Hawk had shown the respect that was expected of him toward a white woman.

But now the barrier that had stood between them was momentarily thrust aside. Mariana's father was now only a speck in her consciousness. There were only Lone Hawk and herself! She had waited too long for this moment. She was going to take full advantage of it!

With intenseness of feeling, Lone Hawk's knuckles whitened on the barrel of the caplock rifle he carried, Mariana's voice reaching his heart like a melodious song. He had prayed to the Great Spirit for this moment. The Great Spirit was now responding. The white woman had surely been summoned by the Great Spirit, sending her to Lone Hawk this morning.

Yet Lone Hawk dared not to blink his eyes, fearing she might be a figment of his imagination and would be gone.

He placed his caplock rifle and heavy gunny sack of traded goods onto the ground beside him, the shadows of the canoe works cabin towering behind him.

"White woman with blazing hair follows Lone Hawk, even speaks Lone Hawk's *name*," he said in fluent English. "Why do you do this thing? What is it you want of Lone Hawk?"

Reverently, she again spoke his name, reveling in the exquisite sensations being near him was creating. She had never known that a man could cause a woman to have such feelings. Not until now.

"Lone Hawk . . ." she murmured. "I have only come to make proper acquaintance with you."

She placed a hand to her mouth and emitted a soft laugh. "I have found that quite impossible in my father's presence. I only hope you don't think me shamefully bold for doing this. I have wanted to speak to you for . . . so . . . long."

Lone Hawk was smothered by her nearness, having for so long wanted to touch her pale, beautiful skin . . . having for so long wanted to kiss her.

But he had learned the art of restraint well in his maturing years. He had never truly believed that he would have this opportunity now being afforded him. It was not in his nature ever to take a woman that could not be fairly his. And knowing this white woman's *gee-ba-ba,* father, Lone Hawk had never expected to speak with her, much less touch and kiss her.

Even now he doubted this would ever be possible. She was, most surely, untouchable to him, he who was what most white man called a . . . heathen . . . savage.

"I have seen that your heart is good toward the Chippewa," Lone Hawk finally said. "It has shown in the kindness of your eyes and smile. This is good, for Lone Hawk's heart is also good toward *you*."

He reached a hand toward her, again tempted to touch the flesh that differed so in color from his, then reconsidered and let his hand move quickly back to his side. He was experiencing every emotion that was good while being in her presence. But again, he must show the restraint expected of him, the next chief-in-line of his village of Chippewa.

"Then you, too, have felt the need to meet me?" Mariana dared to ask, having tensed for a moment when he had looked as though he was ready to touch her. It was not that she feared his touch for fear's sake . . . but because she feared melting with ecstasy from the touch of his flesh upon hers.

"You do not see me as brazen for approaching you in this way?" she quickly added.

Lone Hawk bent his neck so that his face was closer to hers. *"Nee-may-nan-dum-wah-bum-eh-nawn,"* he said thickly. "Lone Hawk is glad you have done this thing today. But do you not fear the wrath of your father? The hate for the Chippewa is dark in your father's eyes. The Chippewa understand that he only tolerates us for the many pelts we bring him from the forest."

Embarrassed at Lone Hawk's being aware of her father's true feelings for the Indians, Mariana lowered her eyes. "I am sorry for my father's attitude toward you," she said in an almost whisper.

Her eyes slowly rose upward, again holding with Lone Hawk's. "But I am glad that you know that it is only my father and not myself who feels this way, Lone Hawk. I have nothing but respect and admiration

40

for you and your people. I am in awe of your people."

She shifted her feet nervously. "I hope it is all right that I confess such feelings to you," she blurted, feeling clumsy in her fight for the proper words to say to Lone Hawk, never having openly spoken with an Indian before. Before now it had been forbidden. It still was.

But she no longer would answer to her father for her each and every movement. She was seventeen! She was no longer a mere child with childish wants and needs. She would follow these feelings that now overwhelmed her, no matter who might try to dissuade her in her search for her own destiny's desires.

"Nee-min-weh-dum-wah-bun-min-ah," Lone Hawk said, no longer fighting the urge to touch her, now doing so as he placed his hand firmly on her shoulder. "It is good to talk with you. Do not be wary of this courage you have found to speak of your feelings to me. You speak with one tongue, your father speaks with two. Let us be special friends, *Bis-kah-no-nay-gee-day."*

Shivers of warmth stirred along Mariana's flesh, feeling a strange possession not in only his words but in the way his fingers pressed into her shoulder. Passion for Lone Hawk again awakened inside Mariana, causing her eyes to waver with a sudden shyness. And he seemed to have addressed her by a name spoken in Chippewa. Her mind was filled with wonder.

"Friends, yes . . . special . . . friends . . ." she said in a clumsy stammer, again embarrassed. "I would love that, Lone Hawk. I would truly love that."

She smiled weakly up at him, still held by his hand and by his hypnotic eyes. "And what did you just call me? You did not address me by my true name."

41

Lone Hawk smiled down at her, knowing that with them there would be more than mere friendship. And he was amused at her lack of knowledge of his language. A time would come, later, for her to know his given name for her. He now knew that there would be a time, soon, when they would be totally alone, to share more than just talk.

He wanted to hold her, to breathe her name over and over again into the tiny loveliness of her ear. He wanted to kindle the passion he saw in her eyes into a burning flame that only he could feed. She was destined to be his. And she seemed to know this as well as he. . . .

"The name Lone Hawk chose to call you will be known by you in time," Lone Hawk said. "We will talk again, lovely one. But for now you must return to your father's dwelling. We do not want him to question your absence. He has seen how you and I have been drawn to each other. He will fight this attraction. You know that as well as I."

Mariana's eyes widened as Lone Hawk took a step closer to her. By instinct she took a step backwards, unaware that she had just stepped into her father's view as he stood at the window of the lodge, having gone there to look for her. Little did she know that he was now glaring at her . . . and little did she know that he was witness to Lone Hawk's quick decision to kiss her. . . .

"Your lips cry out to be kissed," Lone Hawk said, now placing his hands to her waist, moving into her embrace.

Already dizzy from Lone Hawk's declaration of his interest in her, Mariana's senses reeled as he bore his mouth down upon hers in a torrid kiss, then just as

42

quickly released her.

She placed her fingers to her mouth, still feeling his lips there, and watched as he lifted his gunny sack of trade goods and his caplock rifle up from the ground and hurried on away from her without a word of explanation to her as to why he had had that sudden urge to kiss her.

He had said they would be friends. He had surely meant that they would be more than that. And if so? Could she truly be brazen enough to let it go further than what had transpired this morning? Could she let her strange craving for this Indian take her into the unknown realms of love and desire?

And her father! Oh, Lord, he would surely lock her in her room and throw away the key should he find out that Lone Hawk had kissed her.

Or, worse yet, her father might *kill* Lone Hawk.

Yet Mariana doubted that. Her father knew that Lone Hawk had much power of persuasion in the Chippewa community. It was well known that Lone Hawk would be the next chief of his band of Chippewa. It was no secret that Lone Hawk's father was ailing. Soon Lone Hawk would have total power over what the Chippewa did in his community. And Mariana knew that her father would not jeopardize his relationship with the Chippewa by killing Lone Hawk, their soon-to-be-leader!

Standing in an almost daze, not believing what had just happened, Mariana watched as Lone Hawk walked through the large gate and from her viewing range. She still held her hand to her mouth. It seemed that she had melted to the very spot she was standing on, dazzled by how it had felt to be kissed by a man, this kiss, her first. It had stirred so many delicious sensations inside her that she was eager to explore further with these sorts of feelings. And she would. Somehow.

Suddenly noticing the activity about her, the noise of hammers and saws filling the air like thunder in her ears as she came back down to earth, to reality, to life as she had always known it, Mariana looked quickly about her, now worrying about who might have seen her and the Indian together . . . actually sharing a kiss. It could create a major scandal. The outrage could cause her father to do almost anything!

"Father!" she whispered, her insides knotting up with the thought. Turning in jerks, her gaze went to the trading lodge. She was relieved when she saw no one at the doors or windows. She was safe. At least this time she was safe.

In a half run, Mariana began hurrying back to the lodge, avoiding the door that led into the store, going instead through the rear door, which led into their private living quarters. She stopped cold upon finding her father in the kitchen, his brow furrowed as he looked toward her.

Had he seen? Did he know?

Yet Mariana did not want to think the worst. This frown was characteristic of her father more than not. It was his nature to appear to be angry with the world, not only her.

Pretending not to have noticed her father there, Mariana went to the table where the raspberries now lay in a heavy crock, half prepared for the muffins. She sank her fingers into the crock and grabbed a raspberry and thrust it into her mouth, watching out of the corner of her eye as her father poured spiced wine into hot milk, one of his favorite drinks.

Out of the other corner of her eye she watched her mother puttering about the kitchen, placing sugar on the table, along with eggs and butter. The kitchen already smelled of bread baking and coffee brewing. The sun splashed through the window, slanting along the floor in golden streamers.

The living quarters were pleasant enough, at least tolerable. As one entered from the store the large room reached out to the right and to the left giving an open feeling that was enhanced by light flooding through an ample number of windows.

There was a fireplace in the living room, as well as in all the other rooms, double french doors, rich paneling, which shone from Mariana's mother's constant pampering and buffing.

Ceiling beams and molding reinforced the illusion of sumptuousness . . . hardwood floors, bookshelves flanking the fireplace, silver candelabras holding numerous tapers, and cabinets filled with an array of crystal reminders of the luxuries they had left behind in Virginia.

"So you have had another outing this morning, eh, daughter?" Everett said, his abruptness jolting Mariana's nerves.

Swinging around, she licked the juice of the raspberries from her fingers, looking innocently toward her father. "A second outing?" she said, smiling weakly. "I don't know what you mean, Papa."

Everett shook his head. He tipped the tankard of hot milk spiced with wine to his lips and took a great swallow, then wiped his mouth clean with the back of his hand.

"Yes, a second outing," he said smoothly. "Where did you go this time? Haven't I warned you about mingling too much in the courtyard? Many of those men under my employ lack female companionship. You know that many were not accompanied here by a wife. And those women who did come are busy with children and are known to neglect their wifely duties at night. Do you wish to have them pawing at your skirts, Mariana? I would think not."

He couldn't shake the vision of the Indian kissing her! Yet he would not let her know that he had seen. He would just make sure it didn't happen again! He would hurry up the marriage he had planned between her and Eugene South, though she had not yet been informed of his decision.

Mariana gasped, her face turning many different shades of red, having never before heard her father speak so crudely about men in front of her. "Papa!" she said, glancing toward her mother and seeing that she was just as aghast at his comments.

"Everett!" Jewel said, grabbing the edge of the table, feeling suddenly shaken by the abruptness of her husband to their daughter. What could have caused this? It was as though he did it out of desperation. . . .

Everett ignored both Jewel and Mariana's reaction. He slammed his tankard of half-emptied hot milk down on the table. "Tomorrow you will have another outing," he grumbled. "But one planned by me."

Mariana's back straightened. She clasped her hands tightly behind her, never knowing what to expect from her unpredictable father. "What do you mean, Papa?" she dared to ask. "What sort of an outing? What are

46

you talking about?"

Everett scratched his brow idly, only half glancing from Mariana to Jewel. He strolled to the window and stared from it, placing his back to them both.

"I plan to give Eugene South the full day off tomorrow," he grumbled. "Eugene will be taking you for a picnic, across to Deer Island. You will go by canoe. It could be quite a pleasurable outing for you, Mariana."

Mariana grew cold inside. Her eyes showed her distaste of the suggestion as she glowered at her father's back. She crinkled her nose when she spoke.

"Papa, I do not wish to go anywhere with Eugene," she stated flatly. "You know how I feel about him. I do not like him at all. And he whines so when he talks."

Everett turned slowly and challenged Mariana with a set stare. "You will go," he ordered. "And I don't wish to hear any more about it." He smiled crookedly. "And Eugene can't help it if he whines when he talks. It is only a nasal obstruction. You are being vain to let that stand in the way of liking such a dependable man as Eugene."

Mariana unclasped her hands and moved them to her side. She circled them into tight fists. "Dependable?" she fumed. "Perhaps to you, only to get on your good side. But if you truly knew the man you would surely see that all he cares about is his own wants and needs. When he earns enough money he will go elsewhere, Papa."

She angrily flailed a hand into the air. "He won't think another thing about you or this damn trading post!" she uttered contemptuously, half beneath her breath. "He most certainly won't think another thing

47

about me. He is number one on his list of priorities."

Everett's gut twisted at hearing Mariana speak her first profanity, ever. She had become almost too much to handle. But handle her, he would.

He pointed toward the door that led into the other rooms of their living quarters. "Go to your room," he shouted. "And you're lucky I don't wash your mouth out with soap! I don't ever want to hear you say such a word again in my presence. Do you hear?"

Mariana stubbornly tilted her chin. She flung her hair around as she turned and stomped from the room. Yet she knew that she had not won. She would be forced to go with Eugene.

But she would make Eugene's time with her most unpleasant! She would show her father . . . !

Chapter Four

She walks in beauty, like the night of cloudless climes and starry nights.

—BYRON

Sitting proudly erect on his pony, Lone Hawk rode through the forest, eager to present the gifts he acquired at the trading post to his younger sister, Neala. A leather bag hung from the side of his pony, filled with many things that would intrigue Neala. Though Lone Hawk had worried about her insatiable desire for the white man's trinkets, he was always eager to see the shine that entered her dark eyes when he would present them to her.

When Lone Hawk had arrived in his village and had not found Neala there, he thought immediately of another place where he might find her: their secret cave, shared with Sitting Tall, Lone Hawk's Sioux blood brother and Neala's lover. The cave had become their meeting place, so that neither of their fathers would know of their alliance. Sioux and Chippewa

49

chieftain fathers who hated each other would not understand their children becoming friends.

To prove the intensity of this friendship to each other, Lone Hawk and Sitting Tall had, by knife point, made a small opening in their skins from which to draw blood so as to mingle their blood with each others, vowing friendship for eternity.

Neala had only looked quietly on, knowing that there was more than mere friendship between her and the handsome Sioux brave. Their union . . . the promises they had made to each other . . . would be consummated in a much different way from the ritual of the blood brothers. She had promised herself to Sitting Tall, to one day be his wife.

Sending his pony bounding into a gallop through a swift-flowing stream cut deep into the valley, then through a pine forest, Lone Hawk continued to think about his Chippewa father and Sitting Tall's Sioux father. They were both ailing. One day soon Lone Hawk and Sitting Tall would each be the chief of their separate factions of Indians, and, hopefully, there could then be a full alliance between their two sets of people. So there was hope that peace would be finally reached between, at least, these tribes of Sioux and Chippewa.

But even now, despite strain between them, the two tribes respected each other. Before Lone Hawk's father and Sitting Tall's father had each become chief, the Sioux had taught the Chippewa how to hunt buffalo, and the Chippewa had taught the Sioux how to make canoes. The two people had traded religious ideas as well as objects. So they had maintained an uneasy peace, sometimes sharing the same hunting grounds, sometimes flaring up at the memory of an old grudge.

But a personal grudge between Lone Hawk's father and Sitting Tall's father as children had kept them stubbornly apart when they had become chiefs. This had saddened Lone Hawk and Sitting Tall. They both had hoped that peace between the tribes would grow more consistent as both became concerned with the move of the white settlers into their lands.

But not even that had drawn the two stubborn chieftains into peace talks. They had refused to share a peace pipe, even any talk of such a gesture of peace. . . .

"Boo-chee-goo-nee-gah-ee-shee-chee-gay," Lone Hawk mumbled aloud. "It *must* be done between Lone Hawk and Sitting Tall. Sitting Tall's blood now runs through my veins . . . mine runs through his. We made a pact not only for friendship, but also for the future peace for our peoples. *Ay-uh,* it shall be done. Somehow it shall be done."

"Ai-eee," he shouted, thrusting his heels into the flanks of his pony.

The pony answered Lone Hawk's command by moving quickly onward, its hoofbeats echoing through the forest like distant thunder. Lone Hawk inhaled deeply the pine scent of the trees, enjoying this moment alone on his proud steed.

This land of which Lone Hawk was a part was a land of lakes, of rivers full of rapids and waterfalls, of streams and marshes. It was a land of birches and mixed pine, of sudden and severe rock outcroppings. It was a land of rugged and incredible beauty.

His eyes absorbed and appreciated the flowering dogwood, the hills almost completely white with their blooms. Lone Hawk knew that the twigs and buds

51

provided winter browse for deer, that its bright red fruits fed the wild turkeys and other birds. The tree even served his people well. The Chippewa made a scarlet dye from the roots to color their quills and feathers, and used the bitter inner bark as a malaria remedy.

Lone Hawk's gaze captured the redbud casting their splashes into a riot of color in the woodland. This particular tree also served a purpose for the Chippewa. Its purplish-red, pealike blooms were edible, though somewhat sour-tasting. When the flowers were fried, they were eaten as a delicacy. The young fruits, which were small pods, were also edible and were delicious when fried.

The flash and gleam of a waterfall now caught Lone Hawk's eye. The rush of the water through palisades of pine trees at his side alerted him that he was nearing the cave. The cave reached beneath the waterfall, and it was indeed a perfect hideaway, not only for him to meet with his blood brother, but also for Neala to meet with Sitting Tall, as a lover.

Swinging his pony in and about thick clusters of pines, he frowned. It was not the sort of thing to wish on a sister, this having to sneak about like a thief in the night, to be with the man she loved. He would have enjoyed seeing her openly displaying her affections for her beloved. But until full peace became a reality between the Sioux and the Chippewa, only snatches of love could be taken by Sitting Tall and Neala!

Thinking about love and the feelings of a woman placed the perfect facial features of a particular woman before Lone Hawk's eyes. His insides took on a strange quivering when he saw in his mind's eye the white woman with the name of Mariana and with hair so flaming in color it threatened to take his breath away in its unique loveliness. He was fast becoming familiar with how it felt to be enthralled by a woman. None ever before Mariana, whom he had named Blazing Heart . . . had affected him so.

His jaw tightened and his dark eyes flashed with determination. One day soon he would prove his feelings for her. And he would not hide her away as it was required of Sitting Tall to do with the one he loved. Lone Hawk would immediately present Mariana into the village of the Chippewa. He would let everyone know how it must be with him. He would make the Chippewa understand that a woman with the white skin instead of the copper had stolen his heart, and he would be *proud!*

The waterfall flashed and gleamed above Lone Hawk, splashing water into the river at his left side, rushing onward through palisades of pine trees. Nudging his knees into the sides of his pony, he began climbing a steep incline toward the cave opening, his pony's hooves slipping and sliding on the damp earth and grass.

Tightening his shoulder muscles and flicking his reins, Lone Hawk urged his pony upward, cupping a hand over his mouth to warn Sitting Tall and Neala of his approach.

Smiling to himself, he thought a warning was required. He would not wish to find his sister and best friend in too compromising a position.

"*Ingah-bee-dee-gay-nay,*" Lone Hawk shouted. "*Ingah-bee-dee-gay-nay?*"

Through a shaft in the cave roof overhead the sun

53

spiraled downward onto a lover's embrace, sweet and gentle, where Sitting Tall and Neala lay, not yet fulfilled in their lovemaking this day. Sitting Tall stroked easily inside Neala, savoring this rare, stolen moment with the woman he loved.

He kissed the tiny taper of her neck, feeling her rapid pulsebeat against his lips. His hands fit beneath her soft buttocks and lifted her closer, the warm quivering of her response wrapping his manhood in a sensuous bond.

Moss lined the wall and floor of the cave in a plush green, and where the sun broke through in other places in the roof of the cave, yellow buttercups grew through the mossy floor, reaching their satiny arms upward to capture the sun's warmth.

"Did you not hear his warning?" Neala whispered, twining her arms more securely about Sitting Tall's neck. "We must stop, Sitting Tall, for my brother does approach."

Running his hands down the gentle curve of Neala's bare hips, a rush of fire burned at Sitting Tall's loins. "Your brother is not one to think loosely of what he knows is shared here," Sitting Tall said huskily. "If we do not appear at the mouth of the cave, he knows to not enter. More than once he has waited, Neala. More than once . . ."

Weaving his fingers through the black silk of her hair, he drew her mouth to his and ardently kissed her. Neala's breath was stolen from her as his strokes inside her became swift and determined. Her blood surged in a wild thrill as she felt the delicious spinning of her head, that which was only felt when nearing the moment of hot, pulsing desire only shared with Sitting

54

Tall, her lover, oh, hopefully, her future husband.

If only their fathers . . .

The momentary mindlessness that accompanied her release was cause for Neala to think of nothing else but the wonder she had again found in Sitting Tall's arms. She clung to him and placed her cheek against his chest as she felt the familiar stiffening of his body and knew that he was also nearing the moment that could only be described as heaven.

And when he was also spent and was leaning on an elbow, looking down at her loveliness, only then did Neala again remember her brother and why he might be seeking her out this day. He had been to the trading post! Perhaps he had traded for many beautiful items this day for *her*. Had he not promised . . . ?

Under a veil of lashes, Neala looked timidly up at Sitting Tall. "My brother comes," she murmured. "Sitting Tall, we must prepare ourselves for his arrival. We . . . we must get dressed."

"You seem too anxious for your brother this day," Sitting Tall grumbled. He traced the delicate lines of her face with a forefinger. "Why is that, Neala? Do you wish to be with him and not Sitting Tall?"

Neala sighed, hearing Sitting Tall's exasperated tone. She smiled sweetly up at him, tremoring beneath his touch, that touch that forever blossomed passion inside her.

"You are jealous of my brother?" she teased, seeing his handsomeness. He was not so different from her brother, but Sitting Tall was extremely tall and thin whereas Lone Hawk was better built, with muscles abounding at his shoulders and legs, and he was what Neala thought to be the perfect height—six feet.

Sitting Tall's piercing dark eyes were wide set, his lips sensuously full, but there was one major fault with this man that Neala loved. He had a craving . . . a weakness for the white man's firewater. He would almost sell his soul for a bottle of white man's whiskey!

Hopefully, Neala would be able to blot those desires from his mind one day when she could marry him and be at his side at all times to watch out for him. Then let that evil man Jed Fenris and his offering of whiskey even dare to approach Sitting Tall! She would personally pierce his heart with an arrow!

Sitting Tall casually shrugged and rose to his feet, offering a hand to Neala, helping her up from the floor of the cave, which had been spread with furs they kept hidden here for such times as these.

"Jealousy of a Chippewa would never be confessed by a Sioux," he said flatly. Then he chuckled low. "Not even jealousy of a brother."

"I am glad," Neala said, accepting his arms as he drew her fully into his embrace. She hugged him tightly. "Jealously does not become a man *or* woman, Sitting Tall. It can only cause heartache."

"We'd best dress," Sitting Tall mumbled, easing from her arms. "Sitting Tall is also anxious to see Lone Hawk. Visits between blood brothers are too widely spaced apart. That is not good."

"*Ay-uh,* yes," Neala murmured, slipping her white doeskin dress over her head. She smoothed it down over her hips, then stepped into her beaded moccasins. "Should our fathers find out we meet at all, we would be severely reprimanded."

Tossing her waist-length hair back from her shoulders to place an intricately designed headband about

56

it, she sighed languidly. "If we could only announce our desire to be man and wife," she said. "So much depends on this happening."

Sitting Tall stepped into his fringed leggings, his eyebrows forked. "You place emphasis on that word 'depend,'" he said shallowly. "Why do you, Neala?"

Her eyes wavering, Neala looked away from Sitting Tall. She had scolded him enough for drinking the white man's firewater. How could she explain to him that even the future of his people depended on her, a Chippewa?

She was the best hope possible for his people. Only by being totally with him could she make sure he didn't stray, didn't trade for the dreaded white man's whiskey! He could be a great chief to his people only if he placed his back to the one weakness in his character.

Neala would not place her back to him because of this weakness. It was something oh, so innocently begun by him those many years ago when he had accepted that first drink from that fancy white man's bottle. And since then it had kept him as though imprisoned. . . .

Evading his question, Neala lifted the fringed hem of her dress and began running to the entrance of the cave. *"Mah-bee-szhon!"* she giggled. "Come, Sitting Tall! Let's greet Lone Hawk with shared smiles!"

Fixing his headband in place, then his eagle feather in the loop of his hair at the back, Sitting Tall frowned at Neala. He didn't like it when she avoided his questions. It made him look less than a man in her eyes. Yet he had grown used to her stubborn nature and had accepted this quality about her personality that set her apart from most all other squaws.

57

He smiled to himself. Neala was as tiny as a baby doe, yet she moved among her people sometimes as though she was a bear! Lone Hawk often laughed about it also, how his sister was so headstrong and persuasive among the Chippewa.

Sitting Tall nodded to himself, following along behind her. "So shall she be as persuasive in my village of Sioux," he whispered. "My people will accept her. The fact that she is Chippewa will be dimmed in their minds when they grow to know her as I do."

Securing his pony's reins on the low branch of a tree, Lone Hawk removed the leather bag of gifts from the pony and paced not far from the mouth of the cave, watching for Neala or Sitting Tall to make their appearance. He knew they were there. He had seen their ponies grazing farther down from where he now paced, beside the river.

Stopping, he eyed the cave entrance more closely. He wasn't only anxious to give Neala her gifts, but also Sitting Tall his! The white man's sort of pipe found at the trading post had caught Lone Hawk's eye, so different from the calumet peace pipes made by the Chippewa or Sioux. The white man's pipe had a short stem, and its bowl was not made of red sandstone as were the Indians' but from a hollowed-out corncob! Also there were no bright bird feathers to decorate it.

How could any white man think to stir up peaceful feelings between men with such a drab, tiny pipe?

A smile touched Lone Hawk's lips. This gift to Sitting Tall was one meant for amusement, something for which to cause laughter for his best friend, his blood brother. They could share in laughter when comparing pipes throughout the upcoming years!

Lone Hawk's face brightened when Neala ran from the cave, waving and laughing. He returned the wave and moved onward to meet her, smiling across her shoulder now as Sitting Tall came walking tall and erect behind her.

"Nee-may-nan-dum-wah-bum-eh-nawn!" Lone Hawk shouted, waving at Sitting Tall, then stiffened himself against the forcefulness with which Neala lunged into his arms, to heartily hug him.

Neala's eyes were on the bag, yet she would not show her eagerness to her brother. She didn't want him to think that she thought more of gifts than she did of him.

Yet her heart was wildly beating with the promise of what he had chosen for her this time. He was a master of choosing gifts! Everything he had brought to her thus far had sparkled like rare jewels, not only in her eyes, but also inside her heart. He was such a kind, generous brother, a rarity, indeed!

Lone Hawk chuckled as he eased Neala from his arms, then placed his leather bag on the ground and met Sitting Tall's approach with a generous hug.

"My brother, it so good to see you again," he said hoarsely. "The days and nights grow longer between our visits, it seems."

"My father is ailing . . . your father is ailing," Sitting Tall said, returning Lone Hawk's hug. He then stepped away from him and eyed the leather bag that was almost tearing at its seams from its fullness. "Again you bring your sister gifts?"

"Ay-uh," Lone Hawk said proudly, smiling from

59

Sitting Tall to Neala. "I did not want to await her return to the village to give them to her. You know how she craves the white man's trinkets."

"It is insatiable," Sitting Tall grumbled, looking away from the bag in distaste, not from disliking the gifts brought to Neala, but from jealousy, because he was not the one offering them to her, as he should have been, since he was her suitor!

"It could cause her to get in much trouble, this desire for the white man's sparkling beads and soft hair ribbons," he quickly added.

Lone Hawk puffed out his chest proudly, smiling mischievously at Sitting Tall. "Then you would not accept a gift brought from the trading post yourself, Sitting Tall?" he taunted. "You think gifts are frivolous?"

Again Sitting Tall glanced toward the bulging bag, knowing that Lone Hawk would not be frivolous with his words. Lone Hawk had brought Sitting Tall a gift also! And though Sitting Tall detested the white traders and all they stood for, he was as anxious as Neala to see the gift chosen by his blood brother. It had to be grand, this gift chosen by such a brave as Lone Hawk!

Nervously shuffling his feet, Sitting Tall gave Lone Hawk a half smile. "Gifts for *ee-quay,* women, are frivolous," he chuckled. He lifted a shoulder into a casual shrug. *"Mee-suh-ay-oo.* That's all. Gifts between brothers are *special."*

Lone Hawk reached for the bag and placed his hand inside it, feeling around for the corncob pipe. His eyes sparkled with merriment, loving this loose, happy

60

moment with his best friend and his sister. These moments were rare, with the constant need to fend for the Chippewa. If it wasn't the search for food keeping Lone Hawk busy, it was the search for the white man's traps, to destroy them. He had so much driving him these days. And now . . . a . . . beautiful, scarlet-haired woman . . . ! If he let her, she would become the strongest drive inside him, of all. . . .

Pulling the pipe from the bag and handing it to Sitting Tall, Lone Hawk had to force himself not to laugh when seeing the perplexed expression cross his friend's face. He glanced over at Neala, seeing her eyes wide and her perfectly shaped mouth agape with wonder.

Then he squared his shoulders and forced the pipe into Sitting Tall's wide breadth of hand. "Lone Hawk's *mee-nee-dee-win*, gift, to you, my brother," he said, almost exploding inside with need to laugh boister-ously at Sitting Tall's continuing perplexity. "Is not the white man's *ah-pwah-gun*, smoking pipe, a grand gift?"

Sitting Tall turned the pipe from side to side, dwarfed in the largeness of his hand. Then he suddenly understood the meaning behind this sort of gift. It was a gift in jest. A gift to provoke laughter.

Yes, it was something his lighthearted, good-natured, blood brother would do. There were too many days spent in serious thought among all Indian tribes. A time of laughter was welcomed!

Placing the stem of the pipe between his fingers, Sitting Tall put it to his mouth and clamped his teeth onto it, his eyes gleaming merrily as he looked at Lone

Hawk with love and pride.

He nodded and spoke as he still anchored the pipe between his lips, "It is *o-nee-shee-shin,* good, " he said warmly. "The gift is accepted. *Mee-gway-chee-wahn-dum,* thank you, Lone Hawk. This peace pipe is quite unique."

Unable to hold back the laughter any longer, Lone Hawk guffawed, then accepted Sitting Tall into his embrace as Sitting Tall took the pipe from his lips and stuck it into the waistband of his leggings and hugged Lone Hawk, their laughter echoing across the river and through the dense pine forest that stretched out on all sides of them.

And then they were drawn apart when Neala went to them and placed a hand on each of their shoulders. "I am so anxious, Lone Hawk, for my gifts," she murmured. "What have you brought me, big brother? But, of course, whatever it is will be grand."

When Lone Hawk and Sitting Tall broke apart and both eyed her amusedly, she placed a hand to her mouth and giggled. She cast her eyes downward. "Unless my gift was also chosen for the same reason as Sitting Tall's," she said softly. Then her eyes shot upward. "My gifts aren't truly cause for laughter, are they? I so dreamed of . . . of . . ."

Lone Hawk took a quick step toward her and placed a forefinger to her lips, sealing them of further words of worry. "What I have brought you is not cause for laughter," he said thickly, his face now void of amusement. It was stern, with intense love for his sister. "What I have brought you . . . what I always bring you, is brought with much careful planning.

Lone Hawk chose the loveliest of gifts, for the loveliest of sisters."

A sparkle of a tear in the corner of Neala's eye reflected beneath the sun like a minute diamond as she looked up at Lone Hawk, almost choked with emotion, his devotion to her was so fierce.

But she had waited so long! She could wait no longer! *"Wee-wee-bee-tahn!* Hurry up!" she softly cried. "Present them to me, Lone Hawk. Please?"

"Ay-uh, Neala," Lone Hawk said hoarsely. *"Ay-uh."*

Dropping to his knee, with Neala settling on the ground beside him, Lone Hawk began pulling her gifts from the bag. Her eyes grew wide, her hands trembled when she watched as he placed them all on the ground for her to see.

And then, unable to hold back any longer, she began touching, then picking up the items, sighing.

"The ribbons," she said, smoothing her fingers over the velveteen fabrics of them. "They are so *mee-kah-wah-diz-ee*. Oh, so beautiful."

Then she marveled over the colorful fabrics, the spools of thread, and the copper buttons in the shape of hearts. "Everything is *mee-kah-wah-diz-ee*," she whispered.

Then she shot Sitting Tall a half glance, smiling. "Sitting Tall, it is you who should be bringing me such gifts, not my brother," she teasingly scolded.

Sitting Tall flinched, as though shot. He folded his arms across his chest and squared his shoulders. "You have been told many times before that that is impossible," he scolded back. "The Sioux have not made the same sort of peace with the white trader at the trading lodge as have the Chippewa. The Sioux trade with the trappers instead."

Lone Hawk looked quickly over at Sitting Tall, having to force himself not to scold him for what he did get in trade from one trapper, Jed Fenris. The white man's firewater!

But he chose to not spoil the day with another lecture against such practices. In time, Sitting Tall would come to realize the wrong of putting such wicked liquid into his body!

"And, Neala, even you must not let the white man gifts blind you so," Sitting Tall further scolded. "I have also told you the dangers in that. Your lust for the white man's trinkets could get you in much trouble!"

Neala rose quickly to her feet and threw herself into Sitting Tall's arms. "Let us not ruin today with angry words," she softly cried. "Neala sorry for saying you should give such gifts. Neala understands, Sitting Tall."

She looked up into his eyes. "Is Neala forgiven?" she murmured.

Sitting Tall's insides grew warm, his heart raced, seeing the innocence of her wide, dark eyes searching his face for the right answers. He smoothed some dark strands of her hair back from her brow, then lowered his mouth and gently kissed her.

Lone Hawk turned his eyes away, suddenly catapulted into another time . . . another moment. He was remembering the softness of the white woman's lips, the smell of her.

He glanced at the gifts spread out on the ground, smiling to himself. One gift traded for at the trading post had not been brought to Neala. He had chosen it especially for the white woman, knowing that one day he would be given the opportunity to present it to her.

And now, after knowing how she truly felt about him, he would be counting the sunrises and sunsets until he was with her . . . totally with her. Then he would give her his gift of love. . . .

Chapter Five

> *A perfect woman, nobly
> planned to warn, to comfort and
> command.*
> —WORDSWORTH

All the wild splendor that walled Lake Superior lay basking quietly in the cool sunlight and shadow of the forest on either side of Mariana as she traveled with Eugene South toward Deer Island, the tall, pine-covered cliffs facing the lake having now been left behind.

Mariana was finding it almost unbearable to share the canoe with Eugene South. But he had been forced upon her, as had the order from her father to spend the day with the dismal man. She had halfheartedly accepted the prepared lunch basket from her mother for the picnie on Deer Island. And Mariana thought her father absolutely foolish to believe that Eugene could protect her should evil trappers or renegade Sioux Indians happen along on the island while she and Eugene South were sharing the basket lunch!

Her gaze raked over him. He never changed in appearance. His tan hair was always tied at the nape of his neck without a stray lock out of place, and he always wore his suit of black fustian with its brass buttons. His brown leather shoes were, as usual, immaculately buffed, and his linen shirt had ruffles of lace about the cuffs.

Ah, such a simple man, with such pale features. And when he talked, how his voice did grate against her nerves! Her father could make excuses for his voice all he wanted to. Nothing would make Mariana accept it any more readily.

And her father was desperate, it seemed, to get her wed to the dreadful man! Why else would he risk her neck, to throw her into the company of Eugene South in such a way?

Oh! The thought of being with Eugene for an entire day, alone, caused Mariana's insides to curl with distaste. Should the man try to kiss her, how could she keep from retching right before his eyes?

Eugene watched Mariana, seeing more than loveliness. Her lustrous, red hair tumbled down the back of the pearl-gray dress that she wore. It had little puffed sleeves trimmed with a lace ruffle that draped to the elbows, and a bodice that came to a point in front, emphasizing the smallness of her waist, and the inviting swell of her breasts. He was also seeing much happening behind her glum mask. He knew that she did not wish to share the picnic lunch with him this day, but *he* saw it as a rare opportunity, one that could make her see him in a different sort of light.

Away from the demands of her father, perhaps Mariana could see the man Eugene South saw himself as. Though he knew that he was not the handsomest man, he had much to offer her as a husband. He could perform magnificently as a husband in bed! And he had seen how she had looked at the handsome Indian, Lone Hawk, seeing him as a man.

In the depths of her eyes, Eugene had seen Mariana coming alive as a woman does when awakening to the needs of a woman. And now that she felt these needs, she would yearn to have them fulfilled, and it was not decent to even think of her being with an Indian in such a way. She would seek out a man of her own kind . . . her own breeding . . . to experience that first thrill of being fully with a man.

Eugene squared his shoulders and smiled smugly toward Mariana, knowing that he was the best man available for her. The trappers were too filthy. The Indians were worse than that. They were savages.

"I hope you are finding the canoe trip comfortable enough," Eugene said, pulling the paddles through the water, moving the canoe forward in continued jerks. "I would have much preferred offering you a larger, safer craft. But this was all that was available for just two occupants."

Mariana sighed exasperatedly and clasped her fingers more tightly to the sides of the canoe, feeling the roughness of the birchbark through the butter softness of her gloves. "Do not worry yourself over my likes or dislikes," she said dryly. "I am doing my duty being with you. That is all. You are doing yours by being with me. It was just another chore assigned you by my father."

She tilted her chin obstinately and frowned at Eugene. "Have you ever said no to my father, Eugene?

Have you?"

Eugene's face colored with an embarrassed blush. He cleared his throat nervously. "I did not see this as a dreaded chore," he said, laughing softly. "And as to your question as to whether or not I ever tell your father no, an employee must show respect for his employer at all times. That is only a gentleman's way of approaching business."

"I see," Mariana said, drumming her fingers on the sides of the canoe. She looked away from him. "I see."

She ignored him as he again cleared his throat, not wishing to be drawn into further conversation with him. She focused her eyes on the forest and its tranquil beauty. She had explored the floor of the forest often enough to know that the small dots of color that she was seeing were the same sorts of flowers found closer to the trading post. She had clipped several that were now at her bedside in a vase.

These "orchids" of which she was thinking were in truth yellow lady-slippers, found in the oak-hickory woods. Their flower was the same as an orchid's, but much smaller. They were dainty, scarcely an inch long. The yellow lady-slipper was better known to the settlers as nerve root, because the roots were an effective nerve sedative. They were known to be used in domestic medicines, for treating hysteria and nervous disorders.

Mariana had discovered the best way to spot these dainty flowers was to walk along the bottom of a slope and look upward, since the flowers faced downslope.

The other lady-slippers Mariana had found were showy orchids, growing in the moist ledges of the limestone bluffs along the small streams. This majestic orchid grew two to three feet tall, with one or two, sometimes three, blooms topping each stem. The two-inch flowers were white with a tinge of rose-purple, spilling over the slipper as if it were overfilled with wine.

This was Mariana's favorite and she had plucked several on one of her recent outings. While she was in the forest, alone, she had felt as though she was being observed, and her thoughts had immediately gone to Lone Hawk. Yet he had not made himself known to her. . . .

Seeing movement on one side of her at the embankment, Mariana watched as several does and fawns leaped away, over great mats of vines, into the forest. And then she became aware of the rising temperature of the day as the noon sunlight stabbed down through the high canopy of leaves overhead, dappling the lake with shimmering light. It seemed hours since they had left the trading post. Any amount of time with Eugene would feel like too much, she supposed.

She repositioned herself on the seat of the canoe and sighed languidly as the canoe again raced along wider channels. Now Deer Island could be seen in the distance. It looked too isolated to suit Mariana. What had her father been thinking to place her in such a position with Eugene South? She would be completely alone with the man. Should he want to, he could take full advantage of her!

Mariana eased one of her hands from the side of the canoe and reached around to her dress where, against her thigh, her sheathed knife lay waiting, to be used for her protection. Should she have to use it to protect her virginity, she would. If her father didn't worry about such things with Eugene South, it was her duty to!

Again clasping the canoe, Mariana felt an uneasy quivering in its flooring through the softness of her moccasins. It seemed that there was something beneath the surface of the water, pulling at the canoe. And then her eyes widened. She saw vine creepers rise to the surface, tangled with a floating log. And the log was now in the way of the canoe!

Mariana reached her hand to Eugene, her insides cold with fear as the canoe tipped . . . toppled. . . .

"My Lord!" she screamed as she felt herself being tossed into the turquoise blue of the water, the force of her falling pushing her deeper into its inner depths.

Panic-stricken, gulping as water rushed into her nose and mouth, closing in on her lungs, Mariana fought to free herself of the tangle of vines that now suddenly seemed to be wrapping themselves about her like grasping fingers.

She could see the shadow of the overturned canoe above her as the sun outlined it. She struggled. She pulled at the vines, she kicked to raise herself to the surface, all the while wondering where Eugene South was. Surely he would come to her rescue!

Where . . . was . . . he . . . ?

Finally she was able to break free of the vines. She bobbed clumsily to the surface of the water, choking and coughing, gasping for breath. When she was able to finally get her wind, she smoothed her wet hair from her eyes and looked desperately about her, her dress tangling her legs as she tried to tread water.

Her eyes scanned every inch of the water as she now began to wonder about Eugene South's fate. She knew that her own was in question should she not have the strength to swim to the shore. Her battle with the vines had weakened her. The water that had momentarily filled her lungs had stolen too much of her breath, as well as her strength.

But she must swim to safety. It was obvious that she had to save herself. Eugene South had evidently looked first to his own safety, not caring whether or not she lived or died! Anger filled her veins, seeming to give her the needed strength to start swimming. She forced her arms up, then down, the strokes taught her in childhood moving her closer and closer to shore.

And when she was finally able to place her feet on the bottom of the lake, she again felt threatened, because the mud was suctioning her moccasins clean off her. Cursing beneath her breath, again brushing wet strands from her hair, Mariana left her moccasins in the mud and went barefoot through the slimy lake bottom, grimacing when the mud sometimes reached to her ankle.

And then, finally, she was climbing from the lake, hanging on to long stems of grass that bent down into the water. She tugged. She pulled, then fell in a mass of wetness to the ground, panting for breath.

But something drew her quickly back to her feet. On the opposite shore, too far away from her screams to be heard, Eugene South was walking in the direction from whence they had just traveled.

"He . . . *did* . . . only think to save himself," she whispered, clasping her hand to her mouth at the thought of such cowardice. "He didn't even dive beneath the water to search for me when . . . when . . . I was having such a struggle with those

72

terrible vines!"

Combing her fingers through her hair, looking up at the pearl-blue sky, Mariana laughed hysterically. "Papa, you sure know how to pick men!" she shouted.

Then she grew solemn, kicking her feet, trying to get the mud from between her toes. "But perhaps this is all it will take to convince Papa that he is not the man for me," she sighed. "If not this, what?"

Lifting the skirt of her dress, she sat down on the edge of the embankment and dangled her feet into the lake, swooshing them around until the mud was finally gone from them.

And then she pulled her gloves off, a finger at a time. She tossed them into the water, now starting to wonder about how she could manage to return safely to the trading post. It was many miles away now, by canoe.

Looking back in the direction of the tipped canoe, Mariana saw that the current had carried it on downstream. She had no choice but to travel by foot. And being barefoot, this could take some doing!

"Oh, well," she sighed to herself. "If I must, I must."

Rising to her feet, she shook the skirt of her dress out, hating how its wetness clung to her legs. She reached her hands to her hair, feeling its utter tangles. She smoothed it down across her shoulders as best she could, then turned and eyed the forest, then the lake. She should follow the lake back to the trading post, yet something compelled her to work her way further into the forest instead. She wouldn't be as vulnerable as she would be if she was walking alone, in clear view, along the embankment.

And then, too, she could bypass the cliffs by the way of the forest.

"Yes. It is my only choice," she whispered, heading on into the thickness of the trees.

Her only fear was of the traps set by the trappers. So many were unrecognizable by man, let alone by innocent animals. Her father had described many kinds to her, since she insisted on walking in the forest close to the trading post.

He had told her how hunters set deadfalls for wolves. The deadfalls were six-foot-by-eight-foot poles set up at an angle of about forty-five degrees and supported by a two-stick trigger. They were covered with several hundred weight of large stones. When a wolf seized the bait at the back end of the fall, the heavy roof came down and crushed it.

These wolfskins would then be converted into sleigh robes, the prime skins selling at from four to five dollars each.

Another sort of trap was made with a deer used as bait. It was killed and cut open at the back, and into the meat, blood, and entrails, three vials of strychnine— three-eighths of an ounce—were stirred. The merest bite of this deadly mixture was enough to kill, a victim seldom getting more than two hundred yards away before convulsions seized it.

But these were not the sorts of traps Mariana had to keep watch for. There were steel traps that could snap one's leg clean in two. There were deep pits dug into the ground and covered by twigs from trees, grass, and leaves, that could swallow one whole.

Trying to stay brave and keep an eye out for the traps, Mariana inched her way along, her feet already suffering from the briars piercing them.

Fear pressed into her heart the farther she moved

into the forest. She had never felt so alone as she did now. And the slant of the sun's rays through the ceiling of the forest was cause for her alarm. The noon hour was past. Night was not all that far behind.

Hurrying her steps, the need to arrive home before dark the most important drive in her now, Mariana forgot to watch for the traps. Her eyes widened when she heard the snapping of twigs and the splintering of larger branches. And before she even knew what was happening, the ground suddenly gave way beneath her and she found herself falling . . . falling. . . .

Stunned by the blow of the sudden crash of her body against the bottom of the dug-out pit, yet seeing the opening much too high over her head for her to be able to escape from, her fright gave way to a sense of loneliness and isolation, as she realized that she had become victim to one of the dreaded traps. And before she was found by the trapper, she knew that an animal could join her in the dark, smelly pit. . . .

"Papa . . ." Mariana weakly cried, covering her mouth with her hands. "Oh, Papa . . . Mama . . ."

Chapter Six

*Eyes full of starlight, moist
over fire, full of young wonder,
touch my desire!*
—EASTMAN

Attired in only a breechcloth and moccasins, with a bow slung across his shoulder and a quiver of arrows at his back, Lone Hawk led his pony behind him by its reins and moved stealthily through the forest, looking for more of Jed Fenris's traps. He had already disarmed many and had placed them on the travois being dragged behind his pony. Perhaps one day the evil trader would give up and leave! The animals belonged to the forest and the Chippewa!

Stopping abruptly, Lone Hawk spied another trap beneath a cedar tree. Its shine reflected through a scattering of leaves that had been placed over it to hide most of its ugly steel jaws from unsuspecting animals.

With determination, Lone Hawk went to the trap and poked a stick between the open jaws and probed it in the right place. Its loud clank as it slammed closed

76

reverberated through the forest. The stick snapped in two. One end flew up in the air, the other lay where an animal would have lain.

"One less pelt for the white man," Lone Hawk grumbled as he grabbed the heavy trap and placed it with the others on the travois.

Again Lone Hawk began guiding his pony through the forest, his every footstep like that of a panther, so quiet was he in his movements. His eyes were like two sharp points, piercing the underbrush, watching for signs of any other sorts of traps that were ridding the forest of too many animals. He knew that Jed Fenris had many ways of getting his pelts. When he had last been at the trading post, Lone Hawk had seen the finest of pelts piled on the counter to be weighed. Jed Fenris's hunt had been successful.

Lone Hawk had also seen Jed Fenris looking on as Lone Hawk's own pelts had been carried in by the Chippewa braves. In the evil trader's eyes Lone Hawk had seen envy even of those.

"He wishes to see to it that we have no hunt at all," he growled. "He will soon see that he is the one who is to not be allowed to hunt! Even if Lone Hawk has to kill *him*. . . ."

Lone Hawk's spine stiffened, seeing one of those different sorts of traps he had been looking for. The steel traps unmercifully trapped an animal, leaving it to lie suffering for hours before being found and put to its death. This sort of trap that Lone Hawk was creeping up to was not so inhumane. It did not leave an animal suffering while trapped; only sometimes the creature was driven mindless with the efforts of trying to escape the dark pit it had fallen into.

77

Securing his pony's reins to a limb, Lone Hawk moved closer to the pit, seeing that it had again worked quite well for Jed Fenris, for the limbs and twigs that had been placed over the pit were broken.

"Gee-wah-nah-dis," he said sourly. "The animals of the forest are foolish to let this man trap them in such a way. They are no longer as cunning as they once were before the white man came!"

Now wondering just what sort of animal would be awaiting its fate, envisioning a wolf with a great, flossy fur, Lone Hawk placed an arrow into his bow and readied it as he knelt to his knee to begin uncovering the pit. It had become Lone Hawk's practice not only to steal the dreaded traps, but, when he came upon this sort of trap in the ground, he stole the white man's *pelt!*

A slow smile touching Lone Hawk's lips, he lifted one limb, then another. But he heard no growls or commotion of an animal pacing below him in the pit. He studied the break of the limbs and twigs, knowing that only a larger animal could have broken such a number of them. And sounds of complaint were expected from a larger animal!

With an eyebrow forked and now truly anxious, Lone Hawk moved more quickly, his gaze riveted to the spot that he was cleaning away. In only a matter of moments he would see what prize this trap had captured for him this day! Jed Fenris would be furious to lose such a large animal to a Chippewa! It made Lone Hawk proud that he knew the skills of fooling the evil trapper. It had become a game with him . . . game most profitable!

He threw another branch aside clearing the way for him to see. Lone Hawk was taken aback with shock when he saw what lay at the bottom of the pit, curled in a fetal position, asleep.

"Bis-kah-ko-nay-gee-day," he gasped. "Blazing Heart! How . . . did . . . she . . . ?"

Tossing his bow and arrow aside, Lone Hawk's muscles corded as he ripped the rest of the limbs and twigs away until he was able to jump down into the pit beside Mariana.

Mariana awakened with a start. As she opened her eyes and found copper legs next to her face, her insides splashed cold with fear.

But when her gaze shot upward and she discovered that the Indian was Lone Hawk, she broke into a stream of tears, so thankful was she that it was he, instead of another who had no kind feelings for her.

Lone Hawk knelt and swept Mariana up into his arms and carried her from the pit. Beneath a towering elm, he placed her on the ground, still holding her head on his lap.

"How did this happen?" he grumbled, his gaze capturing the smudges of dirt on her face, the blood on the delicate tips of her fingers, and the tangles of her hair.

His gaze moved lower, seeing that her feet were without moccasins, with mud caked between her toes and beneath her toenails.

Again he looked into her tearful eyes, mortified to think about her in the pit alone. It was apparent that she had slept there the entire night. What if a bear . . . or a wolf . . . ?

He would not let himself think about what would have happened if such an animal had fallen into the pit with her.

"I'm so glad you found me," Mariana sobbed, savoring Lone Hawk's closeness. She twined her arms about his waist and hugged him to her from where she lay on his lap.

Her tears wet his abdomen. Her nose picked up the spicy smell of his copper flesh, and she knew that she would forever remember this moment with him. She had dreamed of being alone with him. She was, oh, thank God, she was alone with him *now*.

If he hadn't come along . . .

Lone Hawk's insides were quivering from her closeness. He looked down upon her hair of fire and touched his hand to its tangles. He then moved the hand to her face and touched the softness of her cheek, enraptured by her all over again, and now having the pleasure of actually . . . touching . . . her.

And when her eyes moved upward and locked with his, he felt as though he was drowning in the blue of them. Never had a woman affected him so! Never would one again. She had a magic about her, this woman!

Placing his hands to her waist, he eased her to a sitting position beside him. He then framed her face between his hands, their eyes again locking. "How is it that you are so far from your home?" he said thickly. "Never before have you wandered so far."

Mariana's eyes widened. "Never before . . . ?" she shallowly whispered. "How would you know . . . ?"

"So often Lone Hawk watches from afar," he confessed. "Did you not know?"

Mariana bashfully lowered her eyes. "I had thought perhaps you were there," she murmured.

"Are you offended that Lone Hawk was?"

Mariana's eyes shot upward. "No," she blurted. "How could I be . . . ?"

Lone Hawk took her hands and turned them palmside up, frowning when he saw the blood at her fingertips. "You are wounded," he growled. "Jed Fenris will pay for this!"

"Jed . . . Fenris . . . ?" Mariana said, in her mind's eye seeing the yellow-toothed, bearded trapper.

"He is the reason you became entrapped," Lone Hawk snarled. "He causes much havoc in this forest of the Chippewa!"

"Yes. I should have known," Mariana sighed, wincing with pain as she tried to wiggle her fingers.

Lone Hawk eased her hands down, to her lap. "You were there all night?" he said, nodding toward the pit.

"Yes. All night," Mariana said, shivering at the thought. She held her hands before her eyes, shaking her head as she again studied her fingertips. "I clawed at the side of the pit until my fingers became raw. Then . . . then . . . I gave up. Sleep was my escape. But even then my dreams were troubled by thoughts of animals. . . ."

"You have not told me how you happen to be here," Lone Hawk said, not believing she was. He had pondered over and over again inside his head how this could happen, how he could be totally with her without anyone's coming along to discover them together.

This time Jed Fenris had done him a favor. This time the trapper's pit had captured something even more valuable than pelts. And Lone Hawk had claimed her, instead of Jed Fenris!

Ay-uh. No plan of Lone Hawk's could compare to how this had happened. It was destiny that they should be together. He just hated that she had suffered in any way while being led to him by destiny's plan!

She didn't want to tell Lone Hawk that she had been with another man, on her way to have a picnic with him, alone on Deer Island. She didn't think he would understand. And it was important to her that he not think she had romantic thoughts for another man, even though she had seen Lone Hawk trade for many lovely trinkets for a woman of his own.

This woman of his would just be another challenge for Mariana. She loved challenges. Yet was this one she could not overcome? Though it was obvious that Lone Hawk had feelings for her, was it the custom of the Chippewa that he give his heart to one of his own kind . . . ?

No matter. For now she could not tell him about being with another man!

Feigning lightheadedness, she swept a hand to her brow. "I'm . . . so . . . hungry . . ." she whispered, using this approach to avoid his question. "I must have food, Lone Hawk. It's been so long."

Lone Hawk looked beyond her, into the forest, then back into her eyes. "You have traveled far from your home," he said softly. "You are closer to Chippewa village than your own. Lone Hawk will take you to village. You will be given clean clothes, moccasins and food. And after you have had time to rest, Lone Hawk will return you to your family."

Mariana's pulse raced, her throat went dry at the thought of being taken to an Indian village. Yet in Lone Hawk's company she knew she did not have anything to fear. He had, thus far, shown her nothing but respect. He had been only gentle and very caring to her. This

82

made her midnight dreams of him become real, for in her dreams he had been as gentle . . . as kind. . . .

It was almost unreal, though, that she was even with him. How often had she wondered how she might be given this opportunity? Even now her lips tasted his one kiss. Her rapid heartbeat attested to how his kiss had affected her then, and would do so again, should he try.

"I appreciate your kindness," she said in a rush of words, knowing it best for the moment to erase all thoughts of kisses and feelings from her mind. Jed Fenris could arrive to check on his traps anytime now. She didn't want even to think about Jed Fenris's fate should Lone Hawk come face to face with him. It was Jed Fenris who was responsible for her almost losing her life. She still shuddered at the thought of being assaulted by a bear or wolf!

"You will ride on pony with Lone Hawk," he said, gently helping Mariana from the ground. His gaze swept over her soiled dress, envisioning her in a white doeskin dress and how its softness would mold and accentuate her breasts. He ached with the need to touch . . . to kiss . . . her breasts. Perhaps in time . . .

In one sweep, he had her up in his arms. With his shoulders proudly squared, Lone Hawk carried Mariana to his pony. He heard her gasp when she caught sight of the travois and the traps on it.

"Jed Fenris knows many ugly ways of trapping animals," Lone Hawk grumbled. "Lone Hawk's way is better. The traps I steal are never used again by anyone."

"What do you do with them?" Mariana asked as he lifted her onto his pony.

Lone Hawk bent to get his bow and arrow, slipping his bow across his shoulder and the lone arrow back into the quiver among the rest. Then he swung himself up on his horse and scooted Mariana onto his lap and began moving back into the thickness of the forest.

"Soon you will see the fate of the traps," Lone Hawk chuckled. "There is a grave filled with many. They rust like bones turning to dust. In the end, both are as useless."

A shiver raced across Mariana's flesh. "A . . . grave . . . ?" she whispered, her arm clinging about his waist.

Again Lone Hawk chuckled. "This grave is only a grave dug for the traps," he said. "It is a hole in the ground known only to Lone Hawk. As I said, soon you shall see."

He frowned down at Mariana. "No one knows of my hiding place," he grumbled. "You will be the first. It is my trust in you that leads me to showing you."

Mariana blinked her eyes nervously up at him. "You can trust me," she murmured. "Implicitly, Lone Hawk."

His eyebrows forked with her use of a word he was not familiar with. "Im . . . pli . . . citly . . . ?" he said, slowly mouthing the word. "I do not know the meaning of such a word. Is it good? Or is it bad?"

Mariana giggled beneath her breath, loving this light moment with Lone Hawk. It seemed so natural to be with him in such a way. It seemed only right. To herself she thanked Eugene South for his clumsy canoe steering, and for being too cowardly to rescue her. Otherwise, she would never have found such a valid reason to be with Lone Hawk, in his arms.

Sighing, Mariana cuddled closer to him. "The word used as I have used it today is used for good purposes," she said softly. "Its meaning? It can be defined as meaning unquestioning . . . absolute. It means you can wholly trust me, Lone Hawk."

She looked almost shyly up into his eyes. "Not only now, but for forever," she murmured.

Lone Hawk's insides again quivered at the look of sincere innocence in her eyes and the sound of it in her voice. His heart warmed, melting, it seemed, when he felt her arm tighten about his waist. And when she pressed her cheek against his chest, he feared she might hear the thundering of his heart and understand just how much she held him within a lover's trance! He didn't want to feel threatened by these unique feelings he felt for this white woman. He wanted openly to display them . . . to let the entire tribe of Chippewa see the woman he had chosen to be his wife!

But would she ever consent to be his wife? Their cultures were so different. It was easy for her to enjoy a brief time with him. But a full commitment?

He would have to test this full commitment. Soon.

Though Mariana had feigned a lightheadedness, she wasn't far from the real thing. She had chilled severely in the cold of the night, and her stomach was gnawing even now from hunger. She did not want to think how she might have been should she have spent another night in the dreary, damp darkness of the pit. She owed so much to Lone Hawk. Even her father would have to admit that *he* owed him for saving his daughter.

Perhaps this would draw her father and Lone Hawk into liking each other. Lone Hawk had proven beyond a doubt that he was not the savage that her father saw him as. In Mariana's eyes he was more man than Eugene South, Jed Fenris, *and* her father rolled into one. He was a man . . . a man who had captured her heart.

With its load of traps dragging behind it, the pony moved at a slow pace, yet seemed to cover much ground in a little time. And now it was following alongside a meandering stream, the shafts of sun showing through the tree branches into the water as though golden spikes stretched out, end to end.

"We are nearing the burial spot for the traps," Lone Hawk mumbled, nudging his knees into the side of his pony, urging it on faster. "And not far from there we will then enter my village. My people will be surprised to see a visitor brought to them in such a way."

Mariana again tensed, wondering how his people would react to seeing her with him. Would she be shunned? Or would she be welcomed? She knew how Indians were treated by most whites. Would the Indians be the same toward her? She hoped not. She didn't want anything to spoil this time spent with Lone Hawk. She would memorize each and every moment with him, to draw from in her mind, when again they parted, for this time might be not only their first time together, it might be their last. When she returned to the trading post, her father would most surely keep closer watch on her. Especially after she was returned by an Indian. She knew not to expect her father ever to welcome Lone Hawk as any sort of friend. It was just too much to hope for. She knew her father too well to really hope anything could be different.

Mariana was jarred from her reverie when the pony suddenly stopped and Lone Hawk helped her to the

86

ground. Wide-eyed, she watched him go to a large boulder. As his powerful muscles corded and strained, he pushed the boulder aside, revealing what lay beneath it. It was a hole in the ground just wide enough to drop the traps into. And as she continued to watch, Lone Hawk quickly disposed of at least seven traps.

And when the boulder was again in place, he went to her and drew her onto his lap again on the pony and they proceeded on through the forest.

"It is done," he said blandly. "And until Jed Fenris stops using traps, there will be more added to the grave of traps. The traps are *mah-nah-dud,* bad! No one should hunt in such a way. No one! The arrow is swifter. The animal dies quickly. It is not made to suffer!"

A clap of thunder in the distance drew Lone Hawk's eyes to the heavens. Through the canopy of trees overhead he saw the sky changing from a pale blue to a yellowish-brown color. A zigzag of lightning forked across the sky. The ground beneath the pony's hooves rumbled.

"A storm is near," he said, cupping his hand to look more closely at the darkening sky. "The sort of clouds Lone Hawk sees foretells bad storm, one with much wind and lightning. The rain will continue even into night once it begins."

Mariana tensed, shivering at the thought of the dreadful pit. If she had been still there when the rain had begun . . .

She closed her eyes, not wanting to think about it.

And then her eyes flew wide open. She glanced up at Lone Hawk. If the storm was so severe, and if it was one that might continue for so long, it would be next to

87

impossible for her to return home until it was over. If the rain continued on into the night, that meant that she would have to spend the full night with Lone Hawk.

A sensual thrill coursed through her at the thought, yet there was a trace of fear troubling her. Would ... he ... seduce her ... ? Would she wish ... for ... the seduction ... ? He was the very first man to kiss her. Would he be the very first man to ... to ... teach her fully the ways of a woman?

Her heart vibrated against her ribs, knowing that she wanted him ... fully wanted him.

Chapter Seven

*Who would not love you, see-
ing you move, warm-eyed and
beautiful through the green
grove?*
                    —EASTMAN

Lurid flashes of lightning continued to light the fearfully dark sky. Lone Hawk's pony neighed and shook its mane in fright. But finally it moved out into a clearing and Mariana got her first glimpse of Lone Hawk's village. Sitting in the shimmering shadows of giant cottonwoods along the creek, the wigwams were like looming ghosts as again the lightning illuminated them.

The wigwams were arranged in the shape of a large horseshoe, all facing east, enabling them to bid a welcome to the spirit of the rising sun. Fires burned brightly outside each of the wigwams. Indians were scattering as the first drops of rain began to fall. Dogs were barking and baying.

Mariana had worried about her appearance, this first time she was to be seen by Lone Hawk's people.

But now she did not have that to worry about. Everyone was too involved in getting away from the storm to care about a lone pony entering the village or what that pony was carrying.

Icy pelts of rain began to beat down hard from the sky onto Mariana's face and shoulders. Lone Hawk quickly dismounted from his pony and grabbed her from it and began running, carrying her toward a wigwam.

"The spirits are again angry at trappers," he said scornfully. "The heavens speak with many voices of thunder to frighten the trappers from the land of the Chippewa!"

Mariana looked up into his eyes, seeing them dark with anger. His words of spirits and so much more about him made her realize their total difference in beliefs. Yet she did not feel alien to this village he had brought her to. There was something within her that told her she belonged. It was like other times . . . the strange feelings that overpowered her . . . her desire to know more about the Indians, her awe not only of Lone Hawk, but of all Indians.

Yet she had to believe it was because of Lone Hawk. Her attraction to him had most surely gotten her interest aroused in the Indians in the first place, and now that she was enthralled by them, she hungered to know everything about them. She hungered to be a part of them.

Panting hard, Lone Hawk carried Mariana into his wigwam, his eyes brightening at finding Neala there, keeping the fire in his fireplace burning. He looked about him, smiling. She had even swept his bulrush mats sparkling clean. She had food cooking over the fire. The aroma of wild greens and rabbit rose from the brass kettle sitting in the flames.

Mariana's heart plummeted when she caught sight of the lovely Indian squaw sitting so obediently beside the fire in Lone Hawk's wigwam. And Mariana recognized the colorful yellow velveteen ribbon tied about the squaw's long, flowing black hair, and the necklace of glass beads about her tiny taper of a neck. These were some of the gifts Lone Hawk had traded for at Mariana's father's trading post. This had to be . . . Lone Hawk's . . . woman.

The knowing tore pieces of Mariana's heart away.

Neala rose quickly to her feet, aghast at seeing Lone Hawk entering with a white woman. Who was she? Had he taken . . . her . . . captive . . . ?

"Way-nen-dush-win-ah-ow?!" Neala hissed, smoothing her hands down the lines of her white doeskin dress.

"Ween gee-wee-gee-ah-gun!" Lone Hawk said flatly, easing Mariana to the bulrush-mat floor of his wigwam.

"Weh-go-nen-dush-wi-szhis-chee-gay-yen?" Neala said, her eyes now traveling slowly up and down Mariana.

Mariana tensed, her jealousy of the squaw worsening because she couldn't understand what was being said between her and Lone Hawk. From their tone, it sounded as though they were arguing. Mariana knew from the cold look in the squaw's eyes it was *she* they were arguing over. But why wouldn't they? Surely the squaw did not wish to share the wigwam with Lone Hawk and another woman, especially a *white* woman.

Squaring her shoulders and lifting her chin, Mariana

91

decided she didn't wish to share the wigwam with the squaw. And . . . she . . . wouldn't!

Turning on her heel, she stomped toward the entrance flap, not even caring that the storm was raging in an ugly fury outside the wigwam. Her heart had made a mistake. She should never have let herself get infatuated with Lone Hawk or his ways of life. She would find her way back to the trading post, alone. She didn't need him. She most certainly didn't need an Indian squaw in her life!

A firm hand on her wrist abruptly stopped Mariana. She was jerked around to face Lone Hawk. She firmed her jaw and glared up at him as he continued to hold her in bondage by the tight grip on her wrist. She just challenged him with a set stare as he looked questioningly down into her eyes.

"Andi-aszhion?" he said.

Mariana sighed. She shook her head. "How on earth do you expect me to know what you *or* your woman are saying when you choose to speak in Chippewa?" she said dryly. "Lone Hawk, just let me go. It's obvious I am not wanted here. Why . . . did . . . you even bring me? Your . . . your . . . woman is quite upset by me being here."

Lone Hawk's head jerked back, his eyes widened, and then he laughed throatily as he released Mariana's wrist. He gave Neala a sideways glance, then again looked down at Mariana. "My woman?" he said, again softly laughing. "You think she is my woman?"

Looking from Lone Hawk to Neala, Mariana reached her hand to her throbbing wrist, then was made rudely aware of her raw fingers when she touched them to her wrist, and she recoiled and dropped her

92

arms to her sides.

"She . . . *isn't your woman?*" Mariana said in a near whisper.

Lone Hawk shook his head, his eyes warm with amusement. He stepped to Neala's side and placed an arm about her waist. "She is my *gee-shee-may,*" he chuckled.

Mariana emitted a frustrated breath. She implored Lone Hawk with questioning in her eyes. "Lone Hawk, again you speak in Chippewa," she said. "I know no more than before. What is she to you?"

Nudging Neala to take a step toward Mariana, Lone Hawk nodded toward her. "She is my sister," he said softly. "Neala. Her name is Neala."

A relief swept over her, so keen it felt as though a fresh breeze of morning had touched her all over, and Mariana felt her insides become relaxed in a quivering warmth. This squaw was only Lone Hawk's sister! The squaw he had traded so many gifts for was his sister! The proof lay in the gifts worn by Neala! And since no squaw besides his sister was waiting for Lone Hawk in his wigwam, he most surely had none. His feelings for Mariana were sincere. He was attracted to her in the exact way she was attracted to him. She was so happy over this discovery that she knew she must be beaming like the sun, bright in the heavens!

Neala only halfheartedly approached Mariana, then swung around and totally faced Lone Hawk. "She now knows I am your sister," she said sourly in English. "But Neala not know what she means to you? Why is she here? Why did you bring her?"

"Mee-eewh!" Lone Hawk growled, flailing his hand in the air. "Enough, little sister. Soften your tone of

93

voice. You are in the presence of the woman I have chosen to one day be my *gee-wee-oo!"*

Taken aback by his declaration, Neala's eyes wavered and her knees weakened. She placed her hands to her cheeks. *"Gah-ween!"* she softly cried.

Mariana was becoming frustrated, looking from Lone Hawk to Neala, wondering what was now being said that appeared to have shocked Neala so terribly. It had to be something terrible for Neala to react in such a way. What could Lone Hawk have said? What did he have planned for her? He had chosen her to one day be his . . . what . . . ?

"You will get used to it in time," Lone Hawk said, suddenly drawing Neala into his arms, to hug her. "My sister, you know that everything I do is done with much thought."

"But . . . this . . . ?" Neala said, looking up into his eyes, silently pleading with him. "She is white, Lone Hawk. She does not know any of the ways of the Chippewa. How could she be . . . your . . . wife . . . ?"

The word "wife" came at Mariana like a bolt of lightning from the sky. The loud crash outside the tent as thunder erupted seemed to be an expression of her reaction at knowing what Lone Hawk had planned for her! He was going to marry her? She was going to be his wife? Had he planned this long ago when he had been watching her from afar? Had he been assessing her worth as a woman . . . as a wife?

The thought thrilled, yet frightened her. Could she be transformed from white to Chippewa? Did she really want that complete change? How would one learn the duties of the wife of an Indian if one was only trained in the ways of the white woman . . . ?

Then she shook her head, realizing where her thoughts had taken her. Was this truly happening to her? Was it real? Or would she awaken and find herself back in her bed at the trading post? So often she had dreamed of a life with Lone Hawk. But that had only been a dream . . . a fantasy. . . .

"Do not worry yourself so over what your brother chooses in life," Lone Hawk chuckled, easing Neala from his arms. "Now is not the time. My woman is in need of many things. Her fingers are raw and bleeding. Her dress is ripped and torn. She is shoeless. She needs a bath. She needs food. All of these things we will give her, Neala. You will bring her one of your loveliest dresses, a pair of your moccasins most intricately designed with beads, and a basin of water."

He looked toward the entrance flap, hearing the downpour of rain and the constant claps of thunder. "But move quickly," he grumbled. "The sky spirits are releasing much anger this day. You will get wet, but you can dry later by the fire in your wigwam knowing you have been helpful not only to your brother but also to a woman who soon will be your sister."

Stunned by all of this, Mariana watched as Neala fled from the wigwam. Then her gaze moved about the dwelling, seeing how Lone Hawk lived when he was at home, at peace with himself. The wigwam seemed carefully constructed, a framework of bent saplings, covered with hides and birchbark, secured with willow twigs. A buckskin "sail" was fastened above the chimney vent to guide the smoke from the lodge fire.

The inside walls were lined with bulrush mats and buckskin hides that had been dressed and made smooth enough for the painting of symbols on them.

These represented the moon, the rising sun, and many birds and flowers in various shapes and colors.

Soft robes and warm-looking blankets were spread about along the walls, along with parfleches and cooking utensils, the former well filled with dried berries and choice dried meats and pemmican.

Closer to the fire, which had been built inside a circle of stones, plush furs had been spread above bulrush mats, and farther away still, on the far side of the wigwam, Mariana saw a collection of bows and arrows and the shine of several rifles propped against the wall.

Impressed, finding the wigwam and all that belonged to Lone Hawk quite unique, Mariana moved her gaze and found Lone Hawk silently studying her. "Does my dwelling please you?" he said, chuckling low.

Mariana felt a slow blush rising to her cheek, now aware that Lone Hawk had been observing her while she had been scrutinizing his belongings. She smiled awkwardly up at him. "Yes. It is all so neatly kept," she murmured.

"We can thank my sister for that," Lone Hawk said, taking Mariana by an elbow, guiding her down beside the fire. "My mother fusses, also. She is one who keeps too busy mothering when mothering is no longer needed. She forgets that her son is no longer a child."

"That is the way of mothers," Mariana said, wincing when she leaned her hand against a bulrush mat as she eased down onto a thick fur beside it. Her fingers ached so!

Then she forgot about her fingers. The thought of her mother sent spirals of anguish through her heart. She knew that Eugene South's return to the trading post without her would cause her mother much unnecessary stress. Her mother would believe that she was dead, when all along she was safe! And in her mother's weakened condition, what might the worry do to her?

The continued raging of the storm outside the wigwam made Mariana quite aware of the impossibility of returning home to let her mother know that she was all right. She would have to hope that her mother was much stronger than she had appeared to be of late. Mariana had no other choice. She had tried to warn her Papa that Eugene South was not dependable. It was none of her doing that she had been in the damn canoe when it had tipped!

Lone Hawk settled down beside Mariana. He placed his forefinger to her chin and turned her face so that their eyes could meet. "Your thoughts were suddenly transported to another place," he said thickly. "There is much worry in your eyes. Why is that? You are now safe with Lone Hawk. And soon you will be freed of your wet, torn dress and have food inside your stomach. There is no need for you to be worried. Or is it that you are, instead, afraid? Do I give you cause to be frightened? Haven't I treated you gently?"

Mariana's skin turned to fire where he touched her, his smouldering dark eyes melting her as he looked so intensely down at her. In his voice she could hear passion. His musky, spicy aroma threatened to send her into a strange mindlessness.

"No. I'm not afraid," she murmured. She blinked her eyes nervously, trying to wrench herself from this trance she was being drawn into by being with him, alone. "It was my mother. I was worried about her. Should I not arrive back home soon, she will think I

97

am dead."

"There is no way to send word in such a storm."

"I know."

"Then try and place worries from your mind. Lone Hawk has waited many sunrises and sleeps to be alone with you. In your heart you know you feel the same about me."

Lone Hawk placed his hands to her cheeks and drew her mouth to his in a soft kiss, causing Mariana's head to take on a crazy spinning. Something strange was happening between her thighs. She was experiencing a new sensation . . . a tingling, a sweet sort of tingling never known to her before. And when one of Lone Hawk's hands swept down and cupped her breast through her dress, Mariana did not recognize the sound that came forth from somewhere deep inside her. It was a moan of sorts, something she could not hold back, because the feelings Lone Hawk was evoking inside her could only be described as deliciously beautiful.

And then he drew away from her and rose to his feet just as Neala entered the wigwam in a rush, laughing from the wet strands of her hair tumbling over her shoulders and down an even wetter back.

"The rain is invigorating," Neala giggled, placing a wooden basin filled with water on a bulrush mat beside the fire. She took a dress that had been slung across her arm and placed this beside the basin, and then slipped the moccasins from beneath her arm where they had been secured and handed them to Lone Hawk.

"Your sister obeys well?" she said, smiling up at Lone Hawk.

"This time she does," Lone Hawk chuckled, taking

98

the moccasins with one hand and guiding Neala to the entrance flap with the other. "Now you obey again. Go to your dwelling and change into dry, warm clothes. Leave me and my woman for the remainder of the night."

Neala smiled weakly from Mariana to Lone Hawk, then again fled from the wigwam, her thoughts scrambled about this thing that her brother had chosen to do. But it was not best to question a brother who would one day be chief. He had been instructed well as a child. He had developed well into a man, knowledgeable in all ways of the world. If he wanted a white woman, it was only right that he have her!

Neala hurried on to her wigwam, dripping wet. As she changed into dry clothes, her thoughts were filled with the one chosen by her to be her lifetime mate. Sitting Tall. Oh, how she worried about him when she was not with him. If he were only as wise as Lone Hawk . . . !

Mariana eyed the water, the dress, and the moccasins that were now being offered her. And Lone Hawk's words to his sister had been implanted into her consciousness as a leaf sometimes becomes fossilized into stone. Mariana was to spend the full night alone with Lone Hawk! Would . . . he . . . do more than kiss her . . . ?

But yes, she knew the chances were great that he would try to draw her into a full seduction. And she was afraid that she was not in any frame of mind to deny him. These feelings between them were becoming too strong to deny.

"My sister is generous with her things, is she not?" Lone Hawk said, placing the moccasins on Mariana's lap. "Now you can dress like a Chippewa."

He nodded toward the basin of water. "You will remove the mud from your lovely body," he added, his heart pounding at the thought of touching her all over, testing not only the smoothness of her velvety pink skin, but also her response to his skilled fingers and lips.

Mariana looked around her at the close confines of the wigwam. There was no privacy offered her for a sponge bath. Her face flushed crimson when she looked into Lone Hawk's eyes and saw that it did not matter to him. But to her? She had never even let her father see her in less than a petticoat. How could she let Lone Hawk?

But the command in his eyes told her what was expected of her. She followed him as he went to settle on his haunches across the fire from her, his eyes not leaving her. As though willed to, Mariana placed the moccasins on the bulrush mats beside her and reached for the buttons at the back of her dress, but she flinched with pain when she remembered her raw fingers. She could not even touch the button, much less slip it through a buttonhole.

Smiling awkwardly, she dropped her hands away from her dress. "I can't unbutton my dress," she murmured bashfully. "My fingers. They are too sore, Lone Hawk. They . . . pain . . . me so. . . ."

His long leg muscles knotted and rippled as he rose back to his feet, passion in his eyes. He went unsmiling to Mariana and urged her to her feet before him. And as he reached behind her to unbutton her dress, his eyes again held Mariana speechless. Her insides grew hot as she began to awaken to what it felt like to be a woman in love.

As Lone Hawk smoothed her dress down from her shoulders and then her petticoats, so that both rested about her tiny waist, his eyes first devoured her breasts, and then he lowered his lips, to draw one of the taut tips between them. His tongue flicked out and tasted the sweetness of her flesh, and then his hands swept upward and molded her breasts, setting his loins on fire with need for her.

Mariana scarcely breathed. Her eyes were wide and she was quite aware of the thundering of her heart. It was threatening to drown her in its erratic beats! And the drugged passion that was overwhelming her made her toss aside all thoughts of shame for what she was sharing with this Indian. It was their destiny to be together. Nothing could be wrong that was shared between them.

And she had waited so long for this moment. Always before, dreams had had to suffice. But never in her dreams had she experienced such marvelous sensations! This hot, pulsing desire was something she hardly understood, but she liked the way she felt. Her thoughts were no longer a bundle of confused wonder. With him, everything fit into place. She was . . . going . . . to . . . shamelessly enjoy . . .

But then she was drawn from her reverie when Lone Hawk stepped back away from her and continued lowering her dress. And when he slipped her petticoat away, leaving only her garment covering her private area, she felt her first stirrings of fear. If she let him remove even that, she was silently giving her permission to let him do as he wished with her. Would she regret it—though her heart yearned for this man with the fathomless eyes?

She didn't have any more time to think about it. Lone Hawk soon had her standing totally nude before him and she found herself strangely devoid of shyness as his gaze swept over her, appraising her.

"It is Lone Hawk who will bathe you, since your fingers do not have the ability to do so," he said hoarsely, easing her down on the furs beside the fire. "Do not be bashful, my woman. From this moment on, you will no longer have reason to fear my eyes on your nudity. You will be mine, soon, in every sense of the word. All that will be left to make you fully mine will be words spoken in marriage. And Lone Hawk will not rush you. Lone Hawk knows you have family to consider. You spoke so warmly of your mother. Lone Hawk understands. Lone Hawk's feelings for mother are strong."

Stunned speechless by his declaration of possession and his understanding of her feelings, Mariana stretched out on her back, watching Lone Hawk as he dipped a cloth into the water and began rubbing it, meditatingly, it seemed, along the curve of her neck. Feeling as though she was in a dream, Mariana tremored as he washed even lower, sensuously touching first one breast and then the other.

And when the cloth lowered across her abdomen, Mariana's breath sucked in as her skin tremored beneath the soft wetness of the cloth. Then she shut her eyes to the ecstasy as he went lower still and spread her thighs and touched her softly where no man had ever touched before.

She was glad when at last the cloth went lower, and finally even her toes were rid of the awful mud and she could breathe more easily. Her eyes fluttered open when Lone Hawk eased her shoulders up, and he placed a fur about them.

"All that remains to be made right about your appearance is your hair," he said, smiling warmly down at Mariana. "Lone Hawk has something for you to make even that right. I chose a gift for you from the trading post. It is something that I hope will please you."

Sitting up, drawing the warmth of the fur more snugly about her, Mariana watched Lone Hawk as he went to a leather bag. Her pulse raced as he reached inside. She couldn't believe that when he had been choosing all those lovely gifts he had had her in mind. He had traded his pelts for something especially for *her*. Even then he had known that they would be together, in such a way as now. Had he known that he wouldn't have to force her? Make her a hostage? Had he known that, instead, she would become a hostage of his heart?

Softly gasping, Mariana watched as Lone Hawk brought a hairbrush to place at her feet. She had admired it when she had first seen it on the shelf at her father's trading post. It had been brought from England. It had to be the loveliest of any brush she had ever seen before. It seemed to have been made from some sort of pink shell, and it sparkled even now beneath the glow of the fire.

Picking it up, Mariana could hardly keep her hands from trembling. Her eyes moved slowly up to meet the wonder in Lone Hawk's. Though it pained her to hold it, she held the hairbrush to her breast, knowing that she would always treasure it. "It is so beautiful," she murmured. "And you traded it to give to me?"

"*Ay-uh.* Yes. It is yours," Lone Hawk said, settling on his haunches before her. His eyes went to her hair, and then he lifted his hand to the tangles. "Your hair. Within it there is a hint of fire. It seemed only right that my first gift to you should be a brush with which to make it even lovelier."

He looked at her sore fingers, then at the brush. Without asking permission he took the brush and began drawing it through her hair, loosening the tangles. Mariana sat as though in a trance, again aware of his gentleness, of his feelings toward her. She felt her hair tumbling in long, smooth strands back down to her shoulders, and she looked up into Lone Hawk's eyes just as he placed the brush aside and drew her into his arms.

Easing her down on her back, Lone Hawk stretched out above her. While kissing her he freed himself of his breechcloth and headband, then his moccasins. And when his copper skin was free to touch fully the smoothness of her yielding flesh, he reveled in its utter softness. He had known all along that it would be this beautiful, this perfect, to be with her.

With trembling fingers he smoothed the fur away from her shoulders and let his lips explore her neck, the gentle curve of her jaw, and then lower where her breasts strained up against his chest. He heard her intake of breath as he lowered his lips over the taut tip of her nipple, while his hands sent feathery touches along her abdomen, then lower. His heart thundering, he dared to cup fully the soft vee of her hair between her

104

thighs and then let a finger search for her love bud, which he found pulsing, a sheath in itself, ready to be caressed.

Becoming almost mindless with pleasure, Mariana twined her arms about his neck and urged his mouth to her lips. Dizzy, she kissed him, soaring from the sensations he was arousing by touching a part of her between her legs that she had known nothing of. As his finger caressed and his lips gave her a heated kiss, she found herself growing weak with response.

Lone Hawk momentarily drew his lips away. He placed his free hand to her cheek. "What we do is beautiful," he said in a subdued voice. "What I am about to do will pain you, then become something never experienced before by you. Bear with the pain. I soon will make you forget all pain. It will be even more beautiful than what we have already shared."

Mariana's eyes grew wide. She began to protest, but again his lips claimed all her senses as he kissed her. She again became languorous, as though drugged. And when she felt him impale her with the part of him that he had not yet revealed to her, having somehow managed to undress while kissing her, the pain was only brief, for it soon smoothed out into something wonderful.

A warmth spread through her body, then became heated as he stroked his hardness inside her. By what seemed instinct, Mariana lifted her legs and locked them about his waist, causing her womanhood to be grazed more fully as he rhythmically moved against her.

Lone Hawk's muscles corded and his breathing was harsh as he fulfilled the dreams and passions of his heretofore lonely nights. How often had he hungered for this moment, to be wholly with this woman with hair of flame and skin of velvet? In her eyes he had known that it was not an impossible thing that he wanted. He had seen her want of him. He had felt it in their first kiss. And now to be totally with her! His insides were crazed, it seemed, with this want, with this search for fulfillment! And he must make her enjoy it fully, so that she would ache for more moments like this with him!

Stroking even more eagerly inside her, his hands searching for what he knew to be every woman's pleasure points, he performed the skills he had practiced on many a squaw, always with the thoughts of Mariana in his mind. He placed his hands beneath her buttocks and lifted her closer. He plunged harder. He kissed her ardently. And then he felt her body begin to tremble sensuously. He heard her soft moan of joy as he himself also reached the pinnacle of release. And he had found it in the arms of the one he loved . . . would love *ah-pah-nay,* forever!

Breathless, Mariana clung to Lone Hawk, still tingling where she had felt such an immense pleasure it astounded her!

"Lone Hawk, I never thought it possible for anything to be so beautiful," she whispered. Her eyes closed as she sighed. "I never thought it possible for me to give myself to a man . . . in . . . such a way. My mother. Oh, Lord, what would she think of me, her only daughter?"

Lone Hawk framed her face between his hands. She opened her eyes and looked devotedly up at him.

"Never feel shame when you are with me," he

106

grumbled. "You are my woman, I am your man. We knew it would be so the very first time we made eye contact. It is meant to be. Be happy."

Mariana threw herself into his arms and placed her cheek against his chest. "Oh, I am," she softly cried. "I am."

But tomorrow? When the world became real again, she wondered if she could still be as happy . . . as sure of her decision to give herself totally to a man . . . a Chippewa Indian!

Chapter Eight

Her fairness wedded to a star,
is whiter than all lilies are.
                    —O'BRIEN

A low growl of thunder rumbled in the distance, an occasional, stubborn flash of lightning forked across the heavens as Jewel stood at her bedroom window, peering from it. Shivering, she let the sheer lace-trimmed curtain flutter back over the window, then turned and began pacing. The fact that Mariana and Eugene hadn't returned from their picnic earlier in the evening had already been cause for alarm. And now that the storm had come with such a fury, Jewel's worries were doubled. If Mariana and Eugene had been on their way back from Deer Island in the flimsy canoe, the chances of their surviving the storm were slim.

"Thank God the storm is now past," she whispered, hoping beyond hope that Mariana and Eugene could still be somewhere, waiting out the storm.

108

She wrung her hands, and the tail of her long dress swished around her ankles as she paced from one end of her bedroom to the other. She looked toward the candle on her nightstand, seeing how it had burned halfway to its brass holder. She again looked toward the window, seeing only blackness through the white of the curtain.

"Oh, where are they?" she whispered, tears near.

She went to her dressing table and sat down and busied her fingers at unplaiting her loop of hair at the back of her neck. But her fingers were trembling too severely. She lowered her face into her hands, not wanting to believe that she had lost her Mariana. Mariana was the only good thing left in Jewel's world. In this wilderness, her daughter was a blessing.

Slowly lifting her eyes, Jewel looked toward a drawer at her right side. She flicked a tear from her cheek and swallowed hard, moving a trembling hand to the drawer. With a rapid heartbeat troubling her, she opened the drawer and scooted her fine lingerie aside and stared moodily toward a small book, from which hung a ribbon to which was attached a gold key.

Jewel's eyes focused on the lock at the front of the book. "My diary," she whispered. "Now Mariana may never know. . . . "

"So there you are," Everett grumbled as he walked heavily into the room.

Taken so by surprise, Jewel quickly closed the drawer, almost swooning with fright. She knew that Everett didn't approve of her keeping the diary in her possession. He knew that she no longer made daily entries into the diary, since she had used up the last of the space long ago. Until she had filled its every line he had let her write in it each day. But now that she didn't have the space he felt that the diary was useless and that it should be thrown away, and that she should begin a new one, if she so desired.

But Jewel knew his true reasons for wanting her to throw the diary away. He didn't approve of what she had written those many long years ago. She was sometimes surprised he hadn't stolen it from her drawer and thrown it away himself. But he knew that she would take Mariana and leave should he be so bold as to do that. Jewel had learned to tolerate much about Everett these past years after discovering that he was no more than a cheat to his friends. Only because of Mariana had she chosen to stay with him. Jewel had wanted Mariana to be raised by both a mother and a father. And Everett knew this and treaded lightly around his wife.

Jewel rose to her feet and smoothed the wrinkles from her gathered, plain cotton dress with its long sleeves and high collar. Again she glanced toward the window.

"I'm so afraid," she murmured. Her gaze shot toward Everett. "You know they should have been home long ago, Everett. Do you think they . . . ?"

Everett took two wide steps and drew Jewel into his muscled arms. "Now, now . . ." he crooned, caressing her back. "Don't you get to thinkin' on bad things. Eugene'll look after Mariana. You know how he feels about her. He loves her, Jewel. He wants her to be his wife. He won't let anything happen to our little girl."

Jewel grimaced and withdrew angrily from his arms. "Why did you have to force Eugene on Mariana like that?" she softly cried. "She didn't want to go. She

110

doesn't even like the man. She doesn't want to marry him, Everett. You know she doesn't."

Her gaze swept over Everett, seeing his buckskin attire, the holstered pistol at his waist, and the knife thrust into a sheath at the side of his leg. She looked up at him—he was over six feet tall and weighed at least two hundred pounds. He had changed so much since they had left their Tidewater Plantation. He resembled a savage, dressed in such a way.

She glanced down at her plain dress. Oh, how she hated it! In Virginia she had worn the grandest gowns of silk and satin. She had walked proudly about. Now she was often stooped, in her unhappy frame of mind!

"Do you expect Mariana to be happy with Eugene South, living like . . . this . . . ?" Jewel said in a strained whisper, gesturing toward herself with a sweep of a hand. "Our daughter should be enjoying parties. Men of means could be entertaining her! Eugene South . . . he . . . he doesn't know the first thing about courtesy to a woman. He doesn't even know how to talk. Only a nasal whine, Everett. Only a nasal whine! Our daughter deserves better!"

Then she buried her face in her hands, sobbing. "What am I saying?" she cried. "Mariana may not even now be given a chance to live in any way. Mariana might be . . . dead. . . ."

Everett hurried to Jewel and again drew her into his arms. "Why are you doing this to yourself?" he scolded. "You know your health can't stand stress of any sort. But now that you've said your piece, maybe it's best."

He began ushering her toward her bed. "Darlin', what you need is rest," he said softly. He held her with

111

one arm and bent to throw back a patchwork quilt with the other. Then he eased her down onto the bed, fluffing pillows beneath her head.

"Everett," Jewel fussed, trying to rise from the bed but being held down with the firm press of his hand, "I don't want to rest. How can I with Mariana out there . . . somewhere. . . ."

Giving in to his suggestion, Jewel turned to her side and covered her face with her hand. Again she sobbed. "Yes. I do feel tired," she murmured. "Oh, so woefully tired. My heart feels as though something is tightening around it." She placed a hand to her mouth. "Oh, Mariana," she cried. "Mariana . . ."

Everett eased her shoes from her feet and placed them on the floor, then pulled the blanket over her, his deep-set eyes hazed over with tears. Should anything happen to Jewel a part of his life would be over. Though he had been driven by greed and had caused her life to fall apart, *she* had been *his* lifeline. Without her . . . ? Mariana was too distant most of the time for him to draw any sort of comfort from *her*. It was as though she knew that dark secret of her mother's past. Yet only he and Jewel were supposed to know.

He glanced toward the closed dresser drawer. The damn diary. Hidden between its pages was the truth. Damned if he knew why Jewel was compelled to keep the diary and its ugly truths. It was as though Jewel *wanted* to keep those dreadful days of her past alive!

He lowered his eyes and shook his head. As long as Mariana was alive, so was the past. Destroying the diary would not be destroying the ghastly deed of that damnable Indian all those many years ago . . . !

Bending his stately back, Everett smoothed a lock of

112

hair back from Jewel's face, sighing deeply when he felt how wet it was from her tears. He then bent a kiss to her cheek and turned and walked heavy-footed from the room, feeling useless, utterly useless. He knew as well as Jewel that Mariana and Eugene should have returned by now. And if they survived the storm, could they survive the Indians . . .?

He doubled his hands into fists. "The Sioux," he grumbled. "The damnable Sioux!"

Going to the fireplace, he took his pipe from the mantel and filled it with tobacco, then slumped down into a chair. Taking a twig from the fire, he lit his pipe, then eased his shoulders back against the softness of the upholstered chair and stared into the flames, lost in thought of what life had once been and what it was now. He missed the evenings filled with the challenge of gambling. He missed the horse races . . . the dances. . . .

Kneading his brow, he clamped hard onto the stem of his pipe, missing everything of life that he had once known. He was paying for his corruptness. Yet he knew that he had been lucky to escape Virginia with his life. Even now he suspected he was being hunted!

A low laugh broke the silence of the room. "Guess I showed them a thing or two," he whispered. "Cunning. Yes, I'm a cunning cuss, I am."

Jewel tossed and turned on the bed, in a moment of restless sleep. Then her eyes shot open in remembrance. "Mariana?" she said, quickly sitting upright. "Mariana?"

She looked toward the candle. The wick now lay

113

shimmering in a pool of melted wax, emitting only a faint glow of light about her.

Outside the cabin, a whippoorwill's repetitive call nearly matched the human pulse, with no discernible pause for breath. It was haunting, so clearly defined against the backdrop of night, the thunder still only an occasional rumble in the distance.

Having always loved the whippoorwill's call, which now reminded Jewel of nights in Virginia when she had lain awake counting the times the bird would repeat its beautiful song, she looked toward the window. Her breath caught in her throat, and she was taken aback when she saw the outline of a man as lightning illuminated the sky in ghostly whites behind him.

Jewel was aware of screams, yet oblivious of their being hers, as Everett rushed into the room to hurry onto the bed and to grab her into his arms.

"Jewel!" he shouted, holding her close. "Stop the screaming. You've had a nightmare! Get hold of yourself. You know the condition of your heart. None of this is good for you!"

Jewel pushed at his chest and wriggled free of his embrace. She covered her mouth with her hand and stifled her screams, looking wide-eyed toward the window. With her free hand she pointed a finger toward the window.

"No! It was no nightmare. It was a man!" she cried. "I saw a man at my window. He was there. I . . . saw . . . him. . . ."

Everett moved swiftly to his feet and went to the window to fling the curtain aside. Bending, making his height the same as the window, he peered outside,

114

seeing nothing but the outlines of the outdoor buildings defined by the bright flash of lingering lightning.

Straightening his back and dropping the curtain back in place, he turned and eyed Jewel. "There's nothing there," he said thickly. "Your imagination is playing tricks on you."

Jewel scooted from the bed and slipped her feet into her house slippers. "I saw him," she said stubbornly. "I didn't imagine anything. If I have to I'll go outside and see for myself."

Everett hurried to her and clasped his hands to her shoulders. "You're not in any condition to do anything of the sort," he grumbled. "But what I do insist upon is your coming with me to sit by the fire. It'll warm your bones. And I'll get you some coffee. You've waited on me enough times. Let me wait on *you*."

Sighing heavily, Jewel eased against him as he began guiding her from the room. "I can hardly stand the waiting, Everett," she murmured. "What if . . . ?"

"No what ifs," Everett said dryly. He led Jewel on into the living room, then stopped short, his mouth agape at seeing Eugene South there, standing before the fire, staring down into it, his clothes soaked, his hair sticking up in all directions.

Jewel's heart skipped a beat. She looked wildly about the room, then felt a lightheadedness overcome her when she saw no sign of Mariana. But she forced herself to stay alert, to seek the truth. Yet her legs had suddenly weakened and wouldn't carry her any farther into the room.

She watched as Everett rushed to Eugene and grabbed him by an arm, yanking Eugene around to

115

face him.

"By God, Eugene," Everett stormed. "Where's my daughter?"

Eugene's eyes wavered. He winced as Everett's fingers dug into his flesh. Then he met the challenge of Everett's eyes, head on.

"I don't know what to say," Eugene said in a whine. "Everett, Mariana . . ."

Jewel grabbed for the back of a chair to steady herself. The pit of her stomach felt suddenly weak, her heart becoming engulfed in a slow, nagging ache.

Everett grabbed Eugene by the shoulders and shook him. "What about Mariana?" he shouted. "Has something happened to her?" His gaze shot about the room, then back to Eugene. "Damn you all to hell, Eugene, if you tell me something happened to Mariana while she was entrusted to your care!"

"It wasn't my fault," Eugene cried, trembling. "The canoe. It . . . just . . . tipped."

"The canoe tipped? During . . . the storm . . . ?" Everett said, not wanting to envision his daughter at the bottom of the lake.

"No. It wasn't during the storm."

"What do you mean? It happened in calm waters?"

Eugene hung his head. "Yes, sir," he mumbled. "The canoe got tangled into some floating vines and limbs."

"Damn it, Eugene, are you saying what I think you're saying?" Everett said, his spine stiffening as he stepped back away from Eugene.

Eugene blinked his eyes nervously. "She just disappeared, Everett. Just disappeared," he cried. "I did good saving myself."

Everett's temples pounded. He doubled his hands

116

into tight fists. "God," he said, swinging around, not wanting to face Eugene for fear he would hit him.

Jewel sank down into a chair, numb. She stared into space, seeing nothing, feeling nothing. When Everett came to her, she didn't even see him bend down before her to look into her eyes. The shock of the knowing was transporting her to a place that didn't know grief. Her mind was . . . thankfully . . . blank.

Everett peered into Jewel's eyes. "My God, she's in some sort of trance," he said hoarsely. He placed his hands to her shoulders and gently shook her. "Jewel, darling. Jewel!"

When she didn't respond, he rose angrily to his feet and stormed to Eugene. He placed his hand on Eugene's neck and squeezed, half lifting Eugene from the floor. "You get out there and round up as many men as you can find!" he said between clenched teeth. "We'd better find my daughter if you know what's good for you."

"Everett, accidents happen," Eugene whined. "I'm damn sorry. You know I am. You know how I feel about Mariana."

Everett dropped his hand away from Eugene and lowered his eyes. "Yes, I know," he said, trying to get hold of himself. He had to believe that Eugene had tried to save Mariana. If not, then Everett would hold himself responsible. He had forced Mariana to go with Eugene. Even now Everett saw Eugene as the only man for Mariana! He was the most civilized man in these parts. And should anything happen to Mariana's parents, she would have to have someone to look after her properly.

With this in mind, not wanting to alienate Eugene,

117

knowing that Mariana *would* be found, for she just *couldn't* be dead, not Mariana, he turned and patted Eugene on the back.

"It's not fair of me to accuse you so unjustly," he murmured. "Eugene, I know how you must be feeling. You love her also."

Everett nodded toward the door. "Get on out there, Eugene. Do your damnedest to round up the necessary number of men to go searchin' for her. I've first got to see to making Jewel comfortable. Also, I've got to find someone to come and look in on her while I'm gone."

"I am sorry," Eugene said, then wheeled around and left the cabin.

Everett swept Jewel up into his arms and carried her back to the bed. "Darlin', she's going to be all right," he reassured her, even though he saw that she still was in some sort of self-induced trance. "You're going to be all right. Come morning, you'll see. Mariana will be at your bedside, looking adoringly down at you."

A tear streamed in a silver rivulet down Jewel's cheek.

Chapter Nine

I love your eyes when the love-
light lies lit with a passionate fire.
—WILCOX

A hand circling her breast, gently kneading it, drew Mariana quickly awake. She was aware of the softness of furs beneath her and the warmth of the fire burning low in the firespace. She was not all that alarmed to find that she had slept the full night in Lone Hawk's arms, as though it was a natural thing to be there.

Mariana's insides were growing mushy with a lazy, sensual warmth as she now felt Lone Hawk's hand moving downward, across her abdomen, rippling her flesh beneath the tender touch of his fingers.

And when his hand covered the soft down of hair at the junction of her thighs and began caressing her there, Mariana's breath was stolen away from her in the building ecstasy aglow inside her.

"My beautiful *Bis-kah-ko-nay-gee-day,*" Lone Hawk

said huskily, moving to position himself above her.

He placed his free hand at the gentle slope of her cheek and looked adoringly down into her eyes. "Did you rest well?"

He looked toward her fingers. "Did my herbal ointment draw pain from your fingers?" he said thickly.

Mariana was in such a state of euphoria she could only nod her head in response to each of his questions.

She blushed beneath his steady stare, the fire in his eyes telling her how he wanted to spend these waking moments with her. And she, shamelessly, wanted the same. How had she ever lived without him? Could she even leave him now, to return to her dreary life at the trading post?

Her eyes widened. Trading post! She had momentarily forgotten about her mother and how worried she would be when she still hadn't returned home. A full night had passed. Surely her mother would be thinking the worst . . . that she was dead. And knowing the dangers of her mother's being placed in such a stressful situation, Mariana knew that she must return home . . . at . . . *once* . . . !

Splaying her hands against his chest, Mariana gently shoved at Lone Hawk, but he didn't budge, the muscles of his shoulders and arms corded as he now held himself up by the palms of his hands, over her.

"I must return home," she murmured, gasping lightly when Lone Hawk bent his lips, to suckle on the taut tip of a nipple. "My mother. She will . . . be . . . so worried. . . ."

"We have waited too long to be totally together for you to hurry away from me as though you were only an

120

apparition in my arms through the long night," Lone Hawk said, now kissing the tender hollow of her throat. "Let us make love. Then Lone Hawk will return you safely to your people."

His dark eyes implored her. "You will then tell your mother and father that you wish to be with Lone Hawk, to be his wife," he grumbled. "It is only right, *Bis-kah-ko-nay-gee-day*. It is only right."

Mariana's eyebrows raised inquisitively. "Twice this morning you have called me by a name other than my own," she said, recalling his calling her the same the other time they had been briefly together, at the trading post. "What do you call me? You told me that you would tell me. Please tell me now?"

She was in awe, also, of his having almost ordered her to tell her parents of his intentions for her. He truly wanted her to be his wife! And she knew that she wanted to.

Yet she had her mother to consider. Her mother would have to be made to understand. Perhaps it might have to be done slowly, even if it meant being separated from Lone Hawk for several days . . . several nights.

In the end the wait would be worth it. They had their lifetimes to share!

Lone Hawk swept his hand to her hair. He touched it. "Your hair has captured the sun's fire in it," he said hoarsely. Then he placed his hand to her chest, where her heart thumped wildly against it. "Your heart is also on fire when you are with me."

He smiled warmly down at her. "So Lone Hawk names you Blazing Heart," he said, now weaving his fingers through her hair. "Do you like? It is a name most Chippewa squaws would be proud to claim as

121

theirs. Do you, a white woman, like it as well?"

Mariana's eyes sparkled, and her lips lifted into a quivering smile. "It is beautiful," she whispered. "Thank you, Lone Hawk. It is quite lovely."

Now placing his hands beneath her buttocks, savoring their softness against his palms, Lone Hawk kissed the tiny circle of her navel, then let his lips lower and grazed a kiss across Mariana's pulsing bud of desire.

She sucked in her breath, stunned by his actions, relieved when he again fully positioned himself over her, his mouth now lowering to her lips.

But she was again thinking of her mother. She must return home, now!

"Lone Hawk, please . . ." she murmured, again pushing at his chest. "I must . . ."

His mouth bore down upon her lips, hot and sweet, sealing them of further words. He kissed her with intensity, his fingers traveling along the silken taper of her thighs, then left another trail of fire as they teased their way upward, again cupping her breast.

All thoughts except for those of rapture were stolen away from Mariana as once again she was taught the skills of Lone Hawk as a lover. She twined her arms about his neck and arched her hips as she felt the plunge of his hardness inside her, paining her for only a moment, then blending into something so beautiful she could never think to describe it. All that she was aware of was the power of his lovemaking, drugging her with passion.

She returned the passion, kissing him long and hard, moving her body rhythmically with his. Each stroke inside her fired her desires more. Her pulse raced, her

122

heart was beating with a rapid pounding. She trembled beneath him as his mouth forced her lips apart and his kiss grew more passionate.

His fingers pressed urgently into her flesh as he again placed them beneath her buttocks, to press her closer to him. The passion being exchanged between them was growing more intense, and with a moan of ecstasy, Mariana experienced that moment of mindlessness when only the body was in tune with life.

Soaring, the pleasure having again been so wonderfully keen, Mariana watched as Lone Hawk's mouth lowered from her lips and he buried his face into the depths of her hair, his body still working, shining in a copper, glossy sheen as perspiration rose upon it.

Lone Hawk felt the blood growing hotter in his loins. He inhaled the jasmine smell of Mariana into his nose. His lips pressed against her neck, tasting the sweetness of her flesh.

And then he was beginning to feel the euphoric drifting that meant that release was near, and he gave in to the sensations, feeling as though he was floating as he felt the urge to release his love seeds inside her womb.

He thrust hard, then gently, then hard again. Then, when he was fully spent and his peak of passion finally reached, he leaned away from Mariana and let his gaze take in the full, ripe beauty of her, the beauty that thrilled his inner soul into singing. She was his. He had prayed to the Great Spirit, Wenebojo, that he would grant Lone Hawk this wish, and Wenebojo had heard.

It was something Lone Hawk had thought maybe not appropriate to pray for . . . the loving of a woman with the different-colored skin and culture. But

123

Wenebojo had seen more in Blazing Heart than the color of her skin. It was as though Wenebojo had looked at Blazing Heart as though she were Indian.

Blessed they were that Wenebojo approved! His life would be full, now that Blazing Heart would exchange words of marriage with him. The Chippewa would also feel the blessing in having one so dear and sweet in their midst! It did not worry Lone Hawk at all that she might not be accepted as his wife. Wenebojo would also see to that!

"You look at me so," Mariana said, fluttering her eyelashes nervously up at him. "Did I not please you, Lone Hawk?"

Lone Hawk chuckled low. "You do not read my expressions very well," he said, drawing her up to sit beside him by the fire. "My heart is no longer lonely. Did you not see it in my eyes? You have fulfilled all my desires, my beautiful white woman."

He placed the palm of her hand over where his heart still throbbed so unmercifully. "Do you not feel how you have made my heart come to life?" he said, laughing low. "Never has a woman caused my heart to behave so."

Crawling up on his lap, straddling his waist, Mariana placed her arms about his neck and faced him. "Is this truly real?" she murmured, looking up into his dark, fathomless eyes. "Lone Hawk, how can it be that I am here with you, in such a way? For oh, so long I have wanted you. Tell me you have wanted me as much."

Cupping her breasts, softly kneading them, Lone Hawk looked down at her, his eyelids passion-heavy. "You know this without Lone Hawk telling you," he said huskily. "From afar I watched you. You had to be mine. Nobody else's."

Then he framed her face between his hands. "Now tell me, Blazing Heart, why you were so far from your home when I found you," he grumbled. "Tell me this, for it is only right that Lone Hawk knows. Lone Hawk should know everything about his woman."

Fearing that telling him that she had been with a man before he had found her might shatter their illusion of love, Mariana lowered her eyes and eased her face away from his hands.

"Tell me," Lone Hawk commanded, again forcing her eyes upward, to meet the challenge of his stare. "Why do you turn away from me?"

"Lone Hawk, it's truly not important," she murmured. She looked toward the entrance flap, seeing how it was fluttering in the soft breeze, emitting some pale morning light into the wigwam.

Then she looked back into his eyes. "What is important is that I return home. I so fear for my mother's health. She surely thinks I am dead."

"You tell me why you were far from home, then Lone Hawk return you home," he said matter-of-factly, lifting her from his lap. He placed her on the pile of furs on which they had just made love, then rose to his feet and pulled on his breechcloth.

Mariana was stunned by his abruptness . . . by his threat to hold her hostage if she didn't reveal the events of the day before to him. She didn't like being threatened. Not even by the man she loved!

Rising angrily to her feet, she went and grabbed her soiled dress, out of stubbornness deciding against wearing the white doeskin dress he had given her. She began to fit it over her head, then was stunned speechless when she felt it being yanked away from her.

She turned and watched Lone Hawk as he dropped the dress into the fire. "What . . . do you think . . . you're doing . . . ?" she gasped, paling.

Lone Hawk swung around and glowered down at her. "The doeskin dress was given with loving heart," he said dryly. He motioned toward it. "You wear doeskin dress on your return home."

Mariana's eyes widened. "So you are returning me home, are you?" she said, much too sharply. "For a moment there I thought I was your captive."

"Lone Hawk does not play games," he said, reaching for the doeskin dress, thrusting it into Mariana's hands. "You will tell me why you were so far from home. Then there will be no question as to what Lone Hawk will or will not do. You will be home by the time the sun almost becomes swallowed by the horizon."

"You're so sure I will tell you what you want to know?"

"*Ay-uh.*"

"And I presume that means yes, in Chippewa."

"You are right. *Ay-uh* means yes."

Lone Hawk went to Mariana and took the dress, momentarily looking down at her, then slipped the dress over her head. He smoothed it down across her breasts, then her hips, then smiled warmly down at her.

"Now you tell me?" he said, lifting her hair, letting it then flutter back down to her shoulders.

Mariana felt trapped. She didn't want to tell him about Eugene South. She didn't even want to breathe the coward's name!

But she knew that Lone Hawk would not give up so

126

easily. She must do what she must.

She bent and reached for the hairbrush Lone Hawk had given her, oh, so loving it. She would always cherish it, this, her first gift from the man she loved.

Drawing the brush through her hair in sure, even strokes, Mariana looked down into the fire, evading his eyes. "My father has chosen a man for me to marry," she mumbled, flinching as though shot when she heard Lone Hawk's sudden intake of breath.

She turned her eyes quickly toward him. "But he is a man I cannot stand even to be near," she quickly added.

She worried about his silence, seeing how his eyes had changed into two points of hate and how his shoulder muscles had corded as he had placed his fists to his hips, glaring down at her.

"It is with this man that I was forced by my father to go by canoe yesterday, for a picnic on Deer Island," she said, stammering.

She looked away from Lone Hawk and hurried her brushstrokes through her hair. "It was while I was with him that the canoe tipped and . . . and . . . I swam to shore, then fell into that hideous trap," she murmured.

Then she again moved her gaze quickly to Lone Hawk. "And that is when you rescued me, darling," she said.

She ran to Lone Hawk and threw herself into his arms. "If not for you I would have probably died in that pit. Or Jed Fenris might have found me, and . . . and . . ."

"Who is this man your father has chosen? Who is this man who did not rescue you when the canoe tipped?" Lone Hawk grumbled, easing her from his arms, look-

127

ing down into her eyes.

"He works for my father. You know him, Lone Hawk. Eugene South," Mariana said, wiping a tear from her eyes. "He is a most . . . most despicable man, Lone Hawk. Never could I marry him. Never."

"You marry Lone Hawk," Lone Hawk said flatly. He turned her around and began braiding her hair. "When you return to your home you will look Chippewa. Then let your father deny your wish to marry Lone Hawk!"

Mesmerized by his utter handsomeness and the strength of his words, Mariana's heart raced, envisioning herself as she would be when her father saw her. She would be in the lovely white doeskin dress. Her hair would be braided. On her feet would be the most intricately designed moccasins of all she had ever owned. And she would be riding at Lone Hawk's side. It was as though she already totally belonged to him. . . .

Moisture dripped from every twig in the forest, it seemed, and the air was fresh with the scent of dampened pine cones and earth. Catching the rays of the sun that filtered down through the ceiling of the trees, spider webs sparkled as though diamonds were clinging to each of their spokes.

The pony on which Mariana traveled was moving in a slow, easy canter alongside Lone Hawk's as they followed the stream that led to Lake Superior, and then on to Grand Portage. Red buckeye shrubs grew ten feet tall on one side of them, in the low, moist ground along the stream, their deep red flowers contrasting with the bright green foliage. Tall Norway pines and oak and ash trees were on their other side.

Mariana sat tall and proud, the fringes of her doeskin dress and leggings fluttering in the breeze, her hair hanging in two long braids down her back. Strange how she felt as though it was now only proper for her to be dressed in such a way. Stranger still that she felt this inner peace that came with her transformation.

Glancing over at Lone Hawk, marveling anew at his handsome profile and the shape of the long, muscular limbs and powerful chest sharply defining his leanness, Mariana could not feel ashamed that she had so wantonly given herself to this Chippewa Indian. She had loved him for so long. He had loved her as much. . . .

Her eyes followed him as he nudged his pony forward slightly, then reined it in and swung himself from the colorful blankets used for a saddle and hurried to the stream.

Mariana followed his lead, swinging herself from her pony and then running to the stream where Lone Hawk was already wading, grumbling something low beneath his breath, but not so low she couldn't hear the angry pitch in which he spoke.

"What is it, Lone Hawk?" she said anxiously, bending to her knees on the thick grass that lined the stream.

"Ah-nish-min-eh-wah," Lone Hawk grumbled, wading further into the muck of the stream. "Do you not see?" He gestured to the far bank. "It is the evil traps of Jed Fenris that maims the animals of the forest of the Chippewa! Do you not see the *ah-mik,* beaver? It

crawled to safety only to die."

Mariana rose back to her full height and cupped a hand over her eyes and peered intently across the stream. Her insides grew cold when her gaze settled on a dead beaver. Its right foot was gone, the fur of its leg matted with oozing blood.

Turning her eyes away, Mariana knew how the poor creature had died. Jed Fenris had set a trap under the surface of the water in such a way that the animal would be held under the water and drowned. But, as happened so many times, this particular beaver had managed to escape by gnawing off its imprisoned foot, swum to shore and crawled to safety, only then to bleed to death.

Mariana's father had explained to her how such a trap would be baited with a bit of greenery or a daub of scent, to attract the beavers. Then all that remained for the trapper to do was to check the trap every few days . . . then haul a forty-pound-or-so beaver carcass out of the mud and cold water and then repeat the process.

"*Ai-ee-eee!*" Lone Hawk cried, finding the trap beneath the water, pulling it out and flinging it into the heavy brush at the side of the stream. "That trapper! He is *mah-gay-i-ee,* evil! The spirits of all the animals he has maimed will one day gather together and set one large trap for him. Then he will die a slow death, just like the animals did!"

The sound of approaching horses drew Mariana's head quickly around. Out of the corner of her eye she saw Lone Hawk hurry from the water. She was jolted with alarm as he drew her fully up into his arms and hurried her back to her pony and placed her atop it.

And then in a flash he had swung himself up onto his saddle of blankets and grabbed Mariana's pony's reins and urged it into a gallop alongside his.

But he hadn't moved quickly enough. Suddenly before him and Mariana there was a line of men on horseback blocking their path. And when Mariana saw who was the lead rider, her heart skipped a beat and her face paled.

"Papa . . . ?" she gasped. "Papa . . ."

Everett's insides rolled darkly when he finally realized who the Indian Squaw was on the pony beside Lone Hawk. "Damn . . ." he gasped, tightening his hold on his reins. "Mariana? Is it . . . really . . . you . . . ?"

Mariana could see the puzzlement in his eyes, and then she understood why. He was seeing her attire . . . he was seeing her braided hair . . . he was seeing her with *Lone Hawk*.

"Papa . . ."

Everett's eyes narrowed and he squared his back. He was relieved to find Mariana—but perhaps it would have been better that she had died instead of being found with a damn savage! What if the Indian had robbed her of her virginity? What if she had a half-breed child by him?

He glowered over at Eugene South on horseback beside him, damning him over and over again. If Eugene had found Mariana, this wouldn't have been allowed to happen!

But he could not blame Eugene. Instead, he blamed himself.

"Daughter, let's go home," Everett growled, reaching a hand to Mariana. "Your mother is ailin'."

"Mama? Ailing?" Mariana whispered, covering her mouth with a hand. But hadn't she expected it?

As Lone Hawk returned her reins to her, Mariana gave him a wistful gaze. She would not be sorry for what she had done. She was only sorry that her mother had to be hurt by her absence.

"Mah-szhon," Lone Hawk said thickly. "Go and be a dutiful daughter."

Everett inched his horse closer, glowering at Lone Hawk. "And how is it that you feel you have the authority to tell my daughter to do anything?" he snarled. "Lone Hawk, if you so much as . . ."

Mariana sank her heels into the flanks of the pony and hurried to her father. She took his hand. "Papa, if not for Lone Hawk, I . . . I would probably be dead," she murmured. "You should thank him, Papa. It is not right that you are angry with him." She frowned toward Eugene South, then smiled back at her father. "He rescued me from one of Jed Fenris's pits. I could have been devoured by an animal if one had fallen into the pit with me."

Everett's eyes wavered as he looked Mariana up and down, seeing how she had so easily taken on the appearance of an Indian squaw. It was as though she knew. . . .

"Where's your dress you left the trading post in?" he said in a strain. "Why . . . why are you dressed in such a way? Whose dress is that?"

"My dress was torn and dirty," Mariana murmured. "Lone Hawk's sister loaned me her dress."

Everett's gaze shifted to her hair. "The braids? Did you have to do that? Do you . . . want . . . to look Indian, Mariana?" he said, his voice cracking with the

132

emotion he had kept hidden for so many years whenever he thought of Mariana and how she would react when she found out the truth of her heritage. . . .

Mariana's hand went to the braids, tremoring inside when she recalled Lone Hawk's so devotingly braiding them. "I feel lovely, Papa," she softly said. "I'm sorry you don't think so."

Then she swallowed hard when she thought again about her mother. "Mama? How bad is she?" she murmured.

"We shall see, Mariana," Everett said softly. "Upon our return, we shall see."

Mariana turned and smiled toward Lone Hawk, then felt a part of her go with him when he swung his pony around and began riding away from her. It just didn't seem right that she didn't follow him. The life she had lived at the Grand Portage Trading Post no longer seemed real. Only her feelings for Lone Hawk were real. Only he was real, it seemed.

"Head out!" Everett shouted to the men who had accompanied him on this mission to find his daughter, swinging his horse around with Mariana now following alongside him.

Mariana held her head high, feeling the press of the hairbrush against her abdomen where she had thrust its handle into the band of her fringed leggings. At least she had that with her. While brushing her hair this night she would be catapulted into the world of Lone Hawk again, living in her dreams until they could embrace once more. . . .

Chapter Ten

The midnight hears my cry . . .
I love thee, I love but thee.
                                    —TAYLOR

The room was bathed in a soft golden glow from the lone candle at the bedside. Mariana stiffened as she entered the room, seeing how still her mother lay on the bed, as pale as the dogwood blossoms in the forest!

"You should've taken the time to remove that Indian garb," Everett growled as he moved along with Mariana, at her side. "What's your mother to think, Mariana?"

"She'll be glad that I'm alive and well," Mariana whispered back to him. "The way I am dressed will not bother her one way or the other."

Everett gave Mariana a troubled glance. If she knew the truth that lay hidden inside her mother's heart, then she would know why it would be best not to appear at her mother's bedside in Indian attire. But he had not forced her to change, knowing how anxious Mariana

134

had been to see her mother, and hoping that seeing Mariana would mean Jewel's faster recovery.

At least Everett was glad that Jewel was alert to things about her now. Blanche Lee had informed him of this as soon as he had stepped into the trading post lodge. Blanche still waited in the living room, having offered her assistance for the duration of Jewel's illness. Blanche was the most friendly and outgoing of all the other women at Grand Portage, yet still not the sort to come and visit. Ah, how his Jewel had missed that sort of pastime . . . having someone to chat with . . . or sharing her embroidery time beside the fire.

Tears sparkled in Mariana's eyes as she crept closer to the bed, seeing how helpless and listless her mother was. Asleep, though, didn't she look like some sort of angel? She was still beautiful, and the way her hair lay about her head on the pillow, it looked like some sort of red halo!

"Now, watch that crying," Everett whispered, leaning into Mariana's face. "When your mother wakes up she'll be needing smiles. Not tears. She's had quite a jolt to her nervous system, Mariana."

"I know," Mariana said, placing a fist to her lips as she stepped up to the bedside and peered more intently down at her mother. "If not for the storm I could have been here sooner."

She swung around, her eyes squinting in anger. "Had Eugene South not been a coward, I would have been here even sooner. Mother would have had no cause to be here on this bed only . . . only half alive."

Everett took Mariana's hand and squeezed it. "You're being unfair to Eugene," he whispered back to her. "It's my doing, daughter. Mine alone. I should've

135

never allowed you to go in a flimsy canoe with anyone."

Mariana stared wide-eyed up at him, disbelieving what she was hearing. "You . . . defend . . . him even now?" she harshly whispered. "How could you, Father?"

"Hush!" he scolded. "Show respect for your ailin' mother, Mariana. Arguing can come later. Much later."

Mariana shook her head. "I'll never understand you," she said in a half sob.

Then she focused her full attentions on her mother, jerking her hand away from her father. Kneeling on her knees beside the bed, she searched beneath the patchwork quilt for her mother's hand, grimacing when she felt the coldness of it and the corded veins that reached across the top of the hand, resembling a veined leaf.

Clasping onto the hand and scarcely breathing, herself, Mariana watched for signs of her mother's awakening. And when her mother's eyelids began to flutter and her eyes slowly began to open, Mariana leaned up closer and let her mother see her.

Jewel's breath caught in her throat, her eyes widening when she saw Mariana's smiling face. The ache in her heart smoothed out into a pleasant warmth as she circled her fingers about Mariana's hand.

"Mariana," Jewel sighed, her voice showing strain. "Honey, I thought . . ."

Mariana moved from the floor and positioned herself on the edge of her mother's bed. She placed a hand to her mother's cheek. "Shhh," she encouraged. "No need to even think about your earlier fears. As you see I am here . . . perfectly all right."

136

Now that Jewel could fully see Mariana, her smile faded and she reached her other hand to touch the white doeskin dress. Her heart was no longer calm. It was erratic in its beats. Her voice came out in a shallow whisper. "Mariana, why . . . are . . . you dressed in such . . . a . . . way . . . ?" she said, paling even more at the discovery.

"Don't be alarmed, Mama," Mariana said, tensing when she saw how the dress had affected her mother.

"I told you," Everett stormed. He grabbed Mariana by the wrist and jerked her from the bed. "Now you go and change from that Indian garb. Your mother don't need to be lookin' at you dressed in such a way. It isn't good for her . . . health."

Jewel's eyes went wildly from Mariana back to Everett. "I need to know," she softly demanded. "Where did you get the dress? Why is your hair braided, Mariana?"

Mariana scowled up at her father. "Leave me be, Papa," she spat. "Can't you see you're only making things worse for Mama?"

Jewel bit her lower lip in frustration, then she gave Everett a firm look. "Everett, leave Mariana and me alone for a spell," she said in a tone Everett had become familiar with through the years. Usually a gentle sort, there were times when Jewel spoke with authority. And Everett had never yet denied her anything when she had spoken thus.

Everett's gut twisted, knowing what the Indian outfit had brought to Jewel's mind. But surely she wouldn't tell Mariana. It wasn't the time *for* telling her about the damn Indian who had interfered in his and Jewel's life all those years ago. It was obvious how Mariana felt about Lone Hawk. Should she know the truth about the other Indian, she might even feel free to choose Lone Hawk over Eugene South!

But Everett knew that he had no control over his wife's words, the same as he had no control over her emotions.

He gave Mariana a lingering gaze, then Jewel, and then as he walked from the room he looked toward the drawer where the diary was kept, and he silently prayed that Jewel wouldn't show it to Mariana.

Damn himself all to hell! He should've burned the diary long ago and be damned with Jewel's rantings and ravings when she found out! He was usually a strong and forceful man; it was only his wife who could change him into a blundering idiot!

All of their married lives she had had the upper hand with him. Would she still have it . . . in . . . death?

No longer hearing her father's footsteps, knowing he was gone from the room, Mariana again settled down on the bed beside her mother. She smiled weakly down at her mother when her mother took her hand and held it. She was aware of the trembling of her mother's hand. It even felt colder. And she was seeing that same distant fear in her mother's eyes she had seen many times before. Would she ever understand what haunted her mother? Did she even want to know? Sometimes knowing hurt more than wondering. . . .

Jewel reached her free hand and smoothed it along the doeskin dress. "Now tell me," she murmured. "How is it that you are dressed this way?"

Mariana blinked her eyes nervously, then told her mother of the traumatic moments in the lake, then in the dark pit, and then the wonderful experience of having been taken to Lone Hawk's village. A blush rose to her face as she recalled what had transpired in the village, yet she would never tell this sort of secret to her mother or to anyone. It was a secret she shared with the man she loved . . . with Lone Hawk.

"The Indians were kind to you?" Jewel asked, her voice cracking with hidden emotion.

"Yes," Mariana nodded, acknowledging to herself that she had only been in the presence of two of them . . . Lone Hawk and his sister. "Very kind." She looked down at the dress. "Isn't it beautiful, Mother? The dress is so soft. It touches my skin like a soft kiss."

"It was the Chippewa who did this kindness?" Jewel said, her eyelashes fluttering nervously. "Not . . the . . . Sioux . . . ?"

"Yes. The Chippewa," Mariana said, seeing how her mother had stammered at the mention of the Sioux. "Why, Mother? Is there something you haven't told me about the Sioux? Have you had an experience with them yourself, to make you so frightened of them?"

Jewel turned her eyes away, tormented by remembrances of those nights so long ago. Though the Indian hadn't treated her roughly otherwise, he had forced himself up on her. Over . . . and . . . over again. Over . . . and . . . over again.

Cold sweat suddenly beaded Jewel's brow. Mariana saw its shine beneath the glow of the candle. "Mama, what is it? Did I say something that upset you?" she said, rising quickly from the bed. She went to a basin of water and placed a soft cloth into it and soaked water up into it, then wrung it out and placed the cloth on her mother's brow.

Jewel felt her heart hammering against her ribs. She

139

was beginning to feel lightheaded, as though the blood pumping through her veins was going to drown her!

Wildly, she looked toward the dresser and pointed at it. "Mariana, there's something I have to give you," she said hoarsely. "Go to my dresser. Open the top drawer. Search beneath my things until . . . until you find a small, leather-bound book. Bring it to me, daughter. Bring it to me, now."

Mariana's eyebrows lifted. She glanced from her mother to the dresser. "What sort of book," she murmured, inching from the bed.

Her mother motioned a limp hand. "Just get it, Mariana," she said in a near whisper. "Now."

The soft moccasins she wore made scarcely a sound on the hardwood floor as Mariana went to the dresser and slowly slid the top drawer open. Her eyes searched and then her fingers, finding the small book well-hidden beneath her mother's finery. Her eyes widened as she withdrew the book into full view. The word "diary" was spelled out across its front in flaking gold letters, and a clasp lock secured the pages in place. A key attached to a gold ribbon dangled from the diary.

Mariana turned on her heel and silently questioned her mother with her eyes. And then she spoke. "A diary?" she said softly. "You've been keeping a diary, Mama?"

Jewel slowly shook her head back and forth. "Not for some time now," she said, her voice barely audible. Then she looked up at Mariana, her head still, her eyes burning with tears. "I ran out of pages long ago, Mariana. But there were enough to write of my feelings that you should know about."

Mariana crept back to her mother's bedside and

placed the diary in her mother's hands. "You want me . . . to . . . read your diary?" she said shallowly. "Why would you, Mama?"

Clutching the diary to her heart, Jewel sobbed. "I want you to take the diary to your room and hide it," she murmured. "When I die, only then do you unlock it and read it." Her eyes pleaded with Mariana. "Only then, daughter. Do . . . you . . . understand . . . ?"

Mariana felt a tearing at her heart, seeing her mother so shaken with emotion. And her mother's speaking of death as though it was on the doorstep made Mariana's insides take on a strange coldness.

"Mama, don't talk . . . of . . . dying . . ." Mariana said, smoothing the palm of her hand over her mother's clammy brow. "You'll be all better tomorrow. You'll see. After Blanche feeds you some more of her chicken soup, you'll be as good as new. You've just had a spell."

She leaned down and eased into her mother's arms. "Mama, nothing can happen to you," she softly cried. "I'll feel so . . . so . . . responsible. I should have found a way home, even in the storm."

Guilt feelings were plaguing Mariana's insides for the first time since she had given herself to those wondrous moments with Lone Hawk. She should have never so willingly participated in the seduction! All the while, her mother had been suffering! She should have been here. Her mother would be up now, puttering around in the kitchen, making her delicious jams and sipping on coffee with her husband had it not been for Mariana's wanton ways!

Yes, Mariana now knew that she had been wrong to stay with Lone Hawk in such a way. She should have found a way back to her mother! Could she ever forgive herself should her mother die because of this latest spell brought on by her absence? Could she ever feel free to return to Lone Hawk, with such guilt plaguing her?

"Honey, you should never blame yourself," Jewel crooned, easing Mariana from her arms to look into her eyes. "It's your father's fault, entirely. He should never have encouraged Eugene to take you to Deer Island. I argued with him, but this time he didn't listen. He feels so ... so ... desperate for you to marry the man, Mariana. He's seen how you look at ... at ... that Chippewa Indian, Lone Hawk."

Jewel swallowed hard and looked momentarily away from Mariana, then thrust the diary into Mariana's hands. "You must read this one day," she said dryly. "But for now, Mariana, take it to your room and hide it. Don't let your father know you have it. He doesn't approve of even me keeping it. But I threatened to leave him should he destroy it."

"It's that ... important ... to you, Mama?" Mariana murmured, eyeing the diary questioningly.

"It's important ... to ... you," Jewel said, wiping a tear from her eyes. "It's only right that one day you read it."

"But ... why ... Mama?"

"Now is not the time to tell you, daughter."

"But ..."

Jewel placed a finger to Mariana's lips, sealing them from further questioning. "Now is not the time," she said hoarsely. "Now do as I say. Go and hide it."

"But ... where ... ?"

"In the trunk at the foot of your bed," Jewel said, her eyes again misting with tears. "At the very bottom you ... you ... will find a secret hiding place. For so

142

long I kept the diary hidden away there, myself. But after your father discovered me making an entry one day, I began leaving it in my drawer."

"Can't you give me a hint as to the importance of the diary to me?" Mariana softly pleaded. "Mama, why? Please tell me now."

Jewel looked away from Mariana and placed her hand to her mouth, again flooded with memories that were bitter. "I never wish to speak aloud of those earlier passages in the diary," she said softly. "But you can read them. You need to know. It . . . is . . . only right that you eventually know."

Torn with curiosity, Mariana again eyed the diary. Then her gaze was drawn back to her mother as she felt her eyes on her again. In the depths of her mother's eyes Mariana saw more than the usual haunting. There was more. It was as though her mother's eyes were penetrating clean into Mariana's soul. It made goose pimples ride Mariana's flesh.

"Mariana, the Indian, Lone Hawk," Jewel said in a rush of words. "Did he treat you respectfully? Was he only concerned . . . for . . . your welfare after he found you? Or did he . . ."

Jewel couldn't complete her questioning. The words that she wanted to say seemed stuck in her throat, as though creating a constriction, choking her. She again turned her eyes away, and none too soon, for had she continued studying Mariana's eyes and expressions she would have seen a daughter who was not so easily able to hide the fact that she had been introduced into the ways of love.

"Mama . . ." Mariana gasped.

Jewel continued to look toward the wall. "Mariana,

143

please go on to your room," she said, sobbing. "I shouldn't even have suspected Lone Hawk would. He is supposed to be a kind, gentle Indian. Not like the Sioux I . . . have . . . known."

Mariana blanched. She rose to her feet and edged herself around the bed to face her mother. "Sioux you have known?" she said. "Mama, what Sioux? You've never made mention of knowing any Sioux before. Tell me. Why do you now?"

"Mariana, take the diary and hide it," Jewel said, reaching to touch the diary with shaking fingers. "Your Papa. He shouldn't know."

Knowing that her mother was evading the question about the Sioux, and knowing that when her mother decided against talking about a subject it was done and over with, Mariana bent a kiss to her mother's cheek and hurried from the room to her own bedroom.

Bolt-locking the door behind her, Mariana went and settled down on her bed, luxuriously sinking into the feathers as she studied the diary. It was like a hot coal in her hands, tempting her . . . tempting her. . . .

She eyed the dangling key, rust rough on its edges. Then she eyed the lock on the diary.

"I so want to," she whispered.

But she set her lips firmly in place and squared her shoulders, knowing that she would not defy her mother in any way. If her mother wanted her to read the diary later, then that was the way it must be.

"But after she . . . is . . . dead . . . ?" she whispered, shuddering at the thought of her mother's dying. It seemed impossible that her sweet mother could ever die at all. Yet Mariana knew that it would happen, and probably soon. Her mother seemed weaker with each

144

spell. Mariana knew that she would be lucky to have a mother for even another full year.

Determination in her steps, Mariana went to the trunk at the foot of her bed and opened it, flinching when it squeaked ominously. She glanced toward the door, hoping her father hadn't heard.

Then she began digging through the clothes that lay in the trunk, laying them out on the floor, until she finally had the trunk completely emptied.

When she saw the one corner of the silk-lined bottom of the trunk raised at the one end, she slipped a finger beneath it and found the secret hiding place easily.

And when she had the diary securely in place and the clothes returned in their proper places, only then did she go to the window and peer out, into the darkness of night. With trembling fingers she reached beneath her dress and found the hairbrush secured into the waistband of her leggings. Removing it, she ran her fingers through its bristles, lost in thought, recalling how it had felt when Lone Hawk had stroked the brush through her hair, how it had felt to have his fingers braiding it, and then how his eyes had touched her so admiringly when he had spun her around and had looked at her, transformed into an Indian squaw.

"I mustn't let my guilt stand in the way of my love for Lone Hawk," she said, a tear stinging her cheek as it rolled in a silver rivulet from her eyes. "I love him, oh, so much."

As though drawn to it, Mariana turned and eyed the trunk. "The diary," she whispered. "Why does Mama want me to have her diary?"

She frowned, shaking her head. "And why did Mother make mention of the Sioux tonight? Does it

145

have to do with what is written in the diary?"

Tired from the journey and the strain of finding her mother so ill, and torn with feelings about her mother's illness and wanting to feel free to love Lone Hawk, Mariana placed the hairbrush on her bed and began loosening her braids.

"Mama has always taught me that things all work out for the best," she whispered. "And Mama is most generally right about everything. My being with Lone Hawk was right. It was. . . ."

The distant song of a whippoorwill grabbed Mariana's attention. It sounded so close, just as the whippoorwill had sounded earlier in the morning, when she had awakened in Lone Hawk's arms. She closed her eyes pretending she was there again, his breath warm on her cheek. . . .

Chapter Eleven

> *My steps are nightly driven by*
> *the fever in my breast.*
> —TAYLOR

Growling as though he was an animal himself, Jed Fenris waded in the murky stream, feeling around beneath the water for the trap that he had left there the previous day. His narrow gray eyes were squinting against the rays of the sun burrowing down through the overhang of trees, his dark, bushy hair loosely dangled over his shoulders. His buckskin outfit was soiled with the dried blood of animals and caked mud from his daily treks in and out of streams in pursuit of his trapped victims.

His gaze shifted back to the dead beaver at the embankment, flies hungrily buzzing over its rotting carcass. He had lost another pelt as a result of the cunning of the damn animals. Why hadn't the beaver just accepted its fate beneath the water instead of gnawing its foot off, to then die and rot in the sun? By staying in the water it would have given Jed a pelt worth many dollars at the Grand Portage Trading Post! Now all he had was a carcass of flies, worth nothing at all.

He splashed around in the water, still feeling for the trap, growing angrier by the minute. The trap wasn't there! The damn Injun had stolen it! But which Injun? Jed hadn't yet caught the thief in the act.

Cursing, he left the water, shaking his moccasined feet as he stood on the land, glaring about him. And then his eyes caught the shine of something through the brush on the opposite side of the stream.

"Well, I'll be damned," he snarled, recognizing the shine to be from his trap. "This time he only tossed it away. He didn't steal it." He idly scratched his brow. "Why in tarnation would he do that?"

But it didn't matter why. What was important was that he was not minus another valuable trap.

Wading back into the stream, hurrying to the other side, he smiled wickedly when he withdrew the trap from the weeds, holding it up into the air to inspect it.

"Naw. He didn't hurt it none," he chuckled. "The damn fool. He didn't even know how to hide it well enough for me to not find it. Damn fool Injun."

His eyes narrowed into another squint. "I've got to find out which Injun," he grumbled, moving back into the water to set the trap.

His muscles corded as he armed the trap and again placed it at the bottom of the stream. "And I know just who to ask," he said, laughing throatily. "With enough firewater in 'im, Sitting Tall'll tell me most anything."

He straightened his back and peered through the denseness of the forest. "He'll just about now be waitin' at my place for whiskey," he snarled. "This time I'll give

148

it to 'im with no strings attached. And after he's drunker'n the lord, I'll get answers from 'im, I will."

He got a faraway look in his eyes. "And one day I'll get more'n that from 'im," he chuckled. "One day I plan on gettin' a piece of his squaw."

His loins ached with the thought of that pretty little Injun Squaw's flesh pressed against his own. He had watched Sitting Tall and Neala from afar when they had openly embraced. It had been hard not to go and steal her away from him even then.

But even this had to be done when Sitting Tall was drunk. Jed knew the importance of that squaw to Sitting Tall. Yes, it would have to be done when Sitting Tall was quite drunk!

Chuckling low, Jed went to his horse and swung himself up into his saddle, his gaze proudly assessing the pelts hanging from the saddle horn. The day had been profitable enough.

But he had also had many losses. Many more of his traps had been stolen. He hated to think of what the loss amounted to in dollars. But he could imagine what it would amount to in Injun flesh! And he would have the Injun's hide who had done this to him!

"Sitting Tall, you'd best get ready to enjoy a drinkin' bout with your ol' buddy Jed," Jed laughed, flicking his reins against the rump of his horse. "Ol' Jed here has much talkin' to do today, Sitting Tall. Then you will also say your piece. You'll tell me which Injun, won't you?"

"Giddyap!" he shouted, galloping away from the stream in the direction of his shack. . . .

* * *

149

Squatting down behind bushes, balancing himself on his heels, Sitting Tall watched for Jed to return to his shack. In his possession was a wampum belt made of the most precious of shells, to trade this day for the firewater. His mouth was dry, his pulse raced, awaiting that first taste of whiskey.

Cowering, he looked over his shoulder and from side to side. Sitting Tall did not want to be seen at the filthy trapper's dwelling. None of the Sioux approved of Sitting Tall's relationship with the trapper. Nor did Neala and Lone Hawk of the Chippewa.

But Sitting Tall was driven by the need to experience the lethargy the whiskey allowed him. It was the duties of next-chief-in-line that pressed in on him. It was his lack of confidence in all matters that drove him to drink this liquid, which first set his insides on fire, then caused his brain to lose all worries of the flesh.

"Sitting Tall must have firewater one more time," he grunted, again peering anxiously toward Jed's dreary dwelling. "Perhaps then Sitting Tall will place his back to this need. For Neala, Sitting Tall must."

His smouldering brown eyes remained flat as he watched the shack. His exuberant, glossy black hair was plaited with deer tallow worked into it, to keep it smooth and in place. He wore a breechcloth, tight, hip-high leggings fringed from his waist to his ankles, beautifully beaded, and moccasins on his feet. The beads of his headband matched the beads of his leggings, and a lone eagle feather hung from a loop of his hair at the back. His bare chest was a copper sheen beneath a rivulet of sun winding its way through the trees overhead, his cheekbones handsomely sculpted, his lips generously wide.

150

Jed Fenris's shanty had been built on a spot sheltered by rocks for the double purpose of securing the full warmth of the sun's rays and screening it from the notice of strolling Indians that might happen along. Within a convenient proximity to it stood a grove of trees from which an abundance of dry fuel was always procurable when needed, and equally close was a rippling stream.

The shanty faced a large outdoor firespace outlined by good-sized rocks. The back part of the shanty was made of rough-hewn wood, the front formed of skins carefully extending over an arched framework of slender poles, which were bent in the form of a semicircle and kept to their places by having their extremities inserted into the ground. Near this was a "graining block," planted aslope for the ease of the operator in preparing his skins for the finishing process. Not far removed was a stout frame, contrived from four pieces of timber, tied together so as to leave a square of sufficient dimension to stretch a skin to its fullest extension, so that it could be rubbed with a rough stone or scraper.

This part of the forest was split by a curving stream. Goldfinches darted about overhead, and many striped ground squirrels scurried along the ground, their beady, dark eyes assessing Sitting Tall as they spied him hiding, waiting.

With practiced ears, Sitting Tall caught the distinct sound of hooves approaching in the distance. His pony neighed from where it was reined behind him, drawing a response from the approaching horse.

"He comes," Sitting Tall whispered, his pulse racing. "Jed Fenris comes."

151

But until he knew for sure it was the trapper, Sitting Tall remained hidden. Then when he saw Jed clearly as the trapper wheeled his horse around to rein it to a tree, Sitting Tall rose from the bushes proudly carrying his wampum belt, smiling widely as Jed turned and found him approaching.

Jed chuckled low beneath his breath. He had known Sitting Tall would be there, waiting for him. Sitting Tall was like a moth drawn to fire, his need for whiskey driving him. This always worked in Jed's favor. Always.

Placing his hands on Sitting Tall's shoulders, Jed greeted him. "You have come to have council with me again, I see," he said, smirking. He nodded toward his shanty. "Come. We will share firewater while we sit by the fire."

Jed's gaze lowered as he dropped his hands away from Sitting Tall, his gray eyes sparkling as he saw the wampum belt being offered him. It took all his willpower to not accept it. But this time he had to appear the generous one. To draw answers from Sitting Tall, he had to appear to be a total friend.

"Sitting Tall come to trade with Jed Fenris," Sitting Tall said, lifting his chin proudly. He held the wampum belt closer to Jed. "Wampum belt for whiskey. It is a fair trade, Jed Fenris."

Jed's eyes wavered, then he flailed a hand in the air, his other one grasping the sheathed knife at his left side. "Aw, hell," he said dryly. "You keep your wampum belt, Sitting Tall. This time you just come and have free whiskey with me." He took a step forward and patted Sitting Tall on his back. "What are friends for, eh, if

152

not to share friendly talk and whiskey?"

Sitting Tall's eyes brightened. He smiled clumsily down at Jed. "You are true friend," he said thickly. "Sitting Tall thanks you."

Placing the wampum on a tree stump, leaving it there, Sitting Tall followed alongside Jed until they reached the protective covering of the shanty.

"Sit," Jed said, motioning toward a spread blanket beside the firespace. "Let me get the fire going, then we'll relax and talk."

Sitting Tall sat down, crossing his legs, and watched as Jed busied himself at building a fire. And then his mouth watered as he watched Jed go into the shanty and return with a bottle of whiskey and two tin cups. With trembling fingers he accepted the cup and waited for Jed to pour it full of whiskey.

Jed smiled smugly, seeing how Sitting Tall's hands trembled as he held the cup. Then he filled his own cup and tapped it against Sitting Tall's as he sat down beside him. "Here's to you, Sitting Tall," he laughed. "To our council. Our own, private council, Sitting Tall."

"To *gee-nah-wind,* us," Sitting Tall said, yet not understanding the meaning behind the words. He was too anxious to drink the whiskey, to wonder about anything. He tipped the cup to his lips and swallowed the whiskey, one gulp at a time, at first shivering as it burned its way down his throat, then welcoming it as it began to send pleasurable messages to his brain.

Jed eagerly watched, his eyes gleaming, as Sitting Tall finished the cup, then held it back out toward him, not having noticed that Jed hadn't drunk from his

153

own cup.

"Gee-ah-bi," Sitting Tall said thickly. *"Gee-ah-bi, ah-szhee-gwah!"*

"I take it you're asking for more," Jed chuckled, pouring more whiskey into Sitting Tall's cup. "Well, I ain't one to say no to a friend, Sitting Tall. No siree, I ain't."

Unprincipled as he was, Jed was serving Sitting Tall a special brand of whiskey that he would not drink himself, knowing that Sitting Tall wouldn't even notice, so eager was he to enjoy it. This particular brand of whiskey Sitting Tall was now drinking contained tobacco juice, cayenne pepper, crushed snake heads and various other vile things that would cause Sitting Tall to get drunk faster than if he was drinking whiskey made properly.

It turned Jed's stomach even to think about Sitting Tall's consuming so much of this concoction. But it seemed to be doing the trick. There was already a glassiness entering Sitting Tall's eyes.

"Good stuff, ain't it?" Jed said, grinning as Sitting Tall thrust the empty cup out again toward him.

"O-nee-shee-shin," Sitting Tall said, teetering. He laughed absently as Jed again filled his cup. "Firewater *o-nee-shee-shin!"*

Jed snickered as he held the bottle up before him, seeing that only a trace was left at the bottom. Sitting Tall had consumed enough to cause him to have a loose tongue. Now to get some answers!

"Sitting Tall, we ain't had council yet," Jed said, plopping the bottle down on the ground beside him. "Think we might, eh?"

Sitting Tall drank thirstily from the tin cup, then wiped his mouth with the back of his hand, seeing two Jed Fenrises instead of one as he looked toward him. He emitted a low hiccough, then laughed awkwardly. "We have no peace pipe," he said. "Council needs peace pipe."

"Naw, it don't," Jed grumbled. He leaned into Sitting Tall's face, recoiling when the Indian's breath reached his nose. He wiped at his nose and eased away from Sitting Tall.

"Sitting Tall, how much trappin' do you do yourself?" Jed asked, picking up a twig, scraping ashes in circles at the edge of the fire.

"Trap?" Sitting Tall said loosely, swaying in his lightheadedness. He flailed his hand into the air. *"Ah-mik-un-dah-wah-bun!* Go hunt for beaver? Me no feel like hunting for beaver. Me want more firewater."

Frowning, Jed emptied the rest of the bottle of whiskey into Sitting Tall's cup. "That's all, you fool Injun," he grumbled.

"That should be enough to loosen your tongue, damn you," Jed then said beneath his breath.

Sitting Tall swayed back and forth, his eyes rolling back into his head. *"Mee-eewh, mee-eewh,"* he said thickly. "Sitting Tall has had enough. Must go."

As Sitting Tall pushed himself up from the ground, Jed grabbed him and jerked him back down, beside him.

"You agreed to have council with me if I gave you whiskey," he growled. "Let's talk, Sitting Tall. Now."

Sitting Tall blinked his eyes, wondering how Jed Fenris faded then came back into view as three Jed

155

Fenrises. He laughed. "Sitting Tall has council with many trappers this day," he said.

Jed shook his head. "No. You have council with one," he spat. "With me."

Lifting his shoulder into a casual shrug, Sitting Tall nodded toward Jed. *"Ay-uh.* We talk," he said. "About what, Jed Fenris?"

"Trapping," Jed said in a snarl. "I know of no other topic to talk about. So you talk, also, of trapping."

"Sitting Tall uses bow and arrow," he said, nodding. "You use ugly traps."

"The white man uses traps because it is the way of the white man," Jed grumbled. "You use bow and arrow because you know no better."

Sitting Tall kneaded his chin, then nodded. "Me know no better," he said, slurring his speech. "Sioux know no better." He laughed awkwardly. "Chippewa know no better. But Chippewa hate traps as much as the Sioux. That is true, Jed Fenris."

Jed's pulse raced. He again leaned close to Sitting Tall, grimacing when again Sitting Tall's breath almost scorched his face with its vile stench. He cleared his throat and coughed, then again prodded Sitting Tall into answers.

"You say the Chippewa and Sioux both hate traps," he said dryly. "Enough to steal them, Sitting Tall? Do you steal them, Sitting Tall?"

Sitting Tall's eyes widened. He emitted a lazy laugh. "Me no steal," he said matter-of-factly.

"Then which Indian does steal my traps, Sitting Tall? It happens over and over again. Those traps cost me much wampum. Surely you understand."

"Ay-uh, Sitting Tall understands."

156

"Then tell me who is doing the damn stealing, Sitting Tall. Tell me now."

A frown creased Sitting Tall's brow. He tilted his head sideways, studying Jed Fenris's ugly expression. "Jed Fenris as ugly as traps," he chuckled.

Jed's fingers circled into fists, his face burning with anger. "We're not discussin' my appearance," he spat. "We're discussin' stealin'!"

Sitting Tall pushed himself up from the ground and began teetering away from Jed. "Time to go," he said hoarsely. He picked up his wampum belt from the tree stump and shuffled his feet toward where he had left his pony reined.

"You ain't gettin' no more firewater from me, Sitting Tall, if you don't tell me who it is stealin' from me," Jed shouted after him. "And, Sitting Tall, there ain't no other trapper who'd supply you with the whiskey as I do. You know that, Sitting Tall. You know that."

Sitting Tall's insides splashed cold. Jed Fenris's words came at him like an arrow piercing his heart, sobering him enough to understand the meaning behind Jed's threats.

Slowly turning, he frowned toward Jed. "No more firewater?" he gulped.

Jed rose to his feet and spread his legs, placing his hands threateningly on his hips. "None!" he shouted.

Sitting Tall's heart pounded, his eyes lowered. "It is Lone Hawk," he mumbled.

Jed leaned his ear in the direction of Sitting Tall, his pulse racing, knowing that he had won! He had tricked Sitting Tall into telling him who the thief was!

"Cain't hear you!" Jed shouted. "Speak up, Sitting Tall. If'n you don't, forget ever comin' again to get your whiskey from your ol' buddy Jed Fenris!"

Sitting Tall's gut was twisting. He reached his fingers to touch the scar that had been made when he and Lone Hawk had spoken vows of friendship those many years ago, spilling their blood into each other's wounds.

"Lone Hawk!" he shouted, then turned and stumbled away from Jed, sobbing.

Chapter Twelve

*Let the night-winds touch thy
brow with the heat of my burning
sigh.*

—TAYLOR

The wind whistled through the cottonwoods overhead, serenely rustling their leaves, like a soft whisper. But Mariana felt anything but serene. Her shoulders shook as she sobbed, looking down upon the fresh mound on the ground covered by an assortment of wildflowers.

"Mama," Mariana whispered, bowing her head. The black veil fluttered down away from her shoulders, blending in with her stark black dress. "Why, Mama? You were still so young. Was life so . . . so . . . unbearable that you lost your will to live?"

Mariana's thoughts tarried . . . back to when she was a small child in Virginia. Her mother's sweet, soft laughter rang through the house morning to night, echoing, it seemed, clean from the rafters!

But once they had moved to Minnesota, her

159

mother's laughter had died, and she had only given Mariana occasional weak smiles.

Yet, if Mariana thought hard enough, she remembered times even in Virginia when her mother would get that distant, haunted look, as though a part of her had already died even then.

The hammerings from the canoe makers traveled up to the hillside where a picket fence encircled not only Mariana's mother's grave, but all those others from the trading post who had died in this desolate land. Only plain gray stones marked each grave, with the names of the deceased roughly inscribed on them.

Falling to her knee beside her mother's grave, Mariana ran her finger over the crudely engraved name of her mother. A shiver coursed through her as she felt the hard coldness of the stone. She dropped her hand and turned her eyes away, not wanting to think of her mother beneath that mound of dirt, cold . . . alone. . . .

Her eyes settled on the trading post lodge. Her Papa had already returned there, along with the other mourners, leaving Mariana behind to mourn in her own, silent way.

"Papa," she whispered. "Now it's only you . . . only me . . ."

Lowering her eyes, closing them, she whispered another name, longing for his arms to comfort her. "Lone Hawk," she said. "I don't want to feel responsible for my mother's passing. What we did together, it was . . . out . . . of love."

She raised her eyes to the heavens, tears silver on her cheeks. "Oh, God, let Lone Hawk truly love me," she softly cried. "If not, I will forever be tormented, not only over what I shared with him but also for delaying

160

my return to my mother!"

Mariana then lowered her face into her hands. "Mama, oh, Mama, how I shall miss you," she again cried.

Then her eyes widened as she jerked her head up. "But I have . . . have . . . a part of you left with me, don't I?" she blurted. "Your diary. Your written words will keep you close to me . . . forever."

Scurrying to her feet, Mariana once again looked toward the lodge. Her insides grew cold. The diary! What if her Papa looked and found the diary, also wanting to read his wife's written words to be closer to her. If he searched long enough he would find it, and Mariana had been specifically told by her Mama that her Papa must not know that she had it!

"But if he doesn't find it in Mama's things, he'll know. . . ."

Lifting the skirt of her dress, Mariana rushed from the fenced enclosure, then stopped and turned on her heel and again bowed her head as she took another fast glance at the grave.

"Mama, I'll always love you," she whispered.

Then she turned around and clutched the skirt of her dress up about her, her moccasined feet carrying her hurriedly down the hillside, on around and through the stockade fence, and then on to the lodge. As she entered the living quarters at the rear she grabbed the veil from her head and face and tossed it aside, then stopped to catch her breath, not wanting to raise suspicions should her father find her in such a harried condition.

While she stood there, catching her breath, her gaze swept around her, seeing so much in the living room

161

that was her mother's. The embroidery work left undone, the book of poetry with a satin ribbon hanging from its pages midway through the book, the gold-framed spectacles her Mama had only recently begun to use when sewing and reading.

A remorseful pain stung her heart. Tears again threatened to spill from her eyes. But it was a sort of low growl and heavy footsteps surfacing from her bedroom that grabbed her full attention and caused her insides to grow numb.

"Papa . . ." she harshly whispered. "Oh, Lord. He's looking for the diary. I . . . just . . . know it."

With weakened knees Mariana crept to her bedroom door and looked inside. She covered a gasp behind a hand as she saw her father stomping around the room, his face red, his eyes narrowed in anger.

Mariana's gaze swept around the room, seeing how her father had searched through her dresser drawers and left her clothes rumpled and hanging from them. And her bed clothing had also been mussed, as though her father had searched beneath her feather mattress.

"Papa, what . . . are . . . you doing?" she said, finally getting the breath to speak. She rushed into the room and began to rearrange her drawers, closing them one at a time. She avoided her father's eyes, feeling them almost piercing her back, which she had turned to him.

"Where is it, Mariana?" Everett growled. He went to Mariana and placed his hands on her shoulders, forcing her around to face him. "I looked through your mother's things and didn't find it. That must mean that she gave it to you before she passed away."

Mariana swallowed hard. She had to force her eyes

to not waver, for she would not tell her father where the diary was. She knew that the diary had to be what he was talking about.

"What are you talking about, Papa?" Mariana said, her eyes innocently wide. "Why have you come to my room and gone through my things? I . . . don't . . . understand."

Everett flailed his hand into the air. "The diary, damn it," he shouted. "Your mother's diary. Did she give it to you, or didn't she?"

Lies had never come easily to Mariana, and she felt a strange quivering at the pit of her stomach. Yet she must stay firm. Her mother hadn't wanted her father to know that she had given it to her. So, respecting her mother's wishes, Mariana knew that she must tell a nontruth to her father.

"I know of no diary," she said dryly. "Papa, please leave me be." She cast her eyes downward. "Mama was only moments ago buried. Please leave me be."

Everett dropped his hand from her shoulder then drew her fully into his arms. "It's going to be all right, honey," he said softly. "You'll get used to missin' her."

"I shall never get used to missing her," Mariana said, pressing her cheek hard against his chest, savoring this rare moment in his arms, glad that he had decided to quit pursuing the issue of the diary. It seemed so inappropriate a time to be discussing it, yet she knew that as soon as her Papa was gone from her room, she was going to read the diary herself.

Mariana had waited long enough to see which of her mother's secrets were to be shared with her.

Yet she also feared this knowing. A secret locked away in a diary might change her life. It had seemed

163

that sort of secret when her mother had briefly spoken of it.

"I'm sorry if I troubled you about your mother's diary," Everett said thickly. "But it is missing from your mother's belongings. I think it will be best to quickly remove your mother's things from the bedroom. Only by doing so can I place her from my mind. And the diary must be burned when it is found."

Mariana tensed. She leaned away from her father and looked up into his eyes. "Why would you feel a need to burn Mama's diary?" she murmured, yet she knew she didn't need to hear the answer to that question. She could see a strange sort of tormented look in the depths of her father's dark eyes. And she knew that the secrets within the pages of the diary were the cause.

She now, more than ever, was eager to read the diary. Whatever was written there had not only caused hurt for her Mama, but her Papa, as well.

Everett's eyes narrowed. He turned his face away from Mariana's imploring eyes. "Let's have no more talk of the diary," he said thickly.

He glanced toward the window, having the need to escape. At least for a while. "I'm leavin' for a spell, Mariana," he quickly added. "I'm leavin' Eugene in charge."

He looked back toward her, his lashes heavy over his eyes. "You stay close by. I don't want to hear tell that you went wanderin', Mariana. Do you understand?"

Mariana's eyes widened in surprise. "You're leaving, Papa?" she dared to question. "Now? So soon after Mama's burial? Where are you going? Of late you've slipped away from here more than not. Where

164

do you go?"

"It is not right for a daughter to question a father," Everett said, walking heavily toward the door. He turned and glowered over at her. "Just you stay close by while I'm gone. Do you hear?"

Mariana silently nodded, thinking how much she wanted Lone Hawk. Surely he knew the art of comforting. Just the sound of his voice would soothe her. Her father's comforting arms had been too briefly around her. And now he was leaving? He was not a man so easily understood. He was a man of complex moods and a complicated personality.

"Nodding isn't answer enough," Everett growled. "Tell me, daughter, that you will mind your business . . . that you will stay on the trading post premises while I am gone."

"Papa, why must I be forced to tell you such a thing when you won't even tell me where you are going?" Mariana blurted, without even thinking. She saw rage enter her father's eyes, then was relieved when he didn't lash back at her for her impudence, instead turned and left her alone.

Then she rushed to her bedroom window and drew a delicate sheer curtain aside and watched as he left the lodge and mounted a horse, still in his dark mourning suit. She watched him as his horse thundered from sight, then turned and stared toward the trunk.

Her heart began to pound with anticipation. She clasped and unclasped her hands, her feet seemingly frozen in place, fear now entering her heart at the thought of what she was going to find written in the diary. And wouldn't seeing her mother's handwriting be painful for her? It would be as though her mother

165

were there, with her, when, in truth, her mother was gone forever.

"But I must . . ." she whispered, her voice shaking with emotion. "Mama would want me to. That is why she entrusted it in my care. It was for only my viewing. Nobody else's."

Forcing her feet to move, she went to stand over the trunk, then sank to her knees to the floor before it. Her fingers fiercely trembling, she raised the lid, then began slowly emptying the trunk of its contents, one by one, purposely delaying the moment of truth.

And then as she came to the bottom of the trunk and all that was left to do was to turn back the corner that would reveal the diary to her, she sucked in a deep breath and tilted her head back so that her hair would tumble down her straight back, then again looked downward and lowered her fingers to the satin covering that lined the bottom of the trunk and slowly drew it back, giving her full view of the waiting diary.

Her heart erratic in its beats, from anxiety fused with fear, Mariana at first only touched the diary. And then she circled her fingers about it and drew it upward before her eyes, the dangling key teasing her as it shone in pale gold beneath the splash of the morning sunlight filtering in through the sheer curtains at her window.

"Mama, oh, Mama . . ." Mariana whispered, suddenly placing the diary to her chest where her heart thudded beneath it. "This was yours. It doesn't seem right that I read your private thoughts. Why did you ask me to do this? I'm afraid to. You were so . . . so . . . strange when you told me about it."

She again held the diary out, to study it. "What am I going to find out that was so terrible for you? For

166

Papa? What?" she softly cried.

But determination to get this behind her, as she had done with the short funeral ceremony that separated her from her mother for forever, Mariana grabbed the key and hurriedly placed it in its lock and turned it.

The click of the lock as it became unclasped reverberated around the deadly silent walls of Mariana's bedroom. And when the pages of the diary were eased open as Mariana laid the diary in the palm of her hand, her breath was momentarily stolen from her. She flicked the diary open to its first page of written inscriptions.

It was as Mariana had thought it might be. Seeing her mother's writing, the familiar bends and turns of each of the written letters that connected to make words, made her heart begin a slow aching. She touched her mother's written words. It was as though she was touching her mother . . . as though her mother were there in the room with her, having only just entered these passages in the diary.

A low sob rose from deep inside Mariana. She brushed a tear from the corner of her eye, then went to her bed and plopped down onto it, crossing her legs beneath her. As the sun shone across her shoulder onto the diary, lighting up the pages even more, Mariana began to read. As her mother had said, the first entries had been made many years ago . . . beginning with the year before Mariana had been born. . . .

Tears blurred her eyes as she read of her mother's feelings about having to leave Canada, to go to Virginia with her new husband, Everett, to settle on a plantation there. Jewel hadn't wanted to leave her home in Canada, yet she had not wanted to disappoint

167

her husband of only a few months by letting him know of her feelings about leaving her home and family.

He had promised her a beautiful home . . . a plantation . . . horses . . . entertainment . . . if she would go with him. And, loving him so, she had agreed. She was young. She was vital. And she made friends easily. A new life in Virginia could be exciting, would be a challenge.

And Jewel had never been one to back down from a challenge.

Mariana smiled when reading this passage. In her youth, her mother had been just like her daughter. Mariana loved a challenge. She loved excitement . . . adventure. And only recently had these things been afforded her. After she had met Lone Hawk, her life had become full of many things!

She turned the pages, reading slowly. . . .

And then she began feeling an icy coldness seeping through her veins. Her mother was writing of having been abducted by a Sioux chief as she and her husband had been on their journey to Virginia. She named the Sioux chief . . . a chief by the name of Black Cloud.

Mariana read further, absorbing the words with not only her eyes, but also her heart, now understanding why her father hadn't wanted her to have the diary. . . .

Her mother hadn't only been abducted by Chief Black Cloud. She had also been raped . . . repeatedly raped by him. And when she had escaped and was found by travelers, she knew herself to be already with child by the Sioux.

Mariana bit her lower lip, her heart skipping beats. When Jewel had finally reached her husband in

168

Virginia and told him about the child, he had at first turned his back on her; then, loving her so, and pitying her for what she had gone through, he had accepted her and her daughter, and had raised the daughter as his own.

Numb from the discovery, Mariana slammed the diary closed. She stared into space, seeing the words on the pages over and over again in her mind's eye, knowing now just what they meant.

"My true father . . . is . . . a Sioux chief," she whispered. "I am part Indian."

Dropping the diary onto her lap, Mariana placed her hands before her eyes and slowly turned them, studying their color. "But I . . . am . . . so white. . . ." she whispered harshly.

She rushed from the bed and stared into a mirror over her dressing table, studying the color of her eyes, the shape of her face and its color, and then wove her fingers through her hair, seeing its fiery red coloring.

"Nothing about me speaks of being part Indian," she whispered. "Nothing."

And then she began recalling feelings . . . feelings she had about Indians, her feeling drawn to them. Even when she had been in the Indian village she had felt as though she had belonged.

And when she had been dressed as an Indian, she had felt that it seemed only right that she should be dressed in such a way!

So much of her had hungered to know more about the Indians . . . to be with them.

"And now I know why," she sobbed, placing her hand to her mouth. "Oh, Lord, Mama. How did you keep this to yourself all those years?"

169

Her eyes widened. "And Papa?" she harshly whispered. "You love me as your own. You never did make a difference."

Then she blanched, again studying her face in the mirror. "Oh, Lord, but what if I had been born with copper skin?" she gasped. "What then, Papa?"

A slow warmth began to flow through her veins, a thrill that could not be denied. She now understood so many of her feelings. Since her arrival at Grand Portage she had been utterly fascinated by the Indians, and now, yes, she knew why. She had Indian blood running through her veins! She . . . was . . . part Indian!

"Can it be true?" she said, spinning around, thinking about Lone Hawk and what he might think about the discovery.

Then a frown creased her brow. "But Lone Hawk is Chippewa," she worried aloud. "Will he accept that I am part Sioux? He has spoken so harshly of the Sioux."

Then a smile broke through. "Yet, he has spoken of one Sioux that he has befriended," she sighed. "He is called by the name Sitting Tall."

Mariana rushed to the window and drew the curtain aside, looking toward the forest. "I must know my true father," she whispered. "Though he must be a beast for having raped my mother, I still must try and find him. I will at least observe him from afar. I must."

Looking down at her black mourning dress, she felt a tearing at her heart. Her mother had died such an unhappy, unfulfilled woman. Mariana couldn't let it happen to her. She must go to Lone Hawk. She needed him now for a double purpose. She needed his arms for comforting, and perhaps he could also lead her to her true father.

Though there were many tribes of Sioux in this Minnesota land, and even farther away, most Indians knew each other, and where they made their camps.

But when Mariana spoke the name Chief Black Cloud aloud to Lone Hawk, could she get the courage to tell him why she wanted to know about him? Might he even love her less because she had Sioux blood flowing through her veins?

"It mustn't matter to him," she blurted. "If his best friend is Sioux, the fact that his future wife is part Sioux should matter even less."

Unsnapping her dress from behind and slipping it over her head, Mariana chose a dark riding skirt from her wardrobe, then a long-sleeved white blouse. Carefully she secured the sheathed knife at the thigh of her left leg and positioned a gunbelt about her waist into which she thrust a lone pistol. While her father was gone, she would do her own sort of traveling! And though he had ordered her to not leave Grand Portage, she hadn't verbally promised him anything of the sort!

Picking up the hairbrush Lone Hawk had given her, Mariana quickly pulled it through her hair until it lay in a satin sheen down her back. Then, scurrying around, she hid the diary again and slipped into moccasins. She rushed to her door and opened it, only to find Eugene South there, poised, ready to knock.

Stiffening her spine and tilting her chin, Mariana looked snappishly into Eugene's gray eyes. "What do you want, Eugene?" she said dryly.

Her gaze had taken in his impeccably pressed breeches and the crisp ruffles at his throat and at the

171

cuffs of his sleeves. His thin face was pale, as though it had been bleached, and his voice grated against Mariana's nerves as he began to speak.

"Your father left me in charge of the trading post and you," Eugene said, clearing his throat nervously when spying the holstered pistol at her hip. "I just thought you'd like to know that I'm available should you need me, Mariana."

His eyes lowered. "I know these times are hard for a daughter. You know how sorry I am about your mother."

"Don't speak to me of your feelings for my Mama," Mariana hissed. "Had you not been such . . . such a coward, I'm sure my Mama would be alive today. She thought I was dead, Eugene. And all because of you."

Eugene's gaze shot upward. He clasped his hands behind him. "Can't you forget that day?" he said thickly. "I've apologized. Over and over again."

Mariana slipped on past him. She went to a table and grabbed her riding gloves and smoothed them onto her fingers one at a time. "I don't care to discuss it anymore," she snapped. She swung around and boldly faced him. "And, Eugene, I don't need you to look after me. In fact, I'm leaving. Your duties shall never include me, Eugene. Never."

Eugene took a step forward, reaching a hand out toward her. "Where are you going?" he gasped. "Why are you wearing a pistol? Your father, he'll . . ."

"Father has his life, I have mine," Mariana said in a harsh whisper. "If he had stayed, as he should have, in respect for my Mama, then I would have also. As it is, I've my own places to go. And, by damn, I'm going."

"But your mother . . . ?"

172

"Mama would understand," Mariana said, swallowing hard.

"Your father won't," Eugene said, following her to the door as she stomped on away from him. "My God, Mariana, he'll horsewhip me if I let you go."

Mariana spun around on a heel and looked smugly up into his face. "If . . . you . . . let me go?" she laughed. "Eugene, just try and stop me."

With a thundering heart, hardly able to recognize her own self these days in the way she stood up for herself, Mariana hurried from the house and to the stable.

After choosing a frisky mare and saddling it, she rode it from the trading post and back up to the hill to where the flowers were already wilting on her mother's fresh grave.

Stopping to look at the grave from the saddle, Mariana choked back a sob. "Mama, I now know," she murmured. "And I don't love you less for not having told me sooner. Perhaps if you had told me before I met Lone Hawk and was taught by him how gentle an Indian can be, I could never have accepted my heritage!"

She wiped a tear away with the back of her glove. "But I am proud, Mama," she said softly. "And please be as proud for me?"

Wheeling the horse around, Mariana galloped into the forest, not fearing what the trail ahead offered her. She would find Lone Hawk, then let the rest take care of itself. . . .

Chapter Thirteen

I want your strength to help,
your laugh to cheer, heart, soul
and senses need you, one and all.
—ALFORD

Lone Hawk went with prayer thoughts to the water. His bath was a sacrament, one that he would take alone this day. He had chosen a secluded spot away from the village to have his sweat bath. While he bathed he would be filled with much thought of his Blazing Heart. It was time for him to go to her, demand of her father and mother that she be allowed to return with him, to be his wife.

But first he must receive the blessings of the Great Spirit, Wenebojo. While alone with the Great Spirit, he would receive guidance . . . he would receive courage . . .

Having chosen to build his sweat bath along the banks of a flowing stream, Lone Hawk knew to see in every ripple of the flashing water that came to meet him a shining token of the blessings he would soon be receiving from Wenebojo.

Eagerly he cut the long, supple willow withes that grew on the banks of the stream, pushing the sharpened ends into the soil, bending and tying the feathery tops into an arch. Over the arches he threw his blankets. A sweat lodge was now ready for him to begin his further rituals.

He built a fire close by, in which he placed gathered stones for heating. After the stones were glowing white with heat, he placed four of them in a tiny pit inside the small sweat lodge. He then poured a gourd of cold water over the heated coals, filling the enclosure with steam.

Fully undressing, Lone Hawk positioned himself close to the steaming coals. He folded his arms across his chest and closed his eyes and began silently communing with the Great Spirit.

His heart thundered against his ribs as the sweat poured profusely from his brow. His throat was dry. But still he sat and prayed, feeling the closeness of Wenebojo in the way everything about him was so quiet. It seemed that the birds had ceased to sing outside the sweat lodge. The splash of the water over the rocks in the stream seemed to have been silenced. The swirling, mysterious gray of the steam pressed in on Lone Hawk, making him begin a low chant, which echoed back to him from the walls of the blankets that encircled him.

And then, feeling as though blessed, Lone Hawk threw the blankets aside and stepped out into the fresh air, his nude body a glossy, copper sheen as the sunshine touched him all over in its brilliance.

Lone Hawk stretched out his arms and looked

175

toward the heavens. He again chanted low, thanking his Wenebojo for his blessings this day. He bowed his head, then again looked toward the heavens, oblivious of eyes upon him from the nearby brush.

Having seen the colorful figures of the blankets from a distance and how they were shaped into some sort of shroud over what must be bent sapling poles, Mariana had become intrigued over who might be beneath such a tiny, strange-looking dwelling.

Dismounting from her horse and securing its reins to a tree limb, Mariana had crept stealthily closer to the small tentlike shape, fear having left her as soon as she knew she was close to the Chippewa village. She wasn't afraid even though she had come upon this strangeness in the forest, alongside a stream.

Hearing low chants surfacing from inside the blanket-covered dwelling, Mariana had stooped low behind a thick stand of brush and listened . . . and watched.

Then when she saw the blankets thrown aside and an Indian brave step nude from the enclosure, a blush had fully encompassed her face and she had turned away. She now felt like an intruder. This Indian brave seemed to have been in some sort of trance as he had stepped from the enclosure. She was at least relieved that she had only seen him from his back side . . . for he was quite nude!

The sound of chants rising into the air was cause for Mariana to open her eyes to take another glance. The voice sounded . . . so . . . familiar.

Placing a hand to her mouth, Mariana gasped low.

The Indian brave had turned and his front side was facing her and, though he was looking up as though praying, Mariana was able to see his face.

"Lord, it's *Lone Hawk!*" she whispered, her heart hammering against her chest as her gaze swept over him, seeing the shape of his long, muscular limbs and powerful chest, and the part of his anatomy that could send her senses reeling.

She looked up at his face, seeing his utter handsomeness . . . the high cheekbones, the straight nose, the fullness of his lips. And now that he had lowered his head, ah, how she could see the dark, fathomless loveliness of his eyes!

Her pulse raced. She so loved the copper color of his body, glossy this day from perspiration. She was reminded of her own heritage, and she now wished to have copper skin, to match that of the man she loved. But would he have singled her out to love her if her skin had been the same as his? He had not chosen a squaw to love, and surely there had been many to choose from.

"Will he love me when he finds out that I am part Sioux?" she whispered, not sure how she would find the words to tell him.

"First I shall question him about Chief Black Cloud, then I shall tell him why. . . ." she murmured.

Her insides tremored sensuously as Lone Hawk turned and began moving toward the water. His long muscles knotted and rippled, sharply defining his leanness as he ran splashing into the stream, then disappeared from her sight, diving headfirst into its depths.

If not for still being in mourning for her Mama, Mariana would have been tempted to join him in the

177

water, to surprise him. Even still, she might. It had been proven to her by her mother's sudden death that no one is sure of their tomorrows. If she didn't grasp onto what happiness was handed her today, perhaps she would never get the chance again. For sure, out in this wilderness one must take life a day . . . at . . . a time.

With a racing pulse, Mariana removed her gloves, smoothing them off a finger at a time. Then she daringly slipped her moccasins from her feet, as well as her blouse and skirt, and then the gunbelt from around her waist, leaving her underthings on. She could not be brazen enough to enter the water without her clothes. It was already enough to follow Lone Hawk there, knowing that he was fully unclothed.

"When he finds me there, won't he be surprised?" she said, smiling to herself. She looked to the heavens. "Mama, please understand why I leave my mourning behind me so soon. If you ever loved a man as I love Lone Hawk you would understand. . . ."

Stepping from behind the bushes, Mariana moved gingerly toward the water, now seeing Lone Hawk swimming with expert strokes away from her. So far he hadn't seen her. If he would but turn. . . .

Lone Hawk flipped over, to swim on his back. But when he saw Mariana just beginning to wade into the water, he stopped short and placed his feet to the bottom of the stream, stunned.

"Bis-kah-ko-nay-gee-day?" he whispered. "Blazing Heart? Where did she . . . ?"

Mariana looked up and saw Lone Hawk watching her. Smiling bashfully back at him, she splashed on into the water, its coldness a sting on her thighs as it soaked through the cotton material of her bloomers.

The leather knife sheath grew hard against her leg as it became wet, reminding her that she had forgotten to remove it. But that didn't matter. What mattered was Lone Hawk and the look of passion in his eyes as he grew accustomed to seeing her suddenly there.

And when a slow smile lifted his lips, Mariana knew that he was glad that she had come, even though she seemed to have arrived at a time when he had been in some sort of meditation.

Lone Hawk moved toward Mariana, the lashes heavy over his eyes, knowing that the gods of the wind had most surely sensed his silent needs, for they had brought Mariana to him. And since she had come on her own, it surely meant that she had come to stay. Why else would she have ventured out by herself from Grand Portage? She surely knew the dangers of traveling alone!

Though Sitting Tall was a Sioux and Lone Hawk's best friend, there were others of Sitting Tall's tribe of Sioux who were not as trustworthy. A white woman could even be made to become a slave of a Sioux warrior!

Lone Hawk's gut twisted at the thought of this happening to his woman. If it did, he would kill the Sioux responsible! The Sioux would be made to suffer a slow, agonizing death!

"Lone Hawk, do I surprise you?" Mariana said, laughing softly, moving on toward him. The water was now reaching just beneath her breasts, the cotton material soaking up water at their tips, causing her nipples to strain, defining their darkness through the white of the material.

"My woman comes," Lone Hawk said, touching the

179

gentle curve of her face as they came together. "Why do you?"

Lone Hawk's question jolted Mariana into remembering the pain in her heart. She lowered her eyes, thinking of her mother. It still didn't seem real that her mother should be dead.

Then she raised her eyes slowly upward. "I've much that needs to be said, Lone Hawk," she said thickly.

His gaze captured the swell of her breasts outlined against the flimsy cotton material of her undergarment. And then he smiled down at her, his eyes twinkling. "You follow me into the water to talk?" he chuckled.

Mariana welcomed his lighthearted attitude, not wanting to be burdened with sadness while she was with Lone Hawk. He was now her world! "You were in the water," she softly laughed. "It looked just too inviting to resist."

Lone Hawk placed his fingers to the straps of her undergarment. "It is more refreshing if you swim unencumbered," he said thickly. He slipped the straps over her shoulders. "Enjoy this moment with Lone Hawk. Then we can talk. You can return to my village with me. We shall eat and talk in the privacy of my dwelling."

"I don't have long," Mariana murmured, sensuously tremoring as Lone Hawk continued undressing her. The touch of the water against her bare breasts was a caress of silk. And each place his fingers touched her, she tingled with aliveness.

And then his hands found the sheathed knife at her thigh. "My woman is clever," he said hoarsely. "The knife is a good defense when traveling alone."

180

"Not only a knife," she said dryly. "I've also brought a pistol this time. I knew the dangers, Lone Hawk, of being alone."

"You have the courage of any man, Blazing Heart," Lone Hawk said, loosening the sheath, tossing it on the embankment.

And then he ducked beneath the water and removed the rest of her undergarment, then rose back up and tossed it on the ground.

Lone Hawk's eyes became passion filled, commanding Mariana to move into his arms. As she pressed her breasts into his chest, his breath was momentarily stolen from inside him.

But then his heart resumed its thunderous beatings and his mouth found her lips and bore down upon them in a heated kiss.

Mariana twined her arms about his neck, becoming awash with desire as his hands moved to her breasts, to cup them. She pressed them harder into his hands, her inner thighs painfully sweet with longing. His manhood gyrating against her abdomen spoke of his being ready to take her to the heights of joy she had known only with him.

And as he placed his hands to her waist and lifted her up to slowly impale her, she sighed languidly and placed her legs about him and enjoyed the pleasure his movements inside her evoked.

"Tell me that you love me," Lone Hawk whispered, speaking into her ear. "Tell Lone Hawk that you will stay . . . will be my wife."

Mariana threw her head back in rapture, causing her hair to tumble in fiery red down her back. "I so want that, Lone Hawk," she said, sighing as he pressed a hot kiss on the taper of her neck. "I . . . so . . . want that."

"Then say *ay-uh,*" he whispered. "Say yes, my Blazing Heart. Say that you have come . . . to . . . stay."

Mariana knew the impossibility of that. She still had her father to convince that this was what she wanted most out of life. And she still had Lone Hawk to tell that she was part Sioux. There were too many obstacles in the way of their happiness, it seemed!

"I already told you that I only have a little while," she murmured. "My father doesn't even know that I have come. I must return to Grand Portage before he finds that I am gone."

Lone Hawk stopped his thrusts inside her. He leaned away from her and looked questioningly into her eyes. "Then why have you come, if not to stay?" he grumbled.

Mariana was stunned that he could first make love to her so ardently and then stop and talk scoldingly at her.

"Lone Hawk, please do not spoil the moment by asking questions," she sighed. She placed her hands to his face. "My love, let us talk later. Just love me now, Lone Hawk. Please love me. I've been so filled with sadness. You know how to lift this sadness from my heart. When I'm with you, everything is always so beautiful."

He looked at her with eyes a mixture of ice and fire, then his mouth closed hard upon hers, dazzling her senses. And again he stroked himself inside her, drawing her into his hard frame, leaving hardly any space between them. His fingers wove through the red silk of her hair, his man's strength awakening her every sense into needing him.

She clung. She moaned. She rode with him. Spirals

of pleasure began to soar through her, touching her insides all over with a lazy warmth. And then she felt his thrusts become harder, and together they tremored, finding sheer joy again in each other's arms.

Slipping her from his waist, he held her in his arms and began to splash from the water, carrying her. Mariana placed her cheek to his chest, smiling to herself at hearing the thundering of his heartbeat. Again she had responded . . . again he had enjoyed. It was a surrender . . . a sweet surrender, one that she wished never to end.

As Lone Hawk carried her from the water, onto dry land, his teeth caught the nipple of one of her breasts and gently nipped it. And then his gaze rose and locked with hers, both smiling to the other.

"It was again so lovely," Mariana said in a low murmur. "Even when we are old, it surely will be as lovely."

"Only if we are together when we are old," Lone Hawk growled, placing her feet to the ground. He again wove his fingers through her hair, straightening it to tumble freely across her shoulders and down her back. "Let us now dress and return to my dwelling. We shall then talk of all tomorrows."

"Yes. Let's," Mariana said, her eyes searching for her discarded clothes.

When she began dressing and Lone Hawk discovered that she had not chosen to wear the white doeskin dress, his insides knotted. "You choose white woman's dress over the one Lone Hawk so generously gives you?" he said dryly.

Mariana's eyes lowered, hating to have to tell him the fate of that dress. But she knew that she must. Hurt

183

was thick in his voice. "My Papa . . . he . . . burned it, Lone Hawk," she said in a rush of words, looking up in time to see the total hurt in his eyes.

She went to him and placed her hand to his cheek. "I'm sorry," she said softly. "It was something I had no control over. He took it from my room and burned it. It happened so fast. . . ."

Lone Hawk nodded. "*Ay-uh,* it is something your father would do," he grumbled. "In his heart there is no room for Chippewa. Chippewa dress would not fit into his picture of things."

"Then you understand?"

"More than you know, Blazing Heart. More than you know."

Mariana swallowed hard, eyeing him wonderingly.

Chapter Fourteen

*You gave me wings of gladness
and lent my spirit song.*
— RUSSELL

Now that Mariana was back in Lone Hawk's wigwam, it was as though she had never left. Though small, and nothing to compare with the plantation that she had grown up on in Virginia, or even the trading post where she now resided, Lone Hawk's home lured her, because it was his. One day, hopefully, she would share it with him. It would be enough for her, since every waking hour she would be living for him, sharing everything that was his with him. The longing for the social affairs she'd left behind in Virginia no longer troubled her. Lone Hawk had now filled all the voids in her life.

Sweeping her around and into his arms, Lone Hawk hugged her closely to him. *"Nee-may-nan-dum-wah-bum-eh-nawn,"* he said thickly.

Mariana leaned away from him, to look up into his

magnetic dark eyes. "And what did you just say in Chippewa to me?" she asked softly.

Lone Hawk wove his fingers through her hair, marveling anew at its silken texture. "Lone Hawk says he is glad to see you," he said, smiling down at her. "And did you enjoy your moments in the water with Lone Hawk?"

Mariana's eyes sparkled. "It was a different sort of time spent in water than ever before," she giggled. "It is something I wish to share with you again soon, Lone Hawk."

Then her eyes wavered, as again the thoughts of her mother came to her mind. She lowered her lashes, then blinked them nervously. "But it was not at all proper that I did that at this time," she whispered, feeling a blush rise to her cheeks. "I feel quite wicked, Lone Hawk. I only hope my Mama understands why I do these things with you."

"Your mother," Lone Hawk said in a low grumble. "Does she know you have come alone to the village of the Chippewa?"

Mariana's head moved upward in jerks. She was just now realizing that she hadn't told Lone Hawk of her mother's passing. And he would be the first person she had been put in the position of telling. Speaking of her mother's being dead would make it all so fresh in her mind again, as though she were reliving those horrible moments all over again, when she had discovered her mother lying so lifeless on the bed, her eyes forever closed in sleep.

"Lone Hawk, there's so much I have to tell you," she said, swallowing hard. She glanced down at the blankets and furs spread beside the low embers of the fire in the firespace. "Perhaps we can sit? I'm not sure my knees will hold me up once I begin talking . . . about . . . my Mama."

Lone Hawk's eyes grew serious as he heard the sadness in her voice. Her sadness was his. The ache of her heart seemed to transfer into his, her words touched him so movingly.

"Ay-uh, we will sit," he said, guiding her by an elbow down beside the fire. "Later Neala will bring us food and drink. Or would you rather have it now?"

Mariana shook her head. Her stomach was not quite ready for food. She hadn't eaten that much since her mother's passing. Nothing seemed to taste good, nor did it feel good when it settled into her stomach.

"No. I'm truly not hungry," she said softly, drawing the fullness of her travel skirt around her as she drew her legs up before her.

She clasped her arms about her legs, quite aware of Lone Hawk's presence as he settled down beside her. She could smell the familiar spicy scent of him. She could see the shine of his skin. He had rubbed deer tallow into it as soon as he had returned to his wigwam after their swim.

She averted her eyes and looked down into the fire. The moment of truth was drawing near. When she told him about the passages written in the diary, would he be so glad to have her in his wigwam with him? The part of her that was Sioux was most surely a part of her that would be his enemy.

But first she must tell him of her mother's passing, though finding the words would be hard.

"My Mama," she blurted. "She really wouldn't know anything that I do now, unless she . . . she . . . watches

187

from somewhere in heaven."

Tears rolled in silver rivulets from the corners of her eyes. She could feel Lone Hawk's eyes on her, closely scrutinizing her.

Brushing the tears away, she turned and met his silent stare. "My Mama, she . . . she . . . is dead," she said, again looking quickly away from him as more tears flooded from her eyes.

Lone Hawk's insides grew mellow with understanding. He moved closer to Mariana and drew her fully into his arms as she lowered her knees from in front of her.

She clung to him, sobbing. "Now do you see how shamefully I behaved only a while ago with you in the water?" she sobbed. "I am still in mourning, yet I enjoyed the pleasures of the living."

Lone Hawk placed his hands at her cheeks, framing her face between them. "Nothing you do is shameful," he said dryly. "Our love is true. Love is a way to place sadnesses behind you. *Ay-uh,* it is proper to mourn. But it is also proper to make love. Lone Hawk would even make love to you now. Lone Hawk will again make you forget!"

His mouth bore down upon hers, his hands trembled as his fingers sought out her breasts through the cotton material of her shirt. His tongue sensually crept between her lips, causing her insides to take on a pleasant sweetness.

Mariana sobbed against his lips, she clung about his neck, oh, so wanting this. After she told him all the truth he might never want to love her again. Knowing that Sioux blood ran through her veins, he might think that even touching her was vile. . . .

188

"Wah-nayn-dum gee-mah-szay-dum ee-nayn-dum," he murmured, drawing his lips back a fraction. "Only think good thoughts while with Lone Hawk."

"I . . . so . . . want to," Mariana whispered, becoming breathless as his fingers found the buttons of her shirt and began unbuttoning them.

And soon, when he had her standing perfectly nude before him, she lost sight of what she had come to tell him. For now, there was only he, and these precious moments to share with him. She would forget, for now. Later . . . ?

Removing his breechcloth, now nude before her hazy eyes, Lone Hawk placed his hands to her waist and lowered her gently to the outspread blankets and furs. "Lone Hawk's heart is no longer lonely," he said huskily. "Since you, it beats as though many, it is so filled with thoughts of you."

Smiling languorously, Mariana welcomed him atop her, his hardness already filling her so magnificently. Just the touch of him made her near to swooning. To be totally with him made her senses almost leave her. It was as though the gentle waves of Lake Superior were splashing warmly throughout her.

Smouldering memories of their other times together evoked intense passion inside Lone Hawk. He lowered his lips to the taut tip of her breast, while his fingers were traveling over her, touching her every sensitive pleasure point, to arouse in her something even more beautiful than she had ever experienced before with him. He, too, was feeling it . . . this feverish heat, burning higher, his loins afire with building pleasure.

He stroked evenly into her, his lips now pressed into the hollow of her throat, his hands molding her breasts,

189

fondly squeezing them.

Mariana lifted her hips closer to him, sighing. She closed her eyes and let the feelings take hold . . . feelings she had never experienced before. It was as though her body were a flame, burning. His hands were like heated stones, pressing into her, sending her temperature higher . . . higher. . . .

Shuddering with desire, Mariana softly cried out as Lone Hawk continued to tantalize her with his hands and mouth. She moved sensually with him, savoring his hardness inside her. And then all feelings she was experiencing began to dissolve into a delicious tingling, spreading . . . spreading. . . .

Lone Hawk sensed that she was nearing that point where she would be rendered mindless with the intense pleasure of his skilled lovemaking. He himself felt how her new skills at returning the lovemaking were causing his head to begin a slow spinning. His loins felt near to exploding. . . .

And then they tremored together, in the other's arms, sealing their passion in a fiery kiss as they reached that pinnacle of pleasure found only by those truly in love.

Mariana crept slowly from his arms, still breathless. Yet her mind . . . her thoughts . . . had suddenly been returned to the real world, that world that was filled with remorse . . . death. . . .

Drawing a blanket about her arms, she gazed into the fire, wanting only to remain a part of the world that included Lone Hawk. But she had much on her mind that needed saying. Only by placing all old wounds and doubts behind her could she ever live in total peace with the man she loved.

Lone Hawk sensed how he had again lost his Blazing Heart to sad thoughts. He drew on his breechcloth and settled down beside her and took her hand in his to squeeze it fondly.

"Tell me your thoughts," he said thickly. "My loving you was not enough, it seems. Perhaps once you rid your heart of your grief, it will then belong solely to Lone Hawk."

Fear of telling him about being part Sioux stabbed away at Mariana's insides. She had already told him about her mother; the next thing to tell him about would be the diary! No. She did not want to tell him at this very moment. It surely would be easier later.

Turning her eyes quickly to him, she smiled clumsily up at him. "First you tell me more about your past . . . more about your father," she said in a rush of words. "Tell me more about your people, Lone Hawk? I do not wish, just yet, to speak of my mother's passing. Please understand?"

Lone Hawk picked up a twig and began smoothing it around in the gray ash at the edge of the firespace. "My father? He is not much longer on this earth, either," he grumbled. "He is ailing so, Lone Hawk does not even take you to him, to show you off. My father lies in a half sleep most of the time now. Soon his spirit will be traveling the long trail of the hereafter. Soon Lone Hawk will assume all duties of chief."

"Chief," Mariana murmured. "You will be chief. You will make such a great leader of your people, Lone Hawk."

"None will ever be as great as my father," he said shallowly. "He has fought and won many battles not only of the heart but also of the flesh. In his youth, the

Sioux were a major threat to the Chippewa. Because of my father's wisdom, the Sioux are no longer a threat. Only occasionally do they steal a Chippewa squaw, or a Chippewa horse. And when they do, they are properly dealt with."

At the mention of the Sioux by Lone Hawk, and the bitterness in his voice, Mariana squirmed uneasily on the cushion of blankets and furs. "Do you truly hate the Sioux so much?" she dared to ask. "You have spoken often of your friend . . . Sitting Tall. And he is Sioux."

"We became blood brothers many moons ago," Lone Hawk said, a distant look surfacing in his eyes. "We found together a kinship that even most true brothers do not."

His face was quickly troubled by a frown. "But my blood brother has much to learn about life that Lone Hawk has not been able to teach him," he grumbled. "He chooses firewater over reality, much too often."

Mariana gasped. She drew the blanket more snugly about her shoulders, leaning closer to Lone Hawk. "You mean to say that he drinks whiskey?" she said in a near whisper. "How does he get it?"

"The evil trapper not only causes forest animals to suffer with his traps, but he also causes much infliction upon my blood brother by offering him firewater," Lone Hawk spat. "Jed Fenris not know what he does when he helps my blood brother's mind become warped with white man's whiskey. One day, Jed Fenris will pay."

"Let's speak of pleasant things, Lone Hawk," Mariana encouraged. "Tell me more of your people. I want to know everything about them, because one day I will be a part of them myself."

Lone Hawk looked quickly around. Her words had touched his heart. Though she felt the need to return to her father, to break the news of their marriage to him, she would return again to him to be totally his.

Taking her hand, holding it on his lap, Lone Hawk again stared into the fire, his insides peacefully happy. "Lone Hawk's band of Chippewa are members of the Bear Clan," he said proudly. "The Bear Clan is known for bravery."

He nodded, smiling into the fire. "The Chippewa first lived on the shores of the ocean called the Atlantic," he said. "My ancestors migrated west when told by the Great Spirit that a seashell, or Megis shell, would appear in the west, four times, and that they were to follow it each time. When those sightings occurred, they followed. They were told they would reach our homeland when they found the 'food growing out of the water,' or 'wild rice.' When my ancestors reached this land called by the name *Min-us-so-tuh,* words that mean sky-tinted water, they knew they had arrived in their homeland."

He continued speaking. "This land of the lakes and forests had many bands of Chippewa from the beginning," he said. "Those that had hunted and shared with one another began to compete for trade goods. They began to hunt for the trade rather than for their own use when the white man arrived. The new hunting methods diminished the supply of wildlife. Fewer beavers caused lower water levels and less wild rice. The Chippewa became dependent on trade goods."

"You seem to have accepted the white man into the area generously enough," Mariana said. "Why did you?"

"The white man's items added to the resources of the Chippewa," he said sullenly. "So our people adapted the new tools and materials to their own ways. Kettles saved them work. Beads and cloth gave them new ideas for beautiful crafts far beyond the imagination of the European traders. The fur trade enriched our lives in the same way that centuries of trade always had with other tribes. It was an exchange of gifts that brought honor to both."

"And your father? He is content in this new way of life?" Mariana said softly. "Did he teach you to be happy?"

Lone Hawk tossed the twig into the flames of the fire. "My father adapts well to all changes," he said. "He also taught me the art of adapting well. It is necessary, if I am to lead my people with cunning."

"Your love for your father sounds so strong . . . so special," Mariana said, again thinking of her mother and how empty she was going to feel without her guidance.

Lone Hawk proudly squared his shoulders. A gentle smile touched his lips. "My father was a good teacher," he said, laughing softly. "When I left the wigwam in the morning as a child, my father would tell me to look closely at everything I would see. When I returned, he would ask on which side of the tree was the lighter bark? On which side do they have the most regular branches? He would ask me how I knew there were fish in yonder lake."

He laughed throatily. "Lone Hawk would tell him because the fish jump out of the water for flies at midday in that lake."

Mariana giggled softly. "That's a lovely story," she murmured. "Very, very lovely. Please tell me more."

His heart filled with warmth, enjoying this total sharing with his woman. Lone Hawk drew her into his arms at his side and continued speaking. "My father taught me that whatever the season, the world was filled with a host of Manitog spirits," he murmured. "These spirits controlled the weather, lured game to the hunters, and affected everyone's health. My father told me that the Chippewa focused their religious ideas on pleasing the spirits. If a hunter had bad luck, it was because the Manido, the spirit of the game, was angry. Hunters are careful not to take more animals than they need."

A frown creased his brow. "This is why Jed Fenris will one day pay for stealing so many animals of the forest," he grumbled. "Manido is angry. Manido will one day cast his long shadow over Jed Fenris. Jed Fenris will *die*."

Mariana shivered, hearing the bitterness of his words. Then she became aware of his eyes on her, commanding her to look up at him, and she melted beneath his steady gaze.

"Now you tell Lone Hawk what is troubling your heart. It is more than remorse for your mother. Lone Hawk can see it in your eyes . . . can hear it in your voice when you speak," he said flatly. "You have come to tell me. Tell me now."

Mariana felt color rising to her cheeks, not knowing where to begin. Yet she had to know about Chief Black Cloud. She had to know about her true father.

"Before my Mama died," she slowly began, "she gave me a diary. It was Mama's diary. Many years ago

195

she had kept a daily record of her life. Until recently she had kept the diary a secret from me. But because she somehow knew that death was near, she gave me the diary, telling me to read it after she died."

She lowered her eyes and choked back a sob. "So, Lone Hawk, I did read it," she whispered, her hands trembling. She was glad when he squeezed the hand he held, to transfer his warmth . . . his courage . . . into hers.

"Tell me what was written, Blazing Heart," Lone Hawk said. "It is this that troubles you, is it not?"

With her free hand, Mariana swept a fallen lock of hair back from her brow. Then she nervously placed this hand on her lap. "Yes, it is what I read that troubles me a lot," she said, her voice cracking with emotion.

She shook her head. "It is still hard for me to believe," she harshly whispered.

Lone Hawk saw her struggles. He clasped his hands to her shoulders and turned her to face him. "Until you tell me, your heart will pain you," he softly encouraged. "Tell me now, Blazing Heart."

Mariana's heart pounded. Her throat had become dry. "It . . . is . . . so hard . . ." she said, covering her mouth with a hand. "Lone Hawk, I'm afraid you won't understand. I'm afraid you . . . will . . . no longer want me."

Lone Hawk drew her brusquely into his arms. "Nothing would ever cause my heart to want another," he said hoarsely. *"Gah-ween-geh-goo."*

Squaring her shoulders, Mariana eased from his arms. "Lone Hawk," she said, her eyes wide. "My Mama wrote in her diary of something terrible that happened in her past. It is something that . . . that

196

. . . affects my future."

"Your future is my future," Lone Hawk said, taking her hands, holding them tightly within his. "My future is yours. Whatever it is you are finding hard to say will be shared by both of us."

"It is about my father."

"What about your father?"

"You know him as Everett Fowler."

"*Ay-uh,* Lone Hawk knows him as Everett Fowler."

"I did also, until . . . until . . . I read Mama's diary," Mariana gulped.

"What are you saying?"

Mariana lowered her eyes, finding this even more painful to say than she had expected. Then she looked quickly up and blurted the truth out in a rush of words.

"I now know my true father is a man by the name of Chief Black Cloud!"

Lone Hawk was taken aback. He eyed her with a blank stare, then rose quickly to his feet.

"How can this be?" he said, glaring down at her.

"My Mama was abducted by Chief Black Cloud. When she finally escaped . . . she . . . was with child. She was carrying me in her womb, Lone Hawk. She was carrying Chief Black Cloud's child."

Lone Hawk reached a hand to her shoulders and urged her up to stand before him. His gaze traveled over her, studying the color of her flesh, her eyes, and the gentle lines of her face.

"You must be wrong," he said thickly. "You do not look at all Sioux. You . . . are . . . white."

"You didn't see my Mama," Mariana said softly. "I am an exact replica of her. But, in truth, Lone Hawk, I have Sioux blood flowing in my veins. This Chief Black

197

Cloud. He is my true father. Mama wouldn't have written such a thing in her diary, unless it were true."

Stepping back, away from her, his dark eyes moody, Lone Hawk avoided her searching eyes. "You . . . are . . . part Sioux," he grumbled, kneading his brow. "The Sioux to the Chippewa are nothing but snakelike creatures that crawl through the grass! How . . . can . . . you be Sioux?"

Mariana bit her lower lip in frustration. He was not taking this at all well! Oh, she had feared as much. Yet there was still this one hope.

Rushing to him, Mariana placed a hand on his arm. "Lone Hawk, your best friend is Sioux," she said softly. "Would it matter so much that your woman be Sioux? And I am only part Sioux, Lone Hawk."

His silence angered her. She dropped her hand down away from him and stepped back to glare up at him. "I cannot help but be proud of my heritage," she confessed. "I have felt this strange yearning about all Indians ever since my first arrival at Grand Portage. My love for you all runs deep. And now I know why. I am one of your kind. It makes me proud, Lone Hawk. Please be proud for me."

Lone Hawk squatted down before the fire, balancing himself on his haunches. "Lone Hawk will soon be chief," he said dryly. "My people would not understand a woman who is part Sioux ruling at my side. No one knows of my kinship with Sitting Tall. If they did, they would not accept it. Now how can I expect them to accept you?"

A coldness surged through Mariana's veins. No matter how much they loved each other, he couldn't accept her now, now that she had confessed to being part Sioux. She had expected this. But she couldn't accept it!

Clutching the blanket about her shoulders and falling to her knees beside Lone Hawk, Mariana clasped onto his arm. "You can't be serious," she pleaded. "And if you are, then your people would never need know. It could be our secret, Lone Hawk. Ours alone. Please do not shut me out. I beg you. I love you so."

Lone Hawk turned his eyes slowly around, to look at her. His insides were aching, the truth gnawing at his insides, like a sore festering. He placed a hand to her cheek. "Lone Hawk will have to weigh this in his heart," he said sadly. "You see, it is not right that a chief be less than truthful to his people. It would not be right to begin my reign as chief in a lie."

Mariana rose to her feet, numb. She reached for her clothes and slowly began dressing. And after her holstered pistol was positioned about her waist, she again settled down beside Lone Hawk, having one more question to ask him before leaving.

Once gone, she didn't expect to be welcomed again, and the knowledge cut her as though a million knives were piercing her flesh.

"Lone Hawk, I need to know . . ."

His eyes focused on the low embers of the fire in the firespace, knowing that to look at her would be to grab her into his arms, to not let her go. He had to practice restraint as never before, now that he knew of her relationship with the hated Sioux! More of him wanted to forget this information than not. But he must consider his people's feelings very carefully. He would soon be their leader. . . .

199

"You need to know what . . . ?" he said blandly.

"Where I might find this . . . this Chief Black Cloud," Mariana said, swallowing hard when she saw a look of utter contempt enter Lone Hawk's eyes.

"It's best you not know any more of this Sioux than just his name," he said flatly.

"But, Lone Hawk, I must at least *see* my father."

"He raped your mother and you still wish to look upon his face?" he growled, looking quickly over at her.

"I was born . . . of . . . that rape," Mariana said shallowly. "I must know something of this past of mine that has been kept from me. It is only fair, Lone Hawk."

"It is best to let this part of your past stay dead inside your heart," Lone Hawk growled. "Though I do not even like Everett Fowler, he appears to have been a decent enough father to you. It's best that he remain so."

Mariana rose angrily to her feet. "Lone Hawk, I must find Chief Black Cloud," she argued. "And I will. If he is anywhere close by, I will find him."

Lone Hawk's eyes flamed as he looked up at Mariana. Little did she know just how close Chief Black Cloud made his residence to Grand Portage . . . as well as to Lone Hawk's Chippewa village!

But he would not tell her. She would soon forget this foolishness. And Lone Hawk had more to worry about now that he saw in Mariana more than a woman of his desires. A part of her was Sioux! His heart . . . his mind . . . were wrestling to accept this truth!

Mariana grew cold inside, hearing his silence, seeing his tightened jaw. "You know, don't you?" she gasped.

"You know Chief Black Cloud, don't you?"

Lone Hawk's continued silence was answer enough for Mariana. She stifled a frustrated sob, gave him a lingering look, then turned and fled from his wigwam. She had to get away from him. She felt as though she had lost him . . . totally lost him. . . .

Chapter Fifteen

> *O, beauty, are you not enough?*
> *Why am I crying after love?*
> —TEASDALE

Mariana arrived back at the Grand Portage stockade at what seemed a perfect time. As she rode toward the large gate, all eyes were averted elsewhere. The arrival of many sea vessels from Sault Ste. Marie had just been announced—they were coming into view around Hat Point, the point of land to the left of Grand Portage as one faced the bay. The great "rendezvous" was about to begin.

For the next couple of weeks, Voyageurs would come by the swarms in their large canoes, attired in their colorful sashes, bringing news of the outside world. There would be reunions with old friends, and lots of laughter and storytelling.

Once all the canoes and small sailing vessels— especially the seventy-ton *Otter*, which carried the heavier, bulkier cargoes, arrived at Grand Portage, her

Papa would cast aside all thoughts of Mariana. This would be a time of great profits for him. He would be a king, ruling over his domain, as trade would be at its peak during the "rendezvous."

Her father would be welcoming from six to eight hundred men into his trading post by the time this summer was over. He would even place his mourning aside, for it would not be profitable for him to mourn.

With a set jaw, though bone-weary from the night long travel, Mariana wove her horse through the crowded stockade grounds. After placing it in the stable, she sneaked into the rear door of the private living quarters of the trading lodge.

She was wide-eyed and breathless, fearing being caught. But the living quarters were as silent as a tomb. Mariana was made aware of the absence of her mother. The smells from the kitchen that usually floated enticingly through the air, the smells of coffee brewing over the fire and sweet breads baking, were not there.

There was a sullen atmosphere around her, yet she did not wish to again be caught up in mourning, for she had to put in a quick appearance to her father at the store. Hopefully, after his return from his mysterious outing he would have thought she was already in her bed, sleeping soundly, and would not have checked in on her. But this morning he would expect her. There would be much activity as the Voyageurs arrived to buy their wares.

Hurrying to her bedroom, Mariana quickly slipped out of her travel clothes. She washed, erasing the night smells from her flesh, then chose a dress appropriate for working alongside her father. It was a high-necked gingham dress with a fully gathered waist, long sleeves, and only a trace of lace at the collar and cuffs.

Braiding her hair, she looped it about her head, smiling at her reflection in the mirror, thinking she looked like a proper old maid for sure. But this was exactly what she wanted. She did not wish to have the attentions of any men today. Though she felt as though she had possibly lost Lone Hawk forever, she could not let herself lose complete hope.

A sadness engulfed her when she let her thoughts wander to Lone Hawk. He hadn't understood. He hadn't understood. . . .

"I mustn't think about him," she whispered. "I have my Papa to convince that I haven't been up to any mischief. He must never know I've been to the Chippewa village."

A frown creased her brow. "But what if Eugene South told him?" she said, thinking the terrible man could even use such knowledge as blackmail, to get her to be more attentive toward him.

"But he is too much of a coward to even try that," she softly laughed.

Whisking the skirt of her dress into her arms, fighting off the sleepiness that came in strange sweeps throughout her body, she walked from the living quarters into a hustle and bustle of activity, seeing her Papa through the throngs of men standing about. He was enjoying not only the chance to trade, but also the company of each.

Her Papa was chewing on a fat cigar as he weighed pelts, while Eugene stood dutifully by, recording each sale. Clearing her throat nervously, Mariana went to the long counter and took her place at her father's other side.

"Sleepin' late this morning, weren't you, daughter?" Everett grumbled, his wide lips scooting his cigar from one corner of his mouth to the other.

Mariana's eyes wavered, a blush rising to her cheeks. "Yes, Papa," she murmured. "And even still I don't feel rested enough. After helping you a while, I might have a need to take a short nap."

She hated having to lie to her father, but it was the truth, at least, that she would need a nap. She had pushed herself to travel the full journey from Lone Hawk's village in one night, fearing discovery by her father.

Everett leaned his face down into Mariana's. "That's not like you," he said gruffly. "Why the need for more sleep this morning, Mariana? You know the Voyageurs are arriving. I'll need your help now, more than ever before."

Then he straightened his back and smiled smugly. "But perhaps rest is more important than your helping me this day," he chuckled.

Mariana caught the glimmer in his eyes and the smugness of his words. She didn't like it when her father behaved like this. It had to mean that he had plans for her that she would not agree to. It had been the same sort of plans with Eugene South that had almost cost her her life.

"Why would you say that, Papa?" she dared to ask, stiffening when Eugene's hand brushed against hers as he reached for a ledger that lay close to her left hand.

"You know the first night after the arrival of so many Voyageurs there is always a celebration," he said taking the cigar from his mouth, going to the fireplace, pitching it into the low embers of the fire.

He turned and thrust out his chest and placed his hands inside his front breeches pockets. He was wearing fancy dress breeches and coat today, instead of his usual buckskin attire.

"This great lodge is going to be jumpin' with music and dancin'," he said, his eyes sparkling. "We'll move the counter back against the far wall. The floor will clean bounce from the dancin'!"

Mariana's insides grew cold. She gave Eugene a quick glance, seeing how he was smiling as smugly as her father.

She then gave her father an icy stare. "So soon after Mama's passing?" she said dryly, lifting her chin. "Papa, it . . . would . . . be disgraceful."

Flashes of guilt troubled her, remembering her sensual moments with Lone Hawk so soon after her mother's burial. But those had been private moments that she even believed her mother would understand. That sort of happiness shared with the man you loved were rare in this wilderness. Her mother hadn't had such happiness, it seemed. Her mother hadn't seemed to feel so deeply even about her husband.

Everett stormed back to stand behind the counter and resume his business transactions. "Life is for the living," he grumbled. "Your mother would understand. She knew that during the long winter months most people waited for this time at our trading post. It is a time for celebrating . . . not mourning."

Mariana curled her nose with distaste. "But a dance, Papa?" she worried. "I really am not in any frame of mind for a dance."

"My daughter is going to be the sunshine of the dance," Everett said, winking down at Mariana.

206

"You'll be dancin', Mariana. And it's only right that my daughter be there, to greet the guests."

His eyes lowered. "I've no wife now, you know," he murmured.

"I don't intend to take Mama's place in your life," Mariana snapped, stepping away from her father to stand on the far side of the counter.

Everett gave Mariana a scowl, then laughed boisterously as he greeted some new arrivals into his store. Mariana began straightening bolts of material on a shelf, then felt a presence beside her. Turning with a start, she found Eugene there, smiling.

"Like your father said," Eugene said in an almost whisper, "tonight there's a dance. I plan to be there, dressed in my finest."

Mariana whirled around to face him. She placed her hands on her hips. "And do you think I care?" she snapped. "Eugene, do you forget so easily that I almost died out there alone when you so bravely left me and rescued only yourself?"

"Seems you fared well enough out on your own," Eugene said, poking his face down into hers. "Where did you go, Mariana? You were gone the whole night and even longer. Did you go and meet that savage? Did you?"

Mariana paled, hearing the venom in his words. He was, most definitely, a threat to her. "Where I went and whom I chose to be with is none of your concern," she said, hating it when her voice broke. But Eugene was looking at her much too deviously. If he told . . .

"You're lucky your father was gone as long as you were," Eugene said, chuckling low. "He only arrived home shortly before you did. He just had time to

207

change into a more decent outfit. Apparently he didn't check in on you. Or he would've known, wouldn't he?"

Mariana sighed heavily. "Eugene, let's quit playing cat and mouse games," she said dryly. "Do you plan to tell Papa about what I did, or don't you?"

"Perhaps," Eugene said, chuckling low.

"Oh!" Mariana said, whirling the skirt of her dress around and placing her back to him.

Eugene moved to her side. "Your father and you both have your little secrets, don't you?" he said threateningly.

Again paling, Mariana turned her eyes to him. "What do you mean by that?" she whispered.

"Your father goes one way, you go the other," Eugene said, shrugging. "Now wouldn't you like to know where he goes when he takes these absences from the trading post, Mariana? I know."

Mariana was itching to know, but she wouldn't let Eugene use that to get his way with her. "What my Papa does is none of my business, nor is it yours," she snapped. "If he knew that you are attempting to blackmail him, he would send you on your way, Eugene South!"

Again Eugene lifted his shoulder in a casual shrug. "Seems you have two reasons to dance with me tonight," he said, smiling smugly down at her. "First, for me to keep my silence about you . . . second, for me to tell you where your father goes. You do want to know, don't you, Mariana?"

He turned on his heel and left her standing there, gaping disbelieving after him. Why didn't her father see what a vile creature Eugene South was? Her father was not that easily tricked. Or was it because her father and

Eugene South had been poured from the same mold? They both seemed equally devious. Perhaps her father saw in Eugene a younger image of himself. Eugene South was more of a coward, though, it seemed. And in this instance his cowardice could work in Mariana's favor!

Trying to stay alert, though her weariness was about to get the best of her the longer she worked, Mariana focused her thoughts on the activity about her. The French-Canadian Voyageurs mingled, laughing and greeting each other, discussing the northern border waters that had become their highways.

They were a colorful sort of people, ones Mariana had always enjoyed observing. With the rollicking folk songs they were known for, their lives seemed to be full of fun and gaiety. But they labored hard for their money. They were known to paddle their canoes from dawn to dusk at forty strokes a minute, with short rests every hour. When carrying his cargo and canoe over the Grand Portage trail, each man was often loaded with at least one hundred eighty pounds on his back. His daily ration was a quart of dried peas or corn and two ounces of grease.

There were two types of Voyageurs. There were the "Pork Eaters," a name given to the ones who operated the large canoes that brought trade goods from Montreal to Grand Portage and returned with furs, and there were the "Winterers," who lived west of Lake Superior, trapping and trading with the Indians. In the spring they loaded their canoes with furs and went to Grand Portage. There they were paid, exchanged their furs for trade goods, and returned to spend another winter in the wilderness posts.

The birchbark canoes used by the Voyageurs had been developed by the Chippewa people. They were light and could be made of, and repaired with, materials found along the forest streams. These huge, forty-foot canoes carried ten to fourteen men and held up to three tons of goods. In the more rapid lakes, twenty-five-foot canoes were used by six to eight men.

Everett edged close to Mariana. He patted her hand. "Daughter, it looks as though your eyes will hardly stay open," he said. "Though I don't understand how you could be sleepy after a full night's sleep, I think it best if you get along with yourself and take that nap you made mention of."

He smiled wickedly down at her. "Remember tonight. There'll be no sleepin' beneath this roof."

He smacked her on the behind. "Now get along with you. I want you fresh for the showin' off tonight. Do you hear?"

Mariana felt other eyes on her. She looked slowly to her other side. Eugene was leering toward her. Such a look made her flesh crawl. She feared perhaps he wanted more than dancing from her this night. And if she warned her Papa, then he would find out the truth from Eugene. She was trapped, it seemed.

"Yes, Papa," she murmured. "Perhaps it is best that I do go and take that nap."

She wanted to shout at him that she didn't wish to join in any celebration! She would much rather have returned to Lone Hawk, to convince him that though she had Sioux blood running through her veins, he must still want her! And Lone Hawk could lead her to her true father. He seemed to be the answer for all her woes!

Yet Lone Hawk did not even want her now, in any capacity. If he had wanted her, he would have not let her leave the Chippewa village, let alone himself. . . .

Inching her way through the crowded room, Mariana was glad to finally be in the privacy of her room. Spying the hairbrush on her dresser, she went and got it and held it to her breast. Going to the window, she stared into the forest.

"Somehow, Lone Hawk, I will make you understand," she whispered. "You will want me again. You will love me, forever. I will be your wife. I will. . . ."

Chapter Sixteen

Life is short, so fast the lone hours fly, we ought to be together, you and I.
— ALFORD

The fiddles squeaked at the far end of the room, attempting a minuet. Mariana stood beside her father, welcoming the families of the trading post and the visiting Voyageurs into the store crudely transformed into a ballroom.

Mariana had chosen to attempt to alter her downcast mood by dressing beautifully, transporting herself, if only for a moment, back to the days in Virginia when she had so admired her mother in her beautiful ball gowns and elaborate hairdos. For this evening's festivities, Mariana's hair was upswept in a delicate swirl about her head, and she had placed wild roses in folds above each of her ears. She wore a gown of rich satin, its blue color emphasizing the blue of her eyes. The gown's bodice came to a point in front, emphasizing her tiny waist, its gathers generously garnished with lace and velvet ribbons. At her throat she wore a gold locket hanging from a tiny blue velveteen ribbon. Inside the locket was a picture of her mother.

"My, but don't you look lovely tonight," Blanche Lee said, looking warmly into Mariana's eyes as she stepped up to her, alongside her husband. "Your mother would be so proud."

An ache pained Mariana's heart. She felt a blush rising to her cheek. "But it is too soon," she murmured, casting her eyes downward.

Blanche drew Mariana into her arms. "Honey, your mother wouldn't want you to grieve so," she murmured. "She wanted so much for you. Life is short, Mariana. Take what happiness you can, now."

Tears sparkled in Mariana's eyes as she returned Blanche's warm embrace. "I so appreciate your being there for Mama, when she needed someone," she murmured. "It was so kind of you to leave your family duties to look after Mama. Thank you, Blanche. Thank you."

"Your mother was a fine lady. I only regret that I didn't have more time to spend with her," Blanche sighed, stepping away from Mariana, still holding her hands. "Somehow I feel that if I had been available more often, your mother wouldn't have had to be so lonely. But my family. They keep me hoppin', Mariana. I hope you understand."

"You know that I do," Mariana said, smiling warmly. She nodded toward those who were already dancing in the middle of the floor. "And you deserve this time away from family duties, Blanche. Please enjoy yourself this evening."

213

Blanche leaned a kiss on Mariana's cheek. "You too, Mariana," she whispered. "You, too."

"I'm not sure if that is possible," Mariana said softly. "But I promise that I shall at least try."

Blanche nodded, then walked away with her husband, clinging to his hefty arm. Then Mariana continued at playing the dutiful daughter, until her cheeks felt frozen in place from her forced smiles of greetings. Her hand ached from the tight squeezes from both the men and the women. But finally everyone had arrived and Everett had left Mariana to herself, standing forlornly away from the rest of the merry makers.

"Mariana, shall we have that dance?" Eugene said, suddenly beside her.

When she turned her head jerkily toward him, she grimaced. He was dressed in an impeccably cut evening suit with an abundance of ruffles spilling over his waistcoat and black cutaway coat, his face shining from a clean shave, and he smelled of some rich men's cologne. But he did not appeal to her at all. It was as always before. She detested him. His personality would not even please a fly!

"I really do not wish to dance," Mariana said coldly, clasping her hands tightly behind her. "I am sure you can find a more willing partner, Eugene."

Eugene boldly slipped a hand about her waist and began directing her toward the dance floor. "You know that is not at all what I wish to do," he said dryly. "I've waited all day for this moment, Mariana, and by damn, you are going to dance with me. Not only once, but many times."

He glowered down at her. "Remember? I have much

to tell your father if you don't," he said smugly. "Also, surely you wish to know where your father spends his idle hours, don't you? It is I who can tell you."

"You are not only a coward but also one who practices blackmail," Mariana said, glad at least that the violins were no longer playing a minuet. Instead the dance was a quadrille, the sort of square dance that occasioned no more touching than hands on shoulders.

Not wanting to draw attention to their hostile bantering, Eugene forced a smile as he led Mariana into the midst of the dancers. "My, but haven't we become spiteful, of late," he said. "Mariana, a hateful attitude does not become you."

"I want to cause you to be uncomfortable with me," Mariana said almost beneath her breath, herself forcing a smile, not wishing to have anyone see that she was dancing with a man she despised. "If it is a hateful attitude that causes you to be uncomfortable, then so be it!"

Mariana welcomed his silence. She seemed to have rendered him speechless with her last angry retort. She swept and turned in the movements of the dance. Perspiration soon beaded her brow as she became heated with the crowd of the dancers pressing in on her and the heat of the fire on the hearth where food was being kept warm for the celebration.

She could separate the aromas of roast fowl, boiled potatoes, and mashed turnips. Lobster was bubbling away in a pot, breads were being kept warm, melting with butter, and there was an ample supply of assorted pies.

Silver tankards of brandy were being passed about, and bottles of wine were being opened. And as Mariana could have predicted, her father was sipping on his hot milk amply laced with spiced wine, his gaze proudly following her every movement.

She danced several dances with Eugene, until she became breathless; still, she needed fresh air more to get away from him than to refresh herself. If she didn't find a way of escape soon, she would be forced to be with him the remainder of the night. And any time with him was too much.

Then there was his promise to tell her about her father . . . where he spent some evenings away from the trading post. Even on the night of his wife's burial.

Forcing a laugh, Mariana stepped back away from the dancers, fanning herself with the tail of her dress. "My word, I find this so tiring," she said, giving Eugene a sideways glance. "Perhaps some fresh air would revive me, Eugene. Do you think?"

"Whatever you wish," Eugene said, placing a hand to her elbow, walking toward the opened door at the far end of the room.

There was a strained silence between them as they stepped out into the moon-splashed night. The night air was nipped with chill, causing Mariana to shiver involuntarily. But she wouldn't accept Eugene's arm about her waist. She shoved him away, then hugged herself with her arms. Taking a leisurely stroll, they walked to the wide gate that opened to the bay. Bonfires were lighted along the waterfront, reflecting gold onto the overturned canoes, under which the Voyageurs camped. Several small sailing vessels could be seen farther out in the water, most occupants having been transported on to land by way of canoe.

"It's a lovely night," Eugene said, clearing his throat

216

nervously as he cast Mariana a look of longing. "As you are also, Mariana."

"Eugene, please do not try to flatter me," Mariana said icily. "You know that I am here with you only because I have no other choice."

She then stopped and turned to face him, looking up into the pale features of his face, his gray eyes seeming empty in the darkness of night. "You said that you would tell me about my Papa," she blurted. "Tell me now. You have had many dances with me this night, Eugene. I did as bargained. Now you do the same."

"After the full activities of the evening are over," he said coldly. "Only then will I tell you." He smiled crookedly down at her. "You see, if I tell you now, you will ignore me for the rest of the evening. And the night is long, Mariana. Your father plans to keep the celebration going until morning."

Mariana felt the blood rushing to her face in her anger. She angrily crossed her arms and rose on tiptoe, to speak more fully into his face. "I should have known," she hissed. "You'll never tell me, because you don't even know. You are despicable, Eugene South. Why did I ever trust you?"

"You had no choice," he laughed. "You tend to forget that I could still tell your father where you spent last night. My dear, it most surely was not in your bed."

A movement out of the corner of her eye drew Mariana around. Her pulse raced, not feeling safe this far away from the trading post lodge only in Eugene's company. She already knew the sort of defense he offered a lady in distress. None! And as it was, everyone else was at the lodge, participating in the evening's activities!

Eugene followed Mariana's watchful stare, squinting, trying to see what had made the movement of which he, now, was also made aware. And then his blood turned cold in his veins, recognizing the copper sheen of an Indian's skin through the darkness, standing not that far from where the stockade reached out in two directions.

"A . . . savage . . ." Eugene said, suddenly trembling.

Mariana's eyes widened. Then her heart soared, recognizing Lone Hawk as he stepped out, into full view, beneath the gentle spill of the moonlight.

"Lone Hawk!" Mariana said in a pleasant whisper.

Eugene looked quickly down at her. "Lone Hawk?" he said shallowly. He then stared toward the Indian, now also recognizing the Chippewa brave.

Lone Hawk moved stealthily toward them, the breeze lifting his breechcloth, revealing even more of his muscled thighs.

And when he stood boldly beside Eugene, looking from Eugene to Mariana, his face clouded with a frown. "Your father forces you to be with this man again?" he said, bitterness edging his words. "Or, Blazing Heart, do you decide to choose him as your man after Lone Hawk is so cold to you?"

Mariana was awed at his even being there, even more so at his thinking that she would choose anyone over him, no matter the reason. She wanted to be pleasant to him, even felt a need to apologize to him for being with Eugene South. But she was remembering just how coldly he had treated her after he had found out that she was part Sioux.

"Does it really matter to you why I am in the

218

company of Eugene South?" she asked, stubbornly tilting her chin, folding her arms across her chest. "Seems not, Lone Hawk. Or have you changed your mind about what we discussed?"

Her heart pounded, so wanting to hear him say that he had been wrong. . . .

"The day was long in thought about you," Lone Hawk said hoarsely. "We must be together, alone, Blazing Heart." He gave Eugene a glowering glance. "This man must be made to leave."

Eugene had paled. He glanced from Mariana back to Lone Hawk. "This savage calls you Blazing Heart?" he gasped. "What is your relationship with him, Mariana? Or need I ask . . . ?"

Placing his hand on a sheathed knife at his waist, Lone Hawk took a step toward Eugene. "You call me savage?" he growled. "White man, that is not a word respected by the Chippewa. It would be best if you choose to not use it again in the presence of a Chippewa." He gave Mariana a sudden glance. "Nor even a Sioux," he quickly added.

"God . . ." Eugene said, placing a hand to his throat. Then he gave Mariana a troubled glance. "Mariana, you'd best return to the trading post with me. Should your father . . ."

Lone Hawk clasped a hand onto Eugene's shoulder. "She goes with me," he said flatly. "We talk. You return to the trading post alone."

Eugene felt a lightheadedness sweep through him. He teetered beneath the solid hand of Lone Hawk. "Drop your hand down away from me," he said weakly.

"You return to the trading post. You tell Blazing

219

Heart's father that she has returned to her room. He must not know she is with Lone Hawk," Lone Hawk instructed, his voice cold . . . solemn. . . .

"I can't lie to Everett Fowler," Eugene said in a meek voice. He glanced over at Mariana. "Mariana, you must return with me. I am responsible for you while you are with me. Should your father find out . . ."

Mariana had watched and listened, speechless. A slow smile touched her lips, as she enjoyed Eugene's squirmings. And there was a ray of hope shining inside her, for it seemed that Lone Hawk had changed his mind, that he was going to accept her heritage . . . perhaps even tell her how she could find Chief Black Cloud.

"I think it best you do as Lone Hawk tells you to do," she said, having to force herself to not laugh openly at Eugene and his awkwardness. "What Lone Hawk said . . . about my going to my room. That sounds logical enough. Tell my father that I developed a headache because of the crowd."

"But should he go and look in on you, and not find you there?" Eugene stammered.

"My father is too wrapped up in entertaining to worry one minute about a daughter who has developed a headache," Mariana softly laughed. "Those he entertains tonight will pay dearly for supplies from the trading post tomorrow. My father is only interested in profit. Even more so than he is in his daughter."

But you choose to go with this . . . this . . . sav . . ." Eugene began to say, but Lone Hawk's fingers tightening on his shoulder, actually paining him, caused his words to be cut short.

"You will go," Lone Hawk ordered. "Now."

Eugene nodded his head, sighing with relief when Lone Hawk stepped away from him. "Yes," he mumbled. "I'll go."

His footsteps faltered when he moved away from Mariana, then he turned and began to run, panting harshly.

Mariana covered her mouth with her hand, glad to see Eugene finally put in his place. And she knew that he would not tell her father anything about what had transpired here. The cowardly side of Eugene would make him too afraid to tell. If he did, he would never be able to walk around without looking over his shoulder, watching for Lone Hawk and what he might do to him for telling.

Mariana's insides turned to a mushy warmth when she felt Lone Hawk's hand take one of hers, turning her around to face him. Her heart melted into his when she saw how his eyes burned into hers, smouldering. She could tell that no matter what she had told him about her ties with the Sioux, he still loved her.

"Let us go where we cannot be interrupted by white man," Lone Hawk said, guiding her along the waterfront. *"Gee-mah-gi-ung-ah-shig-wah.* We have much to say, Blazing Heart. Let our hearts again become as one."

As though in a trance, Mariana went with him until they reached a cove, where the cool breeze of the evening was shut out, away from them. She was surprised to see that a small fire had been built and a blanket had been spread. Lone Hawk's pony neighed from a stand of Norway pines further up, on a bluff.

"You knew I would come with you so easily?" Mariana softly asked, no longer angry with him. There

221

was too much hope for the future to still be angry. The fact that he had come meant everything good to her.

"You are my woman," he said huskily. "Lone Hawk your man. *Ay-uh,* you would come."

Mariana blinked back the urge to cry, then threw herself into his arms, her desire for him blocking all doubts from her mind. Surely he had come to tell her all that she wanted to hear. . . .

Chapter Seventeen

*You are the evening star at the
end of the day.*
—WAGSTAFF

"You are glad that Lone Hawk came?" Lone Hawk said, easing Mariana from his arms to look down at her.

The firelight bathed her face in a soft, reflective glow, as well as her delicate neck, tawny shoulders and scented bodice, arousing in Lone Hawk the feelings he always had when he was with her.

There was a whiff of lavender about her this night, and though her hair was upswept from her shoulders, he could still see how it was the color of a burning flame. And as he looked into her wide eyes, feathered by thick, curving lashes, it was as though he was looking into deep, cool water, they were so blue. . . .

"It depends on why you have come," Mariana said, knowing that this was a lie. Her heart was already melting into his, so enraptured was she by his nearness.

It was impossible ever to stay angry with him for

long. Was it the same with him? Did he love her too much to ever let anything stand in the way? Even the thought of her being part Sioux?

She had pondered over and over again in her mind whether or not she should have told him. Yet always, she had decided that, yes, he should know. There should be no secrets between them. Secrets had a way of surfacing at the wrong time. It was best to tell him about whatever could make him unhappy, now, instead of later, after they had made a full commitment to each other.

It would be easier to separate now, than then.

Framing her face between his hands, Lone Hawk leaned down closer to her, to speak. *"Gee-zah-gi-ee-nah?"* he said huskily.

Seeing the keen penetration of his eyes . . . the gentle, yet strong features of his face now modeled by the pale glow of the fire, and hearing the huskiness of his voice, Mariana was aware that he had not asked her a simple question.

Yet she felt as though she shouldn't be so quickly responsive to him. It was he who had treated her as though she were not important to him the last time they had been together. He had the same as banished her from his village, with his utter coldness!

"You answer a question with a question?" she said, trying to force a stubborn attitude. "And you speak in Chippewa so that I could not even understand that question? Lone Hawk, perhaps you have come to see me for all the wrong reasons."

She eased away from him and placed her back to him. Staring down into the fire, she was quite aware of how her pulse was racing. The sweet pain between her thighs was troubling her. Though wanton she surely was, her heart ached again to be swept into his arms, to be totally with him.

Lone Hawk's shoulder muscles corded as he doubled his hands into tight fists at his sides. His woman tested him more than not! No Chippewa squaw would dare to turn her back to Lone Hawk.

Yet it was this difference about his Blazing Heart that always drew him back to her. She would always be one to add a bit of spice to his life. Nothing about her was ordinary!

Knowing that she must be made to understand his hesitancy to accept this that he now knew about her, Lone Hawk relaxed his fingers from their circle of fists and instead, lifted them to Mariana's hair and began loosening it of its swirl atop her head. And when he heard her quick intake of breath, he smiled to himself and continued until her hair tumbled down to lie across the creamy skin of her shoulders.

As one of the roses fell from Mariana's hair, she caught it in the palm of her hand. Encircling her fingers about it, breathless now as she felt Lone Hawk's fingers weave through her hair, she closed her eyes to the ecstasy building inside her. She loved him so dearly. It was hard to stand like stone, with her back to him, when inside she was melting . . . melting. . . .

Lone Hawk lowered his hands, to now cup her breasts through the satin of her gown. "You did not answer my question, Blazing Heart," he said thickly. "Lone Hawk will ask you again. *Gee-zah-gi-ee-nah?*"

His hands on her breasts were dizzying Mariana. "How can I answer a question I do not understand?" she murmured. "You again spoke in Chippewa to me,

225

Lone Hawk."

Placing his hands to her shoulders he slowly turned her around, to face him. He bent a soft kiss to her lips, then again spoke in Chippewa. *"Gee-zah-gi-ee-nah?"* he said huskily.

"Lone Hawk, please. . . ." Mariana sighed.

"In Chippewa I ask if you love me?" Lone Hawk said, now drawing her fully into his arms. "Yet Lone Hawk already knows the answer. It is a wasted question . . . one that is already answered."

His lips sent feathery kisses along the gentle lines of her face, then to the hollow of her throat. "My woman has proven many times her love for Lone Hawk," he said in a husky whisper. "Yet again would make Lone Hawk's heart sing."

Mariana's face and neck throbbed with his kiss. So overcome with love for him was she that she was almost beyond coherent thought. Yet somewhere deep inside her something whispered to her . . . warning her that he had not yet proven that he had come to her with thoughts other than that of fulfilling the desires of his flesh. He had yet to tell her that he no longer cared that she was part Sioux!

"The fire is warm, the sand beneath the blanket soft," Lone Hawk coaxed, his fingers behind her working with the snaps of her dress. "My beautiful one, let us forget all questions . . . all doubts . . . and again share that which our hearts are crying out for."

Mariana's breath caught in her throat when he swiftly lowered the bodice of her dress . . . he even had her silky underthing slipped from her shoulders and was now kissing the soft lobe of her breast.

Yet she had the strength left with which to remember

226

her doubts, no matter how much he tried to convince her that they must be cast aside. She could not share another sensual moment with him if he did not prove to her that he loved her, that he regretted that he had so easily turned his back on that part of her that he did not want to accept.

It cut like a knife . . . knowing that he could accept a Sioux as his best friend, yet could even consider putting her out of his life, with her only being part Sioux!

He had to love her with more intensity than that for her to give herself wholly to him again!

With trembling fingers, Mariana gently pushed Lone Hawk away from her, then clutched the bodice of her dress to her chest to cover herself. "Lone Hawk, please don't," she said, her voice breaking. "This is not the time or the place. I fear you have come to be with me for all the wrong reasons."

Lone Hawk's face furrowed. "You want to be with white man with the pale face and eyes?" he growled, his shoulder muscles tensing. His eyes swept over her. "You prefer fancy white woman's dress to doeskin dress of the Chippewa? Was Lone Hawk wrong to think that you could ever totally turn your back on your way of life?"

Mariana's face flamed in her sudden anger. She waved her hand into the air. "You speak of such things to me when it is *you* who has proved that you cannot accept things about me?" she stormed. "Lone Hawk, you do not even wish for me to be your woman now. You cannot accept that Sioux blood flows through my veins!"

She tilted her chin proudly. "I am proud to be part Indian. You should be proud for me!"

Lone Hawk grabbed her by the shoulders and gently shook her. "Blazing Heart, you must understand why it is hard to accept this knowing of who your true father is," he scolded. "The Sioux are hated by the Chippewa! It will be difficult enough for my people to adjust to a white woman being the wife of their future leader. But for that white woman to also be part Sioux? That will make their adjustment twice harder! I must think about my people's feelings. It is only right. A leader of the Chippewa people must always place the welfare of his people first."

"Then are you saying that you will love me . . . only . . . from afar?" Mariana asked, swallowing hard. "You are not truly free to love me as you wish, because you must place the feelings of your people before feelings for me? Even before my feelings?"

"It will take time, Blazing Heart," Lone Hawk grumbled. "If your love is true, you will be patient. Lone Hawk must find a way to work this out inside his heart. My father is not well. Soon I will be chief. All my decisions must be wise."

Mariana was cold inside. "You *are* saying that we must love from afar, aren't you, Lone Hawk?" she said softly, dying a slow death inside.

"Love as strong as ours will overcome all obstacles," Lone Hawk said, swiftly drawing her into his arms. He burrowed his nose into the depths of her sweetly scented hair. "Let us not dwell, tonight, on what will or not be. Let us not talk of loving from afar. We are together now. My heart soars with feelings for you, Blazing Heart. And the way you cling to me, I know it is the same for you."

"Lone Hawk . . ." Mariana whispered. "I do love

you. That is why the thought of never being fully with you pains me so. My Papa. He will most surely force me to wed Eugene South if I am free for him to do so. I would rather be dead, Lone Hawk. I . . . only . . . want you. . . ."

Overcome with a feverish heat for Mariana, Lone Hawk consumed her mouth with a fiery kiss. He lowered her dress and underthings, and they fluttered down away from her to lie in a heap of frills and satin at her feet.

Then, sweeping her fully up into his arms, he carried her to the blanket beside the fire and spread her out, his eyes dark pools of passion as he looked down upon her pink flesh, drinking in the loveliness of her body, seeing again her perfect breasts, her tiny waist, and her slender legs.

Again he kissed her, leaning down above her. His hands possessing every silken curve of her, he sealed her soft utterings of protest. Even when her fingers splayed against his chest, trying to push him away from her, did he still stubbornly kiss her.

With his knee, he parted her legs, his manhood straining against his breechcloth. He freed the part of himself that ached to join with her body and entered her swiftly and surely, then began his slow, even strokes inside her.

Mariana soon lost the strength in her hands and dropped them down away from him, again being swept up in the silvery flames of desire for Lone Hawk.

She softly moaned, now totally lost to him, feeling how he moved slowly within her, then faster, with quick, sure movements, tantalizing her. She was a moth caught in a web, yet it was a magic web of sweetness, one that she welcomed.

She now knew that he would work this problem out . . . that it would only temporarily separate them. For she knew that he knew, as well as she, that it was their destiny to be together.

Lone Hawk's mouth moved from her lips. He spoke in a whisper against her cheek. "My love for you is as that for the stars in the sky," he said. "One would not exist without the other."

Mariana sighed. "And I so love you," she whispered, twining her arms about his neck. "Never could I ever love anyone as I love you. Without you, I would only be half alive."

His mouth closed hard upon hers. A hot fire shot through him as he felt the tightening in his loins, his explosion so near. . . .

Mariana felt the storm building within as his steel arms enfolded her, holding her close, his taut body against hers stealing all her sense of reason. She hadn't even thought to question where they had chosen to make love. It did not matter . . . that the velveteen sky was their witness.

With the shifting of the wind came the sound of the fiddles squawking . . . the laughter of those dancing. It was a different world to Mariana, so far from reach, while she lay in Lone Hawk's arms, loving him. . . .

And then they tremored against each other, fulfilled again in their feelings for one another. Mariana's breath came in low rasps, and she tingled all over as Lone Hawk's lips worshipped every inch of her body as he slipped away from her to lie on his side beside her.

Again Mariana heard the fiddles . . . the laughter. Her eyes flew wide open, looking in the direction of the sound. "Papa . . ." she harshly whispered. "Should he . . ."

"Your father knows nothing tonight other than the profits he makes tomorrow," Lone Hawk said, leaning up on an elbow, his eyes slowly raking over her. "Even you said that to be so, Blazing Heart. He will scheme to trick the white man as he so often does the Chippewa. He is ruthless. You could not be born of a man such as he."

Lone Hawk's gut twisted, now realizing what he had just said. *Ay-uh,* she was not born of this ruthless white man! She was born of a snakelike Sioux!

Rushing to his feet, he drew on his breechcloth. Again he was reminded of the barrier that was a threat to him and his woman! No amount of lovemaking would make this truth go away. It was as though two people were inside him, wrestling with each other. He felt that torn with knowing who her true father was.

Mariana felt an iciness sweep over her, and it was not from the chill of the night, for the campfire was warm against her flesh. It was Lone Hawk's strange change of mood. And she knew why! He had made mention of her true father! He hated the thought. It was possible that he might never accept the truth, or her!

Shivering, Mariana crept to her feet and moved quickly into her clothes. The silence between her and Lone Hawk was strained. Mariana's heart thundered inside her. She could almost hear it, it was so wildly beating. She felt as though she had lost Lone Hawk again, yet they had just shared the most beautiful moments a man and woman could experience together. It didn't seem possible that so soon this sharing could be shattered. Lone Hawk was her total being!

231

But she would never again confess such feelings to him. She would have to learn to live without him if he couldn't find it within himself to accept her and her heritage . . . a heritage that was not of her doing.

Tossing her hair back from her shoulders, Mariana began to walk away from Lone Hawk and her feelings for him. Suddenly she felt his fingers tightly clasp about her wrist. When she was forced around, to look up into his eyes, she was again almost swallowed whole with rapture. He was looking at her with such devotion. Yet where was this devotion when he spoke aloud . . . ?

"This thing that is tearing us apart," Lone Hawk grumbled. "A way will be found, Blazing Heart, for it to be remedied."

"Perhaps if you . . . if you . . . could lead me to my true father, let me just see him and his way of life, then perhaps *I,* at least, could place all my curiosity behind me," Mariana murmured. "If I never mentioned it again to you, perhaps you could forget it was ever told to you. Then you wouldn't have to worry about truths being kept from your people. It would be as though it had never even existed . . . this . . . truth."

Lone Hawk's expression darkened; his eyes became a silent fury. "You must forget the truth without seeing this Sioux who is your father," he stated flatly. "Only then can you and I place it totally behind us. It is best that you do not even for that one moment look upon the face of the man. Leave it alone, Blazing Heart. Leave it alone."

"You do know Chief Black Cloud, don't you?" Mariana said in a rush of words. "It is as always before. When you speak of him, you speak with much hate

232

from your heart. Why, Lone Hawk? Why do you hate him so?"

"Except for Sitting Tall, Lone Hawk and his father speak with hate of all Sioux," Lone Hawk grumbled. "The chief of whom you speak is no different than another. A Sioux is a Sioux. They are known to steal our women . . . our horses . . . our honor. So it is all Sioux that draw hate from my heart."

His eyes took on a faraway look. "But as I said," he mumbled, "Sitting Tall is different. As boys we discovered a special friendship. As adults, it matures more each time we are together."

He clasped his hands to her shoulders. "You are not the only one whose blood is mingled with the Sioux," he confessed. "Mine also has traces of Sioux. Sitting Tall's blood was mixed with mine many moons ago. But Lone Hawk has had to live with this dread of the Chippewa people knowing. This one secret is enough to be kept hidden from my people. How can I have another? If Lone Hawk brings you into village as wife . . ."

"You refuse to tell me where I can find Chief Black Cloud and again you the same as tell me I can never be your wife," Mariana said, stifling a sob behind her hand. "Lone Hawk, I feel my time with you is being wasted. I should have never agreed to come with you tonight. It seems I have again made a fool of myself. I've made love with a man who cares nothing for me."

Lifting the skirt of her dress into her arms, Mariana turned and began to run away from him. When he spoke her name in Chippewa from behind her, a part of her heart tore away. And when he came to her and tried to stop her, she jerked herself free and hurried on

233

through the gate and to her room.

She flung herself onto her bed, feeling totally empty. She now most definitely had lost him. How could she bear to live without him? Was she to live the same sort of existence her Mama had lived . . . one of sadness . . . unfulfilled sadness . . . ?

Moving from the bed, Mariana searched in the trunk until she found her mother's diary. With trembling fingers she held the diary close to a candle and unlocked it. When she began to read the passages in the diary where her mother had written of Mariana's real father, the words faded before her eyes as tears blinded her.

"I've got to find Chief Black Cloud," she softly cried. "Then perhaps I can make things right, Lone Hawk. This gnawing inside my heart, this strange fascination I've had for the Indians since I first came to Grand Portage, have to be because of my being part Indian myself. Not until I come to grips with this will I be able to relax."

Holding the closed diary to her heart, Mariana went to the window and drew the sheer curtain aside. "Lone Hawk, somehow this will all be made right for us," she whispered. "But until then, I must find a way to make you still care . . . care in all the right ways."

She knew that he was probably already traveling through the forest away from her, but tomorrow she would go to him. She would make him accept her, as she was. She would!

Chapter Eighteen

A soft splash of water, followed by sweet, soft laughter, filtered through the thick stand of cotton-woods beside the flashing, sun-filled river. Jed Fenris's ears perked up, his narrow eyes squinted as he stopped to look about him. He saw a trace of the shine of the river through a thick stand of forsythia bushes. . . .

Neala's breath sucked in when Sitting Tall dove beneath the water and disappeared from her sight. Her heart raced and her lips quivered in a smile when she felt his fingers touch first her ankle, then move on upward, to the juncture of her thighs. When his fingers began a slow caress, Neala threw her head back and closed her eyes, rapture quickly taking hold of her.

And then Sitting Tall surfaced and drew her into his

arms, his kiss warming her cool lips in a gentle kiss, his hands fire upon her breasts as they pressed into them. He swept her fully into his arms and carried her to the riverbank. His eyes adoring her, he stretched her out onto a soft mound of grass. "Neala, Neala . . ." Sitting Tall said in a husky whisper, then entered her with sureness, beginning his possessive strokes inside her.

Neala smiled up at Sitting Tall, running her fingers over the lovely copper sheen of his face. She lifted her hips to meet his thrusts, moving rhythmically with him.

"We should have waited until we got to the cave, Sitting Tall," she couldn't help but whisper. "Anyone could . . . could come upon us. What if someone of my village caught us together? Both our families would prepare for warring!"

"My woman worries too much," Sitting Tall said, bending to brush a kiss across the taut tips of her breasts. "Neala, enjoy your man. It is not every day we can be together. Be my *gee-tay-bee-bee-nay,* my captive, today, Neala. Let Sitting Tall, a proud Sioux, teach Neala, a proud *Chippewa,* more of lovemaking."

He lifted her hair and kissed her neck, his thrusts becoming harder. "Our bodies are again joined," he said thickly. "It should make your worries fade away to nothing, Neala."

He kissed her eyelids, urging them closed. "Close your eyes and pretend we are man and wife, living peacefully in our own dwelling," he whispered. "Pretend we have children busy at play outside the dwelling."

Neala giggled softly, urging his lips away. *"Ah-bee-no-gee?"* she said. "Children? Sitting Tall, that is way into the future." Then she grew solemn. "Even if it is ever possible. My father . . . ? Yours . . . ?"

Sitting Tall placed a finger to her lips. "Hush, my woman," he growled. "This is no time to speak of fathers who do not understand how Sioux and Chippewa could be in love. This is the time to forget."

Sighing, letting Sitting Tall's lips claim hers into silence, she twined her arms about his neck and closed her eyes, feeling the soaring of her mind, *ay-uh,* letting herself become engulfed in the pleasure she only knew with Sitting Tall.

She opened herself more fully to him, feeling how his magnificence filled her. She could feel how he so sensually throbbed inside her. She responded in her own throbbing, feeling the mindlessness engulfing her as the joy of release was suddenly there, as was his, as she knew by the stiffening of his body, and then the more powerful thrust that sent his love seed deep into her womb. . . .

The cracking of a twig close by drew both Sitting Tall and Neala's attention. They drew apart. Neala grabbed her dress and tried to hide her body behind it. Sitting Tall quickly drew on his breechcloth. Just as he began to reach for his sheathed knife, his eyes widened at seeing Jed Fenris suddenly there, standing over him, holding up two jugs of whiskey to entice him.

Jed Fenris leered down at Neala, his loins hot and aching, having seen the full lovemaking being performed right before his eyes as he stooped, hidden close by. Even now he could see the soft peak of one of Neala's breasts, her attempt at covering her full nudity having not fully succeeded. One breast peaked out from behind the doeskin dress, contrasting in its copper color to the white of the dress.

His temple throbbed, knowing now that he had to have her. And knowing that she was Lone Hawk's sister made his plan to abduct her even better! He would teach that damn Injun to steal his traps! If not in one way, then another. And as far as Jed was concerned, this way was the most rewarding to himself.

Sitting Tall's knees weakened, seeing the two jugs of whiskey so temptingly close. It had been too long between drinks. And though Sitting Tall knew that he should be furious at Jed Fenris, knowing that the ugly man must have witnessed Sitting Tall and Neala's lovemaking, it was this thirst for the white man's firewater that made him not complain. If he angered Jed Fenris, the filthy trapper would turn and leave. Sitting Tall couldn't allow that to happen. His mouth already watered for the whiskey. His throat had become dry with need. . . .

"Why have you come?" Sitting Tall said, squaring his shoulders, ignoring Neala who still sat on the ground, breathing shallowly in her fear.

"I've brought firewater. That's all," Jed said, lifting his shoulders into a casual shrug. "Guess I came along at an awkward time, huh, Sitting Tall?" He would act innocent enough . . . get Sitting Tall drunk . . . then take what he had really come for. He would take Neala.

Neala inched back on the ground, her eyes wide. "Sitting Tall, tell him to leave," she said, her voice quivering.

"Come on, Sitting Tall," Jed encouraged, thrusting one jug of whiskey toward him. "Have a drink with me. There ain't no harm in that. And how often do you get such an offer? This drink is free. How about it, Sitting Tall? How about it?"

"Sitting Tall . . ." Neala urged, "you mustn't. Let's leave this place. This man is evil. What he offers is evil."

Sitting Tall's eyes wavered, hearing the pleading in Neala's voice. Yet he saw no harm in taking at least one drink of the whiskey that Jed offered. Jed only wanted to be friendly. There wasn't another white man alive who offered friendship along with whiskey! Sitting Tall couldn't say no. His gut was twisting with the need of the pleasures of the firewater!

"One drink," Sitting Tall grumbled, taking the jug of whiskey. He popped the cork, then turned the jug up to his lips and took a hefty swallow. His body quaked as the whiskey at first left a burning trail to his stomach, and then the burning turned into something smooth, something pleasant, and he knew that one drink would not be enough. Ignoring Neala's continued pleas, Sitting Tall gulped thirstily from the jug, stopping only momentarily to get his breath.

"Go on. Drink," Jed encouraged, slapping Sitting Tall on the back. "Empty that one, then you can have this other jug. I feel generous today, Sitting Tall. Take advantage of it."

Fear stabbing her insides, Neala still clutched the dress to her bosom, afraid to try to lift it over her head, fearing that if Jed Fenris even for a moment saw her nudity as she worked it over her head, she would be raped.

Yet she feared this, anyway. Why didn't Sitting Tall know to worry about it? Surely the wicked man was purposely getting Sitting Tall drunk!

Sad, seeing the man she loved weakened again by the firewater, Neala now wondered if it could ever be any different. Yet she could not find it in herself to not love

239

him. It was a sort of love that was special. She could never love another!

Sitting Tall tipped the jug higher, then felt nothing coming from it into his mouth. He jerked it away from his lips and peered down into the jug, his vision blurring as he tried to focus to see if the whiskey was all gone.

Hiccoughing, laughing loosely, he thrust the empty jug back in Jed Fenris's hand. *"Gee-mah-gah,* gone," he said, teetering in his drunken state. "More. Give Sitting Tall more."

Neala's insides grew cold. She could no longer worry about Jed Fenris's seeing her as she drew her dress over her head. She had to go to Sitting Tall and urge him to not drink any more whiskey. She could tell that he was already mindless!

Hurrying to her feet, she slipped her dress over her head, then spied the sheathed knife not far from Sitting Tall's feet. Her heart pounding, she crept toward it, then stopped when Jed Fenris took a wide step and placed his moccasined foot on the knife, leering down at her.

Neala froze for only a moment, then went to Sitting Tall and clutched onto his arms. "Sitting Tall, don't drink any more of that firewater!" she cried. "Can't you see? Jed Fenris is purposely getting you drunk. Can't you imagine why?"

Only barely hearing Neala, her voice sounding as though coming from inside some deep cave, Sitting Tall brusquely knocked her aside and again teetered as he grabbed the other jug of whiskey and began stumbling away, in the opposite direction from where Neala lay, crying.

Neala tried to run after Sitting Tall, stunned by his rejection, but she was stopped when Jed grabbed her by her wrist and stopped her.

"Where do you think you're going, pretty Injun squaw?" Jed snickered.

Neala jerked at her wrist. "Let me go!" she cried. "Let me go now."

"Now why should I do that?" Jed cackled. "Seems your boyfriend gave you to me on a silver platter. Now don't that seem so to you, squaw?"

Neala swung at Jed with her free hand, only barely scraping his whiskered face with the tips of her fingernails, causing him to emit a soft yelp. "You have rendered Sitting Tall mindless! You know of his weakness," she cried. "You're a vile man!"

Jed's eyes narrowed, his jaw became tight. He lifted his free hand and slapped Neala. "You heathen savage," he growled. "Just shut your mouth. Come along quietly or I'll have to knock you even more mindless than your lover boy."

"You'll be sorry for doing this," Neala sobbed, stumbling as Jed yanked her beside him and led her toward his reined horse. "If Sitting Tall doesn't come after you, Lone Hawk will."

"Sitting Tall ain't in no condition to go nowheres, and let Lone Hawk come," Jed laughed. "Lone Hawk and I have a couple of things to iron out. Squaw, you ain't going to only be mine for a while to do with what I wish, you're also goin' to be bait. When Lone Hawk comes, won't he have himself a surprise?"

Cackling low, Jed grabbed Neala by the waist and lifted her to the saddle, then swung himself up, positioning himself behind her. "We'll show him a

241

thing or two about the wrong of stealin' traps," he snarled, flicking the reins, sending his horse galloping through the forest. "Don't Injuns hold anything sacred? I paid for them traps fair and square, I did. I don't take to someone stealin'. Especially if it's a damned Injun doin' the stealin'."

"You won't get away with this," Neala screamed, her hair flying in the breeze as the horse moved forward. She squirmed, trying to free herself from Jed's muscled arm. But he had her pinioned to him. She could even feel the fretful swell of his manhood as it pressed against her buttocks as he scooted himself closer to her from behind.

Her eyes wild, Neala chewed her lower lip. She looked on all sides of her, hoping for Lone Hawk to suddenly appear. She knew that he was out this time of day, stealing Jed Fenris's traps.

But only moments ago had she discovered that Jed Fenris knew that it was Lone Hawk who was doing the stealing.

Though she wished for Lone Hawk to come and rescue her, she feared for him. This evil trapper was clearly capable of anything if he had gotten Sitting Tall drunk deliberately to steal her away from him!

Her heart ached for Sitting Tall. She was losing hope that he could ever place his lust for the white man's firewater from his life. He had even chosen it over her this day.

Lowering her eyes, Neala felt empty, knowing that Sitting Tall could be so careless in his love for her. He was to be pitied, oh, so pitied. . . .

"Ain't long now," Jed chuckled, tightening his arm even more fiercely about Neala's waist. "Squaw, you

242

don't know how long I've planned this. And watchin' you tangling with that drunken Injun only sent my blood to boilin' more for you. Squaw, you really know how to pleasure a man. Soon you'll be pleasurin' me."

"If you try to rape me I'll cut your heart out," Neala hissed, looking over her shoulder, daring Jed with a dark, steady stare. "Don't you know that a Chippewa squaw knows as much about using a knife as does a Chippewa warrior? Evil white man, Neala even knows the art of scalping."

Her insides rippled fearfully as she spoke so boldly to the man, knowing that he, in truth, would be able to do as he wished with her. Only her words were strong. She wasn't. Beneath the filthy clothes of the white man she knew that he was muscled. To survive in the wilderness, a man had to be well-muscled.

If he didn't give her the opportunity to have a knife for defending herself, he would, indeed, take what he wanted from her. And if he did, she would most surely want to die!

Just the thought of his filthy hands touching her made her want to retch. And if he touched her with his man's private part that surely was as filthy as his hands, she would not ever want to be with a man again. Not . . . even . . . Sitting Tall.

She would never feel clean enough again, to be touched by the man she loved.

Jed's insides were on fire now with the thought of being so near to fulfilling his needs. He could see the spirals of smoke rising from his outdoor fire. Snapping the reins, he urged the horse past towering Norway pines. And then he drew rein beside his lean-to, beneath which were piled pelts ready for trading.

A bitterness rose into Neala's throat, seeing the scattered entrails of slain animals piled against a tree trunk. The stench rose into her nose, causing her to reel and gasp.

Then the shock of this was blotted from her mind when Jed grabbed her down from the horse and began shoving her toward his dwelling, throwing her onto the ground beside his outdoor fire. Wildly her eyes looked about her, seeing buckskin stretched across leaning poles, making a roof over which Jed was now standing, already ripping his gunbelt from about his waist.

"Squaw, the waitin' has been hard, but damn well worth it," Jed hoarsely laughed.

Buttons popped from his shirt as he jerked it away from his chest, then from his arms. His breathing was hard, his loins throbbing. "Undress, squaw, or I'll rip the damn dress from your hide."

He nodded toward his pelts. "Want me to treat you like an animal?"

He laughed. "But that's what an Injun is, ain't it? A damn animal."

He slipped his buckskin breeches down, and his manhood appeared in its swollen strength to Neala. "But ain't seen no animal as purty as you, squaw."

Seeing the part of him that soon would impale her, Neala looked away from him, covering her mouth with her hand. Her gaze swept around her, looking for a weapon to use on him. And when she saw a knife with blood dried on its blade on the ground, not far from her, she began inching toward it.

But she didn't get far. Jed was quickly there, leaning down over her, now fully unclothed.

"Think you're going somewheres?" Jed snickered.

He grabbed one of her hands and forced her to touch his manhood. "This is the only place you're going, squaw. So you might as well decide to cooperate."

Neala winced as her fingers were forced to encircle his swollen shaft. Tears splashed from her eyes as he urged her fingers to move on his hardness. She could feel the throbbing against her fingers. She could hear him breathing hard.

And then he was standing fully over her, flinging her to the ground beneath him. He didn't bother to remove her dress. He lifted it and impaled her in one quick stroke. And as his body began to move, she closed her eyes and began chanting low, praying to the Great Spirit, Wenebojo, that he would send someone to save her. . . .

Sitting Tall stumbled as he walked. He lifted the jug to his lips and thirstily emptied it. And when he couldn't get another drop to wet his throat, he threw the jug angrily aside and fell to the ground, his eyes searching around him.

"Neala . . . ?" he said in a drawl. "Where are you, Neala?"

He began to crawl along the ground, feeling around for her. *"Gah-ween-nee-nee-sis-eh-tos-say-non?"* he said, his head reeling. "Where are you? Neala, I need you. My eyes do not see so well. The firewater. It is now gone, Neala. We can be together again."

He settled on his haunches and lowered his face into his hands. "Neala, I need you," he cried. "Where are you?"

The piercing cry of someone in pain met his ears, yet

he could not distinguish whether it was an animal or a human's cry.

Pushing himself up from the ground, he again began to walk aimlessly about. He squinted his eyes to the piercing rays of the sun beating down upon him. His legs were heavy, his stomach felt as though someone had pierced it with a knife.

"My heart cries for you, Neala!" he shouted, flailing his hands into the air. "Come to me, my woman. Come to me!"

But when he still couldn't find her, Sitting Tall crumpled into a heap beside the river and let tears flow from his cheeks in silver rivulets.

"She is gone," he cried. "In her anger with me over again drinking firewater, she has left me. She'll never love me again. Never. Sitting Tall has lost Neala. Sitting Tall wants . . . to . . . die . . ."

He bowed his head and began a low chant, praying to the Great Spirit, Wenebojo, for forgiveness. He prayed to be given strength to be the man he must be, to one ·day become chief. He needed strength and guidance for all things in life. The firewater had robbed him of everything, it seemed. . . .

Suddenly his eyes grew wild. He stood, staggering, looking desperately about him. He was suddenly recalling Jed Fenris's being there. Jed Fenris had been too eager to give him the two jugs of whiskey. And Jed Fenris had witnessed Sitting Tall and Neala's love-making.

"No!" he shouted, throwing his head back in his sudden grief and understanding. "Neala, no! Were you forced . . . ?"

His legs too weak to carry him in search of her,

Sitting Tall crumpled back to the ground, and wept.

Jed Fenris rose away from Neala, a loose smile on his lips. His face was flushed, his insides finally at peace.

Pulling on his buckskin breeches, he towered over Neala, who had curled up into a fetal position and was pretending to be asleep.

But Jed didn't care. He had gotten from her what he wanted. And soon he would take the same from her again.

His chest thrust out in his pride at having raped a savage squaw, Jed stooped to grab some leather strings from the ground. Then he went to Neala and began tying the strings about her ankles.

He smirked as he watched the flutter of her eyelashes as she looked suddenly toward him.

"You ain't gettin' away, squaw," he laughed. "Not until I get all I need from you. You see, ol' Jed here has only begun to get his pleasures from that luscious body of yours. Maybe tomorrow I'll turn you loose."

"The forest is not a place large enough for you to hide once Lone Hawk finds you," Neala softly cried, paining still between her thighs where he had so roughly assaulted her. "You will become the hunted . . . my brother, the hunter. And no traps will be used on you, evil trapper. My brother will find other ways to make you pay for what you have done to me this day."

"You scare the breeches clean off'n me," Jed cackled. He grew sober and glared down at her. "Now, squaw, if'n you don't want a gag coverin' that lovely mouth of yours, you'd best just keep your opinions to yourself."

"Neala has said all that needs to be said," she said, wincing when he jerked her wrists together and began binding them. "You just try to sleep at night knowing my brother will be hunting you."

"Perhaps it'd be best if I make sure you cain't tell your brother who abducted you," Jed said, standing and placing his hands on his hips.

"Yeah. That would be best. After I have my full fun with you, I'll just do away with you." He chuckled low. "It's for sure Sittin' Tall won't tell. He won't remember nothin' after consumin' those two jugs of my special rotgut."

Lone Hawk was walking along the riverbank, looking for piles of driftwood. Near each pile he poked a stick into the ground. When it sank quickly he knew that he had found an animal burrow. With his stick he opened the burrow up and pulled out a handful of tender wild artichokes that the animals had stored there.

Proud, he rose back to his full height and moved further down the riverbank. . . .

Mariana rode through the forest, now sure of her way to Lone Hawk's village. After the celebration, her father had again mysteriously left. She had spent a restless night of only half sleeping and had risen with the sunrise and left, driven in her need to see Lone Hawk again. She missed him. She couldn't stand their being angry with each other another day. She would be patient with him. He had shown that he was terribly torn and she must try to understand why.

"And perhaps I can find out from Neala who this Chief Black Cloud is," she thought to herself.

Smiling, she flicked the reins against her horse, her hair flying across her shoulders, the dark riding skirt lifting above her ankles. Soon she would be with Lone Hawk again. Hopefully he would welcome her into his village.

Yet, might he hesitate? She was part Sioux!

"But his people don't know this," she reassured herself in a soft whisper.

This time while she was at his village she hoped to learn more about his people ... become acquainted with other members of his family.

Yet she doubted this would happen. Until Lone Hawk came to some sort of peace within his heart about her, she knew to expect him to keep her at arm's length where his family was concerned. His father was chief. One day Lone Hawk would be chief. . . .

Chapter Nineteen

> *I love her with a love as still as a*
> *broad river's peaceful might.*
> —LOWEL

Having found enough wild greens, herbs, and artichokes in the forest, Lone Hawk swung his pony around and began following the stream, making his way back to his village. Though he had busied himself foraging for provisions for his people, his mind had often strayed to Blazing Heart. Again she had turned her back on him and left him as though he were not important!

Had it been a Chippewa squaw being so disrespectful to the future chief of his band of Chippewa, he would have never wasted a moment of his time in thoughts of her. Yet his heart would not be as lonely for a Chippewa squaw as it always was for his Blazing Heart! It seemed he would forgive her anything.

His eyes lowered. "But neither Father nor my people would forgive her for being part Sioux," he worried

250

aloud. "This is a battle that will be hard to win. Yet most battles of the heart are."

He straightened his shoulders and now looked straight ahead, his pony leading him around Norway pines, beneath stately cottonwoods, and then up an incline. The noonday sun was turning the hilltops golden, their long, melancholy shadows thrown over a valley reaching far out, away from the stream.

Lone Hawk's hunting fever was roused as several deer colored the landscape with streaks of brown as they leaped away from him. His hand went to the bow placed at the side of his pony, and then the quiver of arrows, yet something else caught his eye, making him soon forget the deer.

A smile touched his lips, seeing two ponies reined together beneath a maple tree, the sun dappling down upon them like threads of golden-white.

"Neala. Sitting Tall," he whispered, wheeling his pony around, heading it back toward the stream. He would find his sister and blood brother taking refreshment on the banks of the stream. Lone Hawk had swung his pony away from the stream too soon! Had he traveled on just a ways farther, instead of heading toward the low-swept valley, he would have come upon them in their time together!

Then he frowned. "They have become careless," he grumbled to himself. "If it is so easy for Lone Hawk to see them together, so would it be for other wandering Chippewa. Even Sitting Tall's Sioux brothers! Their infatuation with each other would no longer be a secret!"

Lone Hawk would soon hear of the rantings of both his father and Sitting Tall's. Such an alliance between

251

the Chippewa and Sioux would be a disgrace in both powerful chiefs' eyes.

"It will never be different," he whispered. "Not until both Sitting Tall and I have followed our fathers' footsteps in the capacity of chief to our separate peoples. Perhaps then . . ."

"Hay-ah!" Lone Hawk said, flicking the reins, nudging his pony's flanks with the heels of his moccasined feet. *"Ai-eee!"*

He galloped past the reined ponies, and on to the stream, then drew a blank look when seeing no one there. His eyes narrowed into two dark specks as he reined his horse in and began scanning the riverbank over and over again. Still seeing nothing, his heart began a quick erratic beat, fear ebbing its way inside him.

"Ah-nish-min-eh-wah?" he grumbled, his spine stiffening, the copper sheen of his chest and shoulders cording in his added fear. "Where are they?"

Inching his pony along, inspecting every inch of the riverbank, looking occasionally farther down the alley of water for any signs of swimmers, Lone Hawk now began to dread finding the answer to the absence of his sister and blood brother. Surely they had met danger in their careless need to be together!

The sparkle of something in the folds of grass ahead sent Lone Hawk from his pony to run to see what it was. Bending to his knee, he scooped up the empty whiskey jug, his gut twisting at this discovery.

His brow furrowed into a fretful frown, his face growing hot with anger as he placed the whiskey jug before his eyes to study it.

Then he raised it to his nose and whiffed its dreadful

scent, recoiling, it was so unpleasant.

Emitting a low growl, Lone Hawk threw the empty jug away from him, knowing that, again, Sitting Tall had been duped by the evil trapper, Jed Fenris. Only Jed Fenris so generously offered the firewater to Sitting Tall. But it was always for a reason . . . to get something in trade! This time, what had . . . it been . . . ?

A sick feeling suddenly plagued Lone Hawk's insides, and he again looked desperately about him. Neala! Where was his sister? If the evil trapper had been here to give Sitting Tall this jug of whiskey, Neala had to have been with Sitting Tall. The proof was in the fact that her pony was reined with his!

"Where is she now?" he throatily whispered. He flailed his arms into the air and looked into the heavens. "Where is Sitting Tall?"

The only answer that he could come up with was one that he did not want to believe was true. Had Jed Fenris taken Neala in exchange for the whiskey he had given to Sitting Tall? Yet Sitting Tall was also missing.

"Lone Hawk must find them both," he growled, running back to his pony, quickly swinging himself up onto his saddle of blankets.

His jaw tightened, his eyes became two points of hate. "Sitting Tall, if anything has happened to my sister because of your love of the white man's firewater . . ."

Not wanting to think of those possibilities, Lone Hawk thundered away from the stream and began his search. He rode high. He rode low. Up one hill, down the other. He searched beneath deep shadows of trees . . . through thick flowering bushes . . . some with golden blooms . . . some with white.

And then he caught sight of something in the distance. He grew numb inside as he drew closer. There was no denying who it was he was seeing stretched out on the ground, lifeless.

"Sitting Tall!" Lone Hawk gasped. His eyes searched wildly about him for Neala, then his heart ached, seeing no signs of her anywhere.

Quickly dismounting from his pony, Lone Hawk ran to Sitting Tall, seeing out of the corner of his eye another empty jug not that far from where Sitting Tall lay.

Dropping to his knees beside Sitting Tall, Lone Hawk clasped his fingers onto his friend's shoulders and gently shook him, now seeing that Sitting Tall was in no way injured, instead in a drunken stupor.

"Sitting Tall!" Lone Hawk shouted, shaking him more vigorously. "Where's Neala? Where . . . is . . . she . . . ?"

Sitting Tall's eyes fluttered open, the whites red-streaked. When he opened his mouth to speak, his breath caused Lone Hawk to cringe and turn his face away.

"Lone Hawk?" Sitting Tall stammered, licking his parched lips. "Why are you here?"

"Sitting Tall, I found your pony and Neala's," Lone Hawk said in a rush of words. "Where is she?"

Sitting Tall shook his head, trying to clear his thoughts. "Neala? Isn't she here?"

Lone Hawk was trying to hold his temper at bay, yet his temples were throbbing, his anger was so great! "Sitting Tall, look around you," he said, gesturing with his hand as he leaned away from Sitting Tall. "Do you

254

see her?"

Lone Hawk's eyes focused on the empty jug. He went to it and brought it back to Sitting Tall. "Again you are weak, Sitting Tall? You cannot say no to the offering of white man's firewater?" he growled. He bent to his knee and held the jug close to Sitting Tall's face. "Deny that you drank the firewater!" he shouted. He tossed the jug aside. "Its smell is on your breath! Where was Neala while you were drinking the whiskey? Where is she now?"

Sitting Tall blanched, suddenly remembering. It was coming back to him in flashes, Neala so beautiful as she had been swimming at his side. Neala making such sweet love with him! And then Neala watching horrified as he accepted the whiskey from Jed Fenris. The rest was a blur.

"Jed . . . Fenris . . ." Sitting Tall gasped, looking wild-eyed up at Lone Hawk. "Jed Fenris gave me the firewater. Neala looked on. She gone now?"

Sitting Tall hung his head in his hands, suddenly sobbing. "Jed Fenris take her?" he said. "She . . . with . . . Jed Fenris . . . ?"

Lone Hawk rose quickly to his feet, glaring down at Sitting Tall. "You are a pitiful excuse for a man," he hissed. "You do not protect my sister with your life as you should! Instead you choose firewater over her."

Dropping to his knee again beside Sitting Tall, Lone Hawk grabbed him by the shoulders and dug his fingers into his flesh, speaking in a hiss into his face. "If anything has happened to my sister, you will regret ever having tasted that first drop of whiskey," he warned.

Then he shoved Sitting Tall away from him, grimacing. "Sitting Tall, you no longer my blood brother," he said shallowly. "Our friendship is ended." He waved his hand in the air. *"Ah-pah-nay,* forever it is ended, Sitting Tall! You now are just another pitiful Sioux!"

Sitting Tall tried to rise to his feet, but a light-headedness made him stagger back to the ground. He reached his hand toward Lone Hawk as Lone Hawk turned and ran back to his pony, quickly swinging himself onto it. "Lone Hawk!" Sitting Tall cried. "Don't leave me. . . ."

His eyes on fire with hate for Sitting Tall, Lone Hawk silently glared at him, then wheeled his pony around and galloped away, knowing where he must now look to find his sister. And if she was there, Jed Fenris would pay. Not with his life all that quickly, but in a way that would make him wish that he were dead!

"Ai-eee!" he shouted, leaning low over his pony, riding hard in the direction of Jed Fenris's dwelling. Though Jed Fenris wished to keep his location secret, Lone Hawk had observed the filthy trapper many times from afar as Jed had returned home from a day of having discovered his traps missing. It had so pleased Lone Hawk to observe the man's anger, his frustration. Lone Hawk had planned to make the trapper miserable, then later . . . to kill him.

"The time has come!" Lone Hawk shouted. "But it will be a slow death, Jed Fenris. As Lone Hawk sleeps tonight in his dwelling, you will be slowly bleeding to death!"

Thundering onward, Lone Hawk's heart felt as though it was being squeezed, his fear for his sister was so intense. What if he was too late? What if the filthy trapper had raped, then killed her?

An ill feeling sweeping through him at the thought of his beautiful sister at the mercy of the trapper made Lone Hawk now regret that he hadn't taken care of Jed Fenris earlier. If he had, then his sister wouldn't have been placed in danger.

A movement ahead drew Lone Hawk's attention. His eyes widened, his heart raced, seeing the flame of the hair on the rider ahead! And the way the sunlight bathed her face, there was no denying its color! It was not a Chippewa squaw riding on any mere pony! It was Blazing Heart riding straight-backed on a horse, the wind catching the hem of her skirt, baring her ankles and knees to Lone Hawk's wondering eyes.

"She is going to my village," Lone Hawk mumbled to himself. "My woman again changes her mind! She runs hot and cold, my woman!"

Sinking his heels into the flanks of his pony, Lone Hawk galloped toward Mariana, causing her to turn with alarm when she heard approaching hoofbeats. Placing her hand on the sheathed knife at her thigh, she unsnapped the sheath and withdrew the knife, her pulse racing with fear.

And then she sighed with relief, even felt a tremor of rapture, when she discovered the approaching horseman to be Lone Hawk. Had his Great Spirit warned him of her coming? Or had he just happened along? He was everywhere, all of the time, it seemed! And that he had chosen to be here, in this particular spot in the forest at this moment, made her heart race with gladness!

Lone Hawk reined his pony beside Mariana's stately horse. His eyes were cold, yet his insides were warm, feeling that very soon he would have prayed to be with her, for comforting. Should his sister be dead, only his woman could help erase the pain such a loss would cause him.

Yet he could not forget how she had turned away from him the last time they had been together. It was this that caused him to not lend her even that hint of a smile.

"Blazing Heart, you are again alone in the forest?" he grumbled. "Do you not know the dangers?" Had he lost both his sister and his woman in one day to the evils that could be found in the forest now that the white man was there, he could have not lived with that sort of loss!

"I had to come to you," Mariana said, searching his face . . . his eyes . . . for any semblance of a welcome. "Lone Hawk, we must talk. There is so much left unsaid between us. I'm sorry for becoming angry with you last night. But you . . . you . . . seemed to not care for me as sincerely as I thought. After I told you about the fact that I am part Sioux . . ."

Lone Hawk raised his hand. "You have come today," he said thickly. "That is all that matters."

He looked past her, in the direction of Jed Fenris's dwelling, then again into her eyes. "We talk later," he said flatly. "Lone Hawk has much to do now."

A sudden hurt engulfing her, as though a hot coal was at the pit of her stomach, burning her, Mariana's lips curved into a pout. "Isn't it something that can be done later?" she asked softly. "Lone Hawk, I have ridden far to be with you. And I must return almost as quickly. My Papa . . . I never know for how long he will be gone. He must never know that I meet with you like this."

258

"You either wait, or ride with me," Lone Hawk said dryly. "But Lone Hawk can waste no more time. My sister's life is at stake, Blazing Heart."

Mariana swept a hand to her throat as she gasped. "Your sister? What . . . has happened?"

"There is no time to explain," Lone Hawk said, nervously fidgeting on his pony. "You follow? Or will you stay, and wait for my return?"

"I do not wish to stay here, alone, waiting for you," Mariana said, flicking her hair back from her shoulders. "If you don't mind, I'll ride with you, Lone Hawk, if I won't be in the way."

"You are welcome," Lone Hawk said, reaching to touch her cheek. "My sister will welcome you. If she is injured, a woman's gentle hands may be needed."

His eyes narrowed into two points of fire. "If she is dead . . ." he growled.

Slipping his bow from where he had left it hanging at the side of his pony, he placed it over his shoulder and then secured his quiver of arrows at his back. "Jed Fenris will pay, no matter how Neala is found!" he growled.

"Jed Fenris . . . ?" Mariana said in a low gasp.

"Ay-uh, Jed Fenris," Lone Hawk said, giving Mariana a quiet stare, then wheeled his pony around and began riding away from her.

Frightened, bewildered, Mariana flicked her reins and followed along behind Lone Hawk, then finally caught up with him and rode proudly beside him. It was as though she belonged. It was natural to be with him in such a way, to ride alongside him and soon to be facing danger!

Her mind conjured up all sorts of evils that Jed

Fenris could have done with Lone Hawk's sister. And all that she thought of sent spirals of dread up and down her spine. The filthy trapper must have abducted Neala. Why else was Lone Hawk so angry . . . so determined to go after Jed Fenris?

But, of course, if Neala was with Jed Fenris, the yellow-toothed, bearded man could be responsible for many things.

Mariana cast Lone Hawk a sideways glance, somehow fearing what he might do to the trapper if what he thought had happened to Neala had actually occurred. Mariana might even witness a scalping. It gave her a total sense of dread, thinking the man she loved might be capable of such a savage act!

Yet deep in her heart, she knew that Jed Fenris would deserve any sort of punishment set upon him by Lone Hawk if he had harmed Neala in any way.

Feeling almost totally Indian, Mariana held her chin high, proud to be a part of Lone Hawk's revenge, happy that he thought enough of her to include her in the rescue of his sister. . . .

Chapter Twenty

*I love your arms when the
warm, white flesh touches mine
in a fond embrace.*
—WILCOX

When the first signs of Jed's shanty came into view,
Lone Hawk held his hand in the air, cautioning
Mariana into a slow trot. And when he looked at her
with an even more intense hint of fire in his eyes, she felt
her first pinpricks of apprehension at her decision to
accompany him on his mission of revenge. She wasn't
so sure now if she could be a witness to what he had
planned for Jed Fenris. To her, Lone Hawk had always
been a symbol of gentleness . . . of peace. Should she
see another side to his nature, she wasn't sure if she
could love him as much as before. . . .

Lone Hawk wheeled his pony around to face
Mariana. "It is now time to leave our steeds behind," he
said thickly. "We must go the rest of the way by foot."

His gaze softened. "Perhaps you had best stay
behind," he said, reaching to touch the shine of her hair

as the sun spilled down onto it. "It is enough that my sister was forced to be near Jed Fenris. It is not necessary for my woman to also be placed in such a position."

He nodded toward the shade of oak trees. "You stay behind," he flatly ordered. "Lone Hawk will go and rescue Neala, alone."

An involuntary shiver raced across Mariana's flesh. She was pulled in two directions—one to accompany Lone Hawk because she had a silent dread of staying alone with Jed Fenris, somewhere around, already possibly having assaulted one woman, the second, a silent dread of witnessing Lone Hawk in his total anger!

Looking from side to side, then into Lone Hawk's eyes, which had by now grown impatient at her inability to decide, she nodded toward Jed's shanty.

"Lone Hawk, I choose to go with you," she murmured. "I . . . I . . . don't like the thought of being alone. If Jed Fenris is not at his shanty and should happen along while you are there looking for your sister, I just might become his captive."

Kneading his brow, Lone Hawk nodded. *"Ay-uh,* you are right. You come with Lone Hawk," he said flatly. "Let us go now."

He quickly dismounted, then reached and lifted her from her horse. Drawing her into his arms, he held her for an instant, breathing in the sweet smell of her, reveling in the softness of her hair of fire.

And then he eased her from his arms. Mariana silently looked on as he took his bow from his shoulder and then an arrow from its quiver, and positioned the

262

arrow in place on the bow.

Following his lead, feeling the need of a weapon for herself, Mariana lifted her skirt and slipped the knife from its sheath, then, clasping hard onto its handle, began moving stealthily along beside Lone Hawk, occasionally crouching behind a tree, then a thick forsythia or lilac bush.

They were now so close they could smell the stench of the animal entrails piled close by next to a tree trunk. They could see movement beneath the crude lean-to. Mariana got a glimpse of Jed's whiskered face and saw that he was shirtless, displaying a chest thickly covered with fronds of dark hair.

Noting how Jed was now setting himself down beside the outdoor fire and tipping a jug of whiskey to his lips, the muscles at Lone Hawk's shoulders tightly corded, and his jaw became set.

He gave Mariana a silent nod, and she knew to follow stealthily along behind him, her pulse racing, her throat dry, with mounting fear plaguing her. As her foot found a rock thrusting up from the ground, digging into the sole of her foot, which was only protected by the thin barrier of buckskin moccasin, she emitted a sudden cry of discomfort, then jumped with fright as Lone Hawk was suddenly there, covering her mouth with his hand.

"*Bee-sahn!*" Lone Hawk harshly whispered.

Guessing that he had just commanded her to be quiet, Mariana meekly nodded, smiling up at him.

And then again she followed along behind him, her eyes wide, her nostrils flaring as the stench of the trapper's dwelling wafted through the air.

263

Lone Hawk's gut twisted and he placed a hand out to stop Mariana when he caught his first sight of his sister. She was nude, stretched out, her eyes closed, hopefully only asleep, on the opposite side of the fire from where Jed sat. Her wrists and her ankles were bound. She had a bruise below her left eye and there was blood dried on her lips.

The urge to rush Jed and to kill him was so strong, it took all of Lone Hawk's training in restraint to keep him in place. Again he reminded himself of the importance of making this man suffer! One who died so quickly did not suffer long enough! And a man as wicked must be left to suffer, to die a slow death. . . .

Mariana blanched when her gaze found Neala. A sick feeling at the pit of her stomach seized her. She turned her eyes away, shuddering.

"You stay here, Blazing Heart," Lone Hawk quietly ordered. "What Lone Hawk must do will not be pleasant for gentle eyes like yours."

Not having to be told twice, Mariana looked up into his eyes and eagerly nodded. But she couldn't help but watch as he then moved stealthily onward.

What happened then seemed only a blur, Lone Hawk moved so quickly. The swish of the arrows met Mariana's ears. Jed Fenris's screams of pain tore through the peaceful setting of the forest. Mariana covered her mouth with her hands as she saw Jed stagger to his feet, an arrow piercing each of his arms, blood streaming from each wound. She then watched as Jed again plunged, back to the ground.

Lone Hawk draped his bow across his shoulder and bent to untie Neala's ankles and wrists, his heart filled

264

with pain, knowing what his sister had experienced while she was alone with this man. She wouldn't be disrobed had he not taken her sexually. And the way she lay, so limply! Was she going to die?

Seeing Neala's eyes slowly flutter open filled Lone Hawk with relief. "Neala, my sister, oh, my sister . . ." Lone Hawk said softly, releasing her from the last of her bondages. His eyes searched frantically around him, avoiding looking at Jed Fenris who lay, gasping, staring wide-eyed back at Lone Hawk, both his arms rendered helpless by the arrows.

Seeing several blankets only a few footsteps away, Lone Hawk hurried and grabbed one, then placed one about Neala and lifted her gently into his arms.

"You cain't leave me like this!" Jed cried, sobbing hard. "Lone Hawk, I'll bleed to death! Have mercy, Lone Hawk! Have mercy!"

Clutching Neala close to his chest, feeling the weakness of her arm as she draped it about his neck, Lone Hawk glared down at Jed, his lips lifting into a slow, mocking smile.

"And what mercy did you show my sister?" Lone Hawk hissed. "How many times did you abuse her body, filthy trapper? For this, you will die slowly, Jed Fenris. Drop by drop the blood will spill from your body. You are rendered quite helpless with both arms maimed by my arrows."

"I always thought all savages to be heartless heathens!" Jed cried. "Your sister deserved to be raped! She ain't nothin' but a filthy savage herself!"

Anger seethed inside Lone Hawk. He wanted to sit by and watch Jed Fenris die before his eyes. But the

265

filthy trapper would squirm even more if he died alone. Perhaps even a wolf or bear would happen along and corner Jed Fenris and finish him off in the way Jed made so many animals of the forest suffer!

"Lone Hawk, take me home," Neala softly sobbed, clinging about his neck, her tears wetting his chest as she pressed her face against him. "Lone Hawk, he . . . he hurt me. He . . . hurt . . . me. . . ."

"You will soon be resting in your dwelling," Lone Hawk said, turning, carrying her away from the screaming trapper. "Baby sister, how could I ever let this happen to you?"

"Do not blame yourself," Neala said, wiping tears from her eyes with the back of a hand.

"No. I should not blame myself," Lone Hawk growled, now trotting toward Mariana. "Sitting Tall! It is his fault! He chose whiskey over you. He let Jed Fenris abduct you. Sitting Tall is not even a man. He is not at all one who deserves kindness from you, nor from me, Neala."

Neala's heart ached. She closed her eyes and continued sobbing against Lone Hawk's chest, filled with remorse over Sitting Tall and his weaknesses.

But, oh, how she still loved him!

She hurt deeply over his letting this happen to her, yet she so pitied him because of why he had failed her.

She was his only hope. If she didn't still show her love for him, perhaps he would be lost, forever, because of his need to pleasure himself with the white man's firewater. Even now, though she had every reason to hate him, she fiercely loved him and wanted to protect him.

If not her, then who?

Mariana ran and met Lone Hawk's approach. Tears threatened to spill from her own eyes. She felt so much for Neala, yet she didn't know how to express it. All she could do was offer help, then let Lone Hawk guide her in what he would want her to do.

"Lone Hawk, is she . . . ?" Mariana asked, reaching her hand to touch Neala's perspiration-laced brow.

"She is alive," Lone Hawk mumbled. "Outside, that is. Inside? She is dead, Blazing Heart. But in time, she will be able to forget, and her heart will again sing."

Running along beside him until they reached their mounts, Mariana held the blanket about Neala as Lone Hawk mounted his pony with her still in his arms.

"Follow me, Blazing Heart," Lone Hawk quietly ordered. "When we arrive at my village, then, if you will, you can bathe Neala, then help feed her."

His brow creased into a fretful frown. "She has been shamed today by a white man," he grumbled. "It is best that none of the squaws in my village know this. They will hate anyone with the white skin even more than they already do. Even you, my woman."

Mariana swallowed hard. She felt that perhaps she should tell him that this could be the time to introduce her to his people as being part Indian! Then wouldn't that ease the blow that she was white . . . ?

Yet it was the Sioux whose blood ran through her veins!

Oh, if it had only been a Chippewa who had been drawn to her Mama all those years ago, then everything now would be so much simpler!

But it hadn't been a Chippewa. It had been a Sioux

by the name of Chief Black Cloud!

Her gaze settled on Neala. . . .

While she was bathing her, to draw Neala's mind from the horrors of the day, couldn't Mariana talk of Chief Black Cloud, and see if Neala knew of such an Indian? If Lone Hawk wouldn't tell her, surely Neala could! Neala was in love with a Sioux. Surely she knew others!

"I will be glad to help in any way that I can," Mariana said, swinging herself up in her saddle.

Neala smiled weakly over at Mariana. "You are good white woman," she whispered. "Thank you, Blazing Heart. Thank you."

Guilt splashed through Mariana for having schemed to use Neala while making her comfortable. Yet Mariana knew that she had no other choice. Lone Hawk was the cause. If he would give her the answers she needed, she would have no need to bother Neala or anyone else with this need that was now festering inside her like a sore wound.

"My heart goes out to you for what you have been through," Mariana said, smiling back at Neala. "I will be happy to help you in any way that I can. I want to prove to you that all white people aren't bad."

As Lone Hawk wheeled his pony around, holding Neala securely on his lap, Mariana followed. When she heard Jed Fenris screaming blood-curdling screams behind her, she shivered. Lone Hawk, the man she loved with all her heart, had proven to be less than the gentle man that she had always known him to be.

Yet, if she had been he, she wouldn't have been even that gentle! Jed Fenris didn't deserve to live, not even one more moment. He had committed a crime that proved that he was more animal than man.

"*Ai-eee!*" Lone Hawk shouted, galloping into the wind. Mariana nudged the flanks of her horse with her heels and hurried onward until she was riding at his side. Her hair bounced from her shoulders, her heart soared, proud to again be with her man, no matter in what capacity . . . !

Chapter Twenty-One

*There never was a better bar-
gain driven, my true-love hath
my heart, and I have his.*
                    —SIDNEY

Neala's wigwam was quiet, with only the crackling of
the fire in the firespace breaking through the strained
silence. Mariana had felt awkward bathing Neala, yet
she had done it out of sympathy for the beautiful young
thing who had recently traveled to hell and back with
Jed Fenris.

But now Mariana was only occasionally bathing
Neala's fevered brow. A blanket covered Neala to the
pits of her bare arms where she lay on a bed of furs and
blankets. Lone Hawk had left them alone, planning to
return later to take Mariana to the privacy of his own
wigwam.

Sitting with her travel skirt spread about her and her
feet tucked beneath her on furs beside Neala, Mariana
looked down upon the pale face of Lone Hawk's sister,
again reminded of how quickly things could change in

life. One moment Neala was happy, the next, she was wishing to be dead!

Life had many twists and turns, and Mariana knew that she must grasp onto what happiness she could get now, for tomorrow was always so vague, especially in this wilderness of Minnesota.

"Sitting Tall . . ." Neala sobbed, turning her eyes away from Mariana. "Oh, Sitting Tall . . ."

Mariana's heart ached even more for Neala. She now knew that the man Neala loved had forsaken her. His love for whiskey had taken precedence over the woman he loved. It was beyond comprehension for Mariana to understand how Neala cried for Sitting Tall now, knowing how he had neglected her. Neala's love for him must be total . . . a love that nothing could shake! Neala hadn't lost respect for Sitting Tall for his weaknesses.

Mariana wondered if her own love for Lone Hawk was as strong. If he had done the same to her, would she love or hate him? She had so easily become angered with him over much less than what Sitting Tall had done to Neala!

But she knew that in the end, if she had to prove her love for Lone Hawk, yes, she knew that she could only admit to loving totally him, as surely Neala loved Sitting Tall!

"Where are you, Sitting Tall?" Neala further sobbed, tossing her head, her coal-black hair wet with perspiration.

Mariana dipped the buckskin cloth into a wooden basin of water, squeezed the excess from it, then placed it again on Neala's brow. "Now, now . . ." she crooned. "Neala, you're going to be all right. Sitting Tall is going

271

to be all right. He's probably returned to his Sioux village and is feeling dreadful for what happened. You'll be with him again. Soon. Then you can work this problem out between you."

Speaking the word Sioux made Mariana's back stiffen. She was reminded of the question she so hungered to ask Neala. And she must do it before Lone Hawk returned. If he knew that she planned to pump his sister for answers, he would most surely banish her from his village, never to look upon her face again.

But Mariana was driven! The words written in her Mama's diary haunted her, day and night. Her mother had wanted to be fair, to let her know the truth about her father. Mariana would never rest easy until she knew everything about the man who had been half responsible for giving her life.

Though Chief Black Cloud had taken Mariana's mother by force, Mariana still wanted to see him . . . know him. For it was his blood flowing through her veins. She sorely wanted to find out that he wasn't all bad!

Neala moved her eyes back to Mariana. Mariana winced, seeing how swollen they were from crying. But the soft, sweet smile now breaking through Neala's sadness touched Mariana's heart with a warm gladness.

Reaching a hand to clutch onto one of Mariana's, Neala fondly squeezed it. "You are kind," she whispered, winking another tear from the corner of an eye. "My brother chooses a beautiful, kind woman for his future wife." Neala swallowed hard and licked her parched lips. "It is not usual for a white woman to sit at a chief's side, to reign alongside him, but you are different, Blazing Heart. So much of you . . . speaks . . . of not being white. It is as though . . . as though . . . you are part Indian. In my heart, you are one of us. Perhaps one day all of my people will feel the same, and totally accept you."

Mariana was moved deeply by Neala's words . . . by Neala's total acceptance of her. She returned the affectionate squeeze on Neala's hand. "Thank you, Neala," she murmured. "As you must know, there is much questioning in Lone Hawk's mind about how his people will feel about me."

She cast her eyes downward, knowing the depths of Lone Hawk's torn feelings . . . and their source, which Neala did not know.

Then her eyes shot up, recalling what Neala had said about sensing something about Mariana that seemed to speak of her being part Indian! Neala seemed to be able to look into Mariana's soul . . . as though feeling how that part of her that was Sioux was crying out . . . to be accepted by Lone Hawk!

Not wanting to feel guilty for choosing such a time to question Neala, yet feeling that perhaps such an opportune time would not afford itself to her again, Mariana laid the damp cloth aside and leaned closer to Neala.

"Neala, you are aware that I know about Sitting Tall . . . and that he is Sioux," she said carefully. "And you know that this fact can be entrusted to me, that I won't tell anyone."

Again Neala smiled up at Mariana. *"Ay-uh,* Neala knows this," she murmured. "You have proven yourself trustworthy to Neala."

An apprehensive shiver raced across Mariana's

273

flesh, seeing the trust in Neala's eyes. Mariana did not wish to endanger this trust, yet she was compelled to pursue this that she had already begun. She must ask of Neala the question that Lone Hawk would not answer! If not Neala, then there was surely no one else.

"Your people. They do not wish to make an alliance with Sioux, do they?" Mariana asked softly, still not brave enough to ask the question.

"The Sioux and Chippewa have never been able to make a total peace," Neala said, her eyes taking on a faraway cast. "Though they have shared in some ways, they have been farther apart in others, more than not. Most Chippewa look upon the Sioux as snakelike. Even my brother feels this about most Sioux, though in his heart he hungers for peace between the two tribes." She lowered her lashes. "But peace? It can never be total between our two peoples. Unless . . ."

"Unless?" Mariana prodded.

Neala slowly shook her head. *"Gah-ween.* No. It can now never be," she said in a low whisper. "My brother will now never be able to forgive Sitting Tall for what he has done to me. And peace between the Sioux and Chippewa in these close-by forests could only have been achieved when Sitting Tall and Lone Hawk became chiefs. Now . . . now . . . there will never be peace. Lone Hawk will never forgive Sitting Tall. Never . . ."

"I am sorry," Mariana whispered, then, seeing perspiration beading Neala's brow again, she took the dampened cloth and stroked it gently, soaking the perspiration from Neala's brow into the cloth.

"It is not for you to worry about," Neala said weakly, then sighed as she closed her eyes. "It just wasn't meant to be. It is *mee-ee-oo*."

Seeing Neala's lethargic state and how she had closed her eyes, Mariana's heart skipped an anxious beat. She felt that the opportunity to get answers from Neala was quickly slipping away. "Neala? You know about many Sioux, do you not?" she blurted.

Neala's eyes fluttered slowly open again. *"Ay-uh,"* she whispered. "Why . . . do . . . you ask . . . ?"

Mariana squirmed, positioning her feet more comfortably beneath her. "Do you know of a . . . of . . . a Chief Black Cloud?" she asked, her voice breaking. "Neala, do you . . . ?"

Neala's first twinge of nontrust for Blazing Heart troubled her heart. She squinted her eyes, studying the uneasiness reflected in Blazing Heart's eyes. Why would she need to know about the Sioux? Why would she need to know about Sitting Tall's father? It was enough that Blazing Heart knew of Neala's relationship with Sitting Tall. But no other Sioux name must be associated with Neala! Neala never breathed Chief Black Cloud's name. He was a man most hated by Neala's father.

"Gah-ween, no," Neala said, staring blankly up at Mariana. "The name . . . it . . . is not familiar to me."

But though Neala did not confess to knowing Chief Black Cloud, she wished to know why Blazing Heart wanted to know about him. Perhaps this white woman's father wanted to know? Was Sitting Tall in some sort of jeopardy? It was well known how ruthless this Everett Fowler of the Grand Portage Trading Post was! How a daughter like Blazing Heart could be born of him was puzzling to Neala!

Unless . . . unless . . . Neala and Lone Hawk were

wrong about her!

Disappointment made Mariana sigh regretfully. Her shoulders slumped, her smile faded. "Chief Black Cloud must live far away from these parts," she murmured. She lowered her eyes. "Perhaps that is best. Yes, perhaps that is best."

Neala's eyebrows raised, sensing that she had been wrong to suspect Blazing Heart's intentions were unpure. "Why do you wish to know of this Sioux chief?" she dared to ask, leaning up on her elbow, then crumpling back down onto her bed of furs when she felt a lightheadedness sweep through her.

"It doesn't matter," Mariana said, then turned with a start as Lone Hawk came suddenly into the wigwam. She smiled nervously toward him, hoping that he hadn't been outside the wigwam when she had questioned Neala about Chief Black Cloud. He would not appreciate having his sister pumped for answers, especially at such a time, in Neala's weakened state.

In his breechcloth and moccasins, his skin a copper sheen beneath the reflective glow of the fire, Lone Hawk knelt down beside Mariana and wove his fingers through her hair, urging her face around so their eyes could meet.

"My woman's kindness makes Neala's heart sing again?" he said thickly, bending a kiss to the tip of Mariana's nose. "Lone Hawk thanks you. Neala thanks you."

Mariana hoped that he couldn't feel her tenseness. She feared that Neala would mention that she had asked about Chief Black Cloud.

Yet a soft hand on Mariana's arm and Neala's sweet voice breaking through her troubled consciousness made Mariana know that Neala did not want to be the cause of a strain between her brother and the woman he loved.

It was apparent that Neala was a peacemaker. The proof of that was in the fact that she did not hate Sitting Tall, and . . . that . . . in truth, she should.

"She good woman," Neala whispered. "Now take her, big brother, and be happy."

Mariana looked quickly down at Neala. She wanted to thank her for her silence, yet she knew that wasn't necessary. The understanding was in the depths of Neala's dark eyes.

Mariana felt that a bond was forming between her and this beautiful Chippewa maiden . . . a bond that nothing could tear apart.

"Do you feel well enough to be left alone?" Mariana murmured, taking one more last stroke across Neala's brow with the cloth.

"Sleep will be my escape," Neala said "Tomorrow will be a day for my new beginnings. Neala will place all ugliness from her mind."

Neala reached out her hand and touched Lone Hawk's drawn face, which could not hide that he was troubled with worry. "My big brother, do not worry so," she reassured. "Neala is strong. In every way, Neala is strong."

Then Neala touched Mariana's face. *"Mah-szhon.* Go with my brother. You are meant to be together," she murmured. "Some day you will be together, *ay-pah-nay,* forever."

"I just wish there was more that I could do for you," Mariana said, cupping Neala's hand.

"You have done more than you know," Neala said,

277

easing her hand away. She touched the soreness about her mouth and eyes, wincing in pain. "Neala would not want Chippewa sisters to see what a white man did. You were a welcome substitute, Blazing Heart. Neala thanks you again."

Lone Hawk leaned down and hugged Neala. *"Nee-ban,* sleep, *gee-shee-may,* little sister," he said thickly. *"Ah-nway-bin."*

"Ay-uh, gee-gee-kee-wayn-zee," Neala whispered, then broke into sobs as she clung about Lone Hawk's neck. "Sitting Tall, Lone Hawk. Please . . . do . . . not hate him. You know that the whiskey is the cause for his weakness. We must, together, help him. Please?"

Lone Hawk drew away from Neala. "You can speak his name now? Neala, he does not deserve that your lips even are familiar with his name," Lone Hawk growled. Then again he hugged her. "Now is not the time to think about anything. Just sleep, Neala. Sleep."

Neala nodded, then turned her eyes away.

Lone Hawk placed his hand on Mariana's elbow and helped her up from the furs. "It is best she be left alone now," he said softly. *"Mah-bee-szhon,* come. We will now go to my dwelling. You must rest before you make the long journey back to trading post."

Mariana cast him a quick glance, amazed that he seemed so willing to let her go. In his heart, he was obviously still troubled over the truth about her heritage. Perhaps he could never accept it.

Silently nodding, Mariana followed him outside the wigwam, stepping into the bright shine of the sun. The farther she now walked away from Neala's wigwam, toward Lone Hawk's, the more she was made aware of the activity around her. Gaily clad figures darted about. Many women were bent upon their tasks. Great loads of wood were being brought into the village on the Indian women's backs. Some were carrying water from the river, others were tending the outdoor fires and the meat cooking over them. A noisy, gleeful group of children were romping about, playing with their dogs. Elderly men were sitting outside wigwams, shaping gourds into drinking dippers; others were preparing the gourds for dance rattles, putting pebbles inside the gourds already properly cleaned and dried.

Mariana was eager to know all she could about the ways of the Indians. Yet she now wondered if she would ever be given the chance. So much depended on Lone Hawk's ability to win this battle inside his heart . . . the battle that she had caused by telling him the truth about herself.

Chapter Twenty-Two

When sleepy birds to loving
mates are calling, I want the
soothing softness of your hand.
—GILLOM

Entering Lone Hawk's wigwam, Mariana saw a wooden tray of fruit and cooked meats awaiting her, accompanied by a wooden pitcher of liquid refreshment. Her stomach growling hungrily, she was made aware of just how long it had been since she had eaten. So much had happened since to take her mind off the fact that she hadn't had food since late the previous night, before she had gone to bed, too restless, even then, to sleep.

Eagerly Mariana went and plopped down beside Lone Hawk's firespace and slipped her moccasins from her feet, loosening the buttons of her blouse at her throat, having the need now to be altogether comfortable.

"How did you know that I was starving?" she gently laughed, looking at him as he settled down beside her.

"It is Lone Hawk's intention always to know everything of his woman," he said. "When she is sad . . . when she is happy . . . even when she is hungry."

Mariana gave him a half glance, her pulse racing. "If you wanted me to be happy you would tell me what I need to know about Chief Black Cloud," she said softly.

Lone Hawk glowered at her. "That not make you happy," he said thickly.

Anger welled inside Mariana. She rose to her feet and looked down at him, her eyes flashing. "How can you sit there and tell me what would and would not make me happy?" she fumed. "Lone Hawk, perhaps you don't know me at all." She turned and stomped toward the closed entrance flap, but was stopped when he was suddenly there, blocking her way.

"You do not leave angry again," he said flatly. He nodded toward the fire and the food.

"You will forget your temper and be with Lone Hawk with smile on your face," he said dryly. "You much more beautiful when smiling."

"But, Lone Hawk . . ."

"You do not argue," he said, guiding her back down beside the fire.

"My woman too stubborn at times," he said, a twinkle now in his eyes. He offered her a slice of apple. "Eat. Your hunger replaces your anger, *ay-uh?*"

Not able to stay angry with him for long, ever, Mariana smiled weakly up at him, then nodded. When he placed the apple to her lips, she relaxed her shoulders and took a bite, savoring the tangy sweetness as it rolled around her tongue, then down her throat, into her empty stomach.

"You are quite persuasive," Mariana giggled, accepting another bite. "But it is the first time you tempted me with food, Lone Hawk."

Lone Hawk suddenly scowled. He stared into the fire, his jaw tight. Mariana noticed this change in him and reached her hand to his arm. "What's the matter?" she softly questioned. "You are suddenly so lost in thought. Was it something I said?"

"Ay-uh," Lone Hawk grumbled. "It is that word 'tempt' that you chose to use. Sitting Tall. He was tempted by white man's firewater! Because of this my sister . . . was . . . ravished. He no longer friend. He is now my enemy."

He turned his eyes quickly toward Mariana. "So you see how it is with the Sioux?" he growled. "None are trustworthy. It is because of this Lone Hawk wants you to forget this foolishness of wanting to see . . . to be with . . . Chief Black Cloud."

He wanted to tell her that Chief Black Cloud had fathered the weak Sioux, Sitting Tall. Sitting Tall was her brother. Perhaps then she would forget wanting to know any more about them. Wasn't it enough to know the type of person Sitting Tall had become?

But now, even more than before, he believed it best that she didn't know. Though Chief Black Cloud was her father, she in no way resembled him or his son in outward features, nor personality. She was beautiful as well as brave. She had more courage, it seemed, than one hundred Sioux!

Yet then again, he must remember that she was part Sioux herself. . . .

Mariana reached her hand to sweep her hair from

her shoulders. "If you had just found out that you had a different father than the one who had raised you, wouldn't you be curious about this father?" she said, curving her lips into a pout.

"If this father was Sioux? No," Sitting Tall stated flatly.

Mariana knew that it was useless. He would never change his opinion. She was finding that he was as stubborn, perhaps even more so, than herself. In so many ways they were alike, though they were from two entirely different cultures. And the more she was with him, the more she noticed this about them. She was proud of this fact, for she so loved him. . . .

Brushing the platter of food aside, Lone Hawk bent to his knee beside Mariana and began unbuttoning her blouse. "Lone Hawk knows a way to change your thoughts from talk of Chief Black Cloud," he said, his eyes twinkling. "When we share lovemaking, you do not question Lone Hawk about anything."

Mariana's face flamed with color as he pushed her shirt open and took quick possession of her breast with his lips. She placed her hands to his sinewed shoulders, then swept them down his powerfully built chest, savoring even the mere touch of him.

And then Lone Hawk stood up, away from her. His thumbs fit into the waist of his breechcloth and slowly lowered it, his eyes two dark points of fire as he looked down at her.

"Stand," he softly ordered. "Remove your clothes while Lone Hawk watches. You watch as Lone Hawk sheds his own."

Beneath the command of his eyes, Mariana rose to her feet, her heart thundering wildly inside her chest.

283

As she began removing her clothes, she watched his breechcloth being lowered, revealing to her his ready hardness. Always before he seemed to have skillfully undressed without her actually seeing him. And now that he was boldly standing before her, proud of what he had to offer her, Mariana felt a trace of shyness. It was almost as though it was her first time with him. And as she lowered her own clothes completely away from her, she knew that her face was red, because it was hot with a blush.

Lone Hawk feasted his eyes upon her liquid curves, amused at how she seemed to be so suddenly shy in his presence. It was at moments like this that he was reminded of just how young she was. He had been the one to take her across that threshold from girl to woman.

His eyes burning with passion, Lone Hawk reached for Mariana and drew her into his arms, his lips seeming to sear hers as he ardently kissed her, tantalizing her with his hands as they teased her taut breasts, then moved lower, where they found her triangle of flaming hair at the junction of her long, slim legs.

When he skillfully eased his finger inside her and began moving it, Mariana melted against him, their bodies fusing as Lone Hawk began to urge her to the bed of blankets beside the fire.

Feelings of ecstasy overwhelmed Mariana as Lone Hawk again kissed her, lowering his hardness inside her, rhythmically thrusting, awakening her every nerve ending in response.

Mariana sighed. She tremored. Each time with him was better than the last. He always led her into another world, it seemed . . . a world of noncaring. It was a world of total bliss!

His hands again searched her body, moving down her silken thighs and her long, tapering calves. His lips teased first her lips, then the taut tips of her breasts.

And then he laid his head on her shoulder, kissing her softly on the softness of her neck.

"Lone Hawk, I . . . so . . . love you. . . ." Mariana whispered, touching the smoothness of his cheek, tremoring in rapture as he took her hand and kissed its palm.

"Such love is found only once in a lifetime," he said huskily. "Never place your back to this that we share, Blazing Heart."

Mariana looked at him quizzically, wondering about his warning. If anybody placed a barrier between their love, it would be he. In a sense, hadn't he already done so? In not being able to accept that part of her that was Sioux, he was the same as accepting none of her!

Yet this was not the time to ponder over any questions that she knew she would not find answers to. She was already being transported to heaven, it seemed. And she wanted to cherish every moment of this sweetness with her man.

Lone Hawk sought her mouth almost with wildness, knowing that again, soon, she would be separated from him. His dream of having her at his side, forever, had been dimmed by the facts of her heritage. But somehow, he would make the dream come to full life again. It was becoming less and less important in his mind that she was part Sioux. None of his people would ever need know, for nothing about her spoke of her being Indian. It would not be totally wrong to keep

285

this truth from his people, for they would benefit more than not at having her among them. She would set a good example for the young Chippewa women growing into maturity. His Blazing Heart was a symbol of much good that could be taught the young Chippewa maidens!

But until she could place this desire to find her real father from her heart, he would have to be patient. He would not tell her that she would be welcome into his village as his wife while she still hungered to be even that smallest bit a part of the Sioux!

Not wanting to ruin these sensual moments with her, he cast all thoughts and worries from his mind. He moved rhythmically inside her, his hand molding her breast, the palm of his other hand moving soothingly and seductively over her, smiling to himself when she emitted a low moan of pleasure.

Gathering her fully into his arms, he again nuzzled the softness of her neck. His loins were tightening, as her yielding softness cradled his manhood in a wet warmth.

Feverish with desire, Mariana clung to him. Her teeth nibbled at the corded muscles of his shoulder, the sweet pain between her thighs spreading, moving higher.

The wild, sensuous pleasure soaring within her, she felt the beginnings of the reeling of her head, knowing that she had almost reached that moment with Lone Hawk that could be described as magical.

"My woman . . ." Lone Hawk huskily whispered, brushing feathery kisses across Mariana's cheek, her brow, and then again her lips. "Forever Lone Hawk's love will be true. *Ah-pah-nay, Bis-kah-ko-nay-gee-*

day, my Blazing Heart."

His fingers intertwined in her hair, drawing her lips to his in a passionate kiss. Mariana was imprisoned against him, loving it. She didn't wish to leave him. The time away from him was time wasted! Yet until he accepted her . . . fully accepted her . . . she would always leave him. . . .

Lone Hawk's mouth forced Mariana's lips apart as his kiss grew more passionate. She leaned her hips upward, meeting his more eager thrusts. Her head was spinning . . . spinning. . . .

And then they shuddered against each other, the wondrous desire shared again with bone-weakening intensity, fulfilled in their lovemaking.

When Lone Hawk leaned away from Mariana, she placed her forefinger to the cleft in his chin. She traced it slowly—she was so often so caught up in fleeing from him that she did not take the time to notice this part of him that was so unique. It was as though a skilled sculptor had molded this part of his face, to separate him from those who shared the proud title of Chippewa with him. He was unique, and in many more ways than this. For Mariana, there could never be another. . . .

Then she moved slowly to her feet. "Lone Hawk, I really must be going," she murmured. "If my Papa arrives home before I do, I would not even want to imagine what he might do."

Lone Hawk rose to his feet and drew his breechcloth on. "You have not yet told me why you come again to me," he said thickly.

Mariana lowered her eyes, busying her fingers at buttoning her blouse. "You do not wish to speak of the Sioux again, I am sure," she said softly. "So I will not say why I came again to you."

A low growl rose from somewhere deep inside Lone Hawk. *"Ay-uh,* you are right," he mumbled. "Lone Hawk does not wish to speak of the Sioux. It would have been better had you come for other reasons, Blazing Heart."

Her eyes shot upward. "You are sorry I came?" she gasped.

A slow smile touched Lone Hawk's lips. He went to her and drew her into his arms. "Now Lone Hawk did not say that," he chuckled.

He held her away from him, looking into her eyes. "Again Lone Hawk thanks you for helping Neala in her time of need," he said thickly. "She would not have wanted any of our Chippewa women to see her in such a condition. It was good that you were here, to take their place at my sister's side."

"Do you think Jed Fenris is dead by now?" Mariana gulped.

"Jed Fenris will die slowly," Lone Hawk said, moving away from Mariana to stare into the dying embers of the fire. "But he will die. And while he dies he will remember how. It is only right that he will be haunted by remembrances of Lone Hawk while he is taking his last breaths."

Mariana shivered, hearing the cold hate in Lone Hawk's words. But he had reason to hate. She hated Jed Fenris just as much!

Lone Hawk turned to her. "Lone Hawk will return you safely to your father," he said flatly.

"Thank you," Mariana said, slipping her skirt on. Her face became drawn with a frown. "My Papa. I hope he is not home when I arrive there."

Then she quickly looked up into Lone Hawk's eyes. "My Papa. He often mysteriously leaves the trading post," she said softly. "One day I would like to know where he goes . . . who he is with."

Her eyes cast downward. "Yet, I, too leave, just as mysteriously," she murmured.

"Let us now go," Lone Hawk said, offering Mariana a hand. "I will now deliver you home mysteriously."

Mariana giggled; then her thoughts again returned to Jed Fenris. He would no longer be a bother to her or her Papa at the trading post. . . .

Scooting along the ground, Jed felt his brow beaded with perspiration from pain. Though his arms were both as heavy as lead, he forced first one hand and then the other to the arrows. He screamed. The pain was so severe it threatened to make him faint. But he managed to snap first one arrow in two, and then the other, leaving only half of each shaft piercing his arms.

And then he walked, wooden-legged, toward his horse, and drew himself up into the saddle. Fighting off the lightheadedness that was threatening to rob him of his senses, he nudged the horse with his knees. Thankful that the horse followed his lead and began moving through the forest, Jed leaned down and hugged it, clinging. If he could make it to the trading post before bleeding to death, perhaps his life would be spared.

His breath came in rasps, his brow burning as though it was on fire. He knew that he now had a temperature and feared infection. Should he live, would his arms survive with him? Or would he be forced to live a life without them?

Tears rolled from his eyes, the salt from them stinging his burning cheeks. "God, I've not ever been one to pray much," he cried. "But now I do. Let me live. And if you spare my life, please also spare my arms. Without arms a man would only be half alive!"

Bouncing clumsily on the horse, slipping, sliding, Jed breathed hard. Each time the horse's hooves made contact with the ground there was a painful jolt to his arms. He groaned, he moaned. And then he tensed, hearing the sound of horses' hooves approaching him in the distance.

"God . . ." he gasped, fearing the wrath of Lone Hawk all over again should he find him trying to seek help. With all the energy he could muster, he grabbed his horse's reins and urged it in a different direction. When he found a thick stand of cottonwoods to use for cover, he urged his horse behind them and stopped, scarcely breathing as he listened and watched for the horses to come into full view.

Mariana rode proudly beside Lone Hawk, feeling totally at peace with herself, having been able to place the morbid moments at Jed Fenris's shanty from her mind. Life was too short to dwell on sad things.

Leaning her head back so that her hair tumbled in red sheens across her shoulders, Mariana sighed. "This has to be the most beautiful forest in the world," she said. She lowered her head and looked about her. "The maple trees are so lush. And the cottonwoods so lovely as they lose that soft fluff that looks like cotton."

290

She smiled toward Lone Hawk. "But, of course, I don't have to tell you anything of the forest," she softly laughed. "You have been here way longer than I."

"*Ay-uh,* the forest is the home of the Chippewa," Lone Hawk said proudly, squaring his shoulders. "It is good to my people." He nodded toward the maple trees. "The trees give us much sugar. A year's supply of sugar is stored in large birch baskets called *makuks.* The sugar is used to sweeten fruits, vegetables, cereal, and fish. In the summer, the Chippewa dissolve the sugar in water for a cool drink and the children eat hard sugar as candy."

He continued: "The birch bark of the trees, when it's pliable and ready for stripping from the trunks, is used to make canoes. The forest gives my people a place to hunt! A place to fish!" He nodded. "*Ay-uh,* the forest has been good to my people."

And then he frowned. "Until white men like Jed Fenris became a part of it. . . ."

Feeling it harder and harder to cling to his horse, Jed panted. His arms were like two hot coals, painful and feverish. But he had the will of ten men, and he would make it to the trading post!

But he still awaited the arrival of the two horsemen. Only a trace of hope touched his heart. Should those drawing closer be friendly, they could assist him in his time of trouble! The arrows . . . they had to be removed. The bleeding had to be stopped.

Then his gut twisted. He was looking directly onto the face of Lone Hawk as he rode past on his pony.

And then Jed's eyes widened in recognition, seeing who rode alongside Lone Hawk, as though she belonged!

"I'll be damned," he hoarsely whispered. "Mariana Fowler! I'll . . . be . . . damned. . . ."

A crooked smile made Jed's lips lift into a smug smile. "Now I know how to get my revenge once I'm well again," he chuckled. "Lone Hawk, seems I'll have not only your sister, but also your *woman.* . . ."

He watched as Lone Hawk and Mariana rode on past, then urged his horse from the cottonwoods and began to go in another direction . . . a shortcut he knew from way back. But he would wait until Lone Hawk deposited Mariana at the trading post before letting himself be known. And then he would seek the badly needed help from Everett Fowler, knowing that soon Everett Fowler's daughter would pay for ever looking upon the face of that savage Injun, Lone Hawk . . . !

Chapter Twenty-Three

*He loves my heart, for once it
was his own. I cherish his, because in me it bides.*

—SIDNEY

The night was dark, with not even a trace of a moon in the sky. An ominous, low rumble of thunder in the distance reached Mariana as she dismounted from her horse and walked it toward the stable.

Across her shoulder she cast the windows of the living quarters behind the trading post store a quick glance, tensing when she saw no trace of lights at any of them.

She was relieved to know that her Papa wasn't going to catch her on her return from her outing because he wasn't home himself, yet her concern about him and where he might be was greater than her relief at not being caught by him.

Where was he? Was he finding ways to make money other than trading at the trading post? Mariana knew of no other drive within her father than the desire to make money.

Her eyebrows lifted. A . . . woman . . . ? A man's drive to have a woman's attention could sometimes be as strong as greed!

But she shook her head, recalling just how long it had been since her Mama had passed away. Her Papa could not be so crude as to seek out the pleasures of another woman, so soon . . . he had even gone away on the day of her death!

Yet she knew that he had been making these disappearances way before her Mama had died. He could have been meeting a woman then, as he could be now.

"But what women live beyond these walls of the trading post, besides those who are already married . . . ?" she whispered, guiding her horse into a stall, at least glad that a lamp was burning low at the far end of the stable, always a beacon for those who dared to venture out at night.

Her heart skipped a beat, her eyes widened. She turned with a jerk and looked through the open stable door and again toward the dark windows of the cabin.

"Only Indian squaws live beyond these walls," she whispered harshly.

Then she laughed awkwardly. She could never accuse her Papa of being with an Indian squaw. He hated all Indians. Even an Indian squaw wouldn't appeal to him. Surely even the color of their skin would send him into a cold frenzy, knowing that the daughter that he had raised was truly not his, but, instead, an Indian's. He thought of Indians as nothing more than savages.

Another rumble of thunder urged Mariana to hurry.

She removed her saddle, took a few brief strokes with a brush through the horse's tangled mane, then rushed from the stable and into the rear door of the trading post.

Stumbling about in the dark, she finally found a kerosene lamp on the kitchen table. With fumbling fingers she got it lit, then felt the silence around her almost squeeze her in her sudden rush of loneliness.

She looked about her. Except for a few items in the kitchen, everything was the same as when her mother had last labored there. Only the few things required to prepare the brief meals since her mother's funeral were out of place.

Lowering her face in her hands. Mariana emitted a heavy sigh. It still didn't seem real . . . her Mama no longer being there, to touch . . . to love . . . to speak with. It was as if she had lost a part of herself when her Mama had died. Being in the kitchen without her Mama, she felt so misplaced!

Shaking her head, knowing that she couldn't get so caught up in feelings, Mariana raised her eyes upward and swallowed hard. Carrying the kerosene lamp, she went into the living room and soon had several other lamps lighted, then went to a window and stared out into the darkness.

A chill coursed through her, suddenly worrying about her Papa. Suppose something should also happen to him . . . ?

Looking across the courtyard, she saw the wavering of other lights in a window. She frowned. It seemed as though Eugene South had settled in for the night. Just the thought of him made bitterness rise into her throat. Yet hadn't he told her that he knew where her Papa went on these strange outings? If she went to Eugene and asked him, would he tell her now?

"I must find out," Mariana whispered. "Eugene must tell me now. For what if Papa is in some sort of trouble out there? Perhaps Eugene should get some men together and go see if he is all right."

Determination hardening her jaw, Mariana swept up the hem of her travel skirt and ran from the cabin and across the courtyard toward Eugene's cabin. Though she detested him . . . even detested the thought of being in the position of asking his assistance for anything, she knew that he was the only one *to* ask. He knew more of her Papa's affairs than anyone else at the trading post. He had made it his business to know, for Eugene had planned to make much profit from this knowledge.

Mariana shuddered, knowing that Eugene had even planned, had schemed to get *her*.

A low moan surfacing from somewhere close by caused Mariana's steps to falter, and her heart seemed to plummet to her feet. With a pounding heart and sudden weak knees, she stopped and turned to the sound, her eyes squinting, trying to see through the black shield of night, able only to see menacing shadows between the buildings that loomed about her.

"Help . . . me . . ." the voice said, weak and trembling.

The hair at the nape of Mariana's neck rose in her sudden fear. She took a step backward, looking wildly toward Eugene's cabin, then back in the direction from whence she had heard the voice. It was a man's voice. Could it be a trap? Could it be someone pretending to be hurt to lure her to him?

"Anyone. Help . . . me . . ." the voice again said, and this time there was evidence of true pain in the depths of the plea.

"Lord," Mariana gasped, then went searching through the dark.

Then finally she came upon a man curled up on the ground at her feet, a horse close by, neighing low.

Falling to her knee, she studied the man, then jumped back to her feet, speechless at discovering just who it was who was asking for help.

"Jed . . . Fenris . . ." Mariana said in a harsh whisper, covering her mouth with a hand. "How . . ."

Jed's insides grew cold, recognizing Mariana's voice. If he had to depend on her, he could be left to die. She had been with the Indian responsible for the dilemma he was now in, hadn't she? Had she even looked on while Lone Hawk had shot him with his damn arrows?

The way Jed's consciousness was coming and going in sweeps, he knew that he had to be close to dying. If he didn't get help soon, he would. If he had only arrived at the trading post while it had been daylight! Then he would have been discovered. As it was, it was dark. He was only another object in the darkness, nothing more . . . nothing less.

Mariana inched back away from Jed, numb. How could he have survived the wounds inflicted by Lone Hawk? Anyone else would have bled to death way before now. But being that this man was almost the devil himself, he seemed to have powers beyond what most normal men had. Surely his wickedness kept him alive!

"Mariana, get . . . your . . . father. . . ." Jed harshly whispered, groaning as he tried to reach his hand toward her, causing the arrow in his arm to shift and shoot firelike pains through his entire body.

Mariana was torn. She was not the sort to enjoy seeing someone in pain. Yet she must remember that this was not just anyone. It was Jed Fenris. He had brutally raped Neala! He had gotten Sitting Tall drunk purposely, all the while scheming to steal Neala away from her lover.

And had he seen her with Lone Hawk? If so, couldn't he tell her Papa . . . ?

"Mariana!" Jed. said more forcefully. "Don't just stand there. Go get . . . your . . . father. Don't you see? I'm wounded."

He would not let her know that he knew about her being with Lone Hawk. He wouldn't even tell her father! Jed had his own plans for Mariana. As soon as he was back on his feet, he would show Lone Hawk that he was not one to mess with!

Sighing heavily, knowing that she had no choice but to try and get help for Jed, or raise questions in the entire community as to why she hadn't, Mariana knelt to her knee beside Jed.

"My Papa isn't home," she said coldly. "I'll have to go for Eugene South. He'll do what he can."

Jed groaned. "Eugene South?" he harshly whispered. "He don't know nothin' about doctorin'. I need your father. He's taken care of much worse wounds than mine. I've seen 'im. He's as good as any doctor that I've ever been a witness to watch."

"Papa isn't here," Mariana said sourly. "Seems you'll take whatever doctoring you'll get, Jed."

A horse's hooves drawing close made Mariana rise back to her feet. She peered into the darkness, now able

298

to make out the bulky figure of her Papa. Her insides warmed with relief.

Running toward his approaching horse, Mariana reached a hand to her father. "Papa, I'm so glad you're home!" she said. "I've been so worried. Where . . . have . . . you been?"

Then she looked across her shoulder, remembering Jed, then back to her father as he dismounted from his horse and began leading it into the stable. "Papa, Jed Fenris . . ." she began, but was interrupted by her father as his eyes assessed her attire.

"What are you doing out here in the dark? Where have you been?" he said thickly, again looking her up and down. "Mariana, you're dressed in your travel clothes."

He inched his horse next to Mariana's. Reaching over, Everett touched her horse, feeling sweat on its mane. "You've been out riding this time of night, Mariana?" he said, now accusing her with the darkness of his eyes. "Your horse has been recently ridden. Its body is still quite warm."

Knowing that she was about to be caught, Mariana gave a silent thanks to Jed Fenris for at least having arrived when he had, for it would be the attention to Jed that would take attention away from herself.

"Papa, there's no time to discuss me or my horse," she said, going to him to grab his hand. "Jed Fenris is outside. He's injured. He's come for your help, Papa."

Securing his horse in the stall, Everett turned a cocked eyebrow toward Mariana. "Eh? What's that you say?" he grumbled. "Jed? Injured? Where is he? How'd he get injured?"

Mariana gestured with her hand toward the open

299

stable door. "Papa, there's no time for questions," she said in a rush of words. "Jed Fenris is out there on the ground. He's terribly wounded."

Everett gave Mariana a long, silent stare, then swung around her and rushed to where Jed lay. Bending down, he swept Jed's head up from the ground. "Damn, man, what's happened to you?" he said, then shuddered when he saw the arrows in his arms. "Christ. Some Indian has really got a grudge, ain't he, Jed?"

"Just help me, Everett," Jed begged. "I fear I don't have much longer if'n you don't."

Everett gave Mariana a quick glance. "Go and get Eugene," he flatly ordered. "Seems we've got work to do, Mariana." Though it was dark and he couldn't see the redness of Jed's wounds, he knew that they were surely infected, because Jed's body was on fire with fever. He gestured with his hand. "Hurry, Mariana. Tell Eugene to come and help me."

Mariana gave her father a silent scowl, then turned with a swoosh of her skirt and hurried to Eugene's cabin. Was she even going to have to help her Papa? It would not seem right being forced to help a man who didn't deserve spitting on. He was a despicable man . . . surely the son of the devil!

Panting, Mariana went to Eugene's cabin and knocked on the door. When he came and opened the door dressed in only breeches, leaving his pale chest bare, Mariana recoiled, even more positive that she would never let her Papa force her to marry such a pitiful excuse of a man. His chest was not only pale, it was thin, lacking any muscle, and his shoulders were narrow. He did not begin to measure up to Lone Hawk. Not even a fraction!

300

"Eugene," she blurted. "Papa has sent me for you. He needs your assistance. Jed Fenris is injured. He's out there, on the ground. Papa needs you to help get him into our cabin."

Eugene's eyes raked over her. A sneer curved his lips upward. "So you beat your father home again, huh?" he said smugly. "One day you won't be so lucky, Mariana."

Feeling a coldness wash through her, Mariana gave him a silent stare, then turned and fled to her room, now deciding that one day Eugene probably would tell her father about her involvement with Lone Hawk.

Stomping her foot, she circled her fingers into tight fists. "Oh, how could I ever have thought to go to him and ask him about Papa?" she whispered. "He would only use it to get what he wants from me. How could I have so easily forgotten that he knows the art of blackmail?"

Hearing voices and the shuffling of feet, Mariana was suddenly thrust into another sort of world . . . the one she wished to be able to turn and flee from. But her father was too soon shouting out orders to her for her to do anything but obediently obey.

"We'll need lots of hot water, Mariana," Everett shouted, carrying Jed by the shoulders, while Eugene was struggling to carry him by the feet. "But first, Mariana, hurry ahead of us and strip your Mama's bed of its covers!"

Mariana paled. She placed a hand to her throat. "Mama's . . . bed . . ." she stammered. It had been this second bed in a second bedroom that had always made Mariana wonder about the feelings of her Mama and Papa. Her Papa had slept in one room . . . her Mama

301

in another. And now to let a man such as Jed Fenris occupy the bed only her Mama had ever slept in . . . had even died in . . .? It somehow seemed sacrilegious!

But the command in her father's voice and the deep frown he was giving her made her know that no matter how she felt about her mother's room . . . her mother's bed . . . she had no choice but to do as her father ordered.

Her heart aching, she grabbed a lighted kerosene lamp and went to her mother's room. Placing the kerosene lamp on the nightstand, she yanked the bedspread and then the sheets from the bed.

She stood back, wincing, as Jed was placed on this bed, blood dripping from his wounds, coloring the neat feather mattress in blotchy reds.

"Daughter, what are you waitin' on?" Everett shouted. "Go and get us some hot water ready! Get us some clean cloths!"

"Yes, Papa . . ." Mariana said shallowly, then turned and fled from the room. . . .

The room smelled of blood. Mariana's blouse was spotted with it. Her insides curled distastefully as she watched her father remove the second arrow. Eugene fed Jed whiskey, helping to make him become mindless to the pain.

Yet Mariana noticed that Jed was not mindless enough not to stare at her, accusing her over and over again with his squinting eyes. This proved to her that he knew about her alliance with Lone Hawk. She couldn't believe that he hadn't yet told her father, and

302

she began to suspect he had a motive behind his silence.

And then she was relieved when his eyes finally closed and he sank into an unconscious state, spittle rolling from his gaping mouth.

She stared down at him, not believing that she was here, actually helping to save the man's life. Yet she knew that she had no choice, but to do it. To absolutely refuse would cause her father to ask why. And she wasn't prepared to give him any sort of answer. It was her secret that she had witnessed Lone Hawk's anger against Jed Fenris. It was a secret she shared with Lone Hawk.

"Thank God he's passed out," Everett growled, rolling the sleeves of his fringed shirt up above his elbows. "We've got to remove the one arm. It's already showing signs of becoming gangrenous." He nodded toward Mariana. "Daughter, have you got the stomach to help? We need as many hands as possible."

Lightheadedness swept over Mariana at the thought of what he was asking of her. "Papa, I don't know . . ." she said softly. She studied Jed's arms, shuddering. "Are you sure, Papa, that you must remove his arm? That seems so . . . so . . . drastic."

Everett eyed the instruments he had already brought to the bedroom, having suspected something like this would be necessary as soon as they had brought Jed into the light and he had seen how his left arm had discolored.

Looking down at a handsaw and a butcher knife that had been whetted keen, he tensed. Though he had performed this same sort of duty at other times, it never got easier. So far, though, no one had died. . . .

"Ain't got no choice in the matter, as I sees it,"

Everett said, shrugging. He cast Mariana a troubled glance. "Daughter, I do need your assistance. Can you do it?"

Lowering her eyes, wringing her hands, Mariana nodded. "Yes, Papa," she murmured. "If I must, I must."

Everett looked over at Eugene. "You got the stomach for the likes of this?" he growled.

Eugene laughed awkwardly, glancing from Mariana to Everett. He knew that Mariana already considered him a coward. If he left the room now, refusing to help with the amputation, he would be called a coward by Everett also. He couldn't afford to lose any more face than he already had.

"Seems I have no choice, eh?" he said, paling at the thought.

"Then let's get to it," Everett growled.

He nodded to Mariana. "We need one more piece of equipment, Mariana," he said flatly.

"What, Papa?"

"Get your Mama's iron and set it into the fire. Get it damn hot, Mariana. Get it damn hot."

Mariana blanched, having an idea what the iron would be used for. "Yes, Papa," she murmured, then fled from the room. But she couldn't stay away long enough to suit her. Soon she was again at the bedside, assisting her father in what seemed the most gruesome act of her life.

But in less time than it would take to tell it, the arm was opened round to the bone, then was almost in an instant sawed clean off. Everett went and got the hot iron and soon had the whole stump effectually seared, completely closing the arteries. Bandages were then applied and Jed was left to sleep off his drunken state and to awaken to find that he was minus one limb.

Walking from the room, Everett slapped Eugene on the bare back. "Thanks a lot, Eugene," he said, laughing throatily. "Seems we did it. I think the sonofabitch is going to live."

"Seems he just might at that," Eugene said, chuckling. He thrust out his chest, proud that he had fared well enough through the amputation. At times he had felt as though he was on that bed being cut on, the pain was so severe at the pit of his stomach, along with the need to retch.

Glancing over at Mariana, Eugene gave her a slight smile, wondering if his performance had caused her to think more respectfully of him.

But when she gave him a scowl, he knew that nothing had changed her feelings for him, and it seemed as though nothing ever would. She was infatuated with a damn savage! A damn . . . savage . . . !

"Well, you just go on your way and get the stench of blood cleaned off'n you," Everett said, placing an arm about his shoulder, guiding him to the door. Again he patted Eugene on the back. "Again, thanks, Eugene. Sure do appreciate it."

"Anytime," Eugene said, nodding. "Anytime." He gave Mariana another quick glance, then turned and walked away, his head hung. His loins burned. One day he would have her. Everett spoke of wedding plans now more often than not. And if Everett Fowler got something in his mind to be done, by damn, it would be done. Mariana wouldn't have a say in the matter. She would become Mrs. Eugene South. And, hopefully, soon. But if she kept meeting that savage secretly, mightn't she even become with child by the heathen?

The thought of her giving birth to a half-breed gave Eugene cause to wince, as though he had been shot. He hurried to his cabin and washed himself, then took a bottle of whiskey and sat down before his fireplace and began drinking. If Jed Fenris could stand the pain of surgery after drinking enough whiskey, surely Eugene South could drink enough, to enable him to forget the pain of needing a woman so badly . . . !

Mariana turned to go to her room, wanting to remove bloodstained clothes. But the strong grip of a hand on her wrist stopped her. She was breathless with dread of her father's questions.

"It ain't enough that you were brave in there, helpin' Mariana," Everett growled, urging her around to face him. "I need answers." He nodded toward the door. "Where had you been earlier?" His gaze swept over her, again seeing her travel skirt and the white blouse. "You don't dress that way unless you are out riding. And why would you have been so late at night? Mariana, you've been warned of the dangers."

Mariana got a devilish thought. She tilted her chin and yanked her wrist away from her father. "Papa, I went looking for you," she said, rubbing her throbbing wrist. "It seems of late you disappear mysteriously more often than not. I went searching for you. I was worried about you."

She could not believe that the lies came so easily to her. But she was determined to find out where his interests lay away from the trading post. Before her mother had died, it hadn't seemed to matter all that

306

much. Her mother had filled the empty spaces in their house. But now with her mother gone, her home was like a morgue, especially with her father away. Only now did it seem important to Mariana to know where he went and why. Though she hoped soon to be able to live her life with Lone Hawk, she wasn't yet able to, and she felt the need for family close by.

Yet her father's going so often gave her free rein to do as she pleased. Perhaps it was best that he didn't feel the need to stay close by for her sake.

But she had already boldly questioned him. And she could not deny that she wanted the answers as badly now as before.

Everett turned his back to Mariana, easing his shirt from his muscled chest. "It's late," he said dryly. "We can talk about this later."

Mariana grew numb inside. He was evading her question. Now she was more curious than ever to know the answers. But she would not pursue them. She had her secrets . . . let him have his.

"Yes, Papa, it's late," she murmured.

Turning, she went to her bedroom. When she took a glance in the mirror and saw the blood on her clothes, and even beneath her fingernails, she trembled. It was Jed Fenris's blood. He should be dead.

Going to the window, Mariana drew the sheer curtain aside and looked into the distance, where the forest lay dark and foreboding. "Lone Hawk, what will you say when you find out that Jed Fenris is not dead after all? What will you do?"

Then she swallowed hard. "What will you say, when you find that it was I who was forced to help save the filthy man's life . . . ?"

Chapter Twenty-Four

Old as your absence, yet each moment new ... this want of you.

—WRIGHT

Standing before her mirror brushing her hair, Mariana faced the new day with a sense of dread. Again she would have to work alongside Eugene. And though Jed Fenris had been taken to his shanty to mend, having somehow survived both the wounds and his amputation, the smell of him still seemed to linger behind. No matter how much Mariana aired her Mama's room, she could still pick up Jed's scent with every breath that she took.

But Mariana thanked God that only two days of being forced to care for the dreadful man had been required of her. One of Jed's friends had arrived and had taken him back to his shanty, saying that he personally would care for Jed.

This friend of Jed's was another trapper, one who didn't frequent the trading post as much as Jed, and

Mariana guessed that he had the same sort of morals as Jed. Now Lone Hawk would have two trappers to deal with, once he heard that Jed was still alive.

The slamming of the back door drew Mariana from her reverie. Her eyes widened. Where could her father be going now? He was getting more restless each day, it seemed.

But why wouldn't he? Surely he missed his wife as much as Mariana missed her mother.

"But still . . ." she whispered, placing the hairbrush on her dresser to hurry to her window.

Drawing back her curtain, she looked outside just in time to see her father go into the stable. Her heart pounded hard, a plan surfacing inside her mind. If she followed him, then she would finally know.

Her face grew warm and she swung away from the window. "I will," she said, then looked down at what she had chosen to wear. A simple cotton dress with a gathered, flowing skirt, puffed sleeves and a round neckline was not the proper attire for travel on horseback. But there was no time to change. Her father would soon be riding away from the trading post, and if she did not follow close behind him, she would not even know in which direction he had gone.

Slipping into her moccasins and tying a bow about her hair, securing it at the back of her neck, she hurried to her bedside table and withdrew her sheathed knife. After securing it to her right thigh, she went, breathless, from the room. Tiptoeing, she opened the door that led into the store. When she saw Eugene there, dutifully tending to things for his employer, she knew that she would not be missed.

Her pulse racing, Mariana quickly closed the door,

then rushed to the back door and eased it open. She stood with it ajar only enough to watch for her father to leave the stable.

And when he did and was far enough away not to see her, she rushed to the stable and got her own horse. She saddled it quickly, mounted it, then rode after her father.

The encumbrance of the skirt of her dress troubled Mariana as it blew up and about her ankles. The breeze was cool. Another storm was brewing in the distance, the clouds overhead low and gray, making this idea of hers seem ominous . . . even wrong.

Should her father discover her so boldly following him, she knew not what to expect of him.

But he should have been open with her. She was all he had now. It would seem he would treat her more as a woman, than child. And if he knew how much of a woman she really was. . . .

Her heart ached for Lone Hawk at the mere thought of him. Out in the forest, traveling away from the trading post, she should be going to Lone Hawk . . . not following her father. She even felt like a sneak, like a wife following her husband, with thoughts of discovering him with another woman.

"Perhaps I shouldn't . . ." she whispered, having second thoughts. "It doesn't seem proper."

Yet when she watched her father riding onward, only a short distance ahead of her, and the determination with which he traveled, it was impossible for her to turn back. She had wondered for way too long to let this opportunity of discovery pass by her.

Holding her chin high, Mariana rode onward, keeping far back enough for her horse's hoofbeats not to be detected by her father. She looked about her as she rode from the forest into a vast meadow. The ground was a beautiful green turf, graceful and slightly undulating, like the swells of the retiring ocean after a storm. Farther ahead she could see patches and clusters of trees. The sun had broken through the clouds, gilding one side of the valley, throwing a cool shadow on the other. This land was a land of a thousand hills and domes of green, vanishing into blue in the distance.

And then again Mariana was traveling through a dense forest. She tensed her shoulders, keeping watch on all sides of her. Many things could be hidden behind the trees and the many flowering bushes. Even she was guilty of hiding . . . from her father.

Squinting her eyes, looking ahead of her, she watched the fringes of her father's buckskin shirt lift and fall with the breeze. His massive frame was not hard to follow. The horse that he rode thundered its hooves beneath the weight of him onto the ground covered with pine needles and rotted leaves.

And then Mariana saw something else in the distance. Her father was riding toward a small cabin peacefully set into the forest, the land around it neatly cleared, with wood piled high, smoke spiraling from its one chimney.

She wheeled her horse to a stop, her breath catching in her throat when she saw her father's horse stop beside the cabin. Mariana further watched, her eyes wide, as her father dismounted and hurried toward the cabin. He didn't even stop to knock. He went on in, as though he belonged there.

"Whose . . . ?" Mariana whispered, paling.

Quickly dismounting, she secured her horse's reins,

then moved stealthily toward the cabin. The buckskin drawn closed over a window was gaping enough at one corner for Mariana to see through. And its thin material afforded her the opportunity to listen to all that was being said inside the cabin.

When she focused her eyes on the dim lighting of the cabin's interior, Mariana felt her knees grow weak and her insides take on a strange queasiness. There was no denying what she was a witness to. Her father was embracing a woman. He was kissing her.

Mariana turned with a start, covering her mouth with her hands to stifle a loud sob that tried to surface from deep inside her.

She buried her face in her hands. She could not believe that her father was embracing an Indian squaw. She couldn't believe that he was actually kissing her and telling her how much he had missed her.

Then she raised her eyes to the heavens. She had never known anyone who could be as much a hypocrite as her father. He was even more than that. He was a man she could no longer even . . . begin to like. All along, while her Mama had even been alive her father had been meeting his Indian squaw, surely making love to her. Even the day of his wife's burial, he had gone to his Indian squaw!

And all those times when he had cursed all Indians, calling them mangy, savage heathens, he had gone to his Indian and made love to her?

Surely she was wrong! Surely her father had come for trading. Perhaps the embrace was only a ploy!

Slowly turning, Mariana peered again through the window. As her insides grew numbly cold, she listened to the conversation being exchanged between her father and the Indian squaw—a squaw even more beautiful than Neala. She was as dainty as her voice, yet her breasts almost swelled from the doeskin dress. Her hair was not braided, it hung instead long and sleek across her shoulders, tumbling further still down her back. Her copper skin was smooth and clean, shining beautifully beneath the light from the fireplace.

A part of Mariana was dying inside her as she continued to listen. . . .

"Have you told your daughter yet?" Joy asked, cuddling close to Everett as he guided her down beside the fire on to some bear furs. "Your wife now dead. I be your wife, Everett."

"It's too soon," Everett said, drawing her to his side as they now sat, facing the fire. "Mariana wouldn't understand."

"She understand lonely heart," Joy openly pouted. "All squaws understand lonely heart."

"Are you truly that lonely, yourself, Joy?" Everett asked, weaving his fingers through the lustrous black of her hair. "I come as often as I can."

"You build Joy beautiful cabin, but it is not a happy dwelling when you are not a part of it," Joy murmured, looking meekly up into his eyes. "Please take me to your big dwelling. Joy needs to cook your meals for you. Joy needs to tend to all chores for you. It is not meant for a Chippewa squaw to sit idly by, spending days in waiting for her man. She must live with her man, take care of her man."

"This would also make me happy," Everett said, then looked into the fire, haunted by memories.

Jewel seemed there in the flames of the fire, looking

back at him with accusing, blue eyes. But if it hadn't been for her coldness, he would have never had to fulfill his needs with another woman.

When Jewel had requested her separate bed and separate room, that had been the last straw with Everett. And when he had found Joy wandering in the forest one day, having been banished from a Chippewa tribe for reasons he had never understood, it had been too easy to take her as his own. Since that day, he had grown closer and closer to her. The fact that she was Indian did not matter. Before, he had hated all Indians, all savages. But it was easy to separate his feelings for Indians from his feelings for her.

But she was the only one. He could never let Mariana marry the likes of Lone Hawk! His daughter deserved better!

Yet he knew she was not his daughter. He was reminded more of this as each day passed. Even Mariana's temperament seemed to be that of a damn Sioux! He never knew what to expect of her next!

"If it would make you happy to be with me, then Joy does not understand why it cannot be so," she further pouted. She moved to sit directly in front of Everett, on her knees. She placed the palms of her hands at each of his cheeks. "Has not Joy been a good pupil? Does not Joy speak the English language well? Does not Joy prepare meals of the white man for you? Joy has tried hard to please you in every way."

Going to him, settling down onto his lap, Joy embraced him. *"Gee-zah-gi-ee-nah?"* she whispered, then lifted her lips to his. "Kiss me, Everett. *O geem neen."*

His loins on fire with need of her, Everett framed her

face between his hands and lowered his lips to hers and kissed her hard . . . kissed her long. And as she eased her body around so that he could reach her breasts, his large hands cupped them through the buckskin dress.

"Ay-uh neen love *geen,"* Everett said, drawing his lips a fraction away from hers. "Let us make love, Joy. My time will be short this time. Mariana must never know where I go. She is questioning me. She is suspicious."

"Then it is time to tell her," Joy said.

"Perhaps," Everett said, then grew silent as Joy rose to her feet and showed him just why he should put Joy first, Mariana second. Joy stood enticingly before him, drawing her buckskin dress slowly over her head, her eyes passion-dark as she looked down at him.

And as she tossed the dress aside and reached her arms out to him, Everett stood and held his hands out away from himself and let her tiny hands begin to undress him. His heart thudded against his chest, his manhood straining at the buckskin of his breeches, with need to be released. . . .

Mariana stood as though in a trance, having heard all that had been said between them. Even when the Indian squaw so seductively undressed before her father she couldn't move her eyes. But when her father rose to his feet and was letting the squaw begin undressing him, she turned her eyes quickly away, breathing hard.

Then, stumbling away, in a near state of shock, she mounted her horse and rode away, tears scalding her eyes, blinding her. . . .

Everett's practiced ears picked up the sound of a horse's hooves close by, outside the cabin. His trance was momentarily broken. Nude, he went to the door and threw it aside. Squinting his eyes, he looked all about him, then shrugged and closed the door and went back to his woman.

"It must have been my imagination," he said huskily, drawing Joy fully against him, reveling in the touch of her smooth skin against his. He bent and kissed the lobes of her breasts, then lowered her to the floor. He could not believe his good fortune when as he again let his gaze sweep over the loveliness of this copper-skinned wench beneath him. The mere sight of her made him almost reach the ultimate of pleasure. But he knew that it was his age that caused him almost to act prematurely. And knowing this, and realizing that speed was required, he nudged her knees apart and quickly entered her.

Joy emitted a soft sigh. She closed her eyes and tossed her head, living for these moments when his largeness would magnificently fill her. It was her love for this sort of madness with a man that had caused her to be banished from her tribe of Chippewa. She had hungered for men who already had wives. There was a challenge in such men.

And though she had felt more for this white man, Everett Fowler, the fact that his wife was no longer alive as a challenge had made her desires for him lessen. She only pretended with him that he was of uppermost importance to her.

She would one day be gone when he arrived to have these moments with her. If he didn't take her to his village soon, she would leave. She had seen so many possibilities in being in a village of white men! So many would hunger after her!

Full of rage, hating her father, glad that he wasn't her
real father, Mariana rode wildly through the forest.
She would go to Lone Hawk! He seemed to be the only
man she could trust! She never wanted even to see
Everett Fowler again. He was not worth even thinking
about. He had cheated not only his friends back in
Virginia, but also his wife. And also, in a sense, his
daughter!

"How can I ever stand to be around him again?"
Mariana softly cried.

But how could she *not?* Lone Hawk hadn't accepted
her yet. And . . . would he ever . . . ?

Still recalling those moments observing her father
with the Indian squaw, Mariana winced, remembering
how he had even spoken in Indian to her! He had
taught the squaw much about the white way of life, and
she had reciprocated, it seemed.

Riding hard, the ribbon in her hair loosening and
flying away from her, the gray clouds having returned
overhead to make her feel even more gloomy, she
didn't notice the activity in the bushes at her right side.
And when she did, she knew that she had been careless.
She was seeing several Indians on horseback, watching
her. And upon closer observation she recognized none
of them to be Lone Hawk.

She was forced to draw her reins tautly, to stop her
horse when the Indians moved out into the open, in her
way, blocking her further approach.

Her heart skipping beats, Mariana looked from one

to the other. Their faces were painted with different sorts of colored stripes. Some carried rifles, others bows and arrows. They were dressed in the briefest of loincloths, with moccasins on their feet, and great feathers at their locks of hair behind their headbands.

"White woman, you follow . . ." one of the Indians said in distinct English.

"Where . . . are . . . you taking me . . . ?" Mariana said in a near whisper, inching her hand toward the sheathed knife at her leg.

The Indian moved his pony closer and grabbed her wrist, stopping her from getting her knife. "You follow . . ." he growled.

Mariana flinched as his breath reached her. It was touched with the stench of whiskey!

"Sitting Tall . . . ?" she whispered beneath her breath. . . .

Chapter Twenty-Five

> *I want you with your arms and
> lips to love me throughout the
> wonder watches of the night.*
> —GILLOM

Rain was falling in a slow mist. The wind was cold
and damp, probing Mariana's skin like icy fingers as
she continued traveling with the Indians. Sitting stiff
and silent on her horse, Mariana was chilled not only
from the weather, but also from terror. The distance to
the Indian village seemed endless. And though her eyes
had become accustomed to the blackness of night, she
couldn't make out the full figure of the Indian riding
along beside her.

Taking occasional glances, Mariana tried again and
again to see the Indian who appeared to be the leader of
this band. No names had been mentioned among the
group. And when they talked, they used their Indian
language . . . not English.

Mariana's initial suspicion crept into her mind
again, recalling how this Indian beside her smelled so

distinctly of whiskey. Of course this would bring Sitting Tall to mind! And even with the strange designs of paints on this Indian's face, Mariana had seen that the Indian had the marks of handsomeness that he would have had to have had for Neala to have chosen him.

Tensing, Mariana thought to test the Indian by speaking the name Sitting Tall. But she feared this. If it was Sitting Tall, surely he would already know that she was Lone Hawk's woman. Knowing how Lone Hawk and Sitting Tall were such great friends, surely Lone Hawk would have pointed her out to him! So why would Sitting Tall choose to take her as captive?

Shaking her head, Mariana surmised from this that it was not Sitting Tall who had taken her hostage. He had already done enough to endanger his friendship with Lone Hawk. He would not have done anything else as foolish as this! What would even be his reason?

Yet Mariana was also recalling how Lone Hawk had spoken of how the Sioux stole the Chippewa women! Did Sitting Tall or any of the other Sioux braves consider her part Chippewa because she was looked at as Lone Hawk's?

Squinting her eyes, trying to look again about her at each of the Indians, she began to wonder if these really were Sioux Indians? Though she was sorely fearing them, she couldn't help but wonder if any of them knew of Chief Black Cloud.

Then, realizing the foolishness of her thoughts, and that she had better concentrate on how she might release herself from this captivity instead of wondering about a man who had raped her mother, Mariana began to consider ways of escape.

Should this Indian whose breath reeked of whiskey begin to waver on his pony, then she might let her horse fall back, away from him, then find a place to hide until morning.

Or . . . once she was at the Indian village she might find a squaw as friendly to her as Neala had been and convince her that it was not right to hold a white woman hostage, whatever the reason.

Mariana's insides grew cold thinking that she might be treated as her mother had been treated. Mariana knew the chances of being repeatedly raped. She must escape. Somehow . . .

The rain having now stopped, Mariana ran her fingers through the tangles of her wet hair, then smoothed her hand down the front of her dress, straightening its wet folds so that they did not so identify her shape beneath them. But even in the darkness of the night she could make out the distinct shape of her breasts and how the dress clung to them. She could even feel the eyes of the Indian beside her looking at her breasts, as though he had already touched them.

Shuddering, Mariana pushed relentlessly onward, her need to escape strengthening, her determination to escape unwavering. She would watch for every opportunity. Her carelessness would not be repeated.

Then she hung her head, tears near, remembering how she had found her father with the Indian squaw. It still didn't seem real.

Yet what was real in her life?

Sighing, her bones aching, Mariana was becoming weary from traveling through this pathless maze of marshy bottoms, thickets of briar and thorns, and

321

great mats of vines. This region she had been led to was desolate, as though no humans had been there before.

She now even doubted if she could find her way back to the trading post. She was not sure in which direction she had been brought. It seemed that the Indians moved in a maze of circles meant purposely to confuse her.

And then the first signs of fires could be seen ahead, through the denseness of the trees. The Indian at Mariana's side began to shout out orders to the other Indians, speaking in a tongue unfamiliar to Mariana. She had begun to understand some Chippewa words. None of these words being spoken were Chippewa. As each moment passed, Mariana was more sure of having been captured by Sioux!

And when the outdoor fires spread their golden glow, touching these Indians' dwellings, lighting them, Mariana's heart fluttered strangely. She was torn between being afraid and being hopeful. She now saw the first distinct difference between the two tribes. Their dwellings.

Those that she was being directed toward were not wigwams. They were cone-shaped tepees, their outsides colorfully decorated with geometric designs. She was in the company of Sioux Indians. She was part Sioux! Could she be near the village of her father? If she told the Indians that she was part Sioux, could that spare her the indignity of a rape?

But who would believe her? In no way did she look Sioux. . . .

Breathless from anxiety of what the next few moments and hours would bring in life for her, Mariana forced her shoulders back and sat straight on her horse, to show that she was not in any way afraid. Lone Hawk had said that she had the courage of many men. She would prove his statement true!

Being led on into the village, Mariana looked cautiously from side to side. The rain seemed to have sent most of the Indians into the cover of their tepees. The outdoor fires burned low, sizzling in their dampened coals and ashes. In the distance a drum's low beat was a drone through the darkness. The sounds of laughter, mingled with babies crying came from the dwellings.

"Still follow me . . ." the Indian at Mariana's side said in a low grunt, the paint on his face bright and flashy beneath the light of the fires.

But it was the fathomless darkness of his eyes that stirred something familiar inside Mariana. How often Lone Hawk had studied her with the same sort of expression! It was as though this Indian was trying to see clean into the depths of her soul!

Swallowing hard, Mariana turned her eyes away from him and continued on her way to the large dwelling she was being directed toward. It wasn't a tepee. It was a large, bark-covered lodge, with smoke spiraling from four different smoke holes in the roof. It stood at the edge of the forest on level ground, high above a lake, which ran along behind it. It was a long, narrow structure, its ends beautifully rounded, the roof gracefully arched. The snow-white birchbark sides were decorated with striking totemic designs in brilliant colors.

"You now see chieftain father," Sitting Tall said, careful to not speak his own name while in the presence of Lone Hawk's woman. He had to make sure that she

323

did not know to point at him with an accusing finger when Lone Hawk came to sit in council, to speak for her. Sitting Tall would stay behind, with Neala! Lone Hawk would speak in council with the chief of the village, Sitting Tall's father, the one who had given permission for the abduction.

Smiling smugly, Sitting Tall glanced over at Mariana. Lone Hawk didn't know that Sitting Tall knew of her, yet he had watched from afar when they had been together. She was the only way to get Lone Hawk to forgive Sitting Tall! Once Sitting Tall went to Lone Hawk and told of her abduction, making it look as though someone else had done it, wouldn't Lone Hawk be happy? Wouldn't Lone Hawk think that Sitting Tall had again earned the right to his friendship?

It was a scheme that Sitting Tall had thought up all by himself. It was a scheme that had to work!

Dismounting, Sitting Tall went to Mariana and helped her from her horse, his gaze raking over her, admiring his blood brother's choice in women. She was beautiful. Her hair flamed as did the brightest rays of the sun. Her given name, Blazing Heart, fit her well!

Mariana squirmed and jerked away from Sitting Tall. "Let me go," she hissed. "I can manage well enough on my own. I do not need assistance from the likes of you."

Sitting Tall chuckled low, liking not only the fire of her hair, but also of her spirit. He was glad now, for more than one reason, that he had chosen to play this game of "abduction." He would enjoy watching this white woman who had the courage of many men! If not for his love for Neala, Sitting Tall might even challenge his blood brother for this woman with spirit!

"Father waits!" Sitting Tall said, trying to force anger into his words, when in truth he was amused by the white woman's personality. "You come. Now!"

Sitting Tall had instructed his father that he would be bringing home a beautiful white woman, knowing all along that his father would not want to keep her. His health would not allow it. He rarely even had the company of his wives at his side through the night. His father's thoughts now dwelled more on the hereafter than on the present.

But the presence of Blazing Heart could brighten his eyes for a while, at least.

"Why have you brought me here?" Mariana said, now walking alongside Sitting Tall, knowing that she had no other choice. "Don't you have better things to do than go around stealing women? It is not an honorable thing to do."

"Honor is not at question here," Sitting Tall growled, yet knowing that in a sense, it was. Between him and Lone Hawk, honor was in question! Lone Hawk had even said that they were no longer friends! They were enemies, as were most Sioux and Chippewa. Sitting Tall had spent many a night trying to figure out a way to make things right again between them. Hopefully, this was the way. . . .

Sitting Tall placed his hand at Mariana's elbow, guiding her through a wide deerskin flap that hung over the entranceway. Stepping into a lodge well-lighted by the four fires, Mariana glanced over at the Indian at her side and her eyes widened. She was seeing the trace of a scar on the Indian's right arm . . . just the size that would have been created in making a pact in blood with another Indian.

Glancing quickly up at the Indian's face, Mariana tried to see his full features through the paint, then shook her head and focused her eyes and thoughts elsewhere. . . .

On a raised platform spread with bearskins and cushions, with strewn balsam boughs at the base of the platform, was another Indian, thin and aged, yet sitting straight, his shoulders squared. He wore only a breechcloth, the skin spread across his bones resembling stretched leather. His black hair was worn loose and long, down across his shoulders. He sat cross-legged with his arms folded across his sunken chest.

His eyes were dark, looking back at Mariana with a strange sort of wonder, as though he might have seen her before.

He did not rise, but instead bowed graciously, bending from the waist, and raised his hand in greeting.

"My father, the white woman, as promised," Sitting Tall said, pushing Mariana toward the elderly Indian.

She turned with a start when the younger Indian stepped back away from her and then left the dwelling, leaving her alone with the older Indian.

Pale and trembling, Mariana slowly turned her eyes back to the man whom she knew to be chief. She took a bold step forward, though her knees were weak . . . her heart was skipping beats.

"Your son had no business bringing me here," she boldly stated in a rush of words, not believing, even herself, that she could be so brave. But she felt that was her only chance. She had heard that all Indians respected bravery . . . even in a woman!

"It is not for white woman to say what Chief Black Cloud's son does or does not do," Chief Black Cloud said flatly. He unfolded his arms and gestured with a hand. "Come closer. Even though my eyes are weak, they see something familiar about you."

Mariana was stunned by the sudden discovery that she was in the presence of her real father. Her cheeks blossomed with color, her mouth went dry. And if this was Chief Black Cloud and the younger Indian was Sitting Tall, that meant that Sitting Tall was . . . her . . . half-brother!

Her head began to spin. She touched her brow with a hand, she teetered as her knees threatened to buckle beneath her. And this chief had seen something familiar about her.

Oh, Lord, she did resemble her mother in so many ways! Did this chief have the memory to recall the white woman he had taken sexually all those many years ago? Had he felt something besides lust for her when he had raped her? Maybe he hadn't had it in his mind to actually rape her at all, but instead had been thinking that he was making sensual love to her mother.

All these years, had he remembered the white woman who had escaped from him? Perhaps he was even thinking that Mariana was she, having never aged!

"Come closer!" Chief Black Cloud grumbled, again gesturing with a hand.

Mariana edged closer to the platform, the fire's glow playing on the Indian's face in wavering shadows. She looked back at him, now as intensely as he was studying her. Strange that at age seventeen she was meeting her father for the first time. Stranger still, that this father was a full-blooded Indian! Should he know that she was his daughter, what would her fate now be?

What would her fate be, anyway? Why had she been brought here? Perhaps this was a game enjoyed by all Sioux. . . .

"Speak your name to me," Chief Black Cloud grumbled, placing his hands on his knees, seemingly in an effort to hold his lean frame in place.

"Mariana Fowler," Mariana said, boldly lifting her chin. "My . . ."

She stopped short of her intended words, having planned to say that her father was Everett Fowler! In truth, her father sat before her, a powerful Sioux chief.

"And you live where?"

"At the Grand Portage Trading Post."

"Your parents?"

Mariana paled. Should she speak her mother's name, would he recognize it?

"Everett and . . . and . . . Jewel Fowler," she said with a stammer.

Chief Black Cloud slowly lifted his hand and kneaded his chin. He again closely scrutinized her. "Your age?" he grumbled.

Mariana had read in her studies of the Sioux Indians, before moving to this area, that the Sioux say a person is so many snows old.

"I am seventeen snows old," she said, her eyes wavering when she saw his back straighten and his lips become set in a thin line.

"You are familiar to me in appearance," Chief Black Cloud said. "Eighteen snows ago Chief Black Cloud knew of another white woman with hair of flame and eyes the color of the rivers."

328

He nodded. "She called herself by the name Jewel," he said hoarsely. "Woman with the name Mariana, your mother named Jewel. You then could be my daughter."

Mariana felt a weakness seize her. She should have known that a powerful chief would also have to be especially intelligent. But she would never have expected him to realize her true identity so quickly.

Not wanting to admit the truth to him, she took a bold step closer, now having only the small spaces of the firespace between her and the chief.

"My father's name is Everett," she said icily. "Everett Fowler. It is only by chance that my mother's name is the same as another woman of your past."

Chief Black Cloud's eyes narrowed; he again nodded. "My daughter would be as fiery in spirit," he said, chuckling low. Then his gaze flickered over her again. "But my daughter would also have the appearance of Sioux."

Then he again kneaded his chin. "But no two women could look so alike and not be daughter and mother," he said hoarsely. "Yes, you are the daughter of the Jewel of my past. But, yes, you are also the daughter of the white man. It was only my hope that you might be mine. Chief Black Cloud has not been blessed with daughters."

His gaze lowered. "And Chief Black Cloud would have liked to have found in you what he has missed in having lost Jewel," he grumbled. "She was lovely . . . in every way."

Mariana was growing numb inside. She was seeing in Chief Black Cloud what her mother surely hadn't. This man had loved her mother! But her mother had so feared all Indians that she hadn't understood that when he had taken her sexually . . . even repeatedly, as she had written in the diary . . . he had done so with love.

So relieved was she to know that the man who had fathered her was not all bad, Mariana lowered her eyes and exhaled a sigh of relief, feeling the sting of tears of gratitude at the corners of her eyes.

"My son. He did not know how he would stir his aging father's heart by bringing you to him as a prize," Chief Black Cloud said, rising shakily to his feet. He stepped from the platform and went to Mariana. Placing a hand to her shoulder, he spoke with deep respect. "You will be given warm quarters and food."

Mariana raised her eyes slowly upward, choked with emotion, wanting to burst out to this Indian with the news of who she was. She was now proud to have him as a father. He was kind. He was generous. Yet it was not in her to tell him this secret. Perhaps later. . . .

"And then will I be able to return home?" she murmured, looking up, feeling something tugging at her heart when she looked into the depths of his dark eyes.

"You will stay for a while," Chief Black Cloud said solemnly. "Then you will be returned home."

Paling, Mariana eased from his grip. "But why can't I leave now?" she gasped. Did he plan to take her sexually? Perhaps she had been wrong to judge him kindly, so quickly.

"It is this old chief who would like to have you as company, to talk . . . to share things of your world," Chief Black Cloud said softly. "Perhaps when you talk, Chief Black Cloud can remember this other woman of his past. For a while, you will be her."

Mariana's heart skipped a beat. "This woman you speak of," she dared to say. "You loved her? Truly loved her?"

"It was not right in the eyes of the Sioux to love a white woman," he said, his eyes taking on a faraway cast. "So Chief Black Cloud loved in silence."

"But . . . you . . . did . . . ?" Mariana scarcely whispered.

He looked down into Mariana's eyes. "Why is this important to you?" he asked, raising an eyebrow inquisitively.

Feeling as though he was getting too close to the truth with such a question, and feeling the dangers of prodding him for answers, Mariana lowered her eyes. "It's not important," she murmured.

She flinched when he placed an arm about her shoulder and began guiding her toward the closed entrance flap. "Your stay will be one of comfort," he reassured. "And Chief Black Cloud will see to it that his son does not try to claim you as his. You will be mine." He chuckled as he glanced down at her. "But do not worry, Mariana. This body is too old to claim you in ways of a young man. As Chief Black Cloud said, talk is what is asked for from you. Companionship and talk."

Mariana's heart reached out to know him also, but for her own private reasons. Should she tell him the truth, what, then, would be his feelings toward her? Already they seemed . . . special.

Chapter Twenty-Six

> *The winds are left behind in the*
> *speed of my desire.*
>
> —TAYLOR

Lonely and at odds with himself, Lone Hawk rode toward the cave of his and Sitting Tall's youth. So much had been shared there. It was hard to believe that he and Sitting Tall were no longer friends. They had promised friendship forever! Yet Sitting Tall had cast this friendship aside like cottonwood fluff drifting in the wind! When he had turned his back on Neala, he had also turned his back on Lone Hawk!

"But I do miss him," Lone Hawk whispered, his heart empty at the thought of never riding alongside Sitting Tall again, nor ever again challenging Sitting Tall in canoe races. They would never again measure whose arrow was the swiftest!

Sitting Tall's challenge in life now centered about the white man's firewater. And if Sitting Tall lost this challenge, he would lose everything.

"He has already lost much," Lone Hawk said,

nudging his pony's flanks with his heels.

Yet Lone Hawk knew that Neala had forgiven Sitting Tall and was planning to meet him as soon as she had the courage to leave the Chippewa village. Thus far, her fear of the white man kept her hidden away inside her wigwam. Even though Jed Fenris was now dead, Neala feared all trappers.

Raising his fist to the sky, Lone Hawk cursed the day the white man had placed his first foot to the Chippewa soil!

Yet, he quickly lowered his hand, knowing that had the white man not come, neither would his Blazing Heart be there.

Troubled again about his decision about his woman and what she would be to him and his people, Lone Hawk's jaw hardened. He would have to decide soon or possibly totally lose her.

Riding up the incline that reached up to the cave, Lone Hawk's eyes wavered and his insides strangely rolled when he saw a pony reined close by the cave entrance. Lone Hawk was torn with hate and love, recognizing the pony to be Sitting Tall's. A part of him wanted to reach out and love Sitting Tall and a part of him would always hate him!

Yet Lone Hawk knew that Sitting Tall must be pitied. He did not have control of his actions. Not while the firewater burned away at his insides and brain. Sitting Tall was alienated from his own self.

Dismounting from his pony and reining it beside Sitting Tall's, an act so familiar to Lone Hawk, again he was saddened.

Then he was filled with disbelief. Sitting Tall knew Lone Hawk's feeling about his neglect of Neala. And

Sitting Tall would not be expecting Neala to come to the cave. So Sitting Tall was there, expecting Lone Hawk to arrive!

Why? Sitting Tall could even be expected to be killed for what he had done to Neala! He surely was aware of now being only another worthless Sioux in Lone Hawk's eyes! But he knew Lone Hawk well enough to know that even the most worthless Sioux was not in danger while with Lone Hawk. Lone Hawk labored for peace between the two factions of Indians. Not war.

Shaking his head, his shoulders no longer as squared, Lone Hawk moved on toward the cave, stepping over ground tangle, then past flowering rose bushes. He stopped suddenly, his muscles cording as Sitting Tall moved from the cave entrance.

Eyes locked with Sitting Tall's, Lone Hawk placed his hand on the sheathed knife at his right side. His heart thundered wildly, his feelings battling inside him. This was the first time ever that he was facing his blood brother with anything but total love . . . dedication . . . friendship. It was hard . . . this being with Sitting Tall under different circumstances.

"Nee-may-nan-dum-wah-bum-eh-nawn," Sitting Tall said, his arms folded across his chest, his shoulders squared. "Sitting Tall glad to see you. Lone Hawk, my heart is lonely for your friendship." He unfolded his arms and placed a hand solidly over the scar where they had exchanged their bloods. "My scar aches where my blood spilled into yours."

He then placed a fist to his heart. "Lone Hawk, my heart is filled with so much sadness. Tell me we are still blood brothers. Though what I did was wrong, you

334

know that I am sorry. The firewater causes me to do many things."

Lone Hawk's chin lifted, his dark hair spread across his shoulders. "You cannot use that excuse forever, Sitting Tall, for all the wrongs that you do," he grumbled. "You know what you must do. You must never touch firewater again! Only then can we talk of becoming blood brothers again. Lone Hawk will even tell Neala she must never see you again. She is not safe with you. When she was last with you, you allowed her to be ravished by a white man! How could you, Sitting Tall? How could you?"

Sitting Tall's eyes lowered. It was hard for him to recall that day . . . and how anything happened to Neala. He had almost blocked it from his consciousness! All he could recall was his thirst for the firewater. Even now he had the same thirst! Even now he could taste it on his lips . . . could smell it on his breath! Was it going to drive him mad?

Then, recalling why he was there, Sitting Tall raised his eyes upward and took a step toward Lone Hawk. "Lone Hawk, Sitting Tall has come to the cave today hoping you would be here," he said thickly. "Sitting Tall has come to tell you something. After Sitting Tall tells you this, you will become my friend again. You will be so grateful to Sitting Tall, you will even again call Sitting Tall blood brother!"

"Only proving that you no longer drink firewater can make it possible for our friendship to be true again," Lone Hawk stated flatly. "Even then it will be a strained sort of friendship. Sitting Tall, it is not even *right* that I forgive you so easily!"

335

"But you will," Sitting Tall said hoarsely. "After Sitting Tall helps you release your woman from captivity!"

Lone Hawk's eyes widened . . . his gut twisted. He took a step forward, his back stiffened. "What do you say, Sitting Tall?" he grumbled. "What is this about my woman? Sitting Tall, Lone Hawk has never even told you about any special woman!"

"Sitting Tall has watched from afar, many times, while you were with woman with hair of fire," Sitting Tall said, anxiously nodding. "I do know of her. And I also know that she has been taken hostage in my very own village, by one of my very own warriors."

"Ah-neen?" Lone Hawk gasped, his insides growing coldly numb. "What is this you are saying? My Blazing Heart is truly captive? She is in your village of Sioux?"

"Ay-uh, yes. She is," Sitting Tall said, nodding. He watched with an anxious heart for Lone Hawk's further response.

"You . . . permitted this?" Lone Hawk growled, doubling his hands into tight fists.

Sitting Tall's eyes wavered. He alone was responsible for Mariana's capture. In working side by side with Lone Hawk to free her, he hoped, his old camaraderie with Lone Hawk would be revived!

But his fear was of the white woman's pointing an accusing finger at Sitting Tall. Though his face had been hidden behind paint, he was now remembering how foolish he had been to admit that Chief Black Cloud was his father. If this white woman remembered this slip of the tongue, then she would know his true identity. He could only hope that the white woman had been too involved in her own fright to even have heard

336

Sitting Tall calling the chief his father. Sitting Tall knew that all he planned would now work out only by chance. If he lost . . . he had lost no more than he had already lost. If he won, he would again have a blood brother with whom to share life!

Sitting Tall's eyes slowly lifted as he tried not to let his guilt show in their depths. "This abduction was done behind Sitting Tall's back," he lied, swallowing hard. "Before I knew what had happened, your woman was standing before my father, being judged." He shifted his feet nervously. "My father was kind to her. He had her taken to a wigwam. She has been fed. She has spent time with my father, talking. They seemed to form a strange sort of friendship, quite quickly."

Lone Hawk blanched, his heart skipping a beat. He was only now remembering Blazing Heart's connection to Chief Black Cloud! It seemed that her search for her father had ended. Ironically, she had been taken right to him.

"You say your father and my woman have become friends?" he said dryly.

"Ay-uh," Sitting Tall said, his eyebrow quirking. "Seems your woman is not at all uncomfortable in her capacity as hostage. She is a woman of courage, Lone Hawk."

Lone Hawk kneaded his chin, then went to Sitting Tall and clasped onto his shoulder. "Sitting Tall, no matter if she and your father have a friendly relationship between them, she must be allowed to go from your village, and now," he said flatly. "You said you have come to help in her escape. Is that wise? What will your father say or do when he finds out you are responsible for her being set free?"

"Father will never know," Sitting Tall gulped.

"You will shame him, Sitting Tall, by doing this behind his back. If he finds out, you will be less in his heart."

"My father will never know," Sitting Tall again confirmed, no longer thinking the release should be achieved by way of council. It was too risky! The white woman must not be given a chance to wonder about Sitting Tall . . . and who he was.

"And you? Will your guilt lie heavy on your heart?" Lone Hawk prodded.

Sitting Tall placed his hands onto Lone Hawk's shoulders. "My friendship with you is almost as important as feelings between father and son," he said thickly. "Sitting Tall will chance anything, to be friends with you again, Lone Hawk."

"Then tell me your plan, Sitting Tall," Lone Hawk said, easing away from him. He bent to his knee and plucked a weed and placed it between his lips, looking into the distance, puzzled about Sitting Tall and what motivated him. If Sitting Tall could betray his Neala and his chieftain father, wouldn't he one day also betray his best friend?

It was a risky thing, this accepting Sitting Tall as a true friend again!

His heart racing, feeling acceptance by Lone Hawk so near, Sitting Tall lowered himself to balance on his haunches beside Lone Hawk. His eyes gleamed with eagerness. "When it is dark we will steal into my village," he said softly. "You will take Blazing Heart from the wigwam where she is being held. You will then take her away while I stay behind. I will be there for my father when he discovers her gone. It could upset him

338

to find that she has escaped."

"And you are sure you want to do this thing, knowing the weakened health of your father?" Lone Hawk asked, giving Sitting Tall a troubled glance.

"Ay-uh," Sitting Tall said, nodding. "My brother, let me do this for you. Let us again become as brothers."

Lone Hawk looked quickly away from him, the word "brother" bringing to mind the relationship between Blazing Heart and Sitting Tall. They were brother and sister! Perhaps this was the time for Sitting Tall to be told. Most surely Blazing Heart had already told Chief Black Cloud. If they had become as friendly as Sitting Tall said, secrets would have been shared!

Turning his eyes quickly back to Sitting Tall, Lone Hawk quietly studied him, then spoke. "This woman of mine," he said hoarsely. "She is many things, to many people, Sitting Tall."

Sitting Tall looked confused. "What do you mean?" he said, clasping his hands together before him.

"You say she and your father have become friends?" Lone Hawk mumbled. "You think this is strange?"

"Ay-uh."

"It is not so strange, Sitting Tall," Lone Hawk said, frowning. He flicked the weed from his lips, then rose to his feet, watching Sitting Tall as he rose to his feet and came to eye level with him. "You see, Sitting Tall, my woman is also your sister."

Sitting Tall took a staggering step backwards. His cheek twitched. "What is this you say?" he gasped. "How can you call this white woman my sister?"

"Because her true father is Chief Black Cloud," Lone Hawk said, nodding. "She only recently found out, in a book of talking pages. Her mother left a record of her

339

life in these talking pages. Her mother spoke of a time when she had been abducted and taken by an Indian. This Indian was your father, Sitting Tall. It was Chief Black Cloud."

Sitting Tall felt frozen into place, his thoughts taking him back to when he was four snows old. He was recalling a white woman being brought to his village. He was recalling her spending all of her time there with his father. He had heard many soft cries in the night. It was this white woman! Sitting Tall hadn't known if the cries were because she was happy . . . or because she was sad! He had just been bewildered at his father's wanting the woman with the . . .

"Red hair . . ." he said shallowly. "This woman also had the hair the color of the rising sun!"

"You remember the white woman of those many years ago?" Lone Hawk gasped.

Sitting Tall's face became encased in a frown. "My mother was banished from my father's dwelling while this white woman was in our village of Sioux," he growled. "My mother was shamed! It was easy to help this white woman escape!"

"You . . . ?" Lone Hawk said in a near whisper.

"Though only four snows old, Sitting Tall was cunning as a wolf!" Sitting Tall bragged. "I did it for my mother. She was made happy when white woman was taken away!"

Lone Hawk chuckled into his hand. "You do many things that surprise me," he said. Again he clasped his hands to Sitting Tall's shoulders. "Sitting Tall, if you would forget your love for firewater, you could be so beneficial to everyone. You are cunning. We could do many things together again. And when your father and

340

my father are traveling the long road to the hereafter, just imagine what our lives could be like. We could join our two peoples, Sitting Tall!"

Sitting Tall's eyes wavered. Lone Hawk was ready to accept him as a friend, yet would he, if Blazing Heart spoiled it all by telling Lone Hawk that it was Sitting Tall who had abducted her for his own purposes? But now that she knew that Sitting Tall was her brother, surely she wouldn't be so quick to accuse!

A small smile lifted his lips. "You say Blazing Heart is my sister?" he said.

"Ay-uh," Lone Hawk nodded. "She is."

"Though her skin is white, that make me happy," Sitting Tall said softly. "No sisters have been born into my family. I will love her as a sister."

He lowered his eyes, then raised them quickly upward again. "That is, if you so allow, Lone Hawk," he said. "Once you are man and wife, will you allow her to come to the village of the Sioux, to be a part of the Sioux people?"

Sitting Tall's words stung Lone Hawk. He moved away from Sitting Tall toward his reined pony. He heard Sitting Tall scrambling along behind him.

"Lone Hawk, you did not answer me," Sitting Tall prodded, grabbing Lone Hawk by his arm, encouraging him around to face him again.

Lone Hawk stared in silence into Sitting Tall's eyes, reminded of his duty to come to a decision about Blazing Heart. Now it seemed that everything was even more complicated. Now that she knew her true Sioux family and that they were so close to the Chippewa village, it would be even harder accepting her into his village of Chippewa in the capacity of wife. Yet he

341

knew that he wasn't being fair to her. What would the answer be? He was torn, oh, so torn.

"We shall see, Sitting Tall," he grumbled. "We shall see. Let us now go to my woman and set her free." He smiled. "Again you can prove your cunning ways. Again you will set free white woman!"

Sitting Tall's insides quivered. . . .

Chapter Twenty-Seven

*All paths lead to you where e'er
I roam.*

—WAGSTAFF

Feeling peacefully content, Mariana lay beside the fire in her assigned tepee, drifting somewhere between being asleep and awake. The furs snuggled beneath her chin were warm, the doeskin dress that had been given to her by her true father was soft against her skin.

Turning, sighing as she fluttered her eyes open to again look about her, Mariana felt as though she had accomplished what she had set out to do. It was ironic that Sitting Tall had done her this favor, when all along he had abducted her for whatever his own selfish motives were.

Now fully awake, Mariana leaned up on her elbow and gazed into the soft flames of the fire. "Why did he do it?" she whispered. "He hasn't laid claim to me since my arrival. In fact, he left soon after. . . ."

When Chief Black Cloud had spoken of his son, mentioning Sitting Tall by name, Mariana had at once become engulfed in confusion. Sitting Tall . . . Lone Hawk's longtime friend. Sitting Tall . . . having just lost Lone Hawk as a friend.

Was abducting Mariana a way of retaliating against Lone Hawk?

Yet if that were the reason, why *wouldn't* Sitting Tall have claimed her as his? Why would he have handed her over to his father, to use as he pleased?

"He probably didn't really care what happened to me, just as long as he could brag of having abducted me, to torment Lone Hawk with the knowledge," she whispered to herself.

But it no longer mattered to Mariana why Sitting Tall did anything. He, in his mischief, had granted her her wish to meet with her true father. And the meeting had been grand! Though Chief Black Cloud still didn't know that she was his daughter, he had treated her as grandly as though he had known. The time she spent in his large dwelling . . . exchanging talk of customs of his people and hers . . . forming a bond that would be suspicious to Lone Hawk should he find out . . . were moments she would always cherish.

"But tomorrow it will all end," she said, rising to sit with her legs crossed beneath her. "Tomorrow I will go home."

The word "home" was a word that caused her dread. How would she face her father . . . the man who had called himself her father all these years, when she now knew about the Indian squaw with whom he shared more than mere talk! He had blatantly dishonored his wife by going to this Indian squaw! He was the savage that he had always claimed all Indians to be. He was someone she no longer knew.

344

Again sighing, Mariana again crept beneath the warm furs and stretched out with her feet facing the fire. She must get her rest, for the journey back to Grand Portage would be long. . . .

Moving stealthily through the forest, Sitting Tall was familiar with every tree and every rock, since this was the land of his tribe of Sioux. The darkness of night did not impede Lone Hawk and Sitting Tall's plans to take Mariana from Sitting Tall's village.

Lone Hawk rested his hand on the sheathed knife at his waist, his pony neighing in the distance where he had left it and another pony reined, for his and Mariana's quick escape.

Casting Sitting Tall a troubled glance, Lone Hawk still did not know whether or not to trust Sitting Tall's judgment as to how this abduction was to be performed. He had smelled the familiar scent of whiskey on Sitting Tall's breath as they had made their plans. It seemed this scent had become one of Sitting Tall's identifying marks. Lone Hawk knew he still must keep his sister from marrying Sitting Tall! Unless something happened to shake Sitting Tall from this misery that had enveloped him like a moth caught in the snares of a spider web, Lone Hawk could not offer him a dedicated friendship.

This that Sitting Tall was now doing . . . helping Lone Hawk to free Blazing Heart . . . was not enough. Even Sitting Tall's offer to do this troubled Lone Hawk. Something seemed amiss about this abduction of his woman . . . even more so this schemed rescue of Sitting Tall's. Why had Blazing Heart been abducted?

How could a son go against his chieftain father as Sitting Tall was doing? If Sitting Tall's father found out . . .

Sitting Tall placed his hand out, stopping Lone Hawk. "We are near," he whispered. He nodded toward a break in the trees ahead. "Do you not see the outdoor fires of my village?" He gestured. "We will find your woman's tepee at the edge of the village. It will be easy to sneak in, then out. Sitting Tall will keep watch for you, Lone Hawk."

"Is someone in the tepee with Blazing Heart, guarding her?" Lone Hawk grumbled, his knuckles white, his grasp on the sheathed knife was so tight.

"*Gah-ween,* no," Sitting Tall whispered. "My father did not see the need to watch her so closely. Like I said, Lone Hawk, they have reached some sort of friendship that not even a white man has been able to have with my father. Your woman has ways about her that border on the mystical."

Lone Hawk's insides quivered, knowing why the bond had become so easy between his woman and the powerful Sioux chief. They were father and daughter. It tore at Lone Hawk's heart, knowing that his woman had been introduced into the life of the Sioux. He had wanted to do anything possible to keep this from happening.

Before, when she had only spoken of wanting to go to the village of the Sioux—even then it had been a threat to him, to their future. Now it would be harder to introduce her into his village, as his wife. Had she not been brought to the Sioux village, he would have made her his wife tomorrow. His mind had been made up to marry her, to place the knowledge of her being part

346

Sioux into the deeper recesses of his mind. Now he did not know what to anticipate for their future. It depended on her attitude now toward the Sioux. . . .

"Let us move swiftly," Lone Hawk said. "It is best that Blazing Heart be removed from your village quickly, no matter that she has become friends with your father. She belongs in the village of the Chippewa. Not the Sioux!"

"You are right, Lone Hawk," Sitting Tall said, nodding. "Your woman belongs with you." His eyes wavered as he reached his hand to Lone Hawk and clasped it onto his shoulder. "You are happy with Sitting Tall for telling you of your woman's abduction? We are friends again, Lone Hawk?"

Lone Hawk reached out his hand and eased Sitting Tall's hand from his shoulder. "This that you have done for Lone Hawk is good," he said. "But, Sitting Tall, it is not so easy to forget the bad you recently have done. Do you so easily forget my sister . . . and how she was ravished? It is because of you, Sitting Tall. She may never be the same again. She may never want you to touch her again, as a man does a woman. The touch of the white man still burns a path of dread into her heart. When she is with you, do you think it will be different, since it was you who let the white man take her with him to his filthy dwelling? Think about that, Sitting Tall, then tell me whether or not you think I should be ready to fully commit myself to you as friend again."

Sitting Tall was taken aback by Lone Hawk's long speech, a speech that still separated them from a total alliance. It was hard for Sitting Tall to comprehend that what he had done . . . capturing Blazing Heart . . .

chancing his father's finding out that it had all been a plan to save face with Lone Hawk . . . had failed to accomplish what it should have for the risks he had taken.

"You do not mean what you say," Sitting Tall gasped. "Lone Hawk, how many times must Sitting Tall say he is sorry?"

"Lone Hawk does not ask for sorries," Lone Hawk said, glowering over at Sitting Tall, his full outline disclosed to him beneath the brilliant rays of the moon. "Lone Hawk asks for you to never drink firewater again. Then see what sort of man you become. Lone Hawk knows you will be a better man. You will even be welcome as blood brother again . . . as husband for my sister, should she still want you."

Sitting Tall's shoulders squared. "You will see this new man you ask for," he said hoarsely. "Sitting Tall will never touch firewater again!"

Lone Hawk shook his head and sighed to himself. How many times had he heard this sort of declaration from Sitting Tall? Too many times to count on his fingers. And each time Sitting Tall's words had only been wisps of wind, worthless. . . .

Squinting his eyes, Lone Hawk looked ahead, his heart racing at the thought of taking Blazing Heart from the village of the Sioux. His heart ached to see her again, in any capacity! Yet he feared hearing her words about her time with Chief Black Cloud. Chief Black Cloud had ways to charm women. He was noted for that, as well as his wisdom, cunning, and bravery.

"Let us now go," Lone Hawk said shortly, moving stealthily onward, keeping watch for any movement on all sides of him. Though Sitting Tall was knowl-

348

edgeable about this part of the forest, he would not know where each of his father's warriors would be placed to guard the village from intruders. It would be awkward not only for Lone Hawk should he be captured, but also his woman . . . also his father! His father did not yet know about Blazing Heart. . . .

"Sitting Tall will direct you to the tepee, then stand watch," Sitting Tall said softly. "It is my wish that you be happy, Lone Hawk. Take your woman and go. She will not be missed until morning."

Lone Hawk gave Sitting Tall a quick glance. "Lone Hawk thanks you," he said. Then he began running, bending low to shorten his shadow. And as they reached the edge of the village and saw that only a few warriors were positioned about the large outdoor fire, talking and laughing, Sitting Tall nodded toward the tepee that sat at the very edge of the forest. Lone Hawk's spine stiffened, seeing a warrior at the front of the tepee, resting on his haunches, his head bowed in sleep.

"You must move with silence, then speed," Sitting Tall said as he stopped beside Lone Hawk. He gave Lone Hawk a questioning stare, then rushed into his arms and affectionately hugged him. "My friend, how Sitting Tall has missed you. Do not stay away from our cave of friendship. Come. Smoke pipe with Sitting Tall."

Feeling clumsy with Sitting Tall so desperately embracing him, Lone Hawk's breath caught in his throat. His mind was returning to all the embraces of their youth. It was hard to think of a future without them. And now?

Slowly slipping his arms about Sitting Tall, he

349

returned the fond embrace. "Your heart blends into mine," he said hoarsely.

Then Lone Hawk eased away from him. "But now, Lone Hawk must go," he said, glancing toward the tepee, envisioning his woman there in her loveliness, which could not be compared with that of any other woman. He was glad that she had been treated with respect while she was with the Sioux. If she had been harmed in any way, Lone Hawk would not have been fondly embracing Sitting Tall. He would have thrust a knife clean through his heart!

Sitting Tall stepped back into the shadows, his eyes watching carefully all about him as Lone Hawk moved stealthily on toward the tepee.

Removing his sheathed knife, Lone Hawk crept to the rear of the tepee. With a firm hand he began running the blade of the knife down the buckskin material between where it had been drawn tautly between poles.

Breathless, he continued cutting until he had made an opening large enough to step through. And as he did, his heart was swallowed in its beats as he saw Blazing Heart lying there beside the fire, her eyes closed in a peaceful sleep, plush furs covering her, except for her face, resting just beneath her chin. Her hair was spread about her head, like a halo of red roses. The glow from the fire touched her face in gentle shades of gold.

Slipping the knife back into its sheath, Lone Hawk inched his way toward Mariana. He glanced toward the front of the tepee, where the outdoor fire outlined the Sioux who still rested on his haunches outside the tepee.

And then Lone Hawk knelt down beside Mariana, scarcely breathing, for fear she would awaken and find him there, and in the dimmed lighting of the tepee think he was a Sioux, come to assault her.

Raising his hand slowly upward, he inched it toward her face and clasped it quickly over her mouth. She would not be expecting him. He had to protect them both by keeping her from screaming out!

Mariana jumped with alarm, quickly jolted from sleep when she felt the hand on her mouth. She opened her eyes wildly and looked up and in the dim lighting of the wigwam saw the outline of an Indian bending low over her. She had been wrong to trust the Sioux! One had now come to surely rape her!

Throwing the furs off herself, Mariana reached her hand out to try and jerk the hand from her mouth. She tried to speak, then her insides rolled sensuously when the Indian spoke and she recognized his voice to be that of Lone Hawk.

"Be quiet!" Lone Hawk said, bending down into her face so that she could see him. "It is only Lone Hawk. I have come to take you away from this village of Sioux. But it must be done quietly. Lone Hawk would not be welcomed in the village of the Sioux in any capacity."

Mariana closed her eyes and breathed easier, relieved, yet puzzled by Lone Hawk's sudden appearance there. She was not in any danger. Yet he would not know that.

Lone Hawk slipped his hand away from her mouth, then drew her up and fully into his arms, embracing her. "My woman, where will Lone Hawk find you next?" he softly chuckled. "First in a pit in the ground, now, even worse, in the village of the Sioux."

Breathing in the spicy scent of his bare chest, Mariana clung to him. "You are wrong in comparisons," she murmured. "I am safe here, Lone Hawk. Totally safe. Chief Black Cloud . . . my father . . . has been nothing but kind to me. I was to be returned home tomorrow in the company of his warriors. He has treated me grandly, Lone Hawk. Grandly."

Lone Hawk leaned her away from him and looked down into her eyes. "Does he know you are his daughter?" he said thickly.

"No. I never told him," Mariana said, lowering her eyes. "I just couldn't." Then her eyes shot upward. "It would have complicated things for us, wouldn't it?"

Lone Hawk's mouth went agape. He was momentarily rendered speechless. His woman's decision had been guided by her thoughts of Lone Hawk! She had made a choice between her true father and the man who loved her, and she had chosen Lone Hawk!

"I hope this means that it makes it easier for you to make a decision about me," Mariana said, taking his hands in hers. "Does it? Can you now accept me, though I am part Sioux?"

A grumbling outside the tepee and the shadow showing the Sioux guard stretching and rising to his feet caused Mariana to tense and her heart to skip a beat. She glanced quickly at Lone Hawk. When he placed a finger to his lips, encouraging her to be totally quiet, she nodded, then crept with him to the rear of the tepee where the gaping hole showed the darkness of the forest behind it.

Stepping barefoot to the outside, where the dew-dampened grass was cold beneath her feet, Mariana winced. Then her breath was stolen momentarily from

352

her when she was suddenly swept up into Lone Hawk's arms and he began running with her away from the village, further into the forest.

"Soon you will be a part of the Chippewa village, not the Sioux," Lone Hawk grumbled, ducking low beneath branches, stepping high over strewn limbs along the ground.

"How did you even know that I was there?" Mariana asked, clinging about his neck.

"Sitting Tall," Lone Hawk said matter-of-factly. "He has impressed me, Blazing Heart, by choosing me over his father, to please me."

Mariana's eyes widened. She leaned away from Lone Hawk and looked questioningly up at him. "Did you say Sitting Tall told you?" she gasped, not understanding why Sitting Tall would tell Lone Hawk about where she was, when it had been Sitting Tall who had abducted her! She now knew it to be true, for Sitting Tall's name had been mentioned many times in conversation with Sitting Tall's father, Chief Black Cloud.

Chief Black Cloud had even found his son's abduction amusing . . . saying that his son was trying in every way to impress his chieftain father. Abductions were an act of bravery for the Sioux. Chief Black Cloud had longed for the strength himself to abduct again.

But he had savored this choice of Sitting Tall's! He had chosen wisely, this son who would one day be chief himself.

"*Ay-uh,*" Lone Hawk said, his eyes now finding the two ponies reined ahead. "Seems he discovered one of his father's warriors had abducted you. He would have released you himself, except that he felt to tell me, to give me the opportunity, would be to bring friendship between us again."

"But . . ." Mariana said, but she was interrupted by Lone Hawk, again speaking proudly of Sitting Tall's decision.

"Perhaps Sitting Tall and I can become true friends again," Lone Hawk said, lifting Mariana onto one of the waiting ponies. "It is best for both our peoples. One day we will each be chief. It would be best if peace could be reached between the Chippewa and the Sioux. Hopefully, nothing else will happen to draw Sitting Tall and Lone Hawk totally apart again. He has even promised not to drink any more firewater. Until he does, Lone Hawk must believe that he won't."

Though completely stunned by what Sitting Tall had done, Mariana now knew that she couldn't tell Lone Hawk. She didn't want to be the one responsible for causing a rift between Lone Hawk and Sitting Tall again. She understood the importance of what Lone Hawk had said. Peace was important between the two factions of Indians. And peace could possibly be achieved with these two blood brothers as chiefs, but only if each admired and trusted the other.

No. She could not tell Lone Hawk. It seemed that, ironic as it was, there was now going to be a secret between this new sister and brother.

"Let us now go," Lone Hawk said, swinging himself up onto his pony. He looked toward Mariana, whose face was silvered by the softness of moonlight. *"Nee-may-nan-dum-wah-bum-eh-nawn."*

Mariana had learned the meaning of this in Chippewa. She reached her hand to Lone Hawk's face

354

and gently touched it. "I am glad to see you, also," she murmured. "I love you so. Thank you for coming for me. You have proved to me so often, in so many ways, your love for me."

"Where were you when you were abducted by the Sioux?" Lone Hawk said, nudging the flanks of his pony with the heel of his moccasined foot, urging it onward, as Mariana rode alongside him.

"I became careless," Mariana sighed. "But I had seen something that so shocked me. I just didn't think straight afterward."

"What did you see?"

Mariana lowered her eyes and swallowed hard, not wanting to think about it, much less talk about it. Yet she felt she owed Lone Hawk an explanation for her careless actions.

"My father . . . the father who raised me," she slowly began. "When he left the trading post as he has so often mysteriously left of late, I followed him." She looked away from Lone Hawk, then turned her eyes slowly back to him. "Lone Hawk, I found him in a cabin, with an Indian squaw. He had built the cabin for her. He . . . he had even left my Mama to go to be with her. He continues to be . . . be . . . a cheat, Lone Hawk. I am glad that his blood does not flow through my veins. I am so ashamed of him."

"He meets with squaw?" Lone Hawk said, his eyebrows arching.

"She called herself by the name Joy," Mariana said, recalling not only her name, but her loveliness. "She was very pretty, Lone Hawk. But so was my Mama."

"Joy?" Lone Hawk gasped. Then he chuckled low. "Lone Hawk knows of such a squaw. She was banished from our village."

Mariana's eyes widened. "She . . . was . . . banished?" she gasped. "Why was she?"

Lone Hawk cast her a glance, frowning. "Do you truly want to know?" he asked shallowly.

"Yes, I feel I should know. She took my Papa from my Mama."

"She was banished because she was a woman who liked men who already had wives."

"Lord . . ."

"She not stay with your father long. She will move on. You will see. She is only using your father, for her own personal gain."

Mariana was recalling how Joy had begged to be taken to the trading post. A slow smile touched her lips. "Then she doesn't truly love my father," she murmured. "He will be surprised. . . ."

She didn't want to wish everything bad for her father, yet she was finding it hard to wish him anything good.

Riding alongside Lone Hawk, she lifted her chin, still relishing in this newfound feeling of peace with herself. Then she glanced toward Lone Hawk, suddenly remembering Jed Fenris! Surely Lone Hawk didn't know about him yet . . . the fact that Jed Fenris was still alive!

She looked quickly away from Lone Hawk. This was not the time to break such dreadful news to him. She would tell him later. There was no reason to spoil her time with him.

Yes, she would tell him later. . . .

Chapter Twenty-Eight

> With all your gentle ways, so
> sweetly tender, I want you in the
> morning when I wake.
>
> —GILLOM

Again in Lone Hawk's wigwam, resting with him beside the fire after the long ride from the Sioux village, Mariana gazed over at him and smiled. "You would have risked a war with the Sioux over me?" she said, seeing how the fire's shadows danced and played along the sharply chiseled lines of his face and on his firm, sensuous mouth. Her gaze swept lower, to the cleft in his chin.

"Do you not think you are worth warring over?" Lone Hawk chuckled, raising his fingers and drawing them through the brilliant red of her hair. He again took in her soft, perfect features, the fire's glow illuminating her throat, blooming her delicate cheekbones with color.

And then their adoring eyes met.

Mariana could once again feel their hearts melting

357

into one. "I would have doubted your feelings yesterday," she murmured. "But tonight? I believe I know that you would do most anything for me. Am I right?"

"Almost . . ." Lone Hawk said, chuckling low. His fingers went to her shoulders and began scooting the buckskin dress from them. "And you? Blazing Heart, what are you willing to do for me?"

Understanding that he was quite skillfully avoiding the question he would expect from her next, the need to hear him say that he was able to forget that part of her that was Sioux, Mariana thought it best to wait until later to ask him. Somehow she still dreaded the answer. Something deep down inside her warned her that he was not yet ready to make a full commitment to her.

Even though he had taken her from the village of the Sioux, it was not only because of his feelings for her that he had done so; it was also because of his antipathy toward the Sioux. In a sense he had won a battle tonight without even fighting. He surely was feeling victorious in having been able to steal her from the village.

"What would you like for me to do for you?" Mariana teased back, deciding she wanted this sensual moment with Lone Hawk more than she wanted answers. These moments were something she could trust. Something she could keep. Deep within her heart, the memories of these times with Lone Hawk were her own to cherish. No one could take them from her. They were locked within her heart, as her Mama's thoughts were locked inside a diary.

"You need to ask?" Lone Hawk said huskily, drawing the shoulders of her dress downward. The

358

ripeness of her breasts spilled out, golden beneath the fire's glow.

"No, I don't think so," Mariana said thickly, sucking in her breath when Lone Hawk bent to kiss the taut nipple of her breast. She closed her eyes and savored the warmth of his tongue, the coolness of his teeth as he nipped the nipple into an even greater stiffness.

Loosening his headband and removing it, Mariana coiled her fingers through his coarse black hair. And as he continued disrobing her, his lips following her body as it became bared to him, Mariana urged his mouth closer, and he wandered to the juncture of her thighs.

When his tongue flicked between her thighs, Mariana stiffened and emitted a low moan. His tongue . . . his lips . . . worshipping her in this way drove her wild. Writhing, biting her lower lip, Mariana swept her hands from his hair to his shoulders. Not meaning to, she sank her fingernails into his flesh, then opened her eyes wildly when he emitted a loud sound of pain.

Lone Hawk chuckled as he rose up away from her. "Sometimes you have claws of a panther," he said, slipping his breechcloth down and away from himself. "Now we will see if you have energies of panther when we make love."

"Have I before?" Mariana asked, her eyes hazy with rapture as she looked upon his manhood, ready for impaling her.

"Always," Lone Hawk said, now leaning fully over her, leading his hardness between her thighs, where his mouth had just tasted the honey dew of her passion. "Now, my woman, let us not talk anymore. Talk wastes energy. Let us use all energies in making love."

"Yes, let's. . . ." Mariana whispered, her body meeting the demand of his as she lifted her hips to welcome his gentle strokes inside her. She twined her arms about his neck and drew his lips to hers.

With a kiss of fire he answered her, his tongue probing, parting her lips to delve into the soft recesses of her mouth, their tongues intertwining. Again becoming mindless with ecstasy, Mariana floated, reveling in the touch of his hard body pressed into hers. She shuddered sensuously when his lips left her mouth and began showering kisses from one of her breasts to the other.

She tingled with pure joy . . . with utter happiness. There was only now. Time had stood still. All problems past, present and future were cast from Mariana's mind. When she was with Lone Hawk in such a way as now, only happiness claimed Mariana, for happiness was . . . Lone Hawk.

Their bodies fusing, their hearts melting into the other, Mariana felt the depths of her desire rising . . . spilling over . . . as the rush of ultimate pleasure spread throughout her in great splashes of what felt similar to sunshine. She clung to Lone Hawk as her body tremored, feeling his release matching hers.

And then they clung together, beads of perspiration pearling up on their brows, their breaths coming in snatches.

"Again you show your skills as a lover," Mariana whispered, smoothing some dampened locks of hair back from Lone Hawk's brow. "Are you always as masterful in everything you do? It seems that way to me, Lone Hawk."

Lone Hawk leaned away from her, his eyes dark with

spent passion. He traced Mariana's delicate cheekbones with a forefinger. "Stay with me. Be my wife. Then you find out the answer to your question," he said, smiling down at her, laughing low when he saw the surprise light up in her eyes.

"You . . . you have placed all doubts . . . all conflict of my heritage behind you?" she asked in amazement. She leaned up on her elbow, her heart beating excitedly. "Lone Hawk, you . . . truly . . . want me . . . ?"

"Did you ever doubt it, Blazing Heart?"

"You gave me cause to, Lone Hawk."

Lone Hawk drew her into his embrace and hugged her tightly to his hard frame. He burrowed his nose into the depths of her hair, scented as though it had been bathed in rose petals. "Lone Hawk sorry for that," he mumbled. He drew away from her and looked lovingly down at her. "You stay from Sioux village? You no have need to meet with Sioux father again?"

Mariana cast her eyes downward, having been prepared for that question. Oh, how a part of her had enjoyed being with Chief Black Cloud, after having found out what a kind man he was!

Yet she knew that she must relinquish all thoughts of the Sioux, even of her true father, to be able to be with Lone Hawk as his wife. It was wonderful that he was willing to accept her at all. Before, he had left many doubts in her mind. He had been torn, as she was now. . . .

Raising her eyes slowly upward, Mariana nodded. "You own my heart," she murmured. "Only you, Lone Hawk. Yet I wish to share it with your people, if you truly wish me to. Can you forget that I am part

Sioux? Before . . ."

Lone Hawk rose to his feet and drew his breechcloth on. He frowned down at Mariana. "Lone Hawk has thought long and hard about this question," he mumbled. "And Lone Hawk kept coming up with the same answer."

"And . . . that . . . is . . . ?" Mariana said, slipping the doeskin dress over her head.

Lone Hawk leaned and placed his hands to her waist, urging her to stand before him. "Lone Hawk will be chief," he said flatly. "My people will never question any of my decisions. And perhaps, even if they know you are part Sioux, they can see that a possible peace can be had with the Sioux. You see, Blazing Heart, you will represent all things good about the Sioux. You will show my people that peace *is* possible."

Mariana melted into his arms, tears near. "I so want to be with you," she murmured, clinging to him. "Lone Hawk, you are everything to me. Everything."

He urged her away from him. He clasped his hands onto her shoulders. "And you are sure you can separate yourself from the white community . . . the white way of life?" he said thickly. "My ways are different from yours. Totally."

"Lone Hawk, I am willing to adjust in all ways, if it means to be with you," she said softly. "I want to rise in the morning looking upon your handsomeness. I want to go to sleep at night in your arms. You are my only reason for living, Lone Hawk. Surely you know that."

"And you are sure you can place the need to be with Chief Black Cloud from your heart?" he said, frowning down at her. "You have found in him something special, have you not? When you speak his name, it is evident, Blazing Heart."

Mariana met his steady gaze with her own. "I had the need to know my true father," she said, swallowing hard. "I found out. Now I am at peace. I needed to know that he was not all bad. You see, I am of his seed. I wouldn't have wanted to know that a part of me was . . . was . . . totally evil!"

A rush of footsteps outside the wigwam drew Mariana and Lone Hawk from their embrace. Lone Hawk looked toward the closed entrance flap just as Neala was there, speaking in a rush of Chippewa words.

Mariana watched Lone Hawk as his face changed from peaceful to tormented. His eyes wavered, his mouth went slack, his head jerked.

Reaching her hand to him, Mariana winced when he ignored her and rushed from the wigwam. When Neala came into the wigwam, her eyes wet with tears, Mariana knew that something dreadful had to have happened. Lone Hawk had left her as though she didn't even exist . . . Neala was crying as though she had lost her last friend.

Mariana went to Neala and placed her hand to her cheek. "What is it, Neala?" she softly questioned. "What has happened? I couldn't understand what you said to Lone Hawk. You spoke in Chippewa. Where has Lone Hawk gone in such a rush?"

Neala brushed a tear from her cheek with a flick of a finger. "It is our father," she murmured, lowering her lashes. "He . . . he . . . is now gone on his long journey to the hereafter." Her eyes rose slowly upward. "He is dead, Blazing Heart. He . . . is . . . dead."

Mariana was shocked. She hadn't yet had the

363

opportunity to meet Lone Hawk's father, and he was now dead? Her sadness for Lone Hawk and Neala was doubled by her own sense of having been cheated of the opportunity to meet this powerful Chippewa chief.

Then her insides quivered and her eyes widened. Lone Hawk was now chief! She wanted to be proud for Lone Hawk, but she knew this was not the time. One chief had to die for another to be named! This loss was not something to be glad about!

Seeing Neala's frailty, her total sadness, Mariana went to her and drew her into her arms. "I am so sorry, Neala," she whispered. "I'm so sorry."

"My people are already in deep mourning," Neala sobbed. "I must return to them, to mourn jointly with them."

When Neala eased from Mariana's arms, Mariana let her gaze sweep over her. This was the first time she had seen Neala since the fateful day of Neala's dreadful rape. Neala's outward bruises had healed. But Mariana had to wonder about what she carried about inside her. Surely she lived the terrible day over and over again in her mind. Lone Hawk had said that she hadn't yet left the village. She hadn't yet gone to Sitting Tall. Perhaps she never would. . . .

Then, thinking about Neala and what had happened to her, brought Jed Fenris to Mariana's mind again. She hadn't yet taken the time to tell Lone Hawk that Jed was still alive. Now it would be many days before she would again have the opportunity. Lone Hawk would not even want to hear the name Jed Fenris while he was mourning his father's death.

"Neala has already chosen several braves who will accompany you safely back to the trading post," Neala said softly. "My brother will be busy preparing our father for burial. Then he will be busy preparing himself to take over as our people's leader. Surely you will understand. My brother must not have anything on his mind but duties to father and our people for the next several days."

Mariana blanched. She took a step backwards, feeling as though she had been slapped in the face. Her eyes wavering, she turned her back to Neala, not wanting Neala to see how this was hurting her. Mariana wanted to understand! Lone Hawk's feelings . . . his people's feelings . . . were all that was important now. It seemed that the paradise they had planned between them had been suddenly shattered. Again her dreams of being with Lone Hawk were being postponed.

But Lone Hawk would expect her to be strong!

Squaring her shoulders, she turned back to face Neala. "I appreciate what you are saying," she said softly. "Will you please tell Lone Hawk that I will be at Grand Portage whenever his time for mourning is over? I will be waiting for him, Neala. For however long it takes, I will be waiting for him."

What Mariana had said sounded innocent enough, yet a part of her was dying, knowing that she would once again have to return to that part of her life that she hated. And she sorely hated having to face her father, known to her now as only Everett Fowler, with all the truths about him festering inside her!

But it was only a brief delay. Soon Lone Hawk would come for her. They had spoken of total commitment to each other. Then that was how it would be!

"*Ay-uh,* Neala shall give Lone Hawk Blazing Heart's message," Neala said, reaching to fondly take one of Mariana's hands. "You so often show yourself to be woman of courage. Again you prove that you are. Neala understands your true feelings for Lone Hawk. You will be a beautiful wife for my brother. Be patient a while longer, Blazing Heart. So often patience is hard where love for a man is concerned."

Mariana could read between the lines, understanding how Neala was making reference to Sitting Tall without even saying his name. It was evident that Neala still loved him. Perhaps after the Chippewa mourning was behind her, she would go to him and make peace with him again, as lovers knew how to do. It seemed that Neala had more courage than Mariana, for she thought it would be very hard to accept a man like Sitting Tall back into her arms.

"Sitting Tall. My brother . . ." Mariana thought, turning her eyes from Neala. It was still hard to grasp onto, that Sitting Tall was her brother . . . that Chief Black Cloud was her father.

But now was the time to forget her brother and worry about another father, and whether or not he was waiting at the trading post, wondering where she had wandered to.

Mariana feared this next meeting with Everett Fowler. So much had changed in her life . . . in her mind . . . since she had last seen him.

Chapter Twenty-Nine

Lone Hawk's braves had escorted Mariana only as far as the edge of the forest that lay on the one side of the boundaries of the trading post. Mariana had given them back the pony on which she had been riding, the pony only having been lent to her for her return to Grand Portage.

She was now running along the waterfront toward the large gate that would lead her on into the trading post courtyard.

Glancing about her, she saw that many of the Voyageurs had left. By now they were traveling the nine-mile trail that led from Grand Portage to Fort Charlotte.

Even many of the larger sloops that had been anchored out away from the pier had left. Everything was returning to normal about the trading post, yet

Mariana felt that nothing would ever be the same for her again. She was ever-changing, it seemed. She even now felt more Indian, than white. . . .

"Mariana!"

The gruff voice of Everett Fowler resounding from somewhere behind Mariana caused her to cringe, her spine stiffening. She had hoped to find shelter in her room before having to face him.

It was so hard for her to think of Everett Fowler as her father now that she knew so much about him . . . and now that she had met her true father! Yet all these many past years he had been her father in every sense of the word. She would have to think of him that way for at least a while longer!

Horse's hooves drawing closer behind her made Mariana realize that her father was not traveling by foot, but by horse! Was he only now returning from his meeting with Joy? Was he finding it this easy to neglect his duties at the trading post, leaving everything in Eugene South's care?

It had been so obvious, so many times, that Eugene would like nothing better than that. He had shown quite often that he wished to take Everett Fowler's place as the head of the trading post.

Mariana was surprised that Everett Fowler would even allow this to happen. Yet the beautiful Indian squaw most surely had not only captured her father's heart, but also his senses.

"Mariana, look at me when I talk to you!" Everett shouted, reining his horse in beside her. He wheeled the horse around and glared down at her. His eyes were on fire as they crept over her, seeing her attire. Again she had been with the damn Indian! Again he had given her

Indian clothes, in exchange for a dress from her own wardrobe.

He quickly dismounted and stepped closer to Mariana. He leaned down into her face. "Have you no shame?" he hissed. "Mariana, again you show up here at the trading post dressed as an Indian squaw? Have you been with him again? Do you go to Lone Hawk every time you see me leave? How many times have you done this that I don't know about?"

His heated words, the anger in his eyes, made Mariana's own insides grow hot with rage. He could so easily accuse her, when he was guilty of even worse?

She wanted to lash out at him, but the many eyes turned to them in wonder caused her to keep her opinions to herself. She did not wish to be cause for a scandal, yet she felt that perhaps she already was. Everyone must have been eyeing the doeskin dress her true father had given her. As most of them saw it, no decent white woman would wear anything even so much as touched by an Indian, though the white people were ready enough to sell *their* wares to the Indians, for profit.

As always before, Mariana was reminded of what most whites thought of Indians. Indians were looked on as no more than savages . . . as heathens . . . only tolerated in these parts because they were easily cheated!

"Papa, I am tired," Mariana murmured, easing around both him and his horse to walk away from him. "If you wish to talk with me, please let's do so in the privacy of our rooms."

"Mariana, don't walk away from me!" Everett growled, guiding his horse to catch up with her and again glare down at her.

Mariana looked about her, her head bent. "Papa, you're causing a scene," she harshly whispered. "Please. It's not best. There's so much I could say you wouldn't want anyone here at the trading post to hear."

She turned and glared back at him. "Don't push me, Papa, into saying things not even you wish to hear," she said dryly.

Everett paled. His insides coiled tightly, as though ready to snap, his fury at her disrespect was so intense.

"You're a bit out of line, Mariana," he said in a snarl. "Get on to the house. I'll see to you after I tend to my horse."

"I imagine you *would* think I am out of line," Mariana nodded, a sly smile touching her lips. "But, Papa, I've reasons for the way I'm behaving." She nodded toward his horse. "And, yes. It's best you tend to your horse, then me. That is best, Papa."

Boldly lifting her chin, she swung around and pranced on to the house, her insides shivering, knowing that her father was watching her every movement. She had never spoken so disobediently to him before. She had always watched her words much more carefully, never wanting to rile him.

But now, perhaps it was best to get all of this over with instead of leaving the dread to lie heavy on her heart. Once everything was said, then it would be much easier when Lone Hawk came for her.

"Lone Hawk," she whispered, going to the living room and settling down into a plush chair. "Just how long will I have to wait?"

Flipping her hair back from her shoulders, Mariana looked about her. So many things still reminded her of her Mama. The embroidery . . . the eye spectacles . . . the book of poems.

They had all been left in place, as though in memoriam to a sweet, quiet lady, a lady who had not even known when a man had sorely loved her.

"He did love you, Mama," Mariana whispered, taking the book of poems, holding it to her heart. "The Indian who fathered me, truly loved you. He just didn't know how to show you . . . to tell you. When he made love to you, he thought that would be enough. . . ."

"What's that you're sayin' to yourself?" Everett said, walking heavily into the living room. He went and stood over Mariana, his doubled fists resting on his hips, his muscled legs outstretched.

He was a threatening man in his largeness, yet Mariana would not let him be a threat to her any longer.

Placing the book back on the table, Mariana rose from the chair and stood her ground before him. "What was I saying?" she said snappishly, placing her hands on her hips. "I guess I was trying to get Mama to hear me, Papa."

"What?" Everett gasped, dropping his hands to his sides. "What sort of craziness is that?"

"I know it makes one look daft if one talks to oneself, but I was trying to talk to Mama," Mariana said

"I was trying to tell her that Chief Black Cloud did love her when he held her captive all those years ago. When she became pregnant with me, it was out of love, not hate."

Everett felt a lightheadedness sweep over him. He teetered, then reached for the back of a chair to steady himself. "Damn it, girl, what are you saying?"

he stammered.

"I'm saying that I've read Mama's diary," Mariana said, walking away from him and drawing the sheer curtain aside to look from the window toward the hill where her Mama lay at rest beneath the mound of ground. "I'm saying that I have even met by real father."

She let the curtain flutter from her hands and turned to face Everett, her hands now moving silkily along the lines of the doeskin dress.

"It was my father who gave me this dress, Papa," she said dryly. "Not Lone Hawk. I've spent the last two days with my true father, getting to know the man he really is."

She smiled devilishly up into Everett's paling face. "You may call him savage, but he has much kinder traits than you, Papa," she said, her voice trailing off. For so long she had loved this man standing before her, yet she had always found it hard to accept him and his evil ways.

"You must be clean outta your mind talkin' to me in such a way," Everett said shallowly. "And you can't mean it . . . that . . . you've been with the Sioux. Chief Black Cloud and all the Sioux like him are savages. The tales of their ghastly deeds have been spread far and wide. You can't be serious, Mariana. Tell me you're only toying with me? You read the diary, then got upset, then went to Lone Hawk because you couldn't accept the truth about your heritage. Tell me you haven't been with the filthy, savage Sioux!"

Mariana sank down into a chair. She picked up her mother's embroidery work and began running her fingers along the delicate curves of embroidery thread that had been sewn in the shapes of green leaves.

"I haven't only been with the Sioux, but also the Chippewa," she absently murmured, thinking this was the best time to reveal all truths to him. Later it might come hard for her. She already knew to expect some sort of reprimand.

But whatever it was, she would only have a short time to tolerate it. She was only to be a part of her father's life for a short time longer. Soon she would leave with Lone Hawk and never look back again.

Her words were like a bolt of lightning crashing into Everett. His whole body shook from the explosion. He lumbered over to Mariana and grabbed her by her wrist and jerked her up to stand before him.

The embroidery work fell from Mariana's lap as she lunged to her feet. Her heart skipped a beat, thinking that perhaps she had been wrong to be so smug in her telling of truths. She looked onto a face of violence. Her father's face was fiery red, his eyes bulging.

"You're lying," he snarled. "Tell me you're lying."

"I never lie to you, Papa," Mariana said, challenging him with a set stare.

"Then you were with the Sioux and the Chippewa? Are you nothing but a . . . a . . . whore, Mariana? What did I do to deserve a daughter who turns into a whore?"

"But, Papa, I'm not your daughter. Do you forget so easily?"

Everett threw her wrist away from him. He began pacing the floor, kneading his brow. "Something's got to be done about this," he grumbled. "And soon. I can't afford to lose my respect in the community. And with you up to such no good, it'll happen fast."

"Papa, just accept the truths as they are told you," Mariana said, rubbing her sore wrist. "Now if you will excuse me, I plan to go to my room and freshen up. The journey has been long."

She went to Everett and spoke up into his face. "But you must know something else," she said calmly. "If Lone Hawk's father hadn't died . . . if Lone Hawk hadn't been thrust into mourning for his father and into the duties of now being chief, I wouldn't even have returned to the trading post. I would have stayed with Lone Hawk. I would have married him."

She cleared her throat and again began moving toward her bedroom. "As it is, I shall marry him later," she said in a rush of words.

The hair raised at the nape of her neck when she heard her father's heavy footsteps behind her. She emitted a low scream when he grabbed her by the hair and forced her around to again face him.

"You listen to me," he said from between clenched teeth. "You ain't marryin' no Indian. I'll see to it that by tomorrow evening you'll be married to Eugene South. Though you look to him with contempt, he's at least better than a filthy savage Indian!"

Mariana paled. She stared unbelievingly up into her father's narrowed eyes. "You can't force me to marry Eugene South," she softly cried. "I refuse to. I won't marry him."

She winced and closed her eyes when Everett tightened his fingers into her hair and yanked her face closer to his. "You'll do as I say," he grumbled. "I ain't been actin' as your father for all these years to have so little respect from you. By damn, you'll marry the man I see is best for you. By damn, you will marry

Eugene South."

He released her and stormed away from her. "I guess I'll have to see to it that your room is guarded until I return," he shouted.

Mariana combed her fingers through her hair, still feeling the sting at her scalp where the roots had been stretched too tight. "You'll what?" she gasped.

Everett turned around and gave her a haughty smile. "My dear daughter, I plan to go and ride for a preacher," he laughed. "In the meantime, I plan to have you watched. You won't have the opportunity to make a run for it, to go to that damn Indian again." He flailed his hands into the air. "I won't have you marryin' a damn savage! Do you hear?"

Mariana clasped her hands together behind her. She bit her lower lip, tears near to bursting forth from her eyes. Then she took a bold step closer to her father.

"You continue to call Lone Hawk . . . all Indians savages!" she shouted. "Papa, is that Indian squaw you take to bed with you not a savage? What separates her from the rest? As I saw her, her skin was as copper in color . . . her hair as black. She even spoke in Indian."

Mariana's breath caught in her throat. "You even spoke in Chippewa back to her, Papa. And you? You can treat me as some sort of whore because I love an Indian? How about you, Papa? What sort of label must I place on you because you love an Indian? You even left Mama's sick bed to go to the squaw! Did her name . . . the name Joy . . . intrigue you? Or was it her body?"

Everett was stunned numb by Mariana and all that she knew. He had always thought her to have a special intelligence, but how was it that she could gather such information about such intimate things?

"How . . . do . . . you know about Joy?" he said hoarsely.

"I followed you. I saw!" Mariana said, taking a step backwards, expecting to be slapped for her impudence.

Everett hung his head into his hands. "I should've expected it," he mumbled. "Yet, I never thought you could be sneaky. Not my daughter. I thought I taught you better."

"I know that it was not proper for me to do that," Mariana said, her tone softening. "But I couldn't help myself. You . . . you . . . even left the day Mama was buried. It tore at my heart, Papa. I knew there must be a woman. And if there was, I knew that again you proved to be less than an honorable man. Because of this, I felt it wasn't at all wrong to do what I felt needed to be done. So I . . . followed you. I found out."

Her eyes lowered, her hands unclasped behind her. She swept her hair from her brow. "Do you truly love her, Papa? Do you love her more than you ever loved Mama?" she murmured.

"That is something not discussed between father and daughter," Everett said, his voice growing strong, his jaw tightening.

He swung around and walked toward the door. "Now, Mariana, I do plan to go for a preacher!" he shouted. "I do plan to have you watched. This time you won't go runnin' to no Indian for comfort!"

Mariana took several steps toward him. "Papa, about this squaw that you chose over Mama," she said dryly.

Everett stopped and turned to face her, his eyes narrow. "We won't be discussin' her any longer," he said flatly. He pointed to her room. "Go to your room. You may as well get comfortable. You're going to be there for a spell." He smiled wickedly down at her. "At least until I return with the preacher. Then you'll be sharin' Eugene's cabin with Eugene."

Those words stung Mariana's heart. They sent spirals of iciness through her veins. Yet she could not stop what she had started with her father. Not until he was as miserable as he was about to make her.

"I've a few more words to say about your squaw, then I'll never say anything about her again," Mariana said, smiling up at her father. "I promise, Papa."

"Then say it, if you must," Everett growled.

"Papa, seems you've picked a wrong savage to love," she mused. "Though I do not dare call you a hypocrite because you have chosen to bed up with a squaw, with you always calling all Indians savages, I feel you must know the truth about the squaw."

"What . . . truth . . . ?" Everett said, kneading his chin.

"When I told Lone Hawk about Joy, and what she was to you, Lone Hawk told me that Joy had been banished from his tribe of Chippewa," Mariana taunted. "Have you ever wondered why she was banished? Or do you know?"

Everett moved to stand over Mariana. He bent to speak into her face. "Get to it, daughter," he grumbled. "Whatever you have to say, spit it out."

"This squaw? She was forced from the village because she liked playing around with married men," Mariana said softly. "Seems *she's* a whore, Papa. An Indian squaw whore. Even the Chippewa had no use for such a woman in their village."

377

Everett took a quick step backward. Then he raised his hand and slapped Mariana. He left the room in a fury. Mariana placed a hand to her cheek. It was stinging from the slap, yet inside she felt victorious.

Smiling, she went to her room. But her smile didn't last long. When she heard the shuffling of feet outside her door, she crept it open, and her mouth went agape when she saw a man standing there, his back to her, balancing his weight on a rifle that he rested against the floor before him.

Pale, Mariana quietly closed the door. "He meant what he said," she whispered. "I am a prisoner here, more than I ever was in either Indian village!"

Rushing to the window, she swept the curtain aside and watched her father gallop away. "He is going for a preacher," she softly cried.

Chapter Thirty

*Clasp me close in your warm,
young arms, while the pale stars
shine above.*
—WILCOX

Pacing, Mariana kept watching the door. Though she had taken a brief nap, had even been accompanied by the guard outside her door to the kitchen to prepare herself something to eat, she was now anticipating escape. If she waited for her father's return, he would see that she married Eugene South!

And that was a fate worse than death. She could not allow it to happen.

Going to the window, she again tested it. But it was stuck. She couldn't budge it. Always before when she had wanted it raised, her father had had to come to open it for her.

"Damn it," she said, whirling around to again look toward the door.

Again she paced. She looked through the window. The sunset was an orange disc in the sky. Soon it would be dark. Perhaps the man outside her door would fall asleep. Surely he was bored enough to! Then she could slip easily enough from the room.

But the thought of traveling in the total darkness of night caused pinpricks of fear to rise on her flesh. She must remember how easily she had been abducted by the Sioux! It could happen again, but by another tribe . . . a tribe who would treat her as an enemy, not as a friend.

It was a chance she would have to take. She couldn't just sit idly by and let her father ruin her life.

"I must escape," she whispered.

Looking about her, she tried to think of a way she could travel through the forest incognito. If she could only wear a man's breeches. . . .

Her eyes brightening, Mariana went to the trunk at the foot of her bed and threw its lid back. Scrambling through the clothes, she found a pair of man's black breeches. She took them from the trunk and scurried to her feet and held the breeches up next to her. She smiled. Though she knew them to be her father's, they were not the size that he now wore. They had been her father's when he had been much younger . . . much thinner.

"Thank goodness Papa saved them," she sighed.

It was the only time she had known her father to be in the least bit sentimental. Several moth holes in the breeches attested to their age. These were the breeches of the suit that he had worn when he had married Mariana's Mama.

Mariana frowned. She wondered what her Papa would do if he found them missing.

But it would only be another thing added to his list of

reasons to be angry with Mariana. And she cared little now for these reasons. When she left Grand Portage this time, it would most definitely be forever.

Turning, she espied the hairbrush on her dressing table. She laid the breeches across her arm and went to the hairbrush and picked it up. "This is the only thing I will take with me," she whispered.

Then her gaze moved downward, remembering the diary tucked away beneath the bottom lining of the trunk. Loneliness for her mother stabbed at her heart. Perhaps the diary would be a way to keep her mother close to her.

Yet she shook her head, deciding not. The diary had not represented anything good to her mother. The secrets within the diary's pages had not been secrets happily kept. Mariana's mother had lived with the memory of those days spent with Chief Black Cloud in dread. The diary had been written while hate lay heavy in her mother's heart.

"I'll leave it for Papa," Mariana whispered. "He has always wanted to burn it. Well, let him."

Determination sent Mariana into a frenzy of undressing. She again held the breeches out away from her and studied them with a cocked eyebrow, then slipped into them.

She laughed to herself when she discovered how much the waist hung out away from her. Even the length had to be fixed.

Grabbing scissors, Mariana snipped the legs of the breeches off until they were her size. Then she grabbed a long length of ribbon and tied it about her waist, snuggling the breeches tightly about her.

And then she searched further through the trunk and

found the suit jacket. After rolling up its sleeves, she slipped hurriedly into it, buttoned it securely in front, then went to the mirror and looked at herself.

Her gaze went to her hair. With eager fingers she swept it up and secured it into a tight bun atop her head. As she slipped through the trading post store, she could steal a hat, and then she would look like a proper man as she rode into the depths of the forest. People would think she was just another trapper and would leave her be.

She had mainly the larger wild animals to fear. But she would stay on the horse. She would travel without stopping until she reached Lone Hawk. Though he would be in mourning, he would welcome her into his village, knowing that she had finally cut her ties with her father and the way of life that she had always known.

During the time it had taken her to prepare herself for escape, the cover of night had settled in over Grand Portage, as though a giant hawk's wing spread out above it.

Slipping the hairbrush beneath the suit jacket and into the waist of the breeches, Mariana crept to the door and slowly opened it. A kerosene lamp burned dimly across the room, emitting enough light for her to see the guard, who had moved from the door to be more comfortable in a chair.

Mariana's pulse raced, seeing how the man's head was slumped forward, his rifle now resting against the chair instead of in his hand. She had been right to expect him to become bored with his assigned duties. The day had been long for him as well as for her. And thinking that Mariana had resigned herself to the fact that she was to wait for her father to return with the preacher, the man had become careless.

Moccasins on her feet, Mariana tiptoed soundlessly from the room. She moved to the trading post store, finding it dark. Feeling around her, she finally found a hat. Slipping it onto her head, hiding her hair beneath it, she then fled on outside and soon had her horse saddled and was riding through the forest.

The wilderness of thicket and forest was ghostly, with a queer, luminous darkness. It was like velvet, soft and heavy. With every nerve tingling, Mariana pushed on relentlessly, strengthening her determination to reach the Chippewa village unharmed.

She had accustomed her eyes to the blackness, but not to the chill of the night. The air seeped through her clothes like icy fingers clutching. The distance seemed endless, only dark shadows meeting her piercing gaze.

Mosquitoes buzzed . . . the glunk and peep of frogs were all about her. And then she caught the shine of water glowing ahead, with a soft, deep light, as the moon reached down through the overhang of trees.

Nudging her horse's flanks with the heels of her moccasined feet, Mariana urged it onward, thinking that to follow the outline of the water might be a quicker way to get to Lone Hawk. She had done this before. Hopefully she had chosen the right stream. The forest was a maze of waterways. It would be easy to become disoriented. One mistake, and she would be totally lost.

Traveling onward, becoming bone-weary, Mariana was aware that the moon had suddenly disappeared from sight. The forest was now even darker. It was even more threatening. A soft fog had drifted in from the edges of the water, rolling like a giant wave toward her. Somewhere out in the foggy dark an owl spoke its ominous hoot, a whippoorwill echoing its odd, whistling call, repeating it over and over again.

Mariana plowed her way through the cottony fog, riding through a swampy region of thickets, briars and thorns reaching out for her legs, occasionally piercing them.

But then the fog momentarily lifted, revealing to her a campfire just ahead.

Reining her horse to a shuddering stop, Mariana scarcely breathed. Though she had ridden long enough now to be close to the Chippewa village, she knew that she couldn't count on the campfire's being that of a Chippewa. Trappers were known to make camp anywhere . . . anytime. Even Jed Fenris.

"Jed Fenris," she gasped. "Lone Hawk still doesn't know. . . ."

With the fog again swirling around Mariana, seeming to close in on her, she decided to move onward. Inching her horse along, she kept her eyes on the shimmering of the fire through the fog, then, when she was near it, she directed her horse behind a thick stand of Norway pines and dismounted. Securing her horse's reins, Mariana then moved stealthily toward the fire, keeping herself hidden behind trees as she stepped from one to the other.

When she was only a few feet from the fire, enough for her to be able to smell the wood burning, even to feel its warmth on her cooled face, she stopped and peered more intently toward the campsite. When she saw the figure crouched low beside the fire, her heart skipped a beat. Again, it seemed that she had found

Lone Hawk in some sort of meditation! He was chanting something low beneath his breath. He raised his face to the heavens, then to the ground.

Mariana's heart sang with happiness for having found him. Yet a part of her felt his sadness, for she could hear it in his voice, the mournful wail that accompanied each new chant. He was mourning his father in private.

Should she even interrupt?

Yet Mariana could not just stand there, so close to him, without going to him. The journey had been long. The fire was too inviting.

And, oh, how could she just stand by and watch Lone Hawk when she hungered to be in his arms?

But still cautious, she looked farther about her. Her gaze settled on a makeshift sort of wigwam. It was not as carefully constructed as the one Lone Hawk made residence in, in his village. This was much smaller, and the birchbark covering was loosely thrown across the bent sapling poles, instead of being secured against them.

Mariana had to wonder just how long Lone Hawk planned to stay . . . how long he had been there? Had he come as soon as he had seen to his father's burial? Had he planned to stay alone for several days?

Mariana feared that he might not welcome her there.

If not, what then would she do?

Setting her jaw firmly, Mariana crept on toward the fire. She had no choice. And if Lone Hawk loved her, as he had so often confessed, he would not turn his back on her, no matter his reason for now being so strangely alone.

Tripping on a fallen limb, Mariana emitted a loud

385

shriek. She was thrown forward and when she landed she found herself looking up into the wondering eyes of Lone Hawk from where she lay, beside him.

Smiling awkwardly up at him, Mariana leaned up on an elbow. "Lone Hawk . . . ?" she murmured.

Lone Hawk's eyes widened as he saw that the sudden intruder in the night was his Blazing Heart, yet his eyes could not adjust to the way she was clothed! She was in a white man's outfit! The hat that had been thrown from her head in the fall was a white man's hat! Except for the loveliness of her face now revealed to him in the light of the fire, she even looked like a man!

Reaching his hand to the tight bun of her hair, Lone Hawk chuckled low. "Blazing Heart, you do many things which amaze me," he said. "But this that you choose to do makes Lone Hawk *bah-pin*. Lone Hawk welcomes a reason to laugh."

Mariana rose to a sitting position, brushing dirt from her breeches. "Did I fool you?" she said, laughing softly. "Did you think I was a man?"

"If you had not made yourself known to me you would have perhaps been shot," Lone Hawk said, his eyes gleaming. "It is not best to creep upon a man in the night. Most men shoot first, ask questions later."

Mariana's insides splashed cold. "You wouldn't have," she gasped.

Lone Hawk drew her into his arms, his fingers working with the bun of her hair, loosening it. "Tell me," he said thickly. "Why have you come? Why are you dressed in this way? Did not Neala tell you Lone Hawk would come for you when mourning period was past?"

"Yes, Neala told me," Mariana said, melting beneath

386

his steady stare, her head tingling where his fingers touched her anew as he continued to untangle her hair. "And I understood. But . . ."

"But what, Blazing Heart?"

"My Papa, he . . . he . . ."

Lone Hawk's face became shadowed by a frown. "He what?" he grumbled. "Did he threaten you in some way?"

"Yes. He forced me to stay in my room with a guard outside my door." Mariana said in a rush of words, moving to her knees before him, her hair now tumbling across her shoulders and further still, down her back. "He has gone for a preacher. He was going to force me to marry Eugene! Lone Hawk, when the man outside my door fell asleep, I escaped."

Her hands swept down, along the lines of the suit jacket, and then her breeches. "I wore these clothes because I felt it would be safer for me," she further explained. "I was afraid to travel through the forest by night, dressed as a woman. I am quite aware of the dangers for a woman. I've been abducted once. Never do I want the dreadful act to be repeated!"

Then she glanced toward the wigwam, to the fire, and then back to Lone Hawk. "Lone Hawk, why are you here in such a way?" she murmured. "Or need I ask? You are here to be alone, aren't you? Will I be in your way?"

Lone Hawk rose to his feet and stared down into the fire. Mariana could see a deep, haunted look in his eyes. She rose to stand beside him.

"My father's burial has been seen to," Lone Hawk said hoarsely. "Lone Hawk is now chief. This time was needed to prepare myself for the duties. This full day and night has been spent in speaking to the spirits of the forest. Lone Hawk has asked for wisdom ... for strength ... for courage. Lone Hawk wants to be as good a leader as was his father!"

Mariana worked into his embrace. She looked up into his eyes. "Lone Hawk, you will be," she murmured. "You already are."

Framing her face between his hands, Lone Hawk momentarily looked down at her, then lowered his mouth to her lips. He gently kissed her, then slipped his arms about her and lifted her fully up into his arms. Without further words he carried her to the wigwam. Once inside he removed her clothes, then his own.

"You have come. Lone Hawk glad," Lone Hawk said huskily, his hands finding the swells of her breasts in the darkness of his temporary dwelling. "Tonight is ours, Blazing Heart. Tomorrow you will be presented to my people. Tomorrow is theirs."

"I hope they will approve of your choice of wife," Mariana whispered, her insides heatedly stirring as Lone Hawk's hands kneaded her breasts and his hardness found her open to him. When he entered her, she shivered and lifted her hips, again joining him in this sensual way of being together.

"How could they not approve?" Lone Hawk whispered back, his breath hot on her cheek. "Everything Lone Hawk does will be great in my people's eyes! The spirits. They never fail me. . . ."

Sighing, Mariana clung to him, thinking that nothing could be as perfect, as now. . . .

Chapter Thirty-One

> *I arise from dreams of thee in
> the first sleep of night.*
> —SHELLEY

The early morning sun dappling the shaded ground with shimmering light outside the wigwam drew Mariana awake. She yawned and stretched her arms, then looked adoringly over at Lone Hawk, showing his first stirrings of awakening as he tossed from his back to his side, to now be facing her.

Scooting the blanket away from her and Lone Hawk, Mariana slipped into his embrace, fitting her breasts against his chest while she twined her arms about his neck.

"Darling? Are you awake?" she whispered.

When his eyes fluttered open and he looked over at her with passion heating in his eyes, lifting his lips into a blossoming smile, Mariana's insides lit up like a candle, filling her insides with a wondrous warmth.

Lone Hawk didn't answer her. Instead, he placed his muscled arms about her and drew her lips to his. In a torrid embrace, he kissed her with easy sureness. His hands swept over her silken curves, savoring the touch of her slim waist, her slender thighs, and then the softness of the downy hair that lay at the junction of her legs.

Lowering his hardness, his hand then led this throbbing part of himself into her, then moved on around to where her buttocks felt like the softest of doeskins ever touched by him.

Kneading her flesh, he encouraged her hips higher, making his strokes inside her easier. As he plunged, he could almost feel the innermost depths of her! He felt a building heat inside his loins. His head was slowly spinning. He kissed her more ardently, his thrusts becoming faster . . . harder. . . .

The pleasure he was evoking inside Mariana was almost overwhelming her. She felt drugged. Small flames of desire were sparking throughout her. She shuddered with desire as he now bent his lips, to flick his tongue sensually about first one of her breasts and then the other.

"Lone Hawk, my darling . . ." she whispered, twining her fingers through the coarseness of his jet-black hair. "Make these moments last forever. I want nothing more of life than . . . to . . . be with you. . . ."

His night-black eyes looked up at her. His lips moved to the hollow of her throat, his strokes inside her more intense . . . feverish even!

And then their bodies quaked together, their golden web of magic again spinning around them, claiming them.

Mariana sighed contentedly as she pulled free of their lover's embrace. Lone Hawk leaned up on his elbow, running his hand along her flesh anew, finding it hard to keep from still touching her, though he knew they must get dressed and return to his waiting people. From this day forth he would lead his people, and Blazing Heart would captivate them.

Lone Hawk was glad that he had fought and won this battle inside his heart that had momentarily threatened his and Blazing Heart's happiness. That she was part Sioux could benefit him and his people. Perhaps she could lead the way to a complete peace with the Sioux. Now that she and Chief Black Cloud had made some sort of an alliance, perhaps this alliance could be shared with the Chippewa! His woman had special ways about her. She had seemed to have sensed that this alliance with her father would also benefit the man she loved.

"Shouldn't we get dressed, Lone Hawk?" Mariana said, already reaching for the dreadful breeches she had stolen from the trunk.

"Ay-uh," Lone Hawk grumbled, rising to slip his breechcloth on, then his moccasins and then his headband and feather. "We must go to my village. Today is an important one for my people—it is a new beginning. Their future will be free of worry. It is Lone Hawk's place to assure this for my people."

"I only hope that I don't disappoint you or your people," Mariana murmured, now fully dressed. She lifted the hairbrush and began drawing it through her hair, then her breath was momentarily snatched away when Lone Hawk took the brush from her and began brushing her hair for her.

"Your hair the color of flame is *mee-kah-wah-diz-ee*," Lone Hawk said thickly. "It will always be a fascination to me, Blazing Heart. Perhaps our children will have hair the color of the sunrise. That would make me happy."

Mariana trembled. "Children?" she said softly. "Lone Hawk, I . . . have . . . never thought much about children. Do you wish to have children soon?"

"Lone Hawk first wishes to have you all to himself for many sunrises and sleeps, then I will be happy to share you with many children," he said thickly. "Is that what would also make you happy, Blazing Heart?"

Mariana turned and eased into his arms. *"Ay-uh,"* she whispered. "Yes . . . yes! That would make me very happy, Lone Hawk."

Lone Hawk's eyes drank in the sight of her, then kissed her with a fierce, possessive heat. Mariana clung to him, feeling the ecstasy again weaving between them. And when his hand reached up beneath the suit jacket and again claimed her breast, she drew a shaky breath and savored this wondrous joy of being with him. . . .

The sound of horses neighing outside the wigwam drew Mariana and Lone Hawk quickly apart. They exchanged glances, then laughed softly.

"Seems your pony and my horse have taken a liking to each other," Mariana said, bending to get her hairbrush. "Shall we go outside and properly introduce them?"

The sound of shuffling horses' hooves made Lone Hawk's insides roll. His pony was reined. Mariana's horse was reined. They shouldn't be making such sounds unless they were being led away. . . .

"Way-nen-dush-win-ah-ow?" he grumbled, feeling foolish for having left his rifle outside when he had

392

carried Blazing Heart into the wigwam in haste to make love with her.

"What is it? What did you say?" Mariana whispered, seeing the worry in Lone Hawk's eyes . . . having heard it when he spoke.

Lone Hawk stepped in front of Mariana. "You stay here," he whispered. "Someone is out there. Lone Hawk must find out who."

But it was too late. A rifle barrel was suddenly thrust into the wigwam and then a whiskered face as a man stooped to enter. Lone Hawk stepped in front of Mariana to protect her.

"Well, what have we here?" the stranger said, sneering from Mariana to Lone Hawk. His gray eyes, beneath shaggy red eyebrows, danced with mirth as he stepped to Lone Hawk's side and saw the way Mariana was dressed. "Lordy be, is it a female, or ain't it?" he chuckled.

Lone Hawk eyed the rifle and the man's finger poised on its trigger, then the man. "What you want? Who are you?" he said thickly.

"Just happened along," the man said, lifting his shoulder into a casual shrug. "Just thought I'd swipe me a couple of mounts. Couple of beauties reined close by. Guess you two don't mind if'n I borrow them, eh?"

"You not a wise white man," Lone Hawk said, tightening his fingers into fists. "My village close. You will be easily found by my braves."

The man squinted his eyes, nudging Lone Hawk in the stomach with the barrel of his rifle. "Now it just don't seem that's goin to be allowed to happen," he laughed throatily. He bent his head back toward the door of the wigwam. "Hey, Jed! It's just as you

393

expected. It's that damn Injun and the red-haired wench you say he claims to be his."

Mariana's insides went suddenly cold. She and Lone Hawk exchanged quick glances. "Lone Hawk, I never had the chance to tell you . . ." she murmured, but her breath was stolen from her as were her words when Jed stepped into the wigwam.

She glanced from Jed's good arm to where the other sleeve dangled loosely, void of an arm.

Then she looked up into his whiskered face, his teeth yellow as he grinned menacingly toward her. She hadn't had a chance to tell Lone Hawk yet.

And now . . . what did Jed have planned for them? It couldn't be good, for he sorely hated them both!

"Just thought the pony looked familiar," Jed snickered, stepping further into the wigwam, which had become quite crowded. "And though I didn't recognize the horse, jest thought it might be yours, Mariana." He leaned closer to Mariana, the perspiration smell of him curling her nose. "Does your Papa know you're with this Injun again, eh?" His beaded eyes traveled over her. "No. Doubt that he does. Seems you had to use a disguise, this time, to leave Grand Portage."

"My Papa should've let you die," Mariana hissed, stepping boldly closer to Jed, speaking into his face. "When I was helping, I should've seen that the knife slipped. I should've cut your heart clean out of your chest!"

Lone Hawk grabbed Mariana's hand and swung her around to face him. "What is this you are saying?" he said hoarsely.

Mariana's eyes wavered. "Lone Hawk, every time I

started to tell you about Jed, something got in the way," she apologized. "You see, he got back to the trading post quite alive! I was even forced . . . to . . . to help mend his wounds! If I hadn't, he . . . he would have told Papa for sure about me being with you."

She glared over at Jed. "But he didn't," she said sourly. "Seems he had other plans for the both of us all along."

"My friend, George, and I. We're out lookin' for places to set traps this mornin' and to our surprise we happen along two fine and dandy reined mounts," Jed laughed. "And then a lone wigwam? Ain't every day an Injun separates himself from his people. It was too good a chance to pass by . . . this chance to torment an Injun and his playmate."

He threw his head back into a throaty laugh. "Seems ol' Jed lucked out!" he said. "It's not just any Injun, it's Lone Hawk. It just ain't any wench, it's Mariana! Two partners in crime."

Jed sobered. His eyes narrowed into two slits. "Well, lovebirds, seems Jed has plans for you," he growled. "I just might as well get to 'im now as later, whilst the opportunity is at hand."

He nodded toward the man still holding the rifle on Lone Hawk and Mariana. "George, let's get 'em out in the open," he ordered. "I knows of a place not so far from here where we can leave 'em to become a meal for some hungry bear."

Jed leaned into Lone Hawk's face. "You left me to die a slow death?" he snarled. "Well, seems I have the same planned for the both of you."

"You are the one who will be dead. Soon," Lone Hawk warned. "This time, you *will* die slowly. Lone

Hawk will cut pieces from your body, one limb at a time."

Jed paled. He turned and left the wigwam, growling something low beneath his breath. Mariana and Lone Hawk were forced from the wigwam by George, at gunpoint, then made to walk ahead of him and Jed after they mounted their horses, leading Lone Hawk's pony and Mariana's horse behind them.

"Lone Hawk, what can we do?" Mariana said in a harsh whisper. "Where are they taking us?"

"Do not be afraid," Lone Hawk reassured. "Men like these two white men make mistakes. We must be patient. Their fate is already written on the wind."

Mariana's insides quivered with fear. She could not be as confident as Lone Hawk that things were going to work out for them this time. She knew the depths of Jed's hate for them. Minus one arm, he always had a reminder of this hate!

The sun was now hot overhead. Mariana walked alongside Lone Hawk, across a meadow, the bees buzzing hungrily around daisies, a mourning dove cooing ominously from somewhere close by.

Sweat pouring profusely from Mariana's brow, the black, heavy clothes clinging to her dampened flesh, she moved onward, each step now becoming an effort. When Jed would cackle an evil sort of laugh from behind her, she would straighten her shoulders and back, determined to not let him know that she was laboring. She would not add to his enjoyment. If she could keep from it!

The flash and gleam of a waterfall could now be seen through the palisade of pine trees ahead. Mariana thirsted for a drink from the water. She wished to dunk her head into it, removing the filthy sweat from her brow.

She stumbled onward, the splash of water now so close by she could taste it . . . she could feel it.

And then she was standing beside the plushness of the waterfall as it tumbled in effervescent foamy sprays downward into a lake.

When they reached a steep incline, Mariana looked upward and saw the entrance of a cave that was positioned behind the waterfall.

Lone Hawk's soft chuckle caused Mariana suddenly to look his way. She questioned him with her eyes; he responded with a smug smile.

But the question was soon dismissed from her mind when Mariana felt the hard rifle barrel thrust into her ribs.

"Move on up to that cave overhead," Jed said, having dismounted from his horse, now walking directly behind Mariana and Lone Hawk. "Get on with the both of you!"

Her legs aching, her feet burning, Mariana obeyed. Lone Hawk placed his hand to her waist and helped her. And when they reached the cave and were forced inside, Mariana greeted its cool interior, yet feared what sort of plan Jed had for her and Lone Hawk, now that they were there.

"Give me that damn rifle," Jed snarled, grabbing the rifle from George. "I might have only one arm, but by damn, the trigger finger on the one hand never forgets how to work a gun.".

He positioned the rifle beneath his one arm, placing it so that his finger now rested on the trigger. "Tie 'em up, George," Jed commanded. "They're going to be bait tonight. Just let the damn animals come. They'll just get fatter for my traps."

Having brought several leather strippings from the saddlebag of his horse, George forced Lone Hawk to the floor of the cave, then bound both his ankles and his wrists.

Then he went to Mariana and did the same. When the chore was done, he stepped back beside Jed. "Are you sure this is what you want to do with 'em?" he said, kneading his brow. "Damn it, Jed, it's been a long time since I seen a woman so feisty and pretty." He went to Mariana and bent to his knee, jerking the tail of her coat up, getting a look at her breast. "It's a damn shame to let the animals have fun with 'er. I'd sure like to get my chance before she becomes food for some damn animal."

"You don't see so well, George," Jed grumbled. "She ain't worth spit. The Injun's been with 'er."

He nodded toward the cave entrance. "Let's get the hell outta here. We don't want no other Injun comin' along, seein' the horses. Our lives wouldn't be worth spit then."

George gave Mariana another lingering look, then shrugged and turned and left with Jed.

Mariana looked over at Lone Hawk with wild eyes. "Lone Hawk, what are . . . we . . . going to do . . . ?" she softly cried.

Lone Hawk stared toward the cave entrance. He was full of thoughts of Sitting Tall . . . of Neala. It was possible that Neala was ready to meet with Sitting Tall. She had spoken after their father's burial of how she ached to be with the man she loved. Hopefully, now would be the time! Lone Hawk felt that at least one of

398

them would come to the cave, to be alone with their thoughts. Lone Hawk was sure of it!

Turning to Mariana, he smiled toward her. "Your brother? He comes here often," he said softly. "We must hope that he will come soon. . . ."

Mariana tensed. She hadn't seen Sitting Tall since her escape from the Sioux village. She was still keeping hidden inside her heart the truth about Sitting Tall . . . the fact that he abducted her, then helped in releasing her.

If he did arrive and rescue her and Lone Hawk, and their eyes met, what would his thoughts be? She was willing to keep the secret. But he wouldn't know. In his awkwardness, might he reveal his schemes to Lone Hawk, not even meaning to . . . ?

"Do you really believe Sitting Tall will come?" Mariana asked, rolling over to her side to face Lone Hawk.

"*Ay-uh,*" Lone Hawk said dryly. He scooted on his side around to Mariana's back. His teeth began working with the bindings at her wrist. . . .

Chapter Thirty-Two

> It hammers at my heart the
> long night through, this want of
> you.
>
> —WRIGHT

Mourning doves cooed softly from somewhere close by in their hidden nests. The sun was casting its golden streamers through the canopy of trees overhead, reflecting into the lake alongside Sitting Tall's own lean reflection as he rested on his pony, awaiting Neala's arrival at the lake to get her morning jugs of water.

Sitting Tall had watched her from afar many times, wanting her . . . loving her.

Today he had decided he would no longer sit quietly by. He would go to her and make her understand his shortcomings.

He also needed her to help him through his loss . . . and needed her guidance in how to cope with his gain.

His father was now traveling the long path to the hereafter. The burial was now complete. Sitting Tall was now chief.

Hanging his head in his hand, Sitting Tall emitted a low wail of remorse. His father's spirit had drifted away from his lifeless body the very next day after Sitting Tall had helped Lone Hawk in the abduction of Blazing Heart.

It was as though Sitting Tall's father had died because of this white woman's absence from the village.

This side of his father would always puzzle Sitting Tall . . . the side that had so readily accepted the white woman as a friend!

Sitting Tall hadn't expected that. He had thought his father would admire Sitting Tall's cunning for the skills of abducting the white woman. He had thought his father would look upon her with a silent lust, then would cast her aside. Sitting Tall had known that his father would not want her sexually. But he had never expected his father to want her in any other capacity!

"Friends?" he murmured. "Father, why was she so important to you that you took your last breaths because of her? Or is Sitting Tall wrong?"

"Sitting Tall?"

Neala's soft voice stirred Sitting Tall from his troubled reverie. His head moved upward with a jerk. His heart pounded hard against his chest, seeing her dainty loveliness only a heartbeat away.

In her silent moccasins she had moved toward him, and he had not heard, though he had been waiting now since the early morning's rising sun for her.

Swinging himself from his saddle of blankets, Sitting Tall now stood before Neala, yet he dared not yet touch her. He was not sure of her feelings for him, whether or not she had chosen to forgive him for his neglect of her.

401

His eyelids were heavy over his fathomless, dark eyes. In his nervousness, his hands clasped and unclasped behind him.

Neala's pulse raced. She felt swallowed whole by her nervous heartbeats as Sitting Tall looked down upon her, his eyes revealing his love for her in their dark depths.

She longed to reach out and touch him. She longed to rush into his arms. Tears even threatened to spill from the corners of her eyes in her gladness to see him again.

Yet there was this nagging emptiness at the pit of her stomach when she recalled their last time together. If she forgave him, could he again be so thoughtless? Would he exchange her again for a jug of the white man's firewater?

So much of her cried out to him. She knew that he needed someone's guidance . . . someone's encouragement—or he just might never be the man that he had once been before the white man had introduced the firewater to him.

Neala placed her empty water jug down on the ground beside her. The fringes of her white doeskin dress rose and fell with the wind, her braided hair was sleekly black, with colorful satin bows tied at the ends of each.

Her face showed no signs of the bruises inflicted there by Jed Fenris. It was lovely . . . inviting . . . oh, so beautiful to Sitting Tall's feasting eyes!

"You have never come so close to my village of Chippewa before," Neala whispered, looking cautiously from side to side.

She again looked up into Sitting Tall's eyes, knowing

that she had already forgiven him. Deep within her was a peace that she had hoped to achieve when she was again with him. This smooth, warm feeling engulfing her was just what she had hoped to feel. Only now did she know for sure that she had truly forgiven him!

"Many more women will arrive soon for water for their own private dwellings!" Neala softly warned.

When she placed her hand to Sitting Tall's arm, a rush of rapture so keen swept through her that she felt near a swoon.

Yes, she still loved him just as much as before!

Sitting Tall's knees weakened when he felt the sweet softness of her hand against his flesh. But he squared his shoulders and practiced self-restraint—that self-restraint that had seemingly been lost to him after he had tasted the first of the white man's drink!

"Sitting Tall no care about other Chippewa squaws," he grumbled. His hands were trembling in his hesitation to touch her, yet he lifted them and placed them at her shoulders, touching her gently. "Only you are in my mind, Neala. Sitting Tall needs you. Please come with me to our secret cave. So much needs to be said."

Neala felt the magnetism of his eyes as he continued to look down at her. She had always felt this sensation with him, as though her inner self were being pulled into his. She had concluded long ago that this feeling was natural, because they shared a common love.

"Sitting Tall, since that dreadful day with Jed Fenris, I've . . . yet . . . to leave my village, except for water and wood," she said, paling at the thought of leaving the cocoon of her wigwam for any long period of time. "For a while, Neala had thought never to even come to the lake for water!"

Guilt pangs ate away at Sitting Tall's insides. He was responsible for Neala's fright. He lowered his eyes, now feeling only half a man in her presence.

Then his heart skipped a beat when he felt the softness of her arms as she crept into his embrace. He moved his gaze to meet hers as she looked up at him, then wrapped his arms about her and greedily hugged her.

"Neala," he whispered, placing his nose against her perfumed hair. "Sitting Tall never neglect you again. Neala, you . . . are . . . my life."

Low sobs rose from deep inside Neala as she clung to Sitting Tall. Her tears wet his bare chest. "Let us go to the cave," she softly cried. "Sitting Tall, Neala only half alive when not with you."

Sitting Tall eased her from his arms. "You will go with me?" he said thickly.

"*Ay-uh,*" Neala said, nodding. "But we must go now. Soon the other women will arrive. None know of you, Sitting Tall. Only . . . my brother and . . . and . . . his white woman."

More guilt pangs stabbed away at Sitting Tall's insides. It seemed that everything this day reminded him of his wrongdoings! He had gotten a savage thrill when abducting Blazing Heart! But he could not let Neala know that he had done this. Hopefully she would not find out from Blazing Heart. Hopefully Blazing Heart would not ever tell Lone Hawk!

Then he was reminded that he had not yet told Neala about the passing of Chief Black Cloud and that Sitting Tall was now chief! Would her emotions battle inside her? Would she be sad for Chief Black Cloud and glad for Sitting Tall? Surely she would realize that she would have a decision to make! Now that he was chief, he must have a woman at his side!

But he would tell her later. Once they reached the cave, they would share in everything. They would talk . . . they would make . . . love. . . .

Sitting Tall leaned a soft kiss to her lips. "Let us go," he said. "You can return to your water jugs later. Join me on my pony. We will ride together, Neala. It will be so good to have your body pressed against mine while we ride into the wind!"

Neala's insides tremored with ecstasy. When he drew his mouth away from hers, she placed her forefinger to his lips.

"Your breath is sweet like the rain," she said, smiling up at him. "In it there is no stench of white man's firewater. Sitting Tall, Neala . . . so . . . proud."

Squaring his shoulders, his face a mask of pride, Sitting Tall swept Neala up into his arms and sat her on his pony. He swung himself up behind her, then eased her on his lap.

"Neala . . . Neala . . ." he whispered, then held her tightly to him as he whirled his pony around, riding in the direction of the secret cave. . . .

"It is no use," Lone Hawk grumbled, scooting away from Mariana. "The white man secured the leather bindings too tight. My teeth cannot work the knots apart."

He scooted on his side until he was facing Mariana. "Lone Hawk failed you," he mumbled. "No white man should have been able to get away with this!"

Mariana so wanted to reach out to touch him, but her wrists ached where they were positioned behind her. "No man could go against the threat of a rifle pointed toward him," she tried to reassure him. "Lone Hawk, you cannot hold yourself responsible for this dilemma."

"Lone Hawk become careless!" he growled, moving to a sitting position, sitting awkwardly forward with his wrists bound behind him, his ankles throbbing where the leather bindings were cutting into his flesh. "Never should I have left my weapons outside the wigwam."

"And you wouldn't have, had I not come and disturbed your train of thought," Mariana said softly, wriggling until she was able to move to his side. "But, Lone Hawk, I had to come to you. My Papa . . ."

Mariana's eyes widened and she paled. "Oh, Lord," she softly cried. "I forgot my Papa!" She looked wildly over at Lone Hawk. "When he finds me gone he will surely come for me."

Lone Hawk laughed softly. "Seems he won't find us," he said. "This cave is hardly known by anyone."

Then he frowned. "Except now we know that Jed Fenris found it also," he snarled.

His eyes again lit up with amusement. "But also Sitting Tall knows about the cave," he softly chuckled. "If Jed Fenris had known that this was a special cave, shared often by blood brothers . . . he would never have left us here."

Looking toward the cave entrance, Lone Hawk worried to himself. It was one thing to try and encourage Mariana to believe that Sitting Tall might come. It was another thing to believe that the timing could be so right, and that he could actually expect Sitting Tall! Too much had happened in Sitting Tall's life of late to expect him to do anything normal!

"But what if Sitting Tall doesn't come?" Mariana said dryly. "Lone Hawk, do you think . . . a . . . bear will just happen by . . . and find us . . . ? Do you think we will die by such gruesome means?"

Lone Hawk glanced from Mariana to the cave entrance. "We must try to get out of here," he grumbled. "If we scoot slowly, we can at least get outside. Perhaps someone will happen along. Hopefully, a friend."

"Then you don't truly expect Sitting Tall?" Mariana asked, wincing when she tried to move her feet, causing the leather to cut more into the flesh at her ankles.

"One never knows about Sitting Tall," Lone Hawk said scornfully. "We must do what we can for ourselves, Blazing Heart. Perhaps once we are outside we can find a sharp rock with which to loosen our bindings. At least we . . . must . . . try."

Mariana followed Lone Hawk's lead. When he scooted, she scooted. When he stopped to rest on his back, she stopped to rest on her back. Her legs were raw where she had scooted. Her back ached. Her temples throbbed.

But again they scooted together. And as they got to the cave entrance, they looked up, stunned silent at Sitting Tall and Neala, suddenly there, looking down at them.

"*Ah-neen?*" Sitting Tall and Neala said in unison.

Neala fell to her knees beside Lone Hawk. Her

fingers trembled as she began struggling with the bindings at his wrists, while Sitting Tall knelt to loosen Mariana's.

"How did this happen?" Neala said in a rush of words. "Lone Hawk, who did this to you."

Lone Hawk sighed with relief when the leather bindings fell away from his wrists. He rubbed his raw flesh, eagerly waiting for his ankles to be freed.

Then he looked down at Neala, his eyes wavering. Should he speak the name Jed Fenris to her, what would be her reaction?

He glanced over at Sitting Tall. What, for that matter, would Sitting Tall's reactions be when he heard the name?

It appeared that Sitting Tall and Neala had made up their differences. Lone Hawk did not want to be the one to do anything that might interfere. If Neala loved Sitting Tall and wanted him, it was not for Lone Hawk to question!

"A trapper," Lone Hawk blurted, wriggling his toes as his ankles also became freed. "A trapper came across me and Blazing Heart in the forest. He caught us off guard. He led us here by gunpoint."

Mariana gave Lone Hawk a quick glance, then smiled to herself, understanding why he was not mentioning Jed Fenris's name in his sister's and Sitting Tall's presence. The name Jed Fenris seemed to stir all sorts of emotions in many people!

Then she slowly looked up into Sitting Tall's eyes, taking a lingering look at her brother, studying his handsome profile and the guarded look in his dark, fathomless eyes. Without the fancy paints on his face, there was much about him that she immediately liked. She could feel a kinship so keen it caused her heart to skip a beat. This Indian was her brother! And from the way he was looking back at her, it seemed as though he knew of their relationship. She glanced quickly over at Lone Hawk, wondering if he had told Sitting Tall.

Then she again moved her eyes to Sitting Tall, knowing there was no way she could let him know that she was going to keep their secret.

Unless she . . .

"Chief Black Cloud," she said, rising slowly to her feet. "And how is he?"

Sitting Tall rose to his full height, towering over Mariana. His muscles relaxed, his heart sang. Her not referring to Chief Black Cloud as Sitting Tall's father, in Sitting Tall's presence, had to mean that she was not going to reveal the full truth of the day of her abduction! He didn't know why, but he was full of gladness because she had chosen not to!

And then his eyes wavered. He looked past Blazing Heart, to Lone Hawk, and then to Neala. He had yet to speak of his father's passing to either of them. He had dreaded saying the words, for to say them made the knowledge even more painful inside his heart. Sitting Tall had dearly loved his father, though this might sometimes have been hard to tell from the things that Sitting Tall did!

But his love was true. He sorely missed his father. He sorely dreaded having to follow his father as chief, for everyone knew of the greatness of Chief Black Cloud.

Sitting Tall felt he had less than the skills required to . . . be chief.

"Chief Black Cloud . . . he . . . is no longer among his people as their powerful leader," Sitting Tall said, his eyes now locked with Neala's. "My father is traveling the long road to the hereafter. Sitting Tall . . . now . . . chief."

Neala gasped and placed her hands to her mouth. She looked at Sitting Tall in wonder.

Chapter Thirty-Three

*You are the white birch in the
sun's glow.*
—WAGSTAFF

"You are now *en-dah-yen,*" Lone Hawk said,
lowering Mariana to a great pile of furs and blankets
spread out beside the fire in his wigwam. "Home. Does
not it sound grand, Blazing Heart?"

Mariana was glad to be free of the men's clothes. She
had relished the swim with Lone Hawk in a stream
before arriving at his village. Her bare skin tingled with
aliveness where he was now touching her. His eyes
branded her bare flesh as he gazed down upon her. She
savored his copper sheen, revealed to her in his full
nudity.

"*En-dah-ye,*" she repeated after him. "Home. I have
so wanted this, Lone Hawk. Is it truly real? Am I here
with you, to stay? Are you sure you want me? The fact
that I am part Sioux . . ."

His hands gentle at her shoulders, Lone Hawk eased
her on downward until she was beneath him, his body

411

accepting the thrust of her breasts as he fully embraced her.

"Hush, my woman," he said huskily. "Let us no longer speak of your relationship to Chief Black Cloud. He is no longer among the living. Your attraction to the village of the Sioux is no more."

Mariana lowered her eyes. "It is so sad," she murmured. "I only met him to lose him."

"It is not a loss that should weigh heavy on your heart," Lone Hawk reassured her, lifting her chin with his forefinger, directing her gaze into his. "You satisfied your curiosity about your true father. It is *mee-eewh,* finished. Now your thoughts should only be on the wedding celebration soon to be shared with my people! Soon you will become my wife in every way! Tell me you are *gee-mee-nway-dum.*"

"And what did you just say in Chippewa?" Mariana asked softly, trying hard to edge sadness over Chief Black Cloud's death from her mind. She knew she must, for she could not again speak aloud of the remorse she felt to Lone Hawk. It was something that he did not want to have to share with her.

And she understood. It was well known how Lone Hawk's father and Sitting Tall's father's had been ardent enemies. Lone Hawk looked to Chief Black Cloud's death as a victory won! Now he hoped for another sort of victory . . . that of joining the Sioux and Chippewa in friendship, now that he and Sitting Tall had the power to do so!

"Lone Hawk asked if you are glad?" he said, lowering a brief kiss to her lips, his fingers absorbing the sweet flesh of her breasts.

"Ay-uh, I am *gee-mee-nway-dum,"* Mariana said,

412

softly giggling, enjoying learning the lesson of Lone Hawk's language. She would become an apt pupil with him as teacher. She had much to learn!

Lone Hawk leaned momentarily away from her, staring into the flames of the fire in his firespace. "But first, tomorrow something else must be done," he growled.

Mariana crept to her knees and bent over him, twining her arms about his neck. "And what is it you are speaking of?" she asked, looking adoringly up at him, yet flinching when seeing his sudden mask of hate.

"Jed Fenris," Lone Hawk said, a hiss in his words. "Tomorrow his life will end. Lone Hawk will take many warriors and snuff the life from the wicked trappers. Lone Hawk should have rid the earth of the filthy trapper Jed Fenris long ago. The trapper spreads his vermin everywhere he goes."

Lone Hawk picked up a twig and angrily snapped it in two. "Even one-armed, Jed Fenris practices his evil ways!" he grumbled.

He turned his eyes toward Mariana. A smug smile touched his lips as he showed her the two pieces of wood. "But tomorrow, Jed Fenris will be like this twig," he laughed. "Broken."

Mariana leaned away from Lone Hawk. A shiver coursed across her flesh. Then she swept into his arms as he tossed the twigs aside, and she found that his mood could change as quickly as a chameleon changes colors, for he was all sweetness and gentleness as he again lowered her to the bed he had spread for them upon their first arrival at the wigwam.

"My love . . . my woman . . ." Lone Hawk whispered, weaving his fingers through her hair, drawing her to his lips to kiss her. "Tonight we celebrate in private! Let us make love many times tonight, Blazing Heart. Let us place all sadnesses . . . all uglinesses . . . behind us."

As Mariana twined her arms about his neck, she had a sudden memory that, indeed, was ugly. Her father! When he arrived back at the trading post with the preacher and she was not there, what would he do? Would he give up? Or would he come for her?

It seemed that peace was not yet achieved in her heart! She would fear the wrath of Everett Fowler, forever, it seemed. . . .

But as Lone Hawk so sensually kissed her, filling her with a passion she could not deny, she was able to cast worries of her father aside, at least for the moment. She wouldn't even think of how Jed Fenris would die on the morrow. For now, there were only these delicious feelings swimming around inside her.

She clung to Lone Hawk as he entered her, filling her with his magnificent hardness. She crept her legs about him and locked them together at her ankles.

A hazy sort of joy was ebbing its way inside her. She sighed . . . she moaned. And then his lips sealed all her wondrous cries as he kissed her with a hunger fed by her returned kisses . . . her returned rapture.

They rode together as though they were traveling on a great stallion, rising . . . falling . . . cresting. . . .

And then their pleasure was reached, their sighs intertwining, their bodies sensually quaking. . . .

*   *   *

414

"Sitting Tall, I am so sorry about your father," Neala softly said as Sitting Tall led her down to the cave floor. "It happened so suddenly."

Sitting Tall placed his forefinger to her lips, sealing them of further words. "We will not speak of losses tonight," he said thickly. "Let us speak of what we have gained. Neala, I so feared that you would never wish to be with me again. And now that you are, I want to think of nothing else."

When his fingers began raising her doeskin dress, Neala tensed. Her eyes widened. She was remembering another man . . . another man's hands . . . another man's beady eyes leering down at her as she was stripped of her dress.

She could even still feel how he had so roughly penetrated her, as though she was going to be ripped apart.

Splaying her fingers to Sitting Tall's bare chest, she began shoving him away from her. "No . . ." she softly cried, turning her face even away from his kiss. "I can't, Sitting Tall. I . . . can't. . . ."

Sitting Tall rose away from her, his heart thundering against his ribs. His eyes wavered as he watched her rise and edge away from him.

"What are you doing, Neala?" he gasped, reaching his hand out to her. "Why are . . . you . . . denying me?"

"It is too soon," she sobbed, turning her eyes from him. "When I think of that filthy trapper. . . ."

A stabbing pain entered Sitting Tall's breast. He doubled his hands into tight fists, silently cursing himself even more than the trapper. For it was Sitting

Tall's fault more than anyone else's. . . .

Going to Neala, he placed his hands to her waist and turned her to face him. "Let me help erase the bad memory from your mind," he whispered. "It must be done, Neala, now, or you may never be able to. Neala, you must learn to forget. It is necessary to forget quickly. For Sitting Tall has come for you, to take you back to the Sioux village, to rule at my side. Neala, you must forget. You must return with me. Without you. . . ."

Neala lifted her eyes slowly upward, her will bending beneath the pleading in Sitting Tall's eyes. She knew that she meant even more to Sitting Tall than most squaws did to their men. He looked to her as a means of escaping the sort of existence he had found in the white man's firewater. She understood. She nodded her head.

"I am sorry, Sitting Tall, if I for one moment turned away from you," she whispered, placing her hand to his smooth copper cheek.

She looked toward the cave floor, then back at Sitting Tall. *"Ay-uh.* Now is the time for you to make love to me. *Ay-uh,* then I shall go with you. But if your people should turn their backs on me, a Chippewa, what . . . then . . . ?"

"Sitting Tall is now their leader," he said hoarsely. "If Sitting Tall brings a Chippewa maiden to rule at his side, Sitting Tall's people will not question it." He leaned closer into her face. "You will come? We can enter my village together? You will soon become my wife?"

Neala thrust herself into his embrace. She sobbed against his bare chest. *"Ay-uh,* Neala will be your wife," she whispered. "Soon, Sitting Tall. Soon."

Their embrace was long and sweet. . . .

The fire was now only glowing embers in the firespace next to where Mariana lay, snuggled beneath the furs. Lone Hawk had turned his back to her in his sleep and peacefully dozed.

Mariana's eyes drifted shut, her breathing became shallow, her insides still aglow from the aftermath of lovemaking. Her time with Lone Hawk had never been as sweet . . . as fulfilling. She reveled in thoughts of being with him forever, to share such nights of romance . . . such nights of peace. . . .

Sighing, she felt herself drifting somewhere between sleep and waking. She curled to a fetal position, feeling the heat of the embers on her face, enjoying it, for outside the wind howled as if a storm was threatening to break from the heavens.

An occasional clap of thunder rumbled the ground beneath Mariana. A bolt of lightning would occasionally lighten the wigwam through the buckskin entrance flap as it flipped in the wind.

But still Mariana snuggled . . . now lightly snoozing. She was having dreams of tiny children with copper skin running around, laughing . . . some clinging to her skirt, calling her Mama, others chasing after Lone Hawk, calling him Papa! They were beautiful Indian children, all with the traits of their lovely, wonderful father!

A shuffling of feet threatened Mariana's pleasant dream. She tossed from one side to the other, forcing her eyelids to stay shut because she wished to be longer

417

with these children of her dreams.

But she was suddenly jolted from her sleep when a hand was roughly clasped over her mouth, another dragging her from the covers of furs.

Totally nude, Mariana looked wildly about her. She reached out with her hand, trying to hit the person behind her who was abducting her, yet she found only space. She didn't think it was Jed Fenris, for he was not strong enough with his one arm to do this dreadful deed. But perhaps his partner, George?

Another hand shoved a blanket about her, then started forcing her from the wigwam. A lurid flash of lightning lighted the sky. Mariana turned with a start and gasped against the clasped hand as she saw the bold features of her Papa looking down upon her. Everett Fowler had come to claim his daughter! He had eluded all the Chippewa braves . . . had waited until sleep had come to the Chippewa village.

Trying to shake herself free, Mariana only succeeded in causing him to hold more firmly against her mouth and her wrist, which now he squeezed as he led her away from the village and into the darkness of the forest.

Stumbling barefoot over briars and sharp pointed sticks, Mariana winced. She tried to look back in the direction of the wigwam where Lone Hawk still slept, but then even that was taken from her sight as she was led farther and farther away until she saw several men and horses waiting, lightning flashes illuminating their faces.

When she saw the leering face of Eugene South looking toward her, Mariana flinched as though she'd been shot. She knew what was intended for her. Her

Papa had gotten the preacher and he was determined to see that the preacher was used.

"Mariana, damn it, what'd you think you were doing, going to that Indian like that?" Everett growled, removing his hand from her mouth, now that they were far enough away from the Chippewa village.

He nodded toward the waiting men. "What do you think the men are thinkin' of me now? My own daughter choosin' to live the life of a savage? Damn it, I should've left you there, to wallow in their filth and grime! At least the men wouldn't have had to see you taken from the village like you were some sort of savage yourself!"

Mariana clutched the blanket more snugly about her, shaking from anger and humiliation. Her eyes flashed as she looked up at her father.

"Papa, why didn't you leave me with Lone Hawk?" she hissed. "That's where I want to be!"

"It ain't best for you, Mariana," Everett said, going to his horse, removing a dress from his saddlebag.

He went to Mariana and thrust the dress into her hands. He nodded toward a thick stand of bushes. "Go over there and get dressed. You're returnin' home with me, Mariana, whether or not you like it. The preacher's waitin'."

"Papa, I want to marry Lone Hawk," Mariana cried, clutching the dress to her breast. "Why can't you understand that is what I wish? My life with you at the trading post is over."

She lifted her chin haughtily toward Eugene South. "He was never anything to me. And he never will be. I refuse to marry him. You can't make me."

Everett laughed throatily. He placed his hands on

419

his hips and smiled smugly down at Mariana. "We'll see about that," he smirked.

A slow rain began to fall, chilling Mariana. She glared at her father then rushed behind the bushes and hurried into her dress.

Still barefoot, her arms bare, she went to the horse assigned her and mounted it. "Papa, no matter what you say, I won't marry Eugene," she said flatly.

Taking the reins, she flicked them. She shouted to the horse and sank her heels into its flanks and began riding away from her father and the men who gaped openly after her. She ducked her head low, knowing the village wasn't all that far behind her. If she could only get close enough to shout for Lone Hawk!

She tensed when she heard hoofbeats drawing suddenly close behind her. She screamed when she saw her father suddenly there beside her, grabbing her horse's reins.

As her horse came to a quick halt, Mariana was thrown. Landing in a heap on the ground, crying out as her head hit the low-hanging limb of a tree, she felt darkness engulfing her as unconsciousness swept over her. . . .

Everett swung himself down from his horse. He stood over Mariana, his fists on his hips. "Like I said, daughter, you're going to marry Eugene South," he said darkly.

Chapter Thirty-Four

I love your hair when the strands enmesh your kisses against my face.

—WILCOX

Standing before a mirror in her bedroom, Mariana looked at her reflection, turning from side to side, melancholia sweeping through her. The last time she had seen this wedding dress her Mama had modeled it for her. As Mariana looked at herself, she felt as though she was looking at the image of her Mama, she so closely resembled her, especially in the wedding dress.

Smoothing her hands down the gentle lines of the dress, Mariana admired its loveliness, though she had already decided that she would never speak the words required that would make her Eugene South's bride. She was being forced to stand with him before a preacher. But a preacher surely would not seal their union with final words, if the words required of *her* were not spoken!

Smiling smugly, she continued to admire the dress. Yellowed with age, with its triple layers of white silk and Alençon lace, its embroidered bodice, pouf-sleeves, and high, ruffled neckline, it was, perhaps, the most lovely bridal dress in the world! Surely her Mama had worn it with an anxious heart, knowing how lovely she had looked for the man she was to marry. But her Mama had *wanted* to marry Everett Fowler! Mariana did not want to marry Eugene South!

Swinging around, not wanting to see any more of the dress or herself, Mariana began to pace. She kept looking toward the door, knowing that her Papa would arrive at any moment now to escort her to the living room, which had been decorated with wild flowers . . . where the preacher would be waiting. . . .

Looking toward the ceiling, her hair tumbling brilliantly down her back, in bright contrast with the white of her dress, Mariana softly cried. "Lone Hawk, surely you won't let this happen," she whispered. "Can't you please come and rescue me? Papa will force the words from me that will make Eugene South my husband. I know it!"

A knock on the door made Mariana's insides grow tight. Her breath came in low rasps and she bit her lip nervously.

"Mariana? Daughter?" Everett said in his deep voice. "Time's a wastin'. You can't put it off any longer. Come on out here. The preacher's been made to wait long enough. He must get back to Grand Marais. Today!"

Stubbornly folding her arms across her chest, Mariana began tapping her toe, the black leather of her dress shoes peeking out from beneath the folds of her long skirt. She would not answer her Papa. She would not go to the door. He would have to drag her from the room. What would the preacher then think? Would he actually marry a woman to a man knowing she was being forced? If the preacher was a man of God, surely his conscience wouldn't let him!

The door jerked open. Everett, dressed impeccably in a dark suit with ruffles at his throat and sleeves, his face neatly shaved, his hair cut and hanging only halfway to his shoulders, entered the room.

He glowered down at Mariana, then his mood momentarily softened at seeing how beautiful she looked. His insides tremored with remembrance of another time . . . another bride!

If he only closed his eyes he could remember that day he had looked upon Jewel's loveliness in this same dress for the first time. She had, moments later, given herself to him, fully.

It was as though he was going back in time, as though he was looking at Jewel again.

But this wasn't Jewel. This was his daughter.

Yet, she . . . wasn't even his daughter. She was an Indian's daughter.

Oh, if he could only forget the ugly truth of how she had been born into the world! He had willingly accepted her as his. She had accepted him as her father. Until the day she had discovered the truth.

"Daughter, don't make me carry you out there and forcibly stand you before the preacher," he said dryly, forcing his thoughts elsewhere. "Why are you makin' this so hard on everyone concerned? You know that I do this for your own good. You'd never be happy livin' the life of a savage! You're used to comforts, daughter. No Indian heathen can give you comforts!"

423

Mariana clasped her hands behind her. It took all the will power she could muster to not slap her Papa! It was hard to stand by and let him talk so disgustingly of the man she loved . . . of his people!

Oh, how little Everett Fowler knew! If he knew life, as he professed, he would know that he was totally wrong to look at Indians as something to step on! All the Indians she knew, even Sitting Tall, with his weaknesses, were better than Everett Fowler, in every respect!

But because he had raised her as his daughter, when all along he had known that her father was an Indian, Mariana held her temper at bay. "Papa, as I have said, over and over again," she said softly. "I will not marry Eugene South. When it is time for me to say the words, I . . . shall . . . not."

"Then your father will say them *for* you," Everett said, taking her by an elbow, forcing her toward the door. "You *are* going to marry Eugene, Mariana. From this day forth you will be a dutiful *wife* to him!"

Mariana tried to jerk her arm away. "And what do you think Lone Hawk is going to do about this?" she hissed. "You can expect him no longer to behave gently toward you or the trading post should I be forced to marry Eugene."

"So you think your Indian friend will go on the warpath?" Everett chuckled, his eyes twinkling as he looked down at Mariana. "No. I doubt that. All Indians depend too much on the white man's trade goods now. They couldn't exist without 'em daughter."

"They got along just fine before the white man came," Mariana softly argued, stepping out into the living room, seeing Eugene and the preacher waiting.

"That was then," Everett grumbled, guiding her to stand beside Eugene. "This is now."

When Eugene turned and looked down at her, Mariana wanted to scratch his eyes out. He was already seeing her as his bride! She could see the hungry lust in his eyes. He was thinking about later, when they would be alone! Oh, how could she bear it?

The room was quiet. No one else was in attendance. Only the preacher . . . Eugene . . . Everett . . . and Mariana.

Mariana clenched her teeth as her father handed her a bridal bouquet made from wild roses tied together with a pink satin ribbon. She turned and glowered at him and forced them back into his hands.

"It was enough that I was made to wear Mama's wedding dress," she whispered harshly. "I will not make any more mockery of this that you do by carrying flowers as a true bride would be proud to do."

She stood on tiptoe and leaned her face up into her father's. "How can you do this to me, Papa? How?"

Mariana turned with a start and looked toward the door that separated the living quarters from the trading post store. She heard a loud commotion coming from the store, as though someone was there knocking things from the shelves.

Everett's gaze turned to the door, as did Eugene's just in time to see Lone Hawk jerk the door open and enter the room, a rifle poised before him, ready for firing.

Mariana's heart seemed to do a somersault when she saw him, so glad was she that he had come in time. Then she gasped as she looked past him and saw the store filled with many more Chippewa braves and then

425

the emptied shelves, with everything now on the floor. Why . . . ?

His shoulders squared and his chin lifted haughtily, Lone Hawk moved with dignity across the room and pointed the rifle into Everett Fowler's face.

"You steal my woman from my dwelling?" he said sharply. "White man, do you wish to know the wrath of Lone Hawk for such a deed?"

Everett paled and took a step backwards. He swallowed hard. "Lone Hawk, you don't know what you're doing," he said hoarsely, dropping the bridal bouquet to the floor. "Such actions as this will mean punishment for your people. Do you wish to see them harmed? If I must, I will send many white men to your village and destroy it and your people."

Lone Hawk emitted a low growl, thrusting the barrel of the rifle into Everett's gut. "My braves are many," he growled. "Even now they surround your fort. One word from me and they would destroy *your* village and people. White man, do you wish this to be? Or do you take back your threats against my people? And you understand that your daughter is now mine? Do you understand?"

Everett nervously nodded. He glanced down at the rifle, then back up, into Lone Hawk's face. "Yes. I understand," he stammered.

"Your decision is *nee-bwah-kah,*" Lone Hawk chuckled, edging back away from Everett. *"Ay-uh,* your decision is wise."

He glanced over at Mariana. Their eyes met, she returning his gaze openly, fearlessly, lovingly.

Then Lone Hawk's insides rippled sensuously as he took in her loveliness in the white woman's fancy dress.

426

It seemed to be a special sort of dress. Blazing Heart's delicate cheekbones were blooming with color. Her eyes were wide and innocently watching him, ah, this day even more the color of the sky and the rippling rivers! And when she began moving toward him, how strangely her dress rustled!

"Lone Hawk," Mariana said, wondrously happy. "Thank God you have come."

She glanced toward the preacher, seeing his mouth agape, his face pale, and his green eyes bulging in a mixture of awe and fear over what was transpiring here.

Then she looked at Eugene, seeing his shoulders were slumped and defeat written in his pale eyes.

Then she looked at her father, and smiled.

"Mariana, you shouldn't do this," Everett said thickly. "You'll be sorry."

Mariana swept to Lone Hawk's side and clutched onto his arm. "Papa, didn't I tell you that Lone Hawk wouldn't allow this to happen?" she said softly. "Now accept the fact that it is he I love. Not Eugene. Things will be much easier for all of us."

Everett's face darkened. His fingers tightened into fists. "Lone Hawk, you'll pay for this," he threatened.

Then his breath was knocked from him when Lone Hawk thrust the blunt end of his rifle forcefully into his chest.

"You don't listen well, white man," Lone Hawk said icily. "*You* will pay dearly if you ever again try and interfere in Blazing Heart's life. My people are peace-loving people. But they can be pushed so far. There will be a war of wars between the white man and the Chippewa should the white man try to stop Lone Hawk from taking Blazing Heart back to his village to be his woman!"

Everett moaned, clutching his chest. He teetered, then forced himself to stand erect again. He glared from Mariana to Lone Hawk, then back to Mariana.

"So you are now called by the name Blazing Heart?" he snarled. "Mariana, I should have sent you back to your true father the day you were born. You belong with Indians."

His eyes wavered. "I'll never try and contact you again."

He waved his hand in the air. "Go. Get out of here. It makes no difference to me, anyhow. You've never been my daughter. I was a damn fool for even behaving as though you were."

His words stung Mariana's heart. Though she didn't want to, she was recalling those times when she was a small child riding his knee, laughing, too innocent then to know what sort of man he truly was. He had been everything to her! He was her Papa! He had been more special than all other men she had ever known.

And now? It seemed they were no longer anything to each other. All special feelings had died . . . long ago.

Yet she wanted to run to him. Hug him just one more time. Tell him that she was sorry for all the sadness she had brought to his life!

But Lone Hawk circled her waist possessively with his arm, and she knew where she belonged.

Looking adoringly up into his eyes, Mariana smiled. "Lone Hawk, please take me away from here," she murmured. "If you had not come when you did, I would have been married to Eugene."

428

Lone Hawk's eyes widened. He glanced over at Eugene, then at the man standing behind him. "The stranger in this room is the preacher you told me about?" he said hoarsely.

Mariana's eyelashes fluttered, then she laughed softly. "You didn't even know, did you?" she said.

"Gee-kan-dan?" Lone Hawk said, lifting his eyebrow quizzically. "Know what?"

"That you interrupted a wedding," Mariana giggled. "You didn't even know when you came in here that it was a wedding ready to be performed, did you?"

"Gah-ween, no," Lone Hawk grumbled, his eyes growing darker as his anger once again flared. "Lone Hawk come to first destroy your father's store, to prove to him that his wares are no longer important to my people. Then Lone Hawk come to get you."

A smile lifted his lips as he again looked toward the preacher. "He is a strange-looking sort of shaman," he laughed.

Then he placed his arm even more firmly about Mariana's waist. *"Gee-mah-gi-ung-ah-shig-wah,"* he said. "We will leave preacher to your father and Eugene South!"

Mariana walked proudly beside Lone Hawk toward the door, then stopped with him as he turned and gave Everett Fowler another angry stare.

"White man, should you ever again enter the village of the Chippewa uninvited, you will be dead," Lone Hawk warned. "And all of those who accompany you. Hear me good, white man. What I say is true!"

A cold shiver coursed across Mariana's flesh, hearing the savagery of Lone Hawk's words. But then she felt a sweep of victory wash through her as she saw how Lone Hawk's words had humbled her father. Never had she seen him humbled before anyone before! He had always been the powerful one ... the one in authority! He had finally met his match ... and this man who could make Everett Fowler bend to his knees was going to be Mariana's husband!

Lifting the skirt of her wedding dress, she left the trading post lodge with Lone Hawk. She gasped when she looked about her and saw the crowd of Chippewa braves perched threateningly on their ponies, bows and arrows readied by some, rifles by others.

Lone Hawk's threats were real. Hopefully, Everett Fowler would understand this!

"Lone Hawk brought you pony," he said, guiding her toward a black and white spotted pony standing next to his own.

He went to the pony and showed Mariana a leather bag that hung at its side.

"In this you will find appropriate Chippewa attire," he said flatly. "We will travel a while then make camp. You will then remove the white woman's dress and burn it, then exchange it for the Chippewa dress!"

Mariana's insides splashed cold. Her hands went over the softness of the dress, touching the lace, as though she was touching her Mama.

"No," she gasped. "I can never burn this dress. It's a special dress, Lone Hawk."

Lone Hawk's gaze traveled over the dress, again touched by its beauty. "Why special?" he said, cocking an eyebrow.

"It was ... my ... Mama's," Mariana said, casting her eyes downward. "It was special to my Mama."

Her eyes shot upward. "I wish to keep this one

remembrance of my Mama with me forever, Lone Hawk," she said softly. "Please understand?"

Knowing that he was thrusting her so soon into an entirely different sort of world, and understanding her need to cling to at least one thing from her past world, Lone Hawk nodded.

"You can keep it," he said softly. "But after today, you can never wear it again."

Mariana smiled radiantly up at him. "Thank you, Lone Hawk," she murmured. "And, no. I wouldn't want to wear it. It is not the sort of wedding dress I would want to wear to our wedding."

Placing his hands to her waist, Lone Hawk lifted her up onto her pony. "You will have special Chippewa dress for wedding," he said thickly. "Tomorrow, Blazing Heart. You will be totally mine tomorrow."

Mariana's insides curled with warmth . . with happiness. She didn't even give the trading post lodge another glance as she rode away from it, away from the fort, into the forest. . . .

Chapter Thirty-Five

> *I want you more than any
> rhyme or reason . . . I want you,
> want you, want you, all the while.*
> —GILLOM

The campfire burned softly, the sky was dotted with stars overhead, the air had a touch of coolness about it. Mariana lifted her arms as Lone Hawk helped her remove her mother's dress, in awe of him anew, of his powers not only as a man who had captured her heart, but also as a man who could fill other men's hearts with dread.

When she was with him, she always saw only the gentle side of his nature. Yet there were now two times that she had seen him differently. Knowing that he could be fierce didn't frighten her. It thrilled her. She liked knowing that she had chosen a man who possessed both gentleness and strength.

Now totally free of the dress and the soft, frilly finery that she had worn beneath it, Mariana was not bashful beneath Lone Hawk's heated gaze. She even watched him as he removed his breechcloth, revealing to her his readiness to again share with her moments of sensual pleasure, before they rode on to his village, where again his duties of chief would take precedence over even her.

But their wedding day would be hers. His and hers.

What a thrill coursed through Mariana to know that soon she would be able to shout to the sky that she was Lone Hawk's wife! She had waited so long. She had gone through hell, it seemed, to finally reach this point in her life, when she would be joined with the man she dearly loved.

The rustling in the leaves overhead caused Mariana to tense. By instinct she covered her breasts and looked wildly about her, then she felt Lone Hawk's strong arms as he swept her against his hard frame.

"You are afraid?" he said, commanding her eyes to his as he looked possessively down at her.

"We are out in the open for anyone to see," she murmured. "I would have been happier had you offered some sort of shelter, Lone Hawk."

"The sky is our roof, the ground our floor, and I have prepared a bed of blankets," Lone Hawk said, lowering his lips to rain kisses across the gentle lines of her face. "It is good to share you with nature, Blazing Heart. Don't you hear the spirits of the forest whisper your name?"

Mariana giggled. She relaxed against him. "I believe I hear the rustle of the wind through the trees," she said. "That is all, Lone Hawk."

"Then you hear the spirits as I hear them," Lone Hawk said, his fingers causing fires along her flesh as he moved his hand to her breast.

Lowering his lips, he flicked his tongue about the

433

breast, causing its nipple to tighten and Mariana to moan softly.

Yet her worries would not so easily be left behind her. "But, Lone Hawk, should my Papa gather together some men and come after us . . ." she whispered, her face flushing with building passion.

"Did you not see my many braves left stationed close by the trading post?" he said thickly, now easing Mariana to the blankets beside the fire. "They will stay one sleep, then return to the village of Chippewa. If your father does not leave the trading post by then, while his anger is so intense, then Lone Hawk does not expect him to come at all. Everett Fowler knew that Lone Hawk spoke truth when making threats to him. He does not hunger for war. He has given you up, Blazing Heart. He has given you to Lone Hawk."

"I so happily come with you," Mariana sighed, weakening with desire as Lone Hawk's tongue now danced along her body.

Then their bodies entwined as Lone Hawk placed his hardness inside her. He came to her, thrusting deeply. As he kissed her, his mouth was soft and passionate, his hands were cupping her buttocks, drawing her closer to him.

Mariana's body fused with Lone Hawk's as he molded her closely to him. All mysteries of their pasts were being woven together and cast aside, their future bright and full of hope.

Feeling the hunger building in Lone Hawk's kiss, Mariana twined her arms about his neck and lifted her legs about his waist. She was being consumed with rapture. It even seemed more intense because they were sharing it openly.

Somewhere close by an owl hooted. The whipporwill that Mariana had so often heard was again singing its repeated song. Mariana felt as one with nature . . . and she now understood Lone Hawk's feelings when he spoke of spirits of the forest. She felt as though she was a part of the forest. She knew at this moment that she did belong.

An euphoria filled her entire being as Lone Hawk drew his lips from her mouth and instead placed them to her breast. She closed her eyes as the warmth of his tongue flicked and played the nipple into an even greater tautness.

And again his lips moved to her mouth. His tongue brushed her lips lightly, his hands molding and kneading her breasts as he moved with more deliberation inside her, his quick, sure movements setting her afire.

Lone Hawk then cradled her close, placing his cheek against hers. His breath was hot as he spoke into her ear.

"Neen ee-quay," he said huskily. "My Bis-kah-ko-nay-gee-day."

Mariana was quickly learning his Chippewa words. She especially knew when he had spoken her name, Blazing Heart, in Chippewa. And she loved the way he said "my woman" in Chippewa.

"Neen ee-nee-nee," she whispered, her fingers caressing the corded muscles at his back.

She was proud to be able to say "my man" back to him in the Chippewa language. Soon she would know all of his Chippewa words!

"Gee-zah-gi-ee-nay?" Lone Hawk whispered, his tongue tasting the flesh of her neck, his lips kissing the

435

delicate line of her throat.

"Ay-uh," Mariana whispered, then moaned softly as she felt the intense joy of release fill her, as though effervescent waves were splashing throughout her, totally warming her insides.

Mariana breathed hard as she felt his body tightening, then tremoring with the same sort of release she had just been a witness to. They were in tune with each other, in body, as well as in mind. They were one. . . .

And when they both had regained their breath and had drawn apart, Mariana laughed softly as he gave her the leather bag in which she would find her Chippewa dress. He seemed eager to see her dressed as an Indian squaw. She knew that he would be happier if she totally discarded the wedding dress! It would be a true test of her commitment!

Though her heart ached, and recalling that he had said that she could keep the wedding dress, Mariana wanted to prove to him that he was all that was important to her.

Reaching for the wedding dress, feeling its softness against her fingers, flashes of her mother wearing it so intense in her mind's eye, Mariana hesitated a moment, then, feeling wondering eyes watching her, she tossed her Mama's dress into the fire.

"You do not want the dress?" Lone Hawk said, moving to his haunches beside her, his breechcloth on, his headband back in place about his hair, his eagle feathers now numbering two.

Mariana moved to her knees before him. She touched his cheeks gently, then kissed him.

"You do not wish for me to have the dress," she murmured, pulling away from him, to see his expres-

436

sion. "I do this to make you happy."

Lone Hawk beamed. He picked up the doeskin dress and thrust it into Mariana's hands. "You make me happy," he said huskily. "Over and over again you make me happy. My Blazing Heart always knows just how to make my heart sing."

Mariana smiled contentedly up at Lone Hawk. She rose to her feet and worked the doeskin dress over her head, her eyes wavering when she looked into the fire and saw the remains of the dress as melting away right before her eyes. The lace was sizzling. Then like lightning flashing, it was consumed immediately into flames.

"You sorry?" Lone Hawk asked, moving to his feet. He drew her into his arms and wove his fingers through her hair. "Many Chippewa dresses will take the place of that one you just burned. You will see. All dresses of my people will become special to you. Not only one."

"I know," Mariana sighed, clinging.

Then she tensed and something cold grabbed her at the pit of her stomach. She heard the crackling of a twig close by and the nervous neighing of her reined pony, answered by Lone Hawk's.

With speed in his steps, Lone Hawk grabbed Mariana and thrust her to the ground beside him. As they both turned their eyes in the direction of the sound of crushed leaves, the campfire's glow lighted two faces. Jed Fenris . . . and his friend George!

"Lord!" Mariana gasped, seeing the shine of their drawn pistols and realizing that her abduction by her father had postponed Lone Hawk's decision to seek Jed Fenris and his friend out and to kill them.

And now? Was it too late? Would Jed Fenris finish

what he had started when he left her and Lone Hawk at the cave?

Fear grabbed at her heart.

Lone Hawk reached for his rifle which lay close to the spread blankets. He aimed and fired. Jed Fenris fell screaming to the ground as he dropped his firearm and began clutching at his stomach.

The other man's eyes grew wildly open and he emitted a low, scratchy sort of gurgle as he also dropped his firearm and plunged forward, crashing to the ground on his stomach. An arrow was protruding from his back.

Sitting Tall stepped out into the open, clasping onto a large, fancy bow, a quiver of arrows at his back. Pride showed in his dark eyes as he looked from Jed Fenris to George. Both were now lying still. Both were dead.

Then he smiled from Lone Hawk to Mariana.

"Sitting Tall just happened along," he said thickly. "The campfire drew my attention. Then the two men crouching close by in the bushes looked suspicious. I left my pony behind and came to investigate. Sitting Tall arrive just in time, Lone Hawk."

Lone Hawk thrust his rifle aside and went to Sitting Tall. He fondly embraced him. "My friend," he said thickly. *"Mee-gway-chee-wahn-dum*. Thank you, Sitting Tall."

Sitting Tall dropped his arrow and fondly returned the embrace. He became immediately choked with emotion. He felt the strength of Lone Hawk's embrace. He heard the sincerity of his words! Perhaps *this* deed performed for Lone Hawk and his woman would be the deed to bring them totally together again as friends! Sitting Tall felt that he was surely avenged in Lone

Hawk's eyes now.

Lone Hawk drew away from Sitting Tall, still clasping his hands to his shoulders. "You just happened along?" he said hoarsely.

"Sitting Tall on his way to speak with you, Lone Hawk," Sitting Tall said, lowering his eyes. Then he raised his eyes quickly upward and met Lone Hawk's steady gaze. "You see, it is best that you know your sister is now in my village. She is now my wife."

Lone Hawk dropped his hands away from Sitting Tall. His jaw tightened. "So quickly?" he said dryly.

"It is best," Sitting Tall said, then glanced over at Mariana, then back to Lone Hawk. "It is both my wish and your sister's to have your blessing, Lone Hawk."

Sitting Tall clasped his hands to Lone Hawk's shoulders. "It is both my wish and your sister's to have council with you, Lone Hawk, to bring our two peoples together, as one. It is now possible, is it not? You are now chief, Sitting Tall now chief! Everything is possible between us, is it not?"

Sitting Tall's eyes wavered. "You do forgive Sitting Tall for past wrongful deeds?" he asked cautiously. "Sitting Tall never drink the white man's firewater again. I now understand that it controls my ability to think."

Sitting Tall cast Jed Fenris a strange sort of look. "The man who so willingly traded with Sitting Tall, who so willingly gave Sitting Tall firewater is now dead," he said thickly. "Sitting Tall glad."

Lone Hawk placed his hands over Sitting Tall's. "It is very much in my heart to have council with you and Neala," he said throatily. "But, Sitting Tall, Lone Hawk has even greater plan! Tomorrow there is to be a

439

celebration at my village. Let us then introduce our people to a planned peaceful existence between the Sioux and Chippewa! Bring your women! Bring your warriors! There will be games. There will be food."

Lone Hawk moved away from Sitting Tall and placed his arm about Mariana's waist. "There will be a marriage," he said proudly.

Sitting Tall stared openly at Mariana, still fearing her revelation of the truth of her abduction. If she ever told Lone Hawk, he would again have reason to hate Sitting Tall.

"Sitting Tall?" Mariana said, reaching a hand out to him. "Please say that you and Neala and your people will accept Lone Hawk's invitation. I, too, wish for you to be there."

She smiled sweetly at him, again feeling the kinship she had last felt when she was with him. "Sitting Tall, let us become true brother and sister," she said softly, still extending her hand toward him. "Sitting Tall, I've never had a brother or sister before. I would sorely enjoy having one now."

Sitting Tall's insides grew warm with gladness. His eyes gleamed. In two quick strides he was standing before Mariana and had her hand in his.

"It is with great happiness that I can learn of my sister," he said softly. He lifted her hand to his lips. Turning it palmside up, he gently kissed it.

"Gee-shee-may," he said thickly. "Sitting Tall liked the sound of the word sister on his lips. I will enjoy being your brother!"

Mariana glanced from Sitting Tall to Lone Hawk, smiling. She had not only found one Indian to love, but two. . . .

Chapter Thirty-Six

> *Thou lovest; but ne'er knew
> love's sad satiety.*
>
> —SHELLEY

Loud shouts outside the wigwam drew Mariana to her feet. Upon awakening, she had found Lone Hawk gone. She had now only had time to get dressed herself before the commotion had begun.

Combing her fingers through her hair to rid it of its tangles, she missed the hairbrush Lone Hawk had given her as a gift. In the recent upheaval of her life, she had lost it!

Hopefully Neala would have left one behind that she could borrow. Her hair being so long, she could not go long without brushing the witch's knots from it.

Stepping into her moccasins, Mariana went to the entrance flap and raised it. She stepped out into the fresh air and sunshine, then grew pale when she saw Lone Hawk standing over two Chippewa braves, scolding them. He was not only scolding them, it was evident that he had hit them. Blood curled from the braves' noses and mouths.

As though frozen on the spot, Mariana lent an ear to the conversation now being exchanged between Lone Hawk and the two braves. But she couldn't understand anything that was being said. All the words were being spoken in Chippewa.

This made the first twinge of questioning arise inside Mariana. She could often expect to feel like an outsider here in the Chippewa village. The language . . . the customs?

There was so much to learn. . . .

Mariana further watched as several braves entered the village on ponies, with others walking, stumbling along ahead of them. The wrists of those on foot were bound . . . their heads bowed.

Confused, Mariana rushed to Lone Hawk's side. This was to be a day of celebration. This was to be Mariana and Lone Hawk's wedding day. How could either happen with such confusion at the beginning of the day?

Lone Hawk turned on his heel and stared icily down at Mariana as she reached his side. Mariana felt the cold touch of his eyes. She took a step backwards, stunned. This man who was soon to be her husband was looking down at her like he didn't know her. His jaw was set, his lips were tightened into a straight line, his eyes were flat!

"Lone Hawk . . . ?" Mariana said in a whisper, reaching her hand to him, feeling suddenly like a stranger.

"Do not interfere," Lone Hawk grumbled. "Watch, but do not interfere."

"But what is happening?" Mariana boldly asked, not

442

wanting to be cast aside so easily, like an inanimate object. He must be made to understand from the first that she was not an Indian squaw who would look silently on when commanded!

If he didn't understand that she had feelings, then she had made a mistake in coming to his village to be his wife.

Lone Hawk's shoulder muscles corded as his hands formed two tight fists at his sides. He stepped closer to Mariana and spoke down into her face. "Woman, do not show disrespect to chief," he said quietly, only for her to hear. "You listen. You obey. The chief of a village is a most powerful being. Understand this, Blazing Heart. No woman must ever interfere."

He leaned closer. "But if you must know what is happening," he said in an almost whisper, "Lone Hawk will tell you. But hurriedly, understand?"

Mariana anxiously nodded, feeling warm inside now that she saw that he was trying to understand *her* ways, her embarrassment.

She would try to be more understanding of his.

"While you slept, word was sent to neighboring clans of the celebration of Sioux and Chippewa being together this day," he said thickly. "Some do not want to accept this alliance! Chippewa renegades were found close to the Sioux village, ready to attack. They do this though Lone Hawk has spoken. They do not listen. They must be punished."

"But on our wedding day?" Mariana pleaded, her eyes wide.

"This no longer wedding day," Lone Hawk replied sadly. "It has been postponed, because of these braves who have chosen to place their backs . . . their hearts

. . . to the voice of authority!"

Lone Hawk placed a doubled fist to his heart. "Chief Lone Hawk is now voice of authority!" he said more strongly.

Disappointed at hearing that their marriage was to again be postponed assailed Mariana. But now was not the time to speak of such a disappointment. In time, they would be married. Surely nothing *else* could stand in the way!

"What am I to do, Lone Hawk?" Mariana asked fearing the duties of a wife-to-be where punishment of a tribal member by her future husband was required.

"Watch if you wish. But do not speak," Lone Hawk said flatly.

Mariana nodded. *"Ay-uh,"* she murmured, yet she was not so sure she wanted to be a witness to whatever sort of punishment Lone Hawk had chosen to use on the braves who had defied him.

But when Lone Hawk took her by her elbow and guided her alongside him as he approached the other renegades who had just arrived, she knew that she had no other choice. Lone Hawk had chosen that she be a witness. She . . . would . . . be a witness.

Wishing she could understand what was being exchanged between Lone Hawk and the renegades, Mariana watched. Then she watched further as the renegades were guided to a wigwam at the far end of the village.

Mariana was urged to walk beside Lone Hawk, to accompany him to the wigwam, unable to hide the fact that she was trembling. She had seen much hate in the eyes of the braves who were to help in the punishment of those who had wronged Lone Hawk.

444

Yet, when she saw the braves untie the bound wrists of those to be punished, and further, was witness to how these renegades were gingerly led into the wigwam, Mariana had to believe that the punishment would not be so severe, after all.

She relaxed her shoulders. She clasped her fingers together behind her, to steady them. The fringes of her doeskin dress skipped in the wind, her hair fluttered upon her shoulders. It seemed a million years away that she had been Mariana Fowler, living her trading post life. She was now Blazing Heart, soon to be transformed into Chippewa!

The fact that she was part Sioux was fading from her mind, as though she had never known it. Even Sitting Tall's now so openly professing to be her brother would not remind her of her heritage. She would just accept him as "brother," nothing more . . . nothing less. It was important to Lone Hawk that she place this part of her that was Sioux clean behind her.

Lone Hawk led Mariana into the wigwam. Stones circled a fire in the firespace, over which hung a black kettle. The aroma of boiled meat spiraled upward, into Mariana's nose. Hunger pangs gnawed at the pit of her stomach. Her mouth watered. But she would not speak of her hunger. She had been asked to watch, but to not speak. And surely, if food was to be shared by all who were present in the wigwam, she would be included!

Lone Hawk eased Mariana down onto a fur-covered platform and positioned himself beside her. She was amazed at how kindly he was now treating the renegades. He was filling wooden platters with the cooked meat and passing it along to the renegades.

Mariana studied the expressions of the renegades.

Instead of showing joy at being treated kindly, when they could have been reprimanded in many ways that could be painful, they wore masks of fear.

She turned her gaze slowly to Lone Hawk. His eyes were expressionless. His face was glum. There was something strange about this feast suddenly thrust upon the renegades. If it was a feast of friendship, everyone would be smiling. But no one was smiling.

Traces of fear began ebbing their way into Mariana's heart. She saw now that the feast was only for the renegades. None of Lone Hawk's dedicated braves were sharing in the feast. Nor had Mariana been offered anything to eat. Even Lone Hawk was not eating! What did it mean? Was he going to feed the renegades, and then kill them?

Mariana's shoulders tensed. She clasped her hands together on her lap and sat as still as a statue. She couldn't help but see how the renegades' eyes were growing more wild with each bite they took. They looked at Lone Hawk with a silent pleading. The dried blood on some of their mouths and around their noses attested to the brief moments of violence they had experienced before Mariana had emerged on the scene.

But now? She was wondering what would be next. It surely was not to be pleasant, or the braves would not be so frightened. She was wishing for a way of escape. She did not like the atmosphere of fear . . . of dread . . . building around her in the small confines of the wigwam.

Yet she had to be dutiful to Lone Hawk. He had brought her to this wigwam for a purpose. She could not question him or the reason! She had to be fair to him, in every way. She had to remember that he felt

446

that he was being fair to her by letting her be with him at such a time as this!

The renegades ate more heartily. Their mouths and hands were greasy. It was as though they were eating out of desperation. The tension seemed to be mounting in the air.

Mariana looked about her, seeing the braves who stood behind the feasting ones. Their eyes were as fathomless as Lone Hawk's. Their copper chests were shining beneath the glow of the fire. Their arms were firmly crossed over their chests. Knives were sheathed at their waists. Quivers of arrows were on their backs, bows were slung across their shoulders.

Lone Hawk rose suddenly to his feet. He offered Mariana his hand. She eagerly took it and rose to her feet beside him, hoping that whatever sort of trial this was, it would soon be ended.

Easing his hand from Mariana's, Lone Hawk lifted it into the air and began to speak in a drone to the renegades. *"Gah-ween-nee-nee-sis-eh-tos-say-non,"* he said. *"Ah-nish-min-eh-way?* How could you not wish for peace between tribes? Haven't you seen how the white man has come and taken so much of what is ours? The only way to survival now is to work together!"

Mariana felt eyes move to her. She could feel the stares, like icy fingers touching her. She was white. She was part of the culture that had come to threaten all Indians! Surely these Indians were wondering about a chief who spoke so heatedly against the white man and in the same breath could accept a white woman at his side!

But Mariana knew that this was not for them to question. Lone Hawk was now chief! All Chippewa were to look at him as wise, in every decision.

Yet Mariana could not help but wonder just how many Indians would hate her in silence. . . .

"You of Chief Lone Hawk's clan of Chippewa have even caused bloodshed between other clans!" Lone Hawk shouted, his eyes fierce. "You will now take punishment deserved by you!"

Lone Hawk's eyes grew gently soft as he momentarily looked down at Mariana. Then he nodded toward the entrance flap. "We will now go," he said thickly, taking her by her elbow. "The renegades will stay!"

Mariana looked back over her shoulder at the renegades cowering about the fire behind her as she moved with Lone Hawk toward the entrance flap. There were ten. Weaponless, they sat, their legs crossed, their arms folded across their chests, their eyes wild with anticipation!

Mariana wanted to ask what was next in their punishment, but she again recalled Lone Hawk's request that she not speak . . . only watch. . . .

Stepping out into the brightness of the midmorning sun, Mariana was ushered away from Lone Hawk and his braves. She mingled among the crowd that had gathered. Everyone had come to participate in the punishment, it seemed. They were one body . . . one family. Mariana was a part of this family. . . .

Lone Hawk and his braves thrust torches into the flames of the large outdoor fire. Mariana's breath caught in her throat. She clasped her hands to her mouth, watching in horror as Lone Hawk and each of his braves placed the lit torches to the wigwam in which the renegades sat.

"No . . ." Mariana softly cried, not believing the

448

inhumane action of the man she loved. He . . . was . . . going to burn the men alive for what they had done? How could he? He was a gentle, loving man. Was being chief going to change him? Was he a man she had never really known?

Mariana wanted to run to Lone Hawk and plead with him. But she knew not to. She was new to these customs of the Indians. She had no right to question them. Especially the decision of their chief.

The birchbark covering of the wigwam quickly snatched the flames of the fire into it. Mariana took a step backwards, her eyes wide with terror as more and more of the wigwam became engulfed in flames. The entrance flap swayed as flames climbed upward from the bottom. The roof grew in a spreading orange.

And then Mariana gasped. The renegades who had been inside began fleeing, unharmed, one by one, yelping. They ran through the village, still screaming. The screams echoed and bounced through the forest as still they fled!

Lone Hawk came to Mariana, a slow smile touching his lips as he clasped his fingers to her shoulders. "They have proven their cowardice," he laughed. "Never again will they be a threat to anyone. They are the same as dead, Blazing Heart."

He swept his hand about her waist and led her away from the crowd. "Now let us get on with the good things of life," he said softly. "My braves will deliver more invitations to other neighboring tribes to come to our celebration. We will send bundles of tobacco. We have already received acceptances from many in same fashion."

He led her into their wigwam. He turned her around

449

to face him. He framed her face between his hands. "Tomorrow nothing will stand in the way of our speaking words of total togetherness to each other," he said huskily. "The families of these men who just disgraced themselves will be brought into our village. They will be considered as part of our family of Chippewa. Our hearts will beat as one."

Mariana looked up into his eyes, so glad that Lone Hawk had not proven to be the fiend she moments ago thought he might be. If he had meant for the renegades to burn alive in the wigwam, she wasn't sure if she could have remained to be his wife.

But now she knew that all along he had known that the renegades would flee. Their looks of fright had been because they had also known they would flee! And flight meant disgrace.

Smiling, Mariana placed her forefinger to the cleft of Lone Hawk's chin. "I am forever in awe of you," she murmured.

Lone Hawk chuckled, his eyes gleamed. "That is *o-nee-shee-shin,*" he said softly.

Mariana giggled, recognizing the word in Chippewa that meant "good." She tremored sensually as Lone Hawk's lips lowered to hers. Twining her arm about his neck, she knew that everything about him was *o-nee-shee-shin.* . . .

Chapter Thirty-Seven

*All paths lead to you where e'er
I roam.*

—WAGSTAFF

Mariana's heart soared as she sat before the fire, a soft doeskin blanket about her bare shoulders. She looked wide-eyed toward the closed entrance flap, listening to Lone Hawk as he remained outside the dwelling, beating his tomtom, singing his love song to her.

A delicious sort of euphoria claimed Mariana, knowing that Lone Hawk had chosen this particular way to make her his wife! There would be no public ceremony. Their wedding was to be private; the celebration later this morning would spread the word to his people that the deed had been done!

Tears sparkled at the corners of Mariana's eyes. She wiped one from her cheek as it spilled out, a fragile silver rivulet as it traveled downward. She had never heard anything as beautiful as Lone Hawk's song, and it was being sung for her . . . only her. . . .

451

The tomtom's rhythm was steady . . . the voice deep and resonant. . . .

"I will take this woman for my wife," Lone Hawk sang. "I will take this woman for my wife. Oh fair she is! Oh rare she is! Oh dearer still to me! I will take this woman for my wife. I will take this woman for my wife."

Over and over again he sang the song, filling Mariana with such joy that it threatened to steal her senses away!

And then the tomtom spoke no longer. Lone Hawk's voice trailed off to nothingness.

Mariana rose to her feet and swept the blanket back from her shoulders, letting it flutter to rest about her ankles, awaiting Lone Hawk's entrance back into the wigwam. She shook her head so that her hair would tumble across her shoulders and down her back in a brilliant red sheen, glad that she had been given a hairbrush to remove the dreaded tangles.

Shoulders squared, her head held high, proud, Mariana still waited for Lone Hawk to enter. Her cheeks burned with anticipation. Oh, how long had she waited for this moment? She was finally being made Lone Hawk's wife! And the ceremony was so simple! The privacy made the wedding ceremony even more special.

Oh, how she loved it . . . how she loved him.

Lone Hawk entered the wigwam, his eyes hauntingly dark, filled with intense love for her in their depths. The colorful blanket thrown around his shoulders did not prevent Mariana's seeing the shape of his long, muscular limbs and powerful chest.

And as he jerked the blanket off, revealing his full

nudity to her, Mariana's pulse raced. She again saw his long muscles, knotting and rippling as he stepped toward her, all of this sharply defining his leanness.

He took two more steps, lithe as a panther in his movements, and then he had her in his arms, pressing her soft, sweet body into the hardness of his.

Mariana twined her arms about his neck and looked adoringly up into his eyes. "The song was so beautiful," she sighed, her insides tremoring with desire for him. "And it was sung only for me."

"Ay-uh," Lone Hawk said, weaving his fingers through her hair, reveling in its softness, again in awe of its color. "Do you approve?"

Placing her cheek to his chest, Mariana again sighed. "How could I not?" she murmured.

Then she partially drew away from him. "In the song . . . the words . . . they spoke of you making me your wife," she said softly. "Lone Hawk, does that mean that I now am? Is that all that is required?"

Lone Hawk placed his arm about her waist and eased her to the thick cushion of furs and blankets awaiting them beside the fire.

Stretching her out so that he could lean up over her, he looked down upon her face. "You do not know that long ago we did all that was truly required of us to become man and wife," he said, laughing low.

Mariana's eyebrows raised. "And what was that?" she whispered, her insides becoming molten lava beneath his heated stare.

"Some braves only offer food to their chosen women," he said thickly, his hand reaching out to mold her breast. "If the squaw accepts, that means that she has accepted him, not only into her heart, but into her dwelling as her husband."

Lowering a soft kiss to her lips, Lone Hawk's eyes twinkled at Mariana's look of amazement. "You see, Blazing Heart, in a sense we have been married over and over again," he chuckled. "You have shared many meals with Lone Hawk."

Mariana laughed softly. "My word . . ." she said, then her heart thundered wildly inside her when Lone Hawk drew her lips to his and fiercely kissed her.

In one swift movement he had her totally locked against him, his hardness impaling her . . . sending her senses to reeling as he began his strokes inside her.

Her hands went to his face. She placed them gently to each of his cheeks, her thumbs circling downward, tracing the outer lines of his lips as he continued to kiss her with his kiss of fire.

Mariana became aware of hearing soft, repeated moans, then smiled to herself, realizing that it was she making these sounds.

A raging hunger stormed through her. A hunger only Lone Hawk could feed.

Wanting to feel him all over, making her know that he was hers, Mariana crept her fingers to his lean, sinewy buttocks, then across his powerful chest, and then to his corded shoulders.

When his lips set hers free, she placed them to the strong arch of his neck and nipped her teeth into him, smiling to herself when he groaned and looked down at her with a look that burned a path of passion to her heart.

"This is real?" she whispered, her eyes hazy with intense feeling. "We are man and wife? Tell me, Lone Hawk. Tell me. Over and over again."

454

Lone Hawk began to sing his love song again, causing tremors of delight to ride along Mariana's flesh.

"I will take this woman to be my wife. I will take this woman to be my wife. Oh fair she is, oh rare she is, oh dearer to me still. I will take this woman for my wife. I will take this woman for my wife."

A flood of emotions swept through Mariana. She twined her fingers through the coarseness of his black hair and eased his lips to hers. She kissed him long and sweet.

She was floating . . . flying . . . dancing beneath midnight stars. He was everything to her. Her breath . . . her sight . . . her touch!

He was the stars . . . the moon . . . the sun! Mariana knew that he was the total of her being, her existence!

Lone Hawk drew his lips away from her and swept some fallen locks of her hair back from her brow. "My woman," he said huskily. *"Mee-kah-wah-diz-ee gee-wee-oo."*

Mariana knew these words well. He was calling her beautiful! He was calling her his beautiful wife.

"Mee-kah-wah-diz-ee husband," she whispered back, touching his face almost meditatingly with the palm of her right hand.

Lone Hawk chuckled. *"Gah-ween,* no," he said. "Husbands cannot be beautiful. Men are not beautiful. Only women . . . only wives."

"How do you say handsome in Chippewa?" Mariana said, laughing softly.

"Lone Hawk not handsome either," he said, his eyes gleaming. "Lone Hawk only hungry."

Mariana arched an eyebrow, "Hungry?" she exclaimed. "Lone Hawk, what a time to be hungry."

Placing his lips to her neck, he whispered against it. "Hungry for *geen,* Blazing Heart. Only hungry for you. . . ."

He lowered his hands to her hips and pressed the yielding silk of her more up into his thrusts. He kissed her neck, the hollow of her throat, then her lips.

His fingers reached to entwine in her hair, his insides hot and passion-filled. With fierceness he kissed her. He felt their bodies fusing into one as the ultimate of pleasure swept through them, as a fire sweeps through the leaves of trees after being struck by a single bolt of lightning. . . .

And then they lay, still embracing, breathing against the other's cheek.

"Today's celebration will surely be boring after what I have just enjoyed," Mariana giggled, tracing his lips with her forefinger. "My love, oh, my love."

She reached up to hug him. "I hope we will always love each other . . . respect each other . . . as much as now," she murmured. "Tell me that nothing will ever change between us, Lone Hawk. Please tell me."

Lone Hawk leaned away from her, the lashes heavy over his eyes. "Things always change," he said softly.

Mariana paled. "Lone Hawk, what do you mean?" she asked, surprised.

"Love strengthens . . . feelings strengthen . . ." he said, laughing softly when hearing her sigh of relief. "When man and woman love as you and I love, it only gets more beautiful, Blazing Heart."

"Oh, I hope so," Mariana said, scooting to a sitting position as Lone Hawk crept to his feet. "A future filled with such joyous feelings? Lone Hawk, how can I be so lucky as to have found you?"

Lone Hawk began smoothing deer tallow into his hair. He gave Mariana a soft smile. "Lone Hawk found you," he chuckled. "Way before you ever saw Lone Hawk at the trading post, Lone Hawk watched . . . Lone Hawk wanted. So you see? It was I who paved the road to our destiny, Blazing Heart."

Mariana rose to her feet and stretched her arms over her head. "And our destinies have led us here," she said. "We are man and wife. And soon everyone will know." Her eyes sparkled with excitement. "I find it hard to wait for the celebration, Lone Hawk. To be a part of it so excites me!"

"It is the first of many," Lone Hawk said, drawing on white fringed leggings. "Now we must prepare ourselves. Lone Hawk will help ready you. You will help ready Lone Hawk."

Mariana eyed the headdress of many colorful feathers spread neatly on the floor against the wall. Then her gaze traveled farther, seeing the complete white fringed outfit Lone Hawk was going to wear. She had never seen him in full attire. Mainly only a breechcloth. She knew to expect him to be quite handsome! She only hoped that she wouldn't disappoint him with her appearance, though she also had been shown a lovely outfit in which she would appear to his people!

"How do you feel about Sitting Tall and Neala being married?" she asked, picking up the hairbrush, smoothing it through her hair. "How do you think your people will accept it, Lone Hawk?"

"My people have much to accept this day," Lone Hawk said, smoothing down the fringes of his leggings.

457

"They are torn, my people. Most hate the Sioux. But those that do, still love peace more than they hate."

His eyebrows narrowed into a straight line as he frowned. "How they will feel about my sister being married to a Sioux chief troubles me," he scowled. "But loving her as they do, what she chooses will probably be accepted."

Mariana curved her lips into a pout, momentarily feeling her young age of seventeen more than the fact that she was now a married woman. "And what if they do not approve of me?" she worried.

"They already do," Lone Hawk said flatly.

He went to Mariana and drew her into his arms. "They saw how you passed the test of yesterday," he said, looking intently down into her eyes.

"Test?"

"Ay-uh."

"What test?"

"You watched and spoke not a word of protest when Lone Hawk ordered his braves and helped to light the wigwam with the renegade Chippewa. Had you protested, it would have proven that you could never accept the ways of the Chippewa."

He smiled down at her, sweeping her hair back from her brow. "It is good that you did not object to how Lone Hawk and his people tested the renegades," he said softly. "You passed the test. The renegades did not."

"I did not know that . . . I . . . was being tested," Mariana said, her eyes wide.

She recalled how much she had wanted to speak out, to protest. She had thought the renegades were going to be burned alive.

All along it had been only the intention of Lone Hawk and his braves to frighten the renegades into running from the wigwam. Had they remained, to burn, it seemed then they would have proved themselves courageous. But it had been known to all that they wouldn't stay. . . .

"Does such a test offend you?" Lone Hawk said thickly.

Mariana knew that even this question could be a test. It caused an ache around her heart to know that Lone Hawk had a need to test her at all. But she would try to understand. He was taking a chance with her, it seemed, since he was the chief of an important race of people. Had he chosen a weak woman, it could look bad for him in their eyes.

No. She would not even ask him what he would have done should she have failed that test!

"No," she said, lifting her chin proudly. "The test did not offend me."

Then her voice quivered as her chin lowered. "But, Lone Hawk, I hope there are no more like it," she said, laughing softly.

"Gah-ween-geh-goo."

Mariana sighed. She recognized the word "none" in Chippewa. It seemed that she had passed all tests now—but had she really, in the eyes of his people? She knew that only time would be the answer to that question.

"Now. We must ready each other to meet my people," Lone Hawk said. "We must ready each other to meet the visiting Sioux."

Mariana's insides quivered strangely at the mention of the Sioux. She and Lone Hawk had said no more

459

between them about her father, Chief Black Cloud. It was as though the fact did not exist.

But somewhere deep inside Mariana, where memories are stored and cherished, she would always remember those brief moments with the dignified Sioux whose blood ran through her veins.

She would always remember the warmth in his eyes . . . the gentleness in his touch.

Even his voice remained inside her heart, like a song . . . but a song of the past . . . only a memory. . . .

As though Lone Hawk was reading her thoughts, his eyes commanded her to look up at him. "It is good," he said thickly. "It is good that some sort of peace will be shared between the Sioux and Chippewa. Now as never before, it is important to Lone Hawk."

Mariana smiled weakly up at him, reading more into his words than he was willing to speak. He was thinking of her . . . the part of her that was Sioux.

"Peace," she murmured. "Does it not have a beautiful ring to it, Lone Hawk?"

"Ay-uh," he said, then began smoothing red berry juice paint onto Mariana's cheeks. . . .

Chapter Thirty-Eight

*It binds my being with a wreath
of rue . . . this want of you!*
—WRIGHT

With a bit of swan's down at each ear, Mariana's hair had been plaited and wound around her head. She wore a white doeskin dress, garnished with colorful designs of beads, and about her shoulders she wore strips of rabbit fur woven together, every other strip placed with the fur out, each end finished with a tassel of white fur from the breasts of the rabbits.

Lone Hawk wore a headdress, long and full of large eagle feathers. His fringed shirt and leggings were of doeskin, his feet were shod in colorfully quilled moccasins. His hair was neatly braided, the cheeks of his face had been painted with reddish-brown ochre.

The love of his woodland was evident in the floral design beadwork of his shirt.

Walking side by side, Mariana and Lone Hawk moved toward a clearing at the far end of the village

461

where children had taken joy in stomping the grass to lay it flat, readying this stretch of land for the celebration.

A huge fire burned at the one side of the clearing. Over it cooked many an assortment of meats. Some women tended the fires and what was cooking, others tended to the children, who were filled with mischief and merrymaking.

Several braves sat in a circle beating their drums in unison. In the middle of this circle had been placed a platform covered comfortably with many plush furs, and sprays of wild flowers surrounded the platform.

The Chippewa were crowding around the drummers. Some were settling down on the ground, others were dancing, their heads bobbing in rhythm with the beat of the music.

Dogs scampered about, yapping. Ponies neighed from afar in the fields. The air was pulsing with frenzied excitement.

Mariana's heart picked up the beat, beating faster . . . faster. . . .

Lone Hawk eased Mariana on through the throng of Chippewa. He nodded to one, then the other, smiling in a dignified fashion.

And then he helped Mariana to the platform. He sat down beside her, his shoulders squared, his chin proudly lifted.

And then everything grew quiet as all eyes moved to those who were arriving on ponies. Mariana's gaze singled out Sitting Tall and Neala among those approaching.

Sitting Tall looked the chief that he now was, his

headdress every bit as pretty and fancy as Lone Hawk's.

Inside, Mariana felt the special warmth that she was growing used to feeling when seeing Sitting Tall. Her brother. Ah, what a happy ring that word lent to her heart! Though her true father was dead, at least she had a brother.

There was an evident strain in the air as Sitting Tall and Neala dismounted from their ponies, followed by the Sioux who had accompanied them there.

Lone Hawk rose to his feet and awaited Sitting Tall and Neala's approach, his arms folded across his chest, his face void of emotion, though inside he was so pleased to see his sister so peacefully content. Her happiness was evident in the ease in her step and in the depth of her eyes.

She was glowing. Surely Sitting Tall was keeping his promise. If Sitting Tall forgot his love for the firewater, he would make his wife exceedingly happy!

Low murmurs flowed through the crowd of Chippewa, who were separating, making room for the Sioux to approach, to mingle and join them and their celebration.

Mariana looked slowly about her. Her heart skipped a beat when she saw how many of the Chippewa had hate written in their eyes and were clutching the knives sheathed at their sides. If one thing went amiss here, everything could!

Her knees feeling suddenly weak, Mariana rose to stand beside her husband. She placed an arm through one of his and stood there, poised, yet afraid.

But when Sitting Tall and Neala finally reached

them and Lone Hawk greeted them and another Chippewa brave came forth carrying a peace pipe, Mariana began to feel as though everything was going to be fine.

It even seemed that the Indian braves whose hands had sought out their weapons when first seeing the Sioux were now relaxing, their eyes even taking on a more friendly cast.

"We will smoke, then celebrate!" Lone Hawk said, gesturing, as he shouted to his people. "Today is a day that should remain proud in our hearts! We make peace with the Sioux and we accept my woman as one of us! We are blessed, my people! Share the blessing with Lone Hawk, who is now proudly your chief!"

There was a moment of silence as Lone Hawk lowered his hand and began scanning his eyes across the crowd. But, as though a silent command issued from his eyes, one by one the Indian braves and their women began clapping and chanting, their chants rising in pitch until they were shouting!

Mariana's insides tremored. She smiled and clutched harder onto Lone Hawk's arm, so proud for him that he had succeeded in bringing his people to an understanding of what he wanted to achieve!

Smiling at Neala, Mariana swept her eyes over her, seeing her sweetness . . . her loveliness, attired in her clinging doeskin dress, a necklace of beads about her neck, bracelets dangling at her wrists. Her hair hung long and loose across her shoulders in black folds, her cheeks glowed from red berry juice paint.

Neala smiled back at Mariana then moved to Mariana's right side as Sitting Tall moved to Lone Hawk's right side.

Together they sat down. A young brave brought a platter of hot coals for the lighting of the colorfully decorated pipe. And after Lone Hawk got the pipe lit and the lad had returned to the crowd of Chippewa and Sioux who were now sitting on the ground in a wide circle about the fire, Lone Hawk took a puff from the pipe.

He blew the smoke first to the earth, then to the sky. To the north . . . to the south. To the east and west, in token of gratitude for the favor of the spirits.

With many breaths he puffed at the pipe, then handed it down to Sitting Tall.

Exchanging secret smiles, with Lone Hawk, Sitting Tall smoked the pipe, then passed it on to the next Indian, who sat on the ground, away from the platform.

And after the pipe had made its wide circle, each brave having accepted it and smoked it . . . both the Sioux and the Chippewa . . . Lone Hawk rose to stand above them all.

"It is sealed!" he shouted, raising his hands into the air, the long headdress picking up the breeze, stirring the feathers into colorful designs. "Peace is sealed between our two peoples!"

With his dark eyes filled with emotion, Lone Hawk turned and offered Mariana his hand. Trembling, she accepted it and rose to his side.

"And, my people, let me now share with you great news," Lone Hawk said more softly. He raised Mariana's hand with his and again faced his people. "My woman is . . . now . . . my wife!"

Mariana scarcely breathed, watching the faces of the Chippewa for signs of acceptance. All had grown quiet.

Even the beating of the drums in the distance.

Then Mariana saw a blanket being passed from Indian to Indian. As each of them took the blanket by two of its corners and waved it high over their head, then spread it on the ground at their feet, Mariana knew that she was being shown that she was accepted into the village as their tribeswoman. For what they were doing was an Indian sign of friendship!

When the most elderly Chippewa tribesman came forth and gave Mariana a big hug, then threw his robe around her, she knew that this was a sign of warmest greeting! Lone Hawk had told her about these things, hoping they would occur on this day of joy and peace!

Feeling tears near, Mariana bent and hugged the elder tribesman and quietly thanked him. *"Mee-gway-chee-wahn-dum,"* she murmured, knowing the words in Chippewa to say thank you.

As she drew away from him she saw that his eyes were warm . . . his smile touching her heart . . . her soul. If the eldest accepted her, she most surely *was* accepted by all!

"Mee-gway-chee-wahn-dum!" she shouted, waving to the Chippewa. "I so thank you!"

An applause erupted. Chants . . . songs . . . dancing began as the drumbeats resumed.

Lone Hawk circled his arm about Mariana's waist. With his free hand he removed her fur cape, then led her from the platform, then to the large field that had been cleared. Over his shoulder he cast Sitting Tall a smug smile.

"And are you ready to challenge me in games, my blood brother?" he said, chuckling low.

"Your blood brother's head is quite clear to think, to

command legs and arms to work well against you," Sitting Tall said, laughing. He guided Neala alongside him, removed his fancy headdress, and gave it to her, as Lone Hawk removed his to give to Mariana. They left Neala and Mariana and moved on to mingle with the other Sioux and Chippewa braves.

Mariana edged closer to Neala. "I'm so proud of Lone Hawk," she sighed.

"I'm so proud of Sitting Tall," Neala sighed.

"It is a proud day," Mariana said, lifting her head toward the sky, enjoying the touch of the sun kissing her cheeks, the lift of the wind as it stirred her hair. "It is a day I shall never forget."

"Then you are happy with my brother?" Neala asked, touching Mariana softly on the arm.

Mariana's gaze moved and held with Neala's. *"Ay-uh,"* she murmured. "And are you, with mine?"

Neala nodded. They laughed together, then slipped their arms about each other's waists and stood by and watched and enjoyed their husbands at play.

The first game of the day depended chiefly on dexterity. It was a bone game, where the dewclaws of a deer were strung on a narrow strip of deer hide. At one end there was an oval piece of leather pierced with a number of small holes, and at the other end was a needlelike piece of bone taken from the leg bone of a young doe.

Ten was the number of dewclaws used in the game, that being the number obtained from one deer.

Much of the game depended on the balance of the game implement, this being determined by the relative weight of the bones and their order on the string. The heaviest bone was placed, next the bit of leather. The number of holes in the bit of leather was twenty-five.

The braves were divided into two sides. Sitting Tall was the leader of one, Lone Hawk the leader of the other.

And then the game began. A player held the needle between the thumb and forefinger of his right hand, extending his right arm, the needle pointing upward, the bones falling below his thumb.

He then took the bit of leather in his left hand and drew it backward toward his body until the string of cones was in a horizontal position. With a quick motion of his hands he released the bit of leather, swung the string of bones forward, catching one or more of the bones in an erect position on the needle.

The scoring was as follows: to catch the bone next to the needle and hold all the bones erect on the needle counted ten. To catch any bone in the series and hold only that bone counted one, the number in every instance corresponding to the number of bones held erect on the needle.

To catch the bit of leather secured a score corresponding to the number of holes in the leather, and to catch the heavy bone next to the bit of leather counted the value decided upon before the beginning of the game.

The number of points in a game was usually one hundred. The score was shouted by everybody. Sitting Tall's team won this game.

Pride kept the Chippewa from showing their disfavor of the Sioux's being victorious over the Chippewa. They would win the next game!

The snake game was chosen to be next. The implements of this game consisted of four wooden snakes and several sticks used as counters. The wooden snakes were ten inches long and the counters nine inches long. The snakes were scorched brown on the side that represented their backs . . . two were unpainted on the reverse side and two had an undulating red line the length of their bodies. The mouths of all were painted red.

The counters were ten in number. The players were seated around a blanket spread on the ground, the order of playing being from right to left. The manner of play was as follows: the player held four wooden snakes in his right hand and dropped or threw them on the blanket, the score being determined by the position in which they fell.

The counters were laid at one side of the blanket until appropriated by the players; when all the counters were in the hands of players, a person making a score was entitled to take the counters from the other players.

If all snakes fell right side up or all fell wrong side up, the player was entitled to one counter and another play. If he scored on his second play he was entitled to a third play.

If two snakes fell right side up and two showed the white side without the red line, the player was entitled to one counter and another play.

If two snakes fell right side up and the other two showed the white side with the undulating red line, the player was entitled to two counters and another play.

This was the highest score. If he made the same score on his second play he again received two counters, and if he succeeded in making the same score on his third play he returned the four counters, which he then held, giving them to the player who held the one remaining counter and receiving that one in exchange.

The final score of this game was six, the highest, represented by five and one . . . again the Sioux had won!

Low grumblings began to move from Chippewa to Chippewa.

Lone Hawk thrust out his chest and gave Sitting Tall a half smile. "These are child's games," he said. "Let us move to games of warriors."

Races by foot and on horseback were challenged. Lone Hawk and Sitting Tall competed in a bow-and-arrow contest. Trained to shoot without even taking time to sight, they both shot arrows straight up into the sky, one right after the other, as fast as possible. They both knew the object of this sort of game. The one who had the most arrows in the air at one time would win!

As they continued to shoot their arrows, the drums beat wildly in the distance . . . the chanting of the singers rose louder and louder. This was a test between chiefs . . . between tribes. The arrows whizzed into the air. Over and over again. But it seemed that neither Sitting Tall nor Lone Hawk could win. Their skills were equal! The number of arrows in the air were the same!

With their muscles straining and aching, Lone Hawk and Sitting Tall finally cast their bows and arrows aside. Fondly they embraced the other.

"Blood brother, your skills are great," Lone Hawk admitted, patting Sitting Tall on the back. "But now let us play just one more game between our people. My braves must win, to save face!"

"Lacrosse," Sitting Tall said, locking arms about

470

Lone Hawk's waist as they moved to another portion of the playing field.

"*Ay-uh,*" Lone Hawk nodded. "The game that is the most important."

Sitting Tall and Lone Hawk had trained for this game as far back as they could stand. It was a game that took much stamina . . . much determination. They had played many times together with the stick that had a net attached to the curve at the end of it. They had used the net to catch the ball and then to toss it back. Hour after hour the two boys had played catch and had practiced running and trying to knock the ball out of each other's nets.

But now it was not just the two of them. It was many. And it was a combination of both the Sioux and Chippewa. Something they had never thought to experience, only hoped for. . . .

Dozens of players now lined up, standing opposite each other on the long field. Lone Hawk removed his shirt and painted a streak of lightning on his chest. Sitting Tall painted a running deer on his. They said the pictures would help them win.

The smaller of the Indians took their places at the back of the field, where the fastest runners were needed. Lone Hawk and Sitting Tall took their places at the center of the field, where there would be the toughest fighting. The game was rough. Players struggled to get the ball. They could wrestle, trip opponents, bang them over the head with the sticks.

But no one would complain about being hurt. If a player was knocked down, he jumped up laughing, even if he had a bloody nose. Any sign of anger brought yell of "Coward!" from the crowd of people

471

watching. A player felt very much ashamed if he was
hurt so badly that he had to leave the game.

So the game began. Lone Hawk lunged . . . he
kicked. He watched Sitting Tall out of the corner of his
eyes. Smiling, he tripped him. And then Sitting Tall
jumped back to his feet, fire in his eyes. He ran after
Lone Hawk and knocked the ball out of his net! Lone
Hawk ran after Sitting Tall, wrestling him to the
ground.

Muscles corded. Sweat beaded on their brows. But
they laughed . . . enjoying this sport with each other as
never before.

Then Sitting Tall jumped up away from Lone Hawk
and the game continued. It seemed that the game
continued for hours.

But suddenly it was over. Lone Hawk shouted and
chanted, jumping into the air. His braves came to him,
hugging him. They had won the most important game
of all! They had shown the Sioux who was the
strongest . . . the swiftest . . . the ones with cunning!

Panting, Lone Hawk went to Mariana. He took his
fancy headdress from her arms and replaced it on his
head. He turned and watched as Sitting Tall did the
same. They then went together, the four of them arm in
arm, to the platform and watched as a frenzy of dances
began and food began to be passed around in wooden
platters.

The sun was lowering in the sky, tinting the tips of
the trees red; the breeze had a bit of chill in it.

But there was a warmth radiating about Mariana.
Games had been played and won. Hearts had been
sealed with love. Blood brothers had become as though
true brothers again. Two Indian tribes had become as

one family.

Mariana beamed, peacefully content. She glanced up at Lone Hawk. Never had he looked so handsome . . . so confident. Could she ever love him as much . . . as now . . . ? She doubted it. . . .

She looked on, a willing participant in this, her new way of life. Remembrances of times past were becoming fewer and less frequent in her mind. Soon it would all be only a dream. Her Mama beneath that mound of dirt . . . her Papa now alone in his world of greed. She did not want ever to think about him again, yet sometimes . . . sometimes . . . he was there in her memory as she became a small girl again, loving him.

But it would only be a brief thought, for Lone Hawk was always there, to remind her of how life was for her now and would be. Their futures together . . . so magical, their own private paradise.

Chapter Thirty-Nine

> *God's in his heaven—all's right*
> *with the world!*
>
> —BROWNING

Six years later . . . 1795

As the water beat against the rocks below, it was like a pulse, or perhaps even the tick of a clock in its steady rhythm. The years had gone as fast as the water is washed out to sea and back. Six years. They had gone as though in only one blink of an eye. But for Mariana and Lone Hawk they had been good years. Full of love . . . full of wonder of each other!

Mariana clung to Lone Hawk on a high butte, watching a great sloop leave Grand Portage Bay, its sails spread wide, fluttering in the breeze like great wings. She had received word that her father was leaving the trading post. The word had been sent by her father, asking her to come, to say good-bye.

But she had not gone. When she had left the world of the white man to join Lone Hawk and his people, it had been forever. To go back would be to shame Lone Hawk's people, for they would believe that they had openly welcomed a white woman in their midst who had not adapted well enough to be one of them.

A sadness tugged at Mariana's heart, knowing that her father would never see his grandchildren. Sun Hawk, hers and Lone Hawk's son, now one year of age, and the child that Mariana was now growing inside her womb, would never know any of their grandfathers. They would never know their sweet grandmother, Jewel Fowler! That loss was the greatest still to Mariana, though she often thought in silence of her true father, Chief Black Cloud.

"And how do you feel about watching your father leave Grand Portage?" Lone Hawk asked, slipping his arm about Mariana's waist. His eyes savored her loveliness . . . the way her waist-length hair caught the rays of the sun in its tips as it fluttered about with the breeze . . . the way her face glowed in her radiant happiness.

Beneath the soft lines of the doeskin dress that she wore the first signs of the child were showing.

Lone Hawk smiled and placed his other hand on the small swell of her stomach. He would have many months to wait to see if this child was a daughter. He wished for a daughter, to be the mirror image of her mother! Then he would have two women with hair of flame to love!

"My Papa will be followed by others," she murmured. "His new partners of the past year will follow him to Canada because America is now taxing foreign fur traders. The trade centers must move across the border, into Canada, for them to make profits."

Lone Hawk chuckled. "You speak as though you understand this very well," he said.

"I have only recently learned of the new taxation by way of some of your Chippewa who were trading at the Grand Portage Trading Post. I learned about profits from my Papa many years ago. Papa talked much of business at the dinner table," Mariana said, frowning. "There was hardly talk of anything else. No wonder that my Mama became bored with life."

Lone Hawk swept Mariana around to face him. He placed his hands on each of her cheeks, tilting her face so that their eyes could meet and hold. "My woman, are you bored with life?" he asked.

Mariana smiled sweetly up at him. "How can you ask that?" she murmured, reaching to touch his copper cheek. She inhaled the buckskin, spicy smell of him. He was dressed in fringed leggings and breechcloth, his chest bare.

"Then you are happy with Lone Hawk and his people?" Lone Hawk asked, knowing the question was not truly required.

Every day his Blazing Heart showed him in many ways just how content she was. It showed in the way she prepared his meals . . . in the way she sewed moccasins . . . the way she greeted him at the door of their dwelling.

Always she greeted him with a kiss and hug. Even their son was now greeting him alongside her in the same way. She was teaching their son in one way; he would teach him in another. As soon as his son was old enough to go into the forest, Lone Hawk would add to his personality the skills of being a fierce hunter!

"I didn't know one could be so happy," Mariana said

in a soft purr.

She crept into his arms, placing her cheek against his chest. She could hear the pounding of his heart and knew what was on his mind. She was proud that she could stir his heart . . . his mind . . . to wanting her though her body was already taking on another shape.

She now knew that the Chippewa chiefs could take more than one wife! If Lone Hawk ever lost interest in her and took a wife whose body had not yet lost its shape by birthing, Mariana would then find life most unhappy!

Lone Hawk eased her to the ground on a bed of spongy moss. A seagull soared overhead, its wings contrasting white against the brilliant blue of the sky. The aroma of lilacs wafted through the air, touching Mariana's nose. The soft breeze from Lake Superior was cool and refreshing.

"What are you doing?" Mariana teased as Lone Hawk began inching her dress upward.

"It is not every day we are totally alone," he chuckled. "Let us take advantage of such aloneness, Blazing Heart. Let us make love as we did that first time. With much abandonment!"

"Ay-uh," Mariana whispered, holding her arms upward as he drew the dress on away from her.

Then she watched, her eyes becoming misty with tears of joy, as Lone Hawk rose back to his feet and began to undress, slowly revealing to her eyes every inch of his body, so beautiful to her in its copper sheen.

And then he knelt down over her and again drew her into his arms, placing his hardness inside her, beginning his slow, sure strokes.

"Lone Hawk, we are not totally alone as you

wished," Mariana whispered, feeling the pounding of her heart in her ears it was so intense.

"We are not?" he asked, arching an eyebrow.

Placing her hand to her stomach, Mariana softly laughed. "Either a daughter or a son is witness to our moments of ecstasy," she giggled.

Lone Hawk laughed. *"Ay-uh,"* he said. "Our daughter, Blazing Heart. Our Little Flower."

"Little Flower?" Mariana asked, her eyes wide. "You have already named her? You are that sure our child is to be a daughter?"

"If one wishes hard, then the wish is granted," Lone Hawk said thickly.

"Lone Hawk, usually it is the woman wanting a daughter. Not the man."

"It is not every man whose woman is so beautiful. Only daughters borne of such beautiful *ee-quays* are also as beautiful."

Mariana laughed softly, then emitted a low sigh as Lone Hawk kissed her with a loving warmth. She clung to him, returning to him all this love . . . all this warmth. He was her heart. He was her soul. They had found each other in this eden where forest met sky as though they were married to each other . . . where waterfalls sparkled . . . where flowers dotted the land like a colorful patchwork quilt.

Mariana and Lone Hawk would love freely in this, their savage paradise. . . .

Epilogue

The treaty of 1783, ending the American Revolution, set boundaries for the newly independent United States and British North America. The British traders kept control of the Great Lakes region well into the 1790s. But when the young American nation started to tax foreign fur traders, those at the Grand Portage Trading Post moved their business to Fort William, forty-five miles north of Grand Portage on the Lake Superior shore.

The move was complete by 1803. The Grand Portage fur trade heyday was over. Grand Portage was again left to the Chippewa.

But today, visitors can relive the exciting history of Grand Portage. One can hike the Grand Portage Trail and walk in the footsteps of the Voyageurs. One can see the vitality of the outgoing Chippewa Indian community.

The annual gathering of Voyageurs and Indians is reenacted each year during Rendezvous days in August, when one can view the colorful costumes, see the traditional dances, and join games with the Chippewa.

One can see the mountain heights, wildlife, and sparkling view of Lake Superior, unsurpassed in Minnesota.

The Chippewa people ... the land where they reside ... are a people and a land of total enchantment. ...